Revenge, Ice Cream, AND OTHER THINGS Best Served Cold

Broken Hearts and Revenge series

BROKEN HEARTS, FENCES, AND OTHER THINGS TO MEND

REVENGE, ICE CREAM, AND OTHER THINGS BEST SERVED COLD

HEARTS, FINGERS, AND OTHER THINGS TO CROSS

Coming in 2017!

Revenge, Ice Cream, and Other Things Best Served Cold

AND OTHER THINGS

KATIE FINN

Feiwel and Friends
New York

A Feiwel and Friends Book
An Imprint of Macmillan

Feiwel and Friends books may be purchased for business or promotional use.
For information on bulk purchases, please contact the Macmillan Corporate
and Premium Sales Department at (800) 221-7945 x5442 or by e-mail at
specialmarkets@macmillan.com.

Library of Congress Cataloging-in-Publication Data Available

ISBN: 978-1-250-04525-6 (hardcover) / 978-1-250-08018-9 (e-book)

Book design by Eileen Savage

Feiwel and Friends logo designed by Filomena Tuosto

First Edition: 2015

10 9 8 7 6 5 4 3 2 1

macteenbooks.com

For my mother, Jane Finn

PREVIOUSLY . . .

My friend Hallie Bridges smiles at me. We're spending the day at our favorite Hamptons beach, and she's squinting against the sunlight glancing off the water behind her. I'm eleven; we both are. "We'll always be friends, right, Gemma?" she asks. I smile back at her, feeling the sun on my face.

"Of course," I respond easily. "Why wouldn't we be?"

I look over at Hallie, who is biting her lip, the way she does when she's trying not to cry. It's her twelfth birthday party, but I'm the only guest there. It's my doing—I changed the date on the Evite before it went out. I don't feel good about it, but I'm trying to make Hallie miserable enough that her mother will take her away and leave the Hamptons for good. I look across the bowling alley and the lane decorated with streamers and balloons, and see my father and her mother, Karen, standing close. When I found out they were secretly dating—despite the fact he and my mom promised me they were only having a trial separation—I knew what I needed to do. But as I look at our parents, still together, I wonder if I need to do something else. . . .

I stare at the computer screen, feeling dizzy. Karen Bridges is being called a plagiarist by dozens of Web sites—and it's all my fault. I wrote a fake e-mail to my dad's agent about Karen, but I never dreamed it would be interpreted this way . . . never imagined that I would accidentally ruin her writing career. I instinctively reach for the green notebook I stashed in my dad's drawer, the one I've been detailing all my Hallie plans in. "Gemma?" my dad calls from the kitchen. I close his computer and push myself away from his desk, leaving the notebook behind, hurrying out of the room.

※※※※※

I squeeze Teddy's hand and feel myself smile. We're walking into school on the first day of my sophomore year, and I can feel the happy butterflies in my stomach. Teddy's been my boyfriend for a year now, and I'm no longer the anonymous freshman I was last September. I have an identity now—I'm Teddy Callaway's girlfriend. He squeezes my hand back and then opens the door for me as I take a breath and step inside.

※※※※※

"Gemma," Teddy says ten months later, looking across the Target aisle to me. His voice is choked. "I think we should break up."

※※※※※

"You need a makeover," my best friend, Sophie Curtis, says in a tone that doesn't leave any room for disagreements. "You *need one after a breakup. You need to differentiate the person you were in the relationship from the person you are now." She leads me into the salon, and I'm too heartbroken and tired to tell her the truth—that I have no idea who I am now, since I'm no longer Teddy's girlfriend.*

It's so nice to meet you, Sophie," Hallie says, smiling at me on the station platform. Her brother, Josh—no longer just the anonymous cute guy I sat next to on the train—smiles at me as well. I open my mouth to correct the mistake, brought on by my best friend's name scrawled across my coffee cup. I'm about to tell Hallie that she knows exactly who I am and isn't going to be happy when she realizes it. But then I see the way she's smiling at me—like I'm a friend she wants to get to know. The way she used to look when we were kids. I need to apologize to her—I need to make this right—and maybe this is my opportunity.

"Hi," I say with a smile. "It's nice to meet you too."

I look over at Josh in the passenger seat, moonlight falling across his face. It's been a disaster of an evening—Hallie accidentally sent me the wrong text, and I ended up at a pool party in a formal dress. And then the bikini she lent me started to disintegrate in the water, and then I found out someone stole my shoes. But this moment, talking with Josh in my car outside his house, is making up for all the disasters. We sit in

silence that feels so comfortable, I don't even want to breathe, in case I wreck it.

❀❀❀❀❀

Hallie and I are dancing up a storm—or as much as you can dance to a band whose instruments include the didgeridoo— at a bar mitzvah that I've pulled strings so we can attend. She still thinks my name is Sophie, but despite that, it feels like we're really becoming friends. It's her favorite band, and as I watch her dancing, her head thrown back in laughter, I realize that I've been able to do something that makes her happy instead of miserable. And I realize just how much better that feels.

❀❀❀❀❀

Josh and I are standing close, closer than we ever have before. It's the Fourth of July, I'm at the Bridges' party, and my heart is pounding. Not just because of how close we're standing— though partially because of that—but because I'm about to tell him who I really am. "Josh," I say, taking a breath, trying not to notice how near he is, how I could touch him by barely extending my arm. "I—"

But I don't get much further than that, as he leans down and kisses me.

❀❀❀❀❀

You..." I stare at Hallie, standing across from me on the sand, her expression calm and satisfied. She has just introduced me to her boyfriend...who happens to be Teddy. My

Teddy. My thoughts are reeling, but Hallie smiles at me serenely, like everything is unfolding according to plan. "You stole my boyfriend."

"Of course I did," she says, as though this is the most obvious thing in the world. "I have been planning this for years," she says. "And I have been getting you back all summer."

I stare at her, my stomach plunging as all the mishaps and disasters of the summer suddenly become clear.

"Go on home, Gemma," Hallie snaps. "Go on home to Connecticut. This is over. I won." She turns and walks away as, above me, the first fireworks explode, sending down a shower of sparks.

CHAPTER 1

I woke with a gasp, sitting straight up in bed. I was drenched in sweat, my heart pounding. Flashes of memories and dream fragments were swirling around in my head so quickly, it was like I couldn't catch my breath.

And the last dream—make that a nightmare—had been terrible. Hallie had known who I was all along, she'd been playing me all summer, and *she* was the reason that Teddy had broken up with me. . . .

I made myself breathe more evenly, and felt my pulse start to slow. I lay back down again, settling into my pillow. I was just about to close my eyes and try to go back to sleep when I saw the pile of clothes in the corner. There was the white dress I'd worn to the Fourth of July beach party, crumpled on the rug. The clutch I'd picked to go with my dress. There were my flats, tossed in a heap, the soles still sandy. And it hit me, all at once, that it hadn't just been a terrible dream. It had all actually happened. It was worse than any nightmare I would have been able to fabricate, and it was the truth.

I closed my eyes for a minute, hoping against all logic and sense that I could unlearn what I now knew, go back to that restful time when I was just going under my best friend's name and trying to make things right with Hallie, when Josh still liked me. . . .

Josh.

The thought of him, and of the way he'd looked at me when he'd realized my true identity, was enough to jolt me awake. I sat up and squinted at the amber-colored numbers of the digital clock on my bedside table. It was six A.M., but I could tell I wasn't getting back to sleep any time soon. I pushed myself out of bed and headed downstairs in the tank top and shorts I was wearing as pajamas.

Normally, I would have put a robe on, or tried to make myself a bit more presentable, but it seemed like a small comfort this morning that I didn't have to worry about running into anyone, and not just because it was six A.M., or that the house—the beachfront Hamptons mansion of my dad's college roommate-turned-Hollywood-superproducer, Bruce Davidson— was big enough to defy all logic and sense. The real reason was that the only people currently staying in the house were myself and my best friend, Sophie Curtis.

My dad and I had been invited to spend the summer, but I knew Bruce's offer to stay with him was only partially generous. My dad was a screenwriter who worked on a lot of movies for Bruce, and I had a feeling Bruce liked being able to keep an eye on my dad's work progress, with the ability to shut off the Internet if he thought the pages weren't coming quickly enough. But Bruce and my dad—and Bruce's longtime assistant, Rosie—were currently in L.A. taking meetings, so I had the house to myself, since I knew Sophie wouldn't be up for a few hours yet. Bruce's kids, Ford and Gwyneth, were supposed to come to stay at some point this summer, but I'd never gotten an exact date from them. And at the moment I was very glad to be alone. I needed some space to try to get my head around the fact that everything I thought I'd believed this summer had been a lie.

I crossed through the dark empty kitchen, silent except for the subtle hum of the giant silver fridge, and saw the glint of water in the distance. The beach was right outside the house. It was where I'd found myself multiple times so far this summer when I needed to organize my thoughts, and there was nowhere else I wanted to be at the moment. I plucked a sweatshirt that was folded on one of the kitchen stools on the way out—the sun was barely up, and I knew how cold it could be down by the water. The sweatshirt was maroon and soft, and I pulled it on over my sleep tank as I walked past the pool house and down to the water. I had no idea whose it was, but I breathed it in for just a moment, feeling somehow comforted by the scent—like the ocean and dryer sheets and something sweet I couldn't quite place—almost like cinnamon rolls.

I made my way down to the sand in the half-darkness. There was nobody on the beach this early, though there were a few surfers bobbing in the waves, too far away to even make out their faces—just shapes in dark wetsuits. I sat down on the sand and hugged my knees to my chest. I'd come out to this very spot when I'd first arrived in the Hamptons. It was where I'd decided I was going to go along with the misunderstanding at the train station, try to make things right with Hallie. I let out a short laugh as I picked up a handful of sand and then let it trickle through my fingers. So much for that plan.

Even though I knew the facts—knew full well what had happened last night—I still couldn't quite make myself believe it.

Hallie.

It had been Hallie all along.

Hallie had been the reason that Teddy had broken up with me at the beginning of the summer. She had known who I was from the start and had been sabotaging me every step of the way.

And something else she had said last night was echoing in my head. She told me that she had been planning this for *years.* So, she hadn't been moving on with her life, letting go of what I'd done to her when we were kids. Instead she had been plotting revenge on me for who knows how long. I shivered, even though as the sun rose, it was starting to get warmer. It was all just such a reversal of the way I'd understood things that I was feeling like I had whiplash.

Needing a distraction from these thoughts, I stretched my legs out in front of me and looked at the surfers. Most seemed to be staying behind the breakline, just sitting on their boards and bobbing up and down, but there was one surfer who was riding nearly every wave in, and doing it with panache. It was clear he was really great at this, miles better than anyone else who was in the water with him. As he paddled back out, swimming against the current like it was nothing, I weighed my options.

Did I really want to stay here in the Hamptons, where I'd made such a mess of things? Where I apparently had a mortal enemy? Did I really want to put myself through that? I couldn't go back to our empty house in Putnam, Connecticut—my mother and my stepfather, Walter, were still in Scotland. Walter was a former professional fly-fisher and current salmon expert, neither of which I had known were actual things you could be before meeting him. He and my mother were staying in a castle while Walter advised the laird on his salmon. Though my mother had made it pretty clear I wasn't invited, I knew I could call and tell her that I absolutely had to leave the Hamptons, and she'd let me come. Or I could most likely convince Sophie to go back to Putnam and let me stay with her. They were both decent options, but . . .

I dug my fingers into the sand. Somehow, I didn't like the thought of slinking back home and letting Hallie think she'd beaten me, despite the fact that she very clearly had. I knew I wasn't innocent in all this—I had put this thing in motion years ago—but I had been *eleven* then and scared out of my mind. Hallie, on the other hand, had apparently spent the last five years scheming, coldly plotting out how to ruin my life. How best to hurt me. And she had certainly figured it out. The image of her kissing Teddy flashed though my mind, and I closed my eyes tightly as though it would make the memory go away.

Seeing Teddy again—and seeing him with *Hallie*—had been more painful than I'd been prepared for. It was like my broken heart, which I'd just begun to put back together, had been shattered all over again.

I knew I couldn't just stay in the Hamptons and worry that Hallie was about to do something else to wreck my life again. I couldn't spend my summer that way. But I didn't have any other ideas at the moment. Feeling like I wasn't going to be able to make any coherent decisions until I was properly caffeinated, I pushed myself to my feet and brushed the sand off my hands. The sun was almost totally up now, and the beach was slowly starting to get populated with early morning joggers and power-walking senior citizens.

I had just turned to walk back to the house when one of the surfers—the good one—caught my eye. I watched as he rode a wave in then dove off his board and into the water. For a moment it was like the world went into slow motion as the surfer emerged from the water, slicking his hair back and reaching around to unzip his wetsuit. He peeled it down to his waist, and I felt my jaw drop. Then he started walking up to the beach, his surfboard tucked under his arm like it weighed nothing.

I suddenly wished I'd brought my sunglasses with me, even though it had been dark when I'd left the house, and it wasn't really all that bright now. But I would have liked a way to look at this guy without it being totally obvious what I was doing. Even without my sunglasses, it was really hard not to stare. It looked like this guy must surf *a lot*—or else do some other activity where you get crazy-defined abs and arms and shoulders. I expected him to head toward the parking lot, but to my surprise, the guy kept coming closer. I wasn't sure if I should get out of his path, and was just hoping he wasn't going to start lecturing me about objectifying him or something, when he dropped his surfboard onto the sand and started to run right toward me. Before I could even react, I was swept up in a huge hug, and as he set me down—though *dropped* might have been the right word for it, when I was still a few inches off the ground—I realized of course I knew who it was, and that I should have recognized him right away.

"Hey," he said, brushing his hand over the top of his black hair, and turning it into tiny spikes. He grinned at me, but his tone was light, like we were used to seeing each other daily and this was no big deal. "Morning, Gemma."

"Hey," I said in the same faux-casual way as I smiled back, hoping it wasn't obvious how hard my heart was pounding. Ford Davidson—Bruce's son, computer genius, and my longstanding crush—was back in the Hamptons.

CHAPTER 2

"**H**ope I didn't scare you," Ford said as he pushed himself up to sit on the kitchen counter and then take a drink of his orange juice. We'd walked up to the house together, and then Ford had taken a detour into the pool house to shower and change—it seemed he had claimed it as his room for the summer, despite the fact that there were more rooms in Bruce's house than made any rational sense. Now he was wearing long shorts and a T-shirt with an equation written on it. Most of Ford's clothing was like this—obscure insider references that, to understand, you had to be a tech savant, a math genius, or a superfan of the British TV show *Sergeant Which*. But even though I had no idea what his shirt meant, I was happy to see it. It was allowing the surf god on the beach to morph back into the geeky guy who'd been my friend for as long as I could remember.

"Not at all," I said, trying for breezy, trying to hide the fact that Ford's appearance on the beach had been a huge shock. I'd known that Ford and Gwyneth were spending the first part of their summer in Hawaii with their mom and then coming to the Hamptons for the rest of it. Ford had told me they were due to arrive sometime after the Fourth, but I guess I just hadn't expected him to be so literal about it.

I pulled open the fridge door and peered in hopefully. Since it had just been Sophie and me in the house for the last week, it had been our responsibility to stock the fridge, and we were really not very good at remembering to do that. No food had magically materialized, so I shut the door and crossed to the counter.

"You sure about that?" Ford asked, setting his juice down and adjusting his glasses. They were hipster-cool square frames, tortoiseshell, and they brought out his dark eyes. He arched an eyebrow at me, just one, a trick he'd perfected years ago when we were kids. "Because you were *really* staring at me."

I closed the fridge and turned to face Ford. "I guess I was just confused?" I asked. "I mean, I thought you were supposed to be *good* at surfing." I shot him a grin. This was our dynamic, and I could feel myself easing back into it, as comfortable as your favorite pair of jeans.

I couldn't remember meeting Ford or Gwyneth—they were just there, family friends I grew up with, who I saw over the summers and vacations throughout the years. When my dad started working with Bruce, we'd all seen each other more, Ford and I always spending the bulk of our time together. I liked Gwyneth a lot too, but she spent more time in Hawaii with her mom, and wasn't always around. Gwyn was also a year younger than me, and since Ford was a year older, I was always trying to hang out with him.

I might also have been trying to hang out with him because of my long-standing crush. It had been going on so long, I couldn't even remember the moment it had started. I had liked him for what seemed like forever, even back when he was short and stocky, with bottle-thick glasses and headgear. It had been jarring for me, when Ford ditched the braces and turned tall and lanky, to realize that he was suddenly someone the rest of the world (or certain demographics of it, at least) saw as an unequivocal hottie. Because he really was, with his black-black hair and tan skin, and the faintest scattering of freckles across his nose. But I had liked him before all that, despite the fact that practically nothing had ever happened between us.

Well, practically nothing.

He had been the one to give me my first kiss, on my birthday the year I turned thirteen. But aside from that one instance, we'd stayed firmly in the friend zone. After all, it wasn't like we even lived in the same state (if Ford wasn't in Hawaii with his mom, or Los Angeles with his dad, he was at a boarding school for computer geniuses in Silicon Valley) or got to see each other that often. Not to mention the fact that I had been dating Teddy for the last two years.

I realized a moment too late that I was *still* staring at him, and I made myself look away as I crossed back to the fridge, despite the fact that it was still empty. "So, is Gwyneth still sleeping?"

Ford shook his head and took another drink of his juice.

"She's not here for a few days. She's doing a young filmmakers workshop. Some documentary thing."

"Oh, really?" I asked, surprised. Bruce was always trying to get his kids to follow him into the family business, something that they so far had strenuously resisted.

Ford nodded. "She's trying to get into some festival," he said, then shrugged. "She can tell you all about it when she comes. I'm sure I'm getting most of the details wrong." I nodded and saw Ford was looking at me with a small smile on his face. "Nice sweatshirt, by the way."

"Oh," I said, looking down at it, and rubbing the soft fabric between my fingers. "I just found it this morning. It's not mine." I pushed myself to sit on the counter across from him just as Ford stifled a yawn. "When did you get in?"

"Late last night," he said, then yawned again. "*Very* late."

"So what are you doing up this early?" I asked, glancing at the clock and realizing that it was still very early in the morning L.A. time—which meant, I was pretty sure, that it was earlier still in Hawaii.

"I don't know, man, the waves were, like, *calling* to me," Ford said, dropping into the surfer-dude cadence he could adopt when it suited him, usually when he wanted to lull people into a false sense of security by not letting them know how smart he really was, always for his own advantage.

"So what's been happening?" I asked. We'd video-chatted a bit this summer, but they'd been brief conversations, both of us usually pressed for time, nobody going too deep. "How's your summer been so far?"

Ford gave me one of his half-smiles. I think it was because of all the years he spent in industrial headgear, but you rarely saw Ford's teeth when he smiled. When you did, you knew it was because he truly was happy about something. "Not bad," he said. "The island was fun, but it was getting a little boring toward the end. Though it did give me some time to work on my algorithm."

"Your algorithm?"

Ford nodded. "It's called the Galvanized Empathic Multi-purpose Media Algorithm. I started playing around with it as school was ending, and I think I'm getting closer to it being operational. If I can get it right, it might just be a game changer. It would sift through your data, and . . ." Ford started telling me just what this algorithm would do, how it could find patterns and something called metadata, not just for big companies but for your personal use, but I'd stopped understanding most of it after the first few words. I was mostly just nodding, and I think Ford could tell that I was lost, because he stopped talking and shook his head. "But enough about that," he said. "What's been going on with you?"

"Oh," I said. For just a moment I thought about telling him. Telling him *everything*—not just what had happened this summer, but the things that I'd done five summers ago, the things that had put me and Hallie on the path to us facing off on the beach last night. For just a moment I could practically feel what a relief it would be. Ford was one of the most logical people I knew, so I had a feeling that in no time, he'd have a plan all mapped out for me, probably on a spreadsheet, detailing the best decision for me to make.

But this fantasy only lasted for a second. I wasn't going to tell Ford for the same reason that I'd never told Teddy—I didn't think I'd be able to handle it when he started looking at me differently. When who I was changed in his eyes. The only person I'd ever told was Sophie, and that was because when she'd arrived in the Hamptons and found me using her name, I'd been forced to. Sophie didn't seem to think it was a big deal, but I knew I wouldn't get that lucky twice.

"Not much," I said, looking down at the granite countertop with a shrug. "Hanging out. You know."

Ford frowned, and I could feel his dark eyes still on me, and I remembered just a beat too late that he'd always been able to read me when we played poker together. If he could tell that I was lying about the kind of hand I had, he could probably tell that there was something I wasn't telling him. "Gemma," he said, his voice softer. "Are you . . ."

At that moment my phone beeped with a text, and I pulled it from my back pocket. I was thrilled to be interrupted until I looked down and read the message.

Sophie Curtis
6:22 AM
WHERE ARE YOU????!?!?!

My stomach plunged. With all that had been going on, my best friend had not, admittedly, been the first thing on my mind. When I'd left the Bridges' party after Hallie's bombshell, I had texted her that I was going. I hadn't heard from her, so I had just assumed she'd gotten a ride back to Bruce's with Reid, Josh's friend who had a major crush on her, and had been upstairs sleeping this whole time. The fact that she wasn't—that I didn't know where she was and had basically abandoned her—was making me feel faint. I immediately texted back.

Me
6:23 AM
Will come get you ASAP!
Let me know where you are.

"So I might have to go," I said, glancing up at Ford. "My friend Sophie is—" But whatever I was about to say left me as I looked down at my screen, which had just beeped with another text.

Sophie Curtis
6:24 AM
At Hallie's house. COME NOW.

CHAPTER 3

I stood at the edge of the driveway of the Bridges' house, keys in hand, feeling my pulse race. I'd been vague with Ford about where I was going, but he'd started yawning again and was, thankfully, more interested in getting sleep than in asking any follow-up questions. He'd headed off to the pool house as I'd raced out to the driveway, keys to Bruce's giant SUV in hand. I hadn't changed out of the clothes I'd slept in, just kept the maroon sweatshirt on over my tank top. I hadn't wanted to take the time, since my best friend was in distress and needed me. But now that I stood there, I was beginning to regret that I hadn't taken five minutes to just toss on some jean shorts—or, you know, a bra.

I stared at the house—what I could see of it from behind the high hedges—feeling like I was about to return to the scene of the crime. It had only been a few hours ago that Hallie had shattered my world. I really didn't feel prepared to be back here. What if I had to see Hallie? Or—my stomach dropped at the thought—Josh? I honestly had no idea what I was walking into. I didn't know why Sophie was still at the Bridges' house, or why she'd stayed the night there—she hadn't been responding to any of my subsequent texts—but the fact that she was here was making me really nervous. Not only had I inadvertently abandoned her, but I'd left her with the last person that I could trust. I pulled out my phone and texted Sophie once more, hoping that maybe I could get her to come out and I wouldn't have to go any closer.

Me
6:55 AM
I'm here!
Meet me at the bottom of the driveway?

A second later, though, my phone beeped with a response from her that made my heart sink.

Sophie Curtis
6:55 AM
On the beach! Come on back!

I really didn't want to come on back, but at least the exclamation point made it seem like she wasn't being traumatized or anything. I took a breath and let it out, and then made myself walk forward, past the hedges that shielded the Bridges' house from view of the street. The driveway seemed particularly long this morning—though it had nothing on Bruce's, which was long enough to defy all logic—but I made myself keep walking up it until the house came into view in the morning sunlight.

It was as impressive as ever, all steel and glass and sharp lines. But it had a different feel to it, now that I knew it was the place where Hallie had been plotting my downfall. It made it seem less like a modern Hamptons beach house, and more like a supervillain's lair. Hallie's white Jeep was parked in the driveway, but I didn't see Josh's truck anywhere. I was relieved by this, hoping it would mean that maybe I wouldn't have to run into him, when I realized there was a multicar garage to the side of the house that I'd never noticed before. So Josh's truck could have been there—along with whatever car Karen drove, if she was even here. I hadn't seen or really even heard much about her in any of my interactions with Josh and Hallie. They both seemed to be deliberately vague and a little secretive about their mother—which was also one of the reasons I had no clue how a former failed novelist could afford a beachfront Hamptons mansion.

But this was not the moment to be thinking about these things. I needed to get my best friend and get out, fast, hopefully without running into any of the people who actually lived there, all of whom now hated me. I walked around the side of the house to the beach, where I could see some of the tents and tables still set up from the night before. But considering how big the party had been, there was a surprising lack of trash strewn along the beach. Just stacks of chairs and neatly folded tablecloths, anchored by weights against the wind. SOUTH FORK

CATERING, the tablecloths read, with the logo of a stylized fork underneath.

I walked down onto the beach, shielding my eyes against the sun, looking for Sophie. I didn't see her, just people with their dogs and families beginning to set up blankets on the sand, staking out their spots for the day. I walked a few steps along the beach, my eyes scanning the sand, and then the water, for my best friend. She had just texted me—so where was she?

The phone in my hand rang, and as I looked at the number, I realized it was Bruce's landline. "Hey," I said, answering it, figuring that Ford was calling to ask me to pick something up, like maybe some actual food.

"Hi, Gemma!" I froze. It was Sophie, sounding cheerful but still only half-awake. "So I woke up and you weren't here! But I met Ford in the kitchen." Her voice dropped to a register I knew all too well. "*Oh* my god, he's even cuter than in your pictures. He told me you left, but then he went to take a nap, so I'm all alone here. Where are you? What are you doing?"

Walking into a trap. I turned around, my heart hammering, knowing too late exactly what I was about to see.

Hallie was standing in front of me. She was wearing a sundress and flats, her long blond hair swept up into a high ponytail, her makeup perfectly done. She was holding Sophie's phone, a smile on her face. "Morning," she said pleasantly.

"I'll call you back," I said into the phone, then hung up before Sophie could ask any more questions. "Hallie," I said, trying to say this calmly, even though I felt anything but. My heart was pounding hard, and I was trying to get my bearings, wishing she hadn't been able to pull the rug out from under me twice in the last twelve hours.

"Gemma," she replied, her smile widening. "You know, it is such a relief to finally get to call you that. Don't you think? It's nice not to have to *pretend* anymore." She tossed the phone in my direction, and I scrambled to catch it, managing it, but just barely. "Your little friend should learn to watch her stuff," Hallie said. "She just left her phone lying in her purse, right out in the open, where anyone could have gotten to it."

"What do you want?" I asked, still feeling thrown, but trying my best to hide it. I hadn't thought I would have to see Hallie again this soon. Not until I could figure out what I was doing next—or even have some time to wrap my head around the new reality I was living in. Because while she had spent the last five years apparently learning everything about me, I had no idea who she really was. All I knew was what she'd told me when we were spending time together earlier this summer— and I didn't know how much of that was actually true.

"I just wanted to have a chat," she said, her smile hardening into something more fixed.

I just looked at her for a moment, then bit my lip. I knew the facts. I knew that Hallie had done terrible things to me all summer. That she had gone behind my back and stolen my boyfriend. But looking at her, it was hard not to see the girl I thought I'd been friends with for the past month—the person I'd really liked, the person who I'd hoped might be able to forgive me. In that moment, though, I finally realized that girl was just an illusion, like Ford's surfer-dude cadence. It was a put-on, and I needed to stop mourning the fact that I'd lost someone who'd never really existed. "What?" I asked, crossing my arms over my chest.

"I just wanted to go over some things," Hallie said, her voice getting colder. "We didn't really get a chance to talk last night."

"I wonder why," I said, my voice rising, causing a passing jogger to glance over at me. "Considering you walked away from me in stolen shoes."

Hallie rolled her eyes, a look of annoyance sweeping over her face, and I wondered if I was getting to see the real her now—not the mask she'd been wearing in front of me all summer.

I suddenly questioned what all of this was for. Sure, it had probably been fun for her to get me here, to trick me into thinking my best friend needed me. But she had my number and I was pretty sure that whatever she was about to say—ultimatum? Threat?—could also be delivered via text.

"What do you want, Hallie?" I asked, suddenly feeling tired, the weight of my restless night, the early morning, and the shocks I'd been through in the last twelve hours all weighing on me heavily. "Why am I here?"

Hallie looked away, toward the water. When she spoke again, her words came out haltingly, "I just—wanted to make sure that you were going to stay away from Josh. That's all."

It was like my heart constricted when she said his name, and I remembered how he'd looked at me last night, like I'd just broken his heart. Josh had been hurt by his ex-girlfriend lying to him, and he'd thought I was someone he could trust. The expression on his face when he realized I'd lied to him too had been almost more than I could take.

"I don't think that's going to be an issue," I said, even though it was painful to speak the words. "He basically said he never wanted to see me again, so . . ."

A look of relief passed over Hallie's face for just a moment, and then it was gone. "Good," she said. "Then we're done." Her tone was brusque as she turned and started to walk to the house, not looking back at me.

"Was it worth it?" I asked, blurting the words out. Everything she'd done was surprising—but nothing more so than the fact that she'd been willing to let her brother get dragged into this, and then hurt.

Hallie stopped and turned around to look at me. "Was what worth it?"

"The revenge you got on me," I said, my eyes straying to the very point on the beach where I'd been standing when I'd finally understood, much too late, what was actually going on. "Making sure he knew who I really was before I could tell him myself. Was that worth letting Josh get hurt again?"

"That's on you," Hallie said, but I could hear she sounded rattled. "I told you to stay away from him, and you chose not to listen."

"So I guess that's a yes?"

"Look, Josh will be fine," Hallie said, and the confidence was back in her voice. "It's not like you meant all that much to him anyway."

I tried to tell myself that she was just being cruel, but it didn't stop her words from having an impact. It felt like she'd just reached out and slapped me. "Then why get me out here to tell me to stay away from him?" I asked.

"Look," Hallie said, taking another step toward me. "I'm done with you now, Gemma. I did what I set out to do. And now I'm walking away. Okay? We're through."

I just stared at her. "Really," I said, and my voice was heavy with disbelief. "You expect me to buy that? You don't have some new horrible thing in store for me? Another disintegrating bathing suit, perhaps? Another award of Bruce's you want to break?"

"No," Hallie said, and with such conviction that, for a moment, I almost believed her. "I think I've done enough. Have a nice life."

I opened my mouth to say something—I hadn't gotten as far as what—when I heard Hallie's phone ring. She pulled it out of her sundress pocket, and I could have sworn she blushed as she answered it.

"Hi, baby," she said, turning slightly away from me even though I could hear her every word. "I'm down at the beach. I'll be back in just a few minutes. I'm just . . . wrapping something up here. Okay. Okay. Bye."

It took me a few seconds to put it together, but when I did, it was like the world had come crashing down around me all over again. "Who was that?" I asked, and I could hear how high and shaky my voice sounded. "Was . . . was that Teddy?"

"Yes," Hallie said, starting to turn back to the house once more. "Good-bye, Gemma."

"Wait," I said, hurrying to stand in front of her, even though the ground under me was feeling unsteady. "Why are you still even talking to him? Didn't he serve his part in your little plot?" I thought back to the conversation I'd just overheard, and felt my stomach drop. Teddy had called from Hallie's house? Was he staying with her? Did this mean . . . Were they . . .

"What is between me and Teddy is our business," Hallie said, interrupting this train of thought. I could hear she sounded defensive for the first time. "So just stay out of it."

"But why are you even still . . ." I started, and then the penny dropped. There was still a blush coloring Hallie's cheeks, and I put that together with how elated she'd sounded when she'd answered the phone. "Do you actually *like* him?" I asked, incredulous.

"This is none of your business," she snapped.

"Oh, I think it is," I said slowly, my voice laced with disbelief. Hallie steals my boyfriend—and then keeps dating him? I had just assumed she was using him like a pawn, and that he would have been cast aside as soon as she was done with him. I had never dreamed she would try to turn this into an actual relationship. I could feel the anger that was somewhere deep inside, lying dormant while I'd been sorting through my shock and disbelief, starting to bubble up.

"Considering you stole him from me. And considering he has no idea of the real reason that you two actually started dating in the first place." Hallie's head snapped up and she looked at me, her eyes narrowing. "I think that maybe I should be the one to tell him, don't you?"

"Well, then maybe I should tell him all the things you did to me when we were kids," she said, taking a step closer to me and lowering her voice. "How about that?"

I swallowed hard. "I don't think he'd really care what I did when we were *eleven*," I said, even though I had a feeling Teddy—the person with the most unshakable moral compass I'd ever met—would. But Hallie didn't need to know that. "I think he'd care much more about what lies the person he thinks is his girlfriend is telling him."

Hallie stared at me for a moment, like she was trying to see if I was bluffing. "He won't believe you," she finally said. "He'll think you're just being a crazy ex-girlfriend."

My heart sank a little bit as I realized Hallie was probably right—and that I hadn't done myself any favors by desperately trying to get Teddy back in a parking lot, wearing a shirt of Walter's. But we'd been together two years. Surely that had some weight over the month he'd been with Hallie? "I bet he'd listen to me, though," I said, and I saw a flicker of worry crack Hallie's expression of blasé confidence.

"Go for it," she said with a shrug.

"I just might," I said, feeling myself getting angrier as I talked. "I think I'll tell him about how you were just using him as a means to an end, and—"

"Okay," Hallie cut me off, looking a little discomfited. "Try proving it." I opened my mouth but closed it when I realized I had no answer to this. "Also, he's heading out on the Jitney tomorrow, so good luck with that," she said.

I just looked at her for a moment, the morning wind whipping my hair around my face, wondering how we'd come to this, exchanging veiled threats, both of us furious at the other. I took a breath. I didn't know exactly what I was going to say, but I felt like I had to try. After all, less than twelve hours ago, I had thought we were friends. How had we gotten here? "Hallie—" I started.

But before I could say another word, she turned her back on me and started walking up the beach to her house, ponytail swinging.

I watched her go until she disappeared from view. I wasn't feeling sure of anything, and I couldn't begin to sort out my thoughts. So Hallie had said that she was done hurting me. But could I believe her? And should I walk away, be happy she was leaving me alone, and let her continue to lie to Teddy? Just admit that I'd been beaten?

The morning beach didn't seem to provide me with any answers, so I turned and walked down the driveway, feeling more confused than ever, my hands slowly clenching into fists at my sides.

CHAPTER 4

I stepped inside Bruce's house and pulled the door shut behind me as best I could with my hands full of quickly melting drinks from Quonset Coffee.

I had been driving back when I realized that if this was the way my morning was starting off, there was no way I was getting through the rest of the day unless I had caffeine. I'd stopped at Quonset Coffee and picked up my usual iced soy vanilla latte, a lavender lemonade for Sophie, and a blended coffee drink for Ford that seemed to contain as much sugar as caffeine. It was really closer to being a milk shake with espresso than anything else—I was pretty sure I'd seen the barista drop a Junior Mint into it. But Ford had a legendary sweet tooth, so I was pretty sure that he'd like it.

I was glad I'd finished ordering when Sophie had called again from the landline, wondering what was happening. I'd tried to tell her as I collected the drinks, attempting to just relay the facts—Hallie, Teddy, months of deception. But I'd only gotten a few syllables in before I'd started crying, right there by the milk and sugar station. I'd made it out to Bruce's SUV, and then had sobbed to her in the relative privacy of the car. I'd gotten her through the bombshells of the night before, up to my confrontation with Hallie on the beach. Sophie had been shocked and hadn't had much to say besides, "Oh my *god*. Oh my god. *Oh* my god." But it had been comforting to tell someone, at any rate.

I stepped inside and looked around, feeling my eyes widen. I had only been gone an hour, but clearly, in that time things had changed. "Hello?" I called a little fearfully.

This was not the huge empty foyer I'd left this morning. There were now three pyramids of suitcases stacked in a perilous-looking tower, a pile of scripts in a cardboard box, and, for reasons I couldn't begin to fathom at the moment, a huge canvas bag stuffed with what had to be twenty copies of *Once Bitten*, the erotic vampire-love thriller that had been a fixture on the bestseller lists for months now. I'd caught Rosie with a copy before she left for L.A., but couldn't fathom why she would need this many of them. Most perplexing of all, however, had to be the giant stuffed polar bear in the corner. It had a big red bow tied around its neck, and was taking up a pretty good chunk of the foyer. It seemed that while I'd been gone, my father, Bruce, and Rosie had all come back from the coast, but that didn't mean I understood any of the rest of it.

"Gemma?" Sophie stepped out of the kitchen and, seeing me, ran toward me, crossed the foyer (which actually took a little bit of time, as it was bigger than most rooms in my house back home), and gave me a tight hug.

"Hi," I said, hugging her back as best I could without spilling any of the drinks. My best friend and I didn't hug all the time, but it was like she knew I really needed one after everything that had happened.

"*Oh* my god," she said, taking a step back to look at me. Sophie had brown hair cut into a choppy bob, brown eyes, and freckles. We'd looked a lot alike when we were younger, but I was now four inches taller than she was, and lanky where Sophie was curvy. But people still occasionally asked us if we were sisters, which we always got a kick out of. "I still can't believe it about Hallie. And Teddy! He *cheated* on you with her?"

I tried not to wince at this, but I wasn't able to stop myself. "Yeah," I said, shaking my head, which was suddenly playing, like on a horrible loop, Teddy and Hallie kissing on the beach in front of me.

"But when did they meet?" Sophie asked, still sounding baffled. "And *where*? I mean, you and Teddy used to spend, like, every day together. And how did Hallie even know about Teddy in the first place?"

"I . . ." I started, then trailed off when I realized I didn't have the answers for any of these questions. I'd been so focused on the results of what she'd done to me—the boyfriend stealing, the month of sabotage, the letting Josh get hurt—that I hadn't turned yet to wondering about the process. But they were good questions, all of them. How *had* she managed to do it? "I don't know," I finally said.

"So I didn't have to pretend to be you this whole time," Sophie continued on, like she was still putting the pieces together, "because she actually knew who you were from the beginning?"

"She did," I said, "but Josh didn't." His name got caught in my throat, and I swallowed hard, remembering how heartbroken he'd looked the night before when he'd realized the truth.

Sophie gave me a sympathetic smile, and I looked away, somehow feeling like it was going to make me feel worse, not better. "Is my dad here?" I asked, changing the subject as I headed into the kitchen, where I took the drinks out of the carrier and handed Sophie hers.

Sophie shook her head as she picked up her drink. "Some people came and dropped off that stuff, but nobody else is here yet." She took a big sip and then smiled at me. "It's *so* good," she said. "Thank you. Want some?"

I shook my head and placed Ford's drink on the counter, hoping that it would keep for whenever he woke up. Sophie pushed herself up to sit on the kitchen island, her legs dangling over the refrigerated drawers, and raised her eyebrows at me. "So what now?" she asked.

"What do you mean?" I asked, taking a deep restorative sip of my latte, wishing a moment too late that I'd had the foresight to get some food along with the drinks, since I was still starving, and I had a feeling there was still nothing to eat.

"I mean," Sophie said, setting her drink down, "what's the plan? Are you going to stay here?"

I took another sip and looked over at my best friend while I thought about this. It was the same question that had been bothering me on the drive back. Was I really going to stay in the place where so much had gone wrong? "I'm not sure," I said slowly.

"You know, I just intended to stay here a couple of days," Sophie said. "Now that your dad and everyone are here again . . . I mean, I should probably go back to Putnam, right?"

I knew this probably logically made sense—Sophie had come to the Hamptons on an impulse after getting fed up with boy drama, having thrown clothes into a suitcase and hopped on a train. She'd stayed after seeing what a mess I was in here. And I'd been able to have her stay, since it had been just me in the house, and I didn't have to ask permission from anyone. I wasn't sure Sophie would even be noticed in a house this big, but I wasn't sure I wanted to take a chance that she just wouldn't be spotted by my dad or Bruce.

"Well . . . ," I started. I thought about just leaving all this behind, trying to forget it had ever happened. And then I thought about the expression on Josh's face when he'd looked at me the night before. "I'm not sure," I said, tracing my finger down the condensation on my cup. "Can I think about it for a little bit?"

"Sure," Sophie said, pushing herself off the island, taking her drink with her. "Want to think about it by the pool?"

"Absolutely," I said, feeling like after the last twelve hours I'd had, I could use a little time on a lounge chair in the sun.

"Great," Sophie said, heading out of the kitchen. "I'll just change. Meet you in ten!"

I took another drink of my iced latte, almost finishing it. At this point, if Ford didn't emerge soon, I was going to take his drink for myself.

I started to head to my room to finally change out of my pajamas and into my suit, when I heard the front door open and close. A moment later a very sunburned Bruce walked past the kitchen, mid-conversation on his Bluetooth, waving distractedly at me as he went. Rosie was just a few steps behind him, and she broke into a smile when she saw me. I smiled back—you couldn't help it when you saw Rosie, who was so gorgeous, she looked like she should have been in front of the camera, rather than just making sure everything ran smoothly behind it.

"Gem," she said, giving me a quick hug. "Didn't think you'd be up yet. Did you see Ford?"

"Yes," I said, "but—"

"Hey, Gem," my dad said, coming into the kitchen and ruffling my hair in passing. "What are you doing up this early?"

"Hey, Dad," I said. My father looked the same as he always did—rumpled sandy hair, glasses, sneakers, his shirt just the tiniest bit wrinkled, despite all the no-iron shirts I was always buying him for Father's Day. But I couldn't help notice how exhausted he looked, and I didn't think it was just due to the fact that he'd flown in overnight from California. I sometimes wondered if his screenwriting job, wherein he was obligated to take terrible notes about scripts for animated movies about time-traveling animals, was actually that much of an improvement over being a novelist whose work barely got read. "How was the trip?"

My dad just shrugged. "It went as expected," he said, which, it occurred to me, wasn't exactly an answer to the question.

"I'm not sure your father's excited about his new project," Rosie said wryly, raising an eyebrow at him, "despite the fact every writer in town wanted this job."

"What is it?" I asked my father, who was suddenly very interested in his phone.

"It's a novel adaptation," Rosie said, answering when it became clear my dad wasn't going to. "And one that he needs to get started on soon if we're going to make our dates."

"Was that a hint?" my dad asked with a smile as he put his phone away. "Just let me get settled, okay?" He started to head toward the door, then turned and looked back at me. "Actually, I need to talk to you about something, Gem."

"Okay," I said slowly, trying to buy myself some time. These were words that always seemed to indicate that I'd done something wrong, and I mentally scrolled through everything that had happened in his absence, wondering if there was anything I was about to get busted for. I suddenly realized there was one very big potential thing, and added quickly, "But first I just wanted to tell you that Sophie came into town and has been staying here for a little bit. Bruce said it was okay." I mumbled this last part, worried about Rosie, who was much more aware than Bruce himself about what Bruce did and didn't know. I knew she would be able to contradict this in a second—but she was already halfway out of the kitchen when I said this, and it didn't seem like she'd heard me.

"Oh," my dad said, looking surprised. "Well . . . okay. Just as long as Bruce is fine with it."

"He hasn't told me he's not," I was able to reply honestly.

"Okay," my dad said. "Well, that'll be nice for you. And her parents are okay with this?"

"As far as I know," I said, also glad that I was able to respond to this without veering from the truth at all.

"Oh, good," my dad said, raising his glasses and rubbing the bridge of his nose for just a moment. "So I was wondering if you'd gotten any further with your job search."

I was so relieved that this was what he wanted to talk to me about—not the going under an alias, not that he'd found out about what I'd done to Hallie the first time around, not even the fact that Josh had stayed the night here with me while we were both recovering from food poisoning—that I almost laughed out loud. "Right," I said, hoping the relief I was feeling wasn't too obvious. "That. I'm working on it."

"I'm just concerned," my dad said, folding his arms and leaning against the kitchen counter. "You've been spending time with these Hamptons kids, you drop hundreds of dollars on a bathing suit, you don't have a job. . . ." He sighed and shook his head. "I just don't want you to laze the summer away, Gemma."

I bit my lip. I wanted to tell him exactly how I'd spent my summer so far—attempting to make amends, being thwarted at every turn—but knew I couldn't tell him the truth, not yet.

I'd always intended to confess to him what I'd done the

summer I was eleven—but I'd hoped to do it after Hallie had forgiven me. Since that plan was no longer an option, I knew I'd have to come up with another way to talk to him about it. Telling my dad, though, would be different than confessing to Sophie. My dad had been truly, maybe irrevocably, hurt by my actions. He and Karen had fallen hard for each other, in a way that when I was eleven, I'd seen only as standing in the way of my parents getting back together. Now, though, I couldn't help but wonder if Karen had been the last woman—other than my mom—who my dad had truly cared about. In the beginning of the summer I'd tried to ask him if he was dating anyone, in what had been a very awkward conversation for us both. When he'd told me no, it was like he'd found the very idea that he might date someone ridiculous. Telling my dad that I'd deliberately broken up his last serious relationship—especially when I would no longer have a happy reconciliation with Hallie to help smooth things over—was going to be a difficult conversation, and it was one I wasn't sure I was ready to have yet.

"Gem?" my dad prompted.

"Right," I said quickly. "Job. I'll get one. Promise." Even as I said this, though, I realized I had no idea how I was going to go about it. Back home, I was always babysitting, but after encountering Isabella and Olivia, the devil-children who Hallie had foisted upon me out here, I wasn't sure I wanted anything more to do with Hamptons kids. I knew that the twins had only been acting on Hallie's instructions, but still. I gave my dad a smile that hopefully conveyed much more confidence than I actually felt. "Soon."

"Okay," my dad said slowly. I could tell he wasn't impressed by the vagueness of my answers, but I also knew he wasn't going to push me for details. This was what happened after my dad had moved to California—he saw me only a few times a year, and so most of the actual disciplining and, frankly, parenting, had been left to my mom. My father and I were very bad at communicating, something I'd noticed more lately, since I'd been seeing him—when he wasn't off working in L.A., that was—much more than I normally did. "Because, Gem—"

The doorbell rang, and we both looked toward the foyer.

"I'll get it," I said, happy to have an excuse to end this conversation. My dad nodded, looking a little relieved, like maybe he was also glad to be done with playing the role of the disappointed father for the moment.

"All right," my dad said, heading out of the kitchen. "Let me know when you've found something, okay?"

"You got it," I said as I headed for the front door. I stepped around the piles of luggage that seemed to have only increased since everyone had come home, wondered once more about the polar bear, then pulled open the door.

"Hey," said the person on the other side of it, giving me a halfhearted wave. He looked like maybe he was a few years older than me, maybe college-aged. He was wearing a polo shirt and khaki shorts, and he had a professional-looking camera bag over his shoulder.

"Um, hi," I said, easing the door a little more closed behind me. He didn't *look* like the paparazzi I'd sometimes see in Los Angeles—but it would stand to reason that really good paparazzi probably didn't. It would have to be a *really* slow news day, though, for any gossip magazine to want pictures of Bruce. It wasn't even like there was currently anyone famous here for a meeting. Maybe this guy had been misinformed.

"I'm Andy Young," he said, still with utter lack of animation, as he lifted up a laminated ID hung from a lanyard around his neck. "I'm from the *Hamptons News Daily*. I'm here for Bruce Davidson."

"Oh," I said, still not sure if I should let him in or not. Also, while it seemed like this guy had press credentials, I'd heard the stories of aspiring actors and screenwriters pretending to be all kinds of people to get their scripts or head shots or reels into Bruce's hands. His dentist had even tried to pitch him a movie mid root canal. "Um . . ."

The door swung open behind me, and I was relieved to see Rosie standing on the threshold. She'd been Bruce's gatekeeper ever since she'd started working for him, and she was much more capable of vetting this guy than I was. "You're here for Bruce?" Rosie asked, her eyes narrowed.

Maybe even Andy Young could sense Rosie's authority, because he stood up a little straighter. "Yes, ma'am," he said, lifting his badge and showing it again. "I'm just the photographer. But I believe the story is about the local producer and his award collection?"

"What?" I asked, even though I'd heard him perfectly. I was

just hoping that this was either a huge misunderstanding or a huge coincidence. Because otherwise . . .

"I don't think we have you on our media schedule," Rosie said, frowning. "Who did you clear this with?"

Andy Young shrugged. "You'd have to ask them back at the office," he said. "I just go where the assignment is."

"Rosie!" Bruce thundered as he stomped into the foyer. "Why is there no food in the house?" He stopped short when he saw us all clustered around the door. "Did someone order pizza?" he asked, brightening.

"Are you Bruce Davidson?" Andy asked, taking a small step forward. "I'm here to photograph you with your"—he pulled out his phone and squinted at it—"Spotlight award."

I drew in a sharp breath. It confirmed what I'd been afraid of but hadn't quite been able to believe. Despite what Hallie had just told me on the beach, she wasn't done trying to hurt me. She was still doing whatever she could to wreck my life. But I couldn't quite believe the speed at which she'd gone from assuring me she was through to Andy Young's appearance at the house. How had she managed to get a photographer here? And so quickly?

"Um," I said, trying to step in front of Bruce, just praying that Rosie would need to adhere to their schedule today and I could get rid of Andy Young. Hallie knew full well Bruce's Spotlight award was broken—the twins who Hallie had sent here to trash the house had broken it. At the time, of course, I'd thought it was an accident. I'd sent it to Ford, who'd told me he knew a guy who could fix it, but I had no idea if this had been accomplished, or if the award had made the trip back from Hawaii with Ford like he'd promised it would. But either way, the award was no longer in its place of pride in Bruce's brag room, which I knew would come as a surprise to Bruce. "Like Rosie said, if this isn't on the media schedule . . ."

"Oh, what's the harm?" Bruce said, a smile forming on his very red face. Bruce was prouder of his Spotlight award than any of his other trophies. He was unaware of the fact that the whole thing was a clerical error, and the very prestigious award had been meant for acclaimed British documentary producer Marcus Davidman. "I'm sure it's not going to take very long. What did you say your name was? Alex?"

"Andy," Andy said, taking a step inside, then did a double take at the giant stuffed animal. "Uh, nice polar bear."

"Bruce, you have a call in twenty," Rosie said, her eyes still on Andy. It was clear something about this was ringing false to her; she just didn't know what it was.

"I'm sure this won't take that long," Bruce said, already starting to usher Andy toward the part of the house that contained his domain—office, screening room, and brag room. "This way."

"Wait!" I said, jumping in front of them. Everyone stopped and looked at me expectantly, and I cursed myself that I hadn't through of anything to follow this. "Um. Bruce."

"Yes?" he asked, raising his eyebrows at me.

"I . . ." I said, scrambling to come up with anything to stall them, and finally deciding to go with a version of the truth. "I actually think that Ford took it into the pool house. So maybe it's still with him. Want me to check for you?"

"He did *what*?" Bruce thundered. Then, apparently remembering there was a member of the press standing next to him, he forced a smile on his face that was more like a grimace. "Er . . . my son. Little scamp. Gemma?" He tipped his head in the direction of the pool house, and I knew this meant to go get it, and quickly.

I nodded and hurried across the foyer and the kitchen, crossing my fingers on both hands that Ford had, in fact, managed to get the award fixed and bring it back. If this was Bruce's reaction when he thought the award had just been moved to a different part of the house, I couldn't even imagine what it would be if he found out what had really happened to it.

I grabbed the blended coffee drink I'd picked up for Ford on my way, figuring that if I had to wake him up, I could at least provide him with some caffeine. I skirted around the pool to the pool house, opening the door without knocking.

"Ford?" I called.

All the blinds were drawn and the lights were off, and I blinked, trying to get my eyes to adjust. As they did, I understood why Ford had chosen to live in the pool house, despite the myriad other room options available to him in the main house. I hadn't been inside it yet, since, with a room of my own just steps away, I hadn't thought there was any need. But I was suddenly regretting not choosing it for myself as I looked around. It was like a mini-apartment, except minus the "mini" part. There was a pool table, and two brown leather couches facing each other across from a coffee table that was stacked with two laptops and a tablet. There were bookcases lining one wall that seemed equally filled with books and board games. There was a small kitchen, and at the very back of the pool house, an unmade bed.

"Ford!" I called, louder this time. The rumpled sheets moved, and I bit my lip, sorry to have to do this, but not seeing any other options. "Hey," I said, as I speed-walked over to the bed. "Sorry to wake you up."

"Wha?" Ford murmured, still from somewhere underneath the sheets. "Shh. Sleeping."

"I know, sorry about this," I said, wincing slightly as I pulled up the shade right by Ford's bed, then pulled the covers off his head.

"Gah," Ford said, holding up a hand to block the sunlight streaming in, which suddenly seemed incredibly bright in the dark pool house. "Gemma! Dude, what the *heck*?"

"Sorry," I said again. I put the coffee drink into his hand, and Ford looked down at it, then stared at me, baffled. "Here, drink this. It'll—" Whatever I'd been about to say, though, totally left my head as Ford sat up. He was shirtless, and once again the sight of this version of Ford—no glasses, tan, and in crazy-good shape—was incapacitating me. It just didn't seem possible that someone who spent as much time coding as Ford had abs that good.

"Um," I said, turning my head so I was looking fixedly at the bookcase, at the box for the game Shows How Much You Know!

"Bruce is asking about the Spotlight award," I said, talking fast, trying to make up for the delay brought on by the sight of Ford's torso. I figured it might be simpler to leave the photographer out of it for the moment. "Were you able to get it fixed? Do you have it?"

Ford just blinked at me for a second, like he was still hoping this was a very realistic dream, but then nodded and pointed across the pool house. "In the box by the kitchen," he said around a yawn, taking a sip of his drink. I ran across the room, hoping that I hadn't been gone long enough to make anyone suspicious. I opened the cardboard box on the counter, then carefully lifted out the award—the globe on the top firmly in place once again.

"This looks great," I said, relief flooding my system as I carried it back toward Ford and looked at it in the light. "You can't even tell anything happened to it!"

"Just be careful," Ford said as he yawned again. He set the drink aside and lay back down, pulling the covers over his shoulder. "It's more fragile than it was before. And the glue is sensitive to heat—if it melts, it's going to fall apart again. And this guy doesn't give refunds."

"I'll be careful," I said as I dropped the shade down once again. "Thank you *so* much!"

"Don't you mean *mahalo*?" Ford asked, his voice already getting slow and sleepy, but apparently not too sleepy to make fun of the fact that I only knew about four Hawaiian words.

"Mahalo!" I yelled behind me. I walked out of the pool house as fast as I felt I safely could, my hands gripping the base of the

award tightly. The last thing I needed was to accidentally break it when I was on the verge of giving it back.

I was glad whoever had fixed the award had done such a good job—when I gave it back to Bruce, he examined it for what had to be a solid minute before nodding and then motioning for Andy to follow him to the brag room. Rosie went as well, and I hovered in the hallway outside Bruce's domain, half expecting Bruce to come out yelling about the fact that he could tell his award had been tampered with. But only a few minutes later Rosie and Andy emerged again, Rosie using what seemed like pretty serious legalese as she told Andy that they would need to have approval over any quotes in the final piece.

Andy was nodding as she spoke, looking, like he had this whole time, incredibly bored. If he found it at all exciting to be in the home of a big-time Hollywood producer, it was not apparent to the casual observer. "I'll pass the word along," he said, then lifted his camera slightly. "Thanks for the pictures."

Rosie's phone beeped in her hand. "Bruce's call is starting," she said, looking at me. "Gem, walk Andy out, would you?"

"Sure thing," I said as Rosie nodded, then turned and walked back toward Bruce's office. A beat too late I realized I had no idea what this call was about—or what my dad's new project was. He'd finished the revisions on the latest time-traveling animal movie, this time featuring celebrity-voiced penguins. But I didn't know what everyone was working on now—admittedly, I had not been paying a ton of attention to what was happening around here before everyone left for California.

"Thanks," Andy said dryly once I'd walked him across the foyer to the door. "I might not have been able to find it on my own."

I smiled at this. "You're welcome," I said, opening the door with a flourish. "Did you get what you needed?"

Andy Young just looked at me for a moment, then shrugged. "Probably," he said. "I can't imagine they'd need more than that."

"So," I said, trying for casual. I wasn't sure what he knew. Was he in on this with Hallie? Or was he unknowingly being used by her? "You have no idea why the paper decided to do a story on Bruce?"

"Hmm?" Andy was already absorbed in his phone, and blinked at me as he looked up, like he'd forgotten that I was there. "Oh. No. Slow news day, I guess? I just go where they send me." Then he raised a hand in a wave, turned, and ambled across the driveway.

I shut the door behind him and leaned back against it for a moment, trying to process this. So Hallie hadn't even waited a whole day before starting to mess with me again. She'd know soon enough she'd failed—whenever the piece ran about the producer and his award, she'd see she hadn't gotten me in trouble.

But it made me realize that no matter what she'd said on the beach, this wasn't over. Not by a long shot.

CHAPTER 5

"So Gemma swears up and down that she's going to let me teach her to surf," Ford said, leaning back against the red leather booth and looking over at me. I was sitting next to him, and Sophie was sitting across from us. The three of us had headed to dinner at the Upper Crust pizza parlor when it became clear my dad was locked away in his office working for the night, and Bruce was busy with what seemed to be mostly pacing around the pool and screaming at his interns.

Since Sophie was waiting for me to make a decision about whether we were going back to Putnam, I'd thought that there probably wasn't any point in talking to my dad or Bruce about the fact that she was staying there. Bruce had even passed her in the hallways and given her a nod, and then didn't ask who she was or what she was doing in his house, so it seemed like maybe he'd already lost track of how many teenagers were currently living with him. But it also made me glad that he had

Rosie around, otherwise I had a feeling he probably would have been robbed years ago.

Ford had woken up late that afternoon with bedhead and a pillow crease across his face, and announced he was starving. I was happy that he and Sophie seemed to be getting along. He was treating her the way he treated his sister—which I was relieved to see, since Sophie was a total knockout and most boys lost the ability to form complete sentences around her.

I looked over at Ford, and I could feel the blush starting to creep into my cheeks. The ill-fated surfing lesson had happened a year ago, but we'd never really discussed it since. But I supposed there was no rational reason not to bring it up. . . . After all, it wasn't like anything had really happened. "We really don't need to talk about this."

"Yes, we do," Sophie said, leaning forward, then making a face and pushing my pizza closer to me. Both she and Ford groaned when I tried to order my favorite pizza, pineapple-sausage-pepperoni. Ford thought that putting pineapple on pizza and calling it "Hawaiian" was an insult to his home state, and Sophie was a fan of plain extra-cheese, nothing on it. They both claimed they didn't even want any of my toppings migrating, so they'd made me order my own pie. I didn't mind, despite the fact that ordering a pizza for one was just slightly embarrassing. But my dad was the only other person who liked pizza this way, and I knew he'd appreciate the leftovers.

"So we've gone all the way down to my favorite spot in Malibu," Ford said, looking over at me again with a grin. "I've brought all the gear. I'm prepared to teach her the basics. And then at the last minute Gemma chickens out."

"I wouldn't put it quite like that," I said, feeling my face get hotter than ever. "I just *realized* the extreme folly of going out into the open ocean with only some wood and fiberglass. That's all."

"Chickened out," Ford said, shaking his head at me. "And if you weren't going to surf then—a deserted beach, perfect conditions, private instructor—you're never going to."

"That's not true," I said automatically. I didn't know what the circumstances would be that would get me to change my mind on this, but I was sure there had to be some.

"Sure," Ford said, rolling his eyes theatrically. "I'll believe it when I see it."

"Maybe we should tell Sophie about how the rest of the night went," I said, raising an eyebrow at him, preparing to turn the tables.

"Um, we don't have to," Ford said, his smile falling away. "Oh, look, you still have some of your disgusting pizza left."

"What happened?" Sophie asked, looking from Ford to me, her expression clearly saying *What happened?!?*

"Ford locked the keys in the trunk of his car, along with our phones," I said, and noticed to my delight that it looked like Ford was beginning to blush now. "And we didn't have any money, so we had to walk to this gas station. . . ." I looked over at Ford, who was now very busy pretending to read the menu, despite the fact we'd already ordered and had finished eating.

"And then what?" Sophie asked, raising an eyebrow.

Ford looked over at me, and our eyes met for a moment. Nothing had happened, which was what I'd told myself firmly over the last year, when I was still with Teddy, wondering if I'd done anything wrong. We'd just walked to a mini-mart, used the phone, bought candy, and walked up the road together in the moonlight, talking and sharing a Slurpee as the sound of the waves crashed next to us. We weren't sure if anyone was going to come and get us, and we'd prepared ourselves for the possibility we'd have to sleep in the car. We'd tilted the seats back as far as they would go, and there had been a moment—I was sure of it—when we'd been looking at each other, lying down in the car, just a foot apart, when I'd felt that things could have gone another way. That moment the very air in the car had felt charged—like if either of us had said anything, or moved an inch, something would have happened.

But then my dad came and picked us up, the moment disappeared, and we'd never spoken about it since. Because there wasn't anything to talk about, really. Not at all.

"And then my dad came and picked us up," I finally said.

"Wow," Sophie said, deadpan, "that's a really great story, you guys." She shot me a look that let me know she thought there was something I wasn't telling her.

"Do you want dessert?" I asked, taking the menu out of Ford's hands. "They have cannolis here that're great." I glanced around for our waitress, and then stopped. I looked—and then looked again.

It was Josh.

He was standing with the crowd of people waiting to be seated, looking down at his phone.

"Which cannoli?" Ford asked, taking the menu back from me.

"Um, I don't know," I said, sliding out of the booth. "I'll be right back."

"Gem?" Sophie asked, and I could hear the confusion in her voice, but I ignored it as I walked across the restaurant. I hadn't thought it through; I just knew I had to try to talk to him, try to get him to listen to me in a way he hadn't been willing to do the night before.

I crossed from the restaurant into the area by the hostess stand, where people were crowded onto two benches or standing around, staring at the hostess and sighing loudly. Josh was still looking down at his phone, leaning against the wall, and hadn't seen me yet. I took a breath as I walked a few steps closer to him, trying to gather my thoughts, and figure out what I was going to say. . . .

"Hi, Gemma!" Reid Franklin was suddenly standing right in front of me, looking thrilled to see me and speaking much more loudly than was necessary. "It's so funny to see you here. Are you trying to get a table too? Is Sophie with you?" Reid looked around, the expression on his face lovestruck. Reid had fallen for Sophie pretty much on sight, whereas her feelings toward him could be described as indifferent, at best.

"No," I said, trying to look around him to see Josh. "I mean, yes, but . . ."

Josh looked up at me, and I felt my breath catch in my

throat. He looked stunned to see me, and I couldn't help but notice the faint blue circles under his eyes, like maybe he'd passed the same sleepless night that I had. I opened my mouth to say something, when Josh shook his head and walked out the restaurant's front door, pushing it a little harder than he needed to.

I didn't even think about staying, just followed him outside, where he was striding across the parking lot. "Josh," I called as I hurried after him. "Wait a second. I—"

"What do you want?" he asked, and I could hear that the hurt in his voice was just as raw as it had been the night before. "Seriously. I have nothing to say to you."

"I just . . ." I started, taking another step toward him, but then stopping when I saw how he tensed up as I came closer. I felt myself falter as I looked up at him. He was as cute as ever— dark hair, tan skin, green eyes. Memories of the Josh I'd spent the first part of the summer with flashed through my mind, unbidden—Josh holding flowers, coming to pick me up for dinner; Josh, rumpled in oversize meerkat sweatpants, laughing as he watched *The Princess Bride*. Josh, touching my face so gently, leaning down to kiss me. I blinked as I tried to focus on who was in front of me now—Josh, his expression distant, looking at me like I was a stranger. "I just wanted to try and explain."

"Explain," he echoed. His voice was cold and clipped, and just the sound of it was enough to make me want to cry. Josh had only sounded like that a few times this summer, always when he was talking about his ex-girlfriend, who had broken his heart with her lies. And now I was in that category too. I was also getting bitter-voiced. "Explain how you lied to me all summer?"

"No," I said immediately, then hesitated. "I mean, yes, there were some things that . . . um . . ."

"God, Sophie, I—" Josh stopped and shook his head. "I don't even know what to call you. Gemma?" He said my name like it was a particularly ugly foreign word he wasn't going to bother saying again.

"Gemma," I confirmed. "But—"

"I don't even know who you are," Josh said, sounding as baffled by this as he was upset. "I mean, you pretended to be someone else. Who *does* that?"

"You do know me," I said, but my stomach was starting to clench, and this conversation was not at all going the way I had hoped it might. I had wanted Josh to just be willing to hear me out, and maybe, possibly, consider forgiving me. But it was very clear that wasn't about to happen.

"No," he said, shaking his head again. "I don't. Who are you, really?"

I opened my mouth to reply, then hesitated. The question, as simple as it was, had hit me in my core. For years I'd carried the guilt of what I'd done to Hallie when we were kids, how I'd wrecked my father's life. And then I'd poured myself into being Teddy Callaway's girlfriend. And then, reeling from that, I'd gone immediately into being Sophie Curtis as I'd tried to make things right with Hallie. I had been all these other things for so long now, I wasn't sure who I was without them. Which meant I wasn't exactly sure how to answer this very simple question.

Josh shook his head yet again, and started to walk back to the restaurant, but then stopped with his hand on the door handle and turned back to me. "I just want to know why," he said, and I could hear hurt and confusion through the anger in his voice. "You pretend to be someone else, you get me to fall for you—and why? Was it just some big joke?"

"*No,*" I cried. I could feel myself on the verge of tears. I started to take a step toward him, but something in his expression stopped me. "Josh. Please. You have to understand. I never meant to hurt you. I was just trying to make things right."

"Well, you did a great job of that," he said sarcastically.

I swallowed hard and nodded. *This* was the hardest thing to grasp—that all my efforts this summer, all my trying and stress and worry, had not only been for nothing, they'd actually made things worse. And though Hallie had stacked the deck against me, it still didn't change the fact that I'd failed. "But it wasn't intentional," I said haltingly. "I mean . . . I wasn't trying to hurt you. That's the last thing I ever wanted." Josh looked down for a moment, then away. I wondered if, just maybe, my words were getting through to him. "And—"

"Hey!" Reid stepped outside, smiling big. "Our table's ready." A minute too late, he picked up on the vibe, and his smile faltered and fell as he looked from me to Josh. "Um. Am I interrupting?"

"No," Josh said. He looked away from me and took a step back toward the restaurant. "We're done here." He pulled open the door and stepped inside. Reid followed a moment later, shooting me a sympathetic look, and then I was alone in the parking lot, feeling worse than ever.

❦❦❦❦❦❦

"You okay?" Sophie asked as we walked into the house. I hadn't had much to say once I'd returned to the table, and had only picked at the cannolis that Ford and Sophie had devoured.

I nodded, not making eye contact. I hadn't wanted to try to explain to her what had happened, not with Ford there. Telling him why I'd been so quiet on the ride home would involve telling him about Josh, which meant I'd have to explain what was going on with Hallie.

Ford had started yawning hugely again, and he called good night to us as he headed toward the pool house.

"Talk to you in the morning?" Sophie asked, looking up at me. She'd taken off her shoes (the only flats Sophie ever wore were flip-flops) and was standing at the foot of the staircase.

"Definitely," I said, shooting her a smile. She looked at me for a moment longer before nodding and walking upstairs. I knew Sophie could tell that something was wrong, but I also knew that she'd wait until I was ready to talk about it.

I headed to the kitchen to get myself some water. I pulled a bottle out of the fridge door and was thrilled to see that, sometime today, Rosie had stocked the kitchen once again. I sat down at the counter and rolled the bottle between my palms. I couldn't get the argument with Josh out of my head. Did

I really want to stay here and have a summer filled with scenes like that? But on the other hand did I really want to leave town, knowing I wouldn't have a chance to change his mind—that he would always think the worst of me?

I was starting to get warm despite the air conditioner that was constantly running, a quiet hum in the background. I pulled off my jacket—only to realize a second later that it wasn't mine. It was Ford's—he'd given it to me in the restaurant, when I'd been shivering in my sundress, not realizing that the Upper Crust kept their air conditioners set to arctic. I looked across to the pool house and saw all the lights were still on, then grabbed my water and headed for the sliding door that led to the patio.

The warm night air hit me as soon as I stepped outside, and I could hear the sound of the waves from the beach that was just steps away. I knocked on the pool house door, and when I heard "Yeah?" I stepped inside.

I was glad I wasn't going to wake Ford up for the second time that day. He was sitting on one of the leather couches, an acoustic guitar across his lap, strumming it softly. "Hey," I said.

"*Aloha,*" he said with a smile. "Miss me, huh?"

I threw the jacket at him, and was happy to see it hit him on the head. "Wanted to return this."

Ford just raised an eyebrow at me. "Oh, *that* you return?"

"What are you talking about?" I asked, but he just smiled and started playing his guitar again. "I'm surprised to see you're not on your laptop," I said. Ford's two modes for as long as I'd known him seemed to be surfing and coding. It was a little disconcerting to get to see this much of his face.

Ford shrugged and played a minor chord. "Ran into a little problem with the algorithm," he said. "Right now it's having trouble distinguishing between real information about people and misinformation on the Internet," he said. "It's causing an issue, because then it starts to build metrics based on the false data."

I nodded, a little amazed that I seemed to be following him so far. "So you have to correct the misinformation," I said slowly.

"Of course," Ford said, now just plucking the strings. "Otherwise, the whole model will be unfounded and eventually cause a crash. You always have to start with a foundation of truth."

I nodded, turning over his words in my head. "I guess that makes sense," I said. I pulled the door open. "I'll leave you to it."

"Hey, Gem?" Ford called when I was about to step outside. He glanced up at me for a moment before focusing down on his guitar again. "I'm glad you're here. It'll be nice to see you for more than a few days."

"Right," I said, making myself smile back at him. I was on the verge of telling him that I was very much considering leaving the Hamptons, and soon, but at the last minute I decided against it. "Night, Ford."

"Night, Gem," he said, and as I stepped outside, I heard the playing start up again in earnest.

I walked through the house to the upstairs where all the bedrooms were, and went right to the guest room that was

Sophie's. "Hey," she said when I opened the door. She was sprawled on her bed, flipping through a gossip magazine.

"Hey," I said as I sat down on her bed. "Got a second?"

"I have five seconds," she said with a smile, and I made myself more comfortable on the bed, then took a deep breath and told her what had happened at the restaurant with Josh. When I'd finished, she looked at me sympathetically. "I'm so sorry, Gem."

"Thanks," I said, my voice coming out hoarse. I pressed my palms against my eyes. I could feel tears back there, lurking somewhere, and I didn't want to let them escape. I lowered my hands and shook my head. "You should have seen the way he looked at me," I said. "It was like he didn't even know me."

"Of course he knows you," Sophie said with such authority that I felt slightly better. "And he'll remember that at some point. Just maybe not right away."

"I just . . . really messed things up here," I said in a small voice, looking down at the blue stripes on Sophie's bedspread.

"So," Sophie said after a moment, her voice hesitant. "What are you thinking?" she asked. "Do you want to go home?"

I took a breath before I answered her. I knew that it would, logically, make more sense to just go back to Putnam and stay with Sophie until my mom and Walter were back from Scotland. But Ford's words were reverberating in my head, and there was a part of me, overriding the logic, that needed to try to fix things here. "I think we should stay," I said. Sophie's eyebrows flew up, and I hurried to explain. "I can't just slink away and leave Josh to think the worst of me," I said. "And if I leave now, he'll only ever think that."

Sophie looked at me for a long moment, then smiled. "Well, I guess if we *have* to stay in a beachfront mansion with a pool, we have to." She gave me a measured stare. "What are you going to do about Hallie?"

"Nothing," I said, and Sophie's jaw dropped.

"Seriously?" she asked. "After what she did all summer? After the thing today with the photographer?"

"The last thing I want is to be drawn into some revenge war with her," I said even as Sophie looked at me skeptically. "I'm serious. It's the stronger thing to stay above it, and just walk away."

"She stole your boyfriend," Sophie pointed out in a patient voice.

"I know," I said, trying again not to wince, and failing. "And I'm going to have a little chat with Teddy and tell him the circumstances. I think when he hears what happened, and how she manipulated him, they're not going to be together for much longer."

Sophie frowned. "But I thought he wasn't answering your texts."

"He isn't," I admitted. I'd been texting him throughout the day, telling him we needed to talk. I had a feeling that either Hallie was holding on to his phone, or the prospect of talking to an ex-girlfriend—one who had just found out you'd cheated on her—was keeping him from responding to me. "But," I said, feeling myself start to smile, "I know where he'll be tomorrow."

CHAPTER 6

"Explain it to me again," Sophie said over the phone as I walked up the sidewalk, trying not to draw any attention to myself, then wishing I knew what exactly that involved.

"It'll be simple," I said, hoping even as I spoke the words that they would turn out to be true. "I'll find Teddy before he gets on the Jitney. I'll explain to him what Hallie did, and how she's been using him. And then he'll break up with her." I could say this last part, at least, with full confidence. Teddy tended to see things in black-and-white, which had occasionally been frustrating when we were together, but was now something I found I greatly appreciated. Once he found out what Hallie had done, he would end it with her immediately. I knew that for him, it would be that clear.

"And you're doing this because you want him to know," Sophie said, and even through the phone I could hear the doubt in her voice. "And not for any other reason?" I could practically feel her expectant silence, and I couldn't help thinking that now would be a really great moment for her train to lose cell service. Since we'd decided to stay, she had headed back to Putnam for the day to pick up more clothes, and also her car.

"What do you mean?" I asked, even though I was pretty sure I knew what she meant.

"Is this just your way of making sure Teddy is single so you can get him back?" she asked, and the tone of her voice was enough to make it clear what she thought about this prospect. "I remember how upset you were when he dumped you, Gem. I remember the stress-baking. And it would be understandable if you still have lingering feelings. More than understandable. In fact, I think it's called identity regression, and it's when—"

"Have to go," I said quickly. Both of Sophie's parents were shrinks, and I could always tell when she was about to launch into one of their theories. "But call me when you're heading back." I hung up, then looked at the Jitney stop at the end of the street.

The Jitney—the bus that ferried people from the Hamptons to New York City and back again—had been the way I'd gotten to the Hamptons five years ago the first summer I'd spent here, but I hadn't taken it since. There were pickup spots in all the different townships, and they were pretty frequent in other parts of the Hamptons, but in Quonset there were only two a day. Hallie hadn't realized the gift she'd given me when she'd told me that Teddy would be taking the Jitney back today. I knew that there was a possibility he would be on the evening bus, but there wasn't much of a chance that he'd be at any stop other than this. It was the closest one to Hallie's house, and knowing Teddy, he would be concerned enough about his carbon footprint that he wouldn't have wanted to travel any farther than necessary. The Teddy I'd known would already have purchased credits to try to offset the carbon he'd use for the ride into New York City (and then the train ride to Putnam).

I looked at the pickup stop with its round green sign and wondered if I should duck into Quonset Coffee and get an iced latte, not only because I wanted one, but to use as a prop. My running into Teddy needed to appear accidental, a twist of fate, nothing but coincidence, like I'd just happened to pass the bus stop heading out of the coffee shop.

I looked at the time on my phone and decided against it. I only had about ten minutes before this next bus was departing, and I didn't want to miss my window. People had already started to gather with duffel bags and overstuffed carry-ons, milling about near the pickup spot, making small talk or scrolling through their phones. But Teddy was not among them, and I had just resigned myself to the fact I'd have to come back later tonight, when I saw a white Jeep speed down the street and double-park. I recognized it as Hallie's car and I watched, my heart starting to beat harder, as she got out of the driver's side. A moment later Teddy got out of the passenger seat, carrying his beat-up duffel. I realized a moment too late that they were heading right toward me, and if Hallie saw me now, it would derail this plan entirely—there was no chance she'd leave me and Teddy alone with a chance to talk. As they started to come closer to me, I panicked, looked around, then ducked into the closest store to me—the ice-cream parlor Sweet & Delicious.

A bell jangled over the door as I stepped inside. The store was empty, which wasn't that surprising, considering it wasn't even noon yet. I had once been a regular customer here, the summer that I was eleven. But I hadn't been inside yet this summer, just passed by it. I had only a vague memory about what it had looked like when I'd been here before, but from what I could recall, not much had changed.

It was still decorated like an old-fashioned soda shop. There were three booths against the walls, an ancient jukebox in the corner, and the whole color scheme seemed to be bright white with red trim. There was a bulletin board near the door with flyers, notes, and pictures of happy customers eating ice cream pinned to it. There was nobody even standing behind the counter, which seemed strange, but I was grateful for it at the moment, since I knew I was not behaving like a normal ice-cream parlor patron. I flattened my back against the wall and tried to peer out the glass door to the street, but the writing that covered it—*Sweet & Delicious* in stylized script, along with the hours of operation—was making it hard for me to see out. I crossed to the glass window that looked onto the street, and the only thing hampering my view now was the HELP WANTED sign in the corner.

Trying to keep myself hidden from view as much as possible, I peered out. Teddy was now standing at the back of the haphazard Jitney line, and Hallie was next to him. I felt my stomach twist as I saw that Teddy's arm was around Hallie's shoulders, that she was leaning against him, her head resting on his chest.

"Hello?" a voice from the back called. "Is someone there?"

For a moment I debated not saying anything, since this might buy me more time to skulk by the window. But then what if the employee came out and thought I was robbing the place or something? Which I very well could have been, by the way. Not that I had any intention of knocking over an ice-cream parlor, but this one would seem to make it particularly easy.

"Yes," I called back, "but no rush or anything." I didn't exactly want ice cream, but I figured I could just stall, pretend I was undecided, and try a bunch of flavors. I looked outside again, but now Hallie and Teddy were obscured by a family with four kids, all of whom seemed to either be crying or punching each other, or both. One of the kids went for a headlock, and in the scuffle that ensued, I saw that Hallie was still next to Teddy. I pulled out my phone and checked the time. The bus was due to leave in ten minutes, and this whole plan hinged on Teddy being alone. Why hadn't I factored in that Hallie might be there until the bus departed, waving after him like war brides did in old movies?

Leave, I thought as hard as I could. *Just go.*

"Sorry," the employee called again, sounding more stressed this time. "I'm actually in the freezer. I might need you to . . . um . . . ." There was the sound of banging on metal, and then the sound of a door swinging open and hitting a wall. "Never mind!" The voice sounded somewhat familiar, and as the employee ran from a side door to stand behind the counter, I realized why—it was Reid. He was wearing an all-white outfit with a red apron over it. Reid stared at me, clearly as surprised to see me as I was to see him. He blinked fast a few times. "Oh. Hey, Gemma."

"Hey," I said. I hadn't known that Reid had been working here, but most of my interactions with him so far this summer—except for the one last night—had involved trying to keep him from accidentally revealing who I was, so maybe there just hadn't been the opportunity to talk about the state of his employment.

"Nice to, um, see you again," he said as he scrambled to put on a red baseball cap with *Sweet & Delicious* etched across it. Since Reid's hair was red, and his face had a tendency toward redness, I wasn't sure this hat was going to be the best look on him. He gestured toward the back. "Sorry about that. The freezer door keeps locking, and this one time I was trapped in there for, like, fifteen minutes. They said I nearly had frostbite!"

"Wow," I said, leaning over to look out the window once more. "That's really . . ."

Whatever I'd been about to say died on my lips as I realized what was happening. The bus was pulling up to the Jitney stop, and the haphazard line was starting to get more organized, people jostling to claim their spots. And Hallie was still firmly pressed to Teddy's side.

"Actually, I'm glad you're here," Reid said as he adjusted the brim of his hat, moving it up and down and then returning it to exactly the same spot. "I was hoping to talk to you about . . . I mean, this is kind of awkward, but . . ."

I could hear Reid, but all my attention was focused out the window. The bus doors were still closed, but the driver was opening the storage doors underneath and starting to load people's luggage onto it. From what I remembered, once all the luggage was loaded, the bus was only a few minutes away from leaving, which meant my window for talking to Teddy before the bus departed was now rapidly closing. I watched, panicking, as Teddy handed his duffel to the driver, Hallie still looking like she had no intention of going anywhere. I needed to get her out of there *now*. But how? If she saw me, the whole plan would be blown. But it's not like I could magically become someone else and convince her to get out of line. . . . An idea suddenly hit me, and I whirled around to face the counter.

"Reid!" I said, taking a step toward him. "Can I use your phone? It's an emergency."

"Oh," Reid said, looking a little startled. "Um, sure. Is yours not working?"

"I just . . . I need it now," I said, glancing back outside again and seeing how full the under-bus storage was getting. "Please?"

"Sure," he said, and I ran across to the counter, grabbing the phone from Reid's hand as soon as he held it out.

"Thanks," I said as I ran back to my spot by the window, already scrolling through his texts. Thankfully, he had texted a little with Hallie—it looked like mostly brief exchanges about logistics, and a few from the night of the party, when he was trying to locate Josh. I started typing as fast as I could, while also hoping I was doing a believable Reid impression. It wasn't lost on me that it was Hallie who, by stealing Sophie's phone, had given me the idea to do this.

Reid Franklin
11:55 AM
Hi Hallie! Sorry to bother you, but I'm over at the ice-cream parlor and it looks like maybe your car is being towed??

I pressed myself back against the wall and watched as Hallie reached into her pocket and pulled out her phone. It seemed like fate had decided to be on my side for that moment, since there was a huge delivery truck in the middle of the street, blocking Hallie's view, and mine. So maybe her car *was* about to be towed, and I was just helping her out.

I saw Hallie look up in alarm, toward the street. She said something to Teddy, and I stared down fixedly at Reid's phone screen when she stretched up to kiss Teddy good-bye, not wanting to have to see it. When I looked up again, Hallie was hurrying up the street, her long blond hair streaming behind her.

"Thanks," I called to Reid as I hustled out the door.

"Uh, Gemma—" I heard him start, but the rest of whatever he was going to say was lost as I dropped the phone in my bag and let the door slam behind me. It looked like the bus driver was closing the luggage storage, which meant I only had minutes to make this happen.

I dashed full-out toward the Jitney line, only slowing down when I got close, and then I adopted a leisurely walk, like I was just out enjoying a morning stroll, hoping my labored breathing wasn't going to give me away. I kept my eyes straight ahead as I passed by Teddy, willing him to notice me.

"Gemma?"

Bingo. I stopped and turned around. I'd fixed what I hoped was a believable expression of surprise on my face, but it faltered a little as I looked at him.

Teddy Callaway.

I'd seen him the night of the Fourth, but so much had been going on—and I'd been struggling to wrap my head around what was happening—that it felt like this was the first time I'd properly seen him in over a month. He was more tan than when he'd broken my heart in the gardening aisle of Target, and his blond hair was lighter—both were probably a result of the Colombian volunteering trip he'd gone on without me. He was wearing the same light blue T-shirt he'd worn on our last date together (not that I'd had any idea of this at the time, of course), and it brought out his pale blue eyes.

He was so achingly familiar to me, and my instinct still kicked in, the one that told me this was my boyfriend, who I loved, and why wasn't I kissing him?

"Gem?" he asked, looking at me with his head tilted to the side. "You okay?"

I blinked and tried to get my thoughts back in some kind of order. I had to focus. I had a job to do here. "Yes," I said quickly. The most disconcerting thing of all was the way he was looking at me—like I was an old friend he'd just happened to run into. There was a distance to his expression, and it felt like he was breaking my heart all over again. "I mean, hi! So crazy to run into you like this."

"Yeah," he said as he nodded toward the Jitney. "I'm just heading back to Putnam."

I nodded, like this was brand-new information that I was hearing. "Oh, cool," I said. "Right." I looked up at him and took a breath. I couldn't let myself get distracted by the fact that he looked so much cuter than I'd remembered. He had lied to me. He had *cheated* on me. Remembering this, and the rush of anger that came with it, was enough to help me focus. "So I'm actually glad to see you. I wanted to talk to you about something."

"Oh, yeah?" Teddy asked, suddenly looking wary as he took a step closer to the bus.

"Manhattan!" the driver yelled as the bus doors opened and there was a collective impatient sigh from the people in line all around us. "Twelve o'clock for Manhattan is boarding." The people in line started to surge forward, and Teddy glanced over to them.

"Yes," I said quickly, taking a step closer to him. "It's about Hallie."

"I don't—" Teddy looked toward the bus and took a breath. "Gem, I'm really sorry about what happened. And I'm sorry you had to find out the way you did. But I'm not going to talk about Hallie with you."

"But . . ." I said. I noticed, my pulse picking up, that there were only a few people left standing on the curb, and that the bus's engine had sputtered to life. I took a breath and started speaking faster. "You have to listen to me. Your relationship isn't what you think it is. Hallie's just using you—"

Teddy let out a short laugh and shook his head. "You know, I told Hallie she was wrong about you," he said.

"You . . . did?" I asked, trying to follow this turn in the conversation.

He nodded. "She told me that you'd probably get in touch. That you'd try and spread lies about her. That you would say whatever you had to." He looked at me sorrowfully and shook his head. "I told her she was wrong. I told her you wouldn't sink that low."

Of course she had. I could feel my anger toward Hallie rising, but knew this was not the moment to vent it. "It's not that," I said, speaking faster than ever as Teddy was jostled to the side by the last remaining passenger, an older man with a fedora, who was struggling to get on and snapping at anyone who tried to help. "It's *true*. Hallie was just trying to get me back; she never—"

"Are you coming?" the bus driver yelled, leaning half out the open door. "Got a schedule to keep here."

Teddy turned back to me, his expression sympathetic. "I know the breakup has been hard for you," he said. "But you're better than this. Take care, okay?" And before I could reply, he leaned down and kissed me on the cheek, his lips brushing it gently.

"Wait," I started, trying to get my bearings. "Don't—" But Teddy had turned and walked away, giving me one last glance before boarding the bus.

The door closed behind him, and the bus rumbled down the street. Even though there was no reason to any longer, I watched it until it faded from view, feeling like I should have expected this. Of course Hallie had realized I would try to talk to Teddy. She'd played me perfectly, just like she'd been doing all summer. And now Teddy was gone. I could keep calling or texting—or show up at his house in Putnam—but now I knew that would only make me look crazy. And he certainly wouldn't listen to me.

I started to walk back to the car, feeling like there wasn't anything to do now except head back to Bruce's. I had made it most of the way up the street before I heard an unfamiliar ringing coming from my purse. I lifted it out and saw that it was Reid's phone—the one I'd taken and then forgotten to return to him.

⁂

"Sorry about that," I said as I handed Reid his phone back. I had made certain to delete the text I'd sent from his phone. Reid was staying with Josh and Hallie, so I had a feeling that Hallie would be asking him all about it later tonight, if by then she hadn't already figured out my part in things.

"Sure," Reid said, still looking baffled. "Were you . . . I mean, was everything okay?"

"Oh, sure," I said, but even as I did so, realizing how strange my behavior must have looked—ducking into the ice-cream parlor, demanding his phone, running out. "I just saw someone I knew on the Jitney line and wanted to say hi."

Reid nodded and moved his baseball cap up and down again. "Gotcha." He gave me a quick smile and then pocketed his phone.

I suddenly felt a wave of guilt hit me. Reid was a nice guy—did he deserve to be pulled into this, used without his knowledge? But then again, had Sophie? "Listen," I said haltingly, trying to gather my thoughts even as I spoke. "I wanted to apologize. . . ." I took a breath to explain but suddenly realized I didn't even know where or how to begin. I also had no idea what Josh had told him, how Hallie might have spun this.

Reid just looked at me expectantly. "Apologize for what?"

I looked around the store, like I would be able to discover some answer I could give him—and there, unexpectedly, leaning against the window, I found it. And this would also get my father off my back, so it was two birds with one stone. "Apologize for not wanting any ice cream," I said quickly as I gestured to the HELP WANTED sign. "Are you guys still hiring?"

CHAPTER 7

"Ice cream?" my dad asked as he turned around in his chair to face me. He was blinking at me like he wasn't entirely sure who I was, which I knew meant he'd been working all morning.

"Yes," I said as I held up my new Sweet & Delicious hat. While I'd been in the store, talking to Reid about the job opening—he had no idea if they were still hiring, which probably shouldn't have surprised me, since he also hadn't realized I'd kept his phone until I gave it back to him—Kendall, the manager, came to deliver that week's paychecks. She'd given me an application and then walked me through the particulars of the job—they needed someone three days a week, and one of the days had to be a weekend. They also sometimes partnered with The South Fork, the catering company, and provided ice cream if an event needed a sundae bar. If that was the case, Sweet & Delicious employees were asked to step in (for regular pay plus the possibility of free food). This had all sounded fine to me—it didn't seem like it was going to take up too much time or be too taxing, and best of all, it would get my father off my back—so when she offered me the job, I accepted on the spot. "I start tomorrow."

"Wow," my dad said, nodding, and I could tell I was coming a little bit more into focus. "That's great, Gem. I'm proud of you."

"Thanks," I said, perching on the edge of his office couch. "What are you even working on right now?" I tried to crane my neck to see my dad's computer screen. "Rosie said something about a novel adaptation?"

My dad nodded, and I noticed that for some reason, he'd started turning bright red. "Yeah," he said, clearing his throat. "That's right. And then the studio wants me to write the next animal movie."

"What is it this time?" I asked, a little surprised that he had to start it right away, since he'd just finished the one about penguins.

"*In the Nick of Time*." He grimaced. "They want this one to be a Christmas movie. About Santa. And, somehow, also about time travel and polar bears."

"Oh," I said, finally putting the pieces together. "So that explains why there's a giant stuffed one in the foyer."

He nodded. "They're not exactly subtle."

I sat back on the arm of his couch. I couldn't help but notice that my dad seemed markedly unexcited about this movie. "Are you going to do it?"

My dad took off his glasses and set them down on the side of his laptop. "You know," he said, a note of surprise creeping into his voice, "I'm thinking about turning it down. The studio wants me to, but I'm just not sure I can handle another one of these."

"Then say no," I said, giving him a smile. "If you don't have to, why do something that's just going to make you unhappy?"

"Very wise," he said. "I'll take it under advisement."

"So if you're not writing about polar bears, what are you working on?" I asked. "That novel adaptation Rosie was talking about?"

"Uh," my dad said, moving to close his laptop screen. "I'm not sure that you should—" As he moved his computer, I saw that there was a book on the desk next to it—a book with a familiar black-and-red cover.

"Dad," I said, horrified, as I looked from the copy of *Once Bitten* and back to my father. "You're not . . . ?"

My dad nodded and put his glasses back on, but not before I noticed that he looked distinctly uncomfortable. "Yeah," he said. "I'm adapting the screenplay."

"Oh," I said. I realized this explained why there had been a huge number of copies in the foyer, and also, when I'd seen Rosie with a copy earlier this summer, she'd said it was for work. But that didn't change the fact that my *dad* was going to be writing the screenplay for one of the most controversial books of the last few years. I mean . . . did he even know what this book was *about*? I certainly didn't want to be the one to tell him.

"Yeah," he said. "Bruce spent a fortune on the rights, but there were a lot of writers up for the job. The author had final say, though, and she chose me for some reason. So that's what I'm working on, to answer your question."

I nodded, still reeling from this revelation. "Not exactly time-traveling penguins," I pointed out.

He gave me a ghost of a smile. "I know," he said. "And I've got to be honest with you, I'm worried about the process. Bruce had to promise all kinds of things to get the author to sell the rights. I haven't met her yet, but apparently she wants to be very involved. So I might be gone a bit over the next few weeks. If she's as demanding as it seems like she's going to be, I have a feeling I'm going to be going to her and not the other way around to get to hear her 'thoughts.'"

I nodded and picked up the book to look at the back cover—no photo, just a brief bio stating that Brenda Kreigs lived on a remote island with her family. "So where does she live?" I asked, looking up from the book. "Where's her island?"

My dad smiled and took it back from me. "Manhattan," he said. "I think that part was probably dreamed up by someone in the publicity department."

"Got it," I said. I supposed it was better than having my dad constantly leave to go to Newfoundland or something. But I couldn't help but feel like I'd barely seen him this summer.

"When I turn this draft in, I'll have more free time," my dad said, apparently sensing what I was feeling—or maybe even feeling the same way.

"Especially if you don't have to write a polar bear movie," I pointed out.

"Exactly," my dad said. "I think I've amassed enough

goodwill with the studio to pass on it and not have it damage my future career prospects." He opened his laptop again, which was enough to get me moving toward the door. It had been traumatizing enough to find a copy of that book in my mom's closet—I didn't even want to get a glimpse of what my dad's interpretation of a vampire-love story would look like.

"Good luck with the writing," I said as I started to head out.

"Thanks, Gem," he said. But before I had left the room, he called after me, "No more credit card charges, right?"

"Nope," I said immediately. I had learned my lesson as far as that was concerned—I had no desire to see my dad's face turn that red ever again. "And as soon as I start getting paid, I can pay you back."

"That's my girl," my dad said, giving me a smile before turning back to his laptop screen. I shut the door behind me, trying not to do the math of just how many hours I was going to have to work at the ice-cream parlor to pay for the bikini Hallie had given me, knowing full well that it would disintegrate and that I'd have to buy a replacement for her.

I walked away from my dad's office and went looking to see if anyone was around. After wandering around the house for a while (and then texting when wandering started to feel like too much effort—I always forgot just how massive Bruce's house was until I really started to walk through it), I determined that I was the only young person there. Sophie was still en route from Putnam and stuck in traffic, and it seemed like Ford was still surfing—he'd told me that was his plan when I'd passed him on the way to the kitchen this morning. I was at a bit of a loose end, which was actually something of a novelty in a summer that had been already filled with more emotional peaks and valleys than I ever could have anticipated. Feeling like I should take advantage of the moment, I headed to my room, flopped down on my bed, turned on my laptop, and logged on to Friendverse.

When I'd been going on under Sophie's name, I'd had to put crazy privacy controls up on my own profile so you couldn't even find me if we weren't already friends. But there was no longer any need for that, so I switched my privacy settings back to what they normally were and scrolled through my news feed. I paused for a moment at the status update of Abby West-Smith. She was Sophie's friend, but I'd become Friendverse friends with her a few years back after I'd seen her comments on Sophie's profile. Unlike most people, who only seemed to update incredibly boring or braggy statuses, Abby's were always just funny. She hadn't updated much this summer, but I read through some of her older statuses, feeling myself smile. Reading through her status updates—and then looking back at my profile, which I hadn't touched in months—was like looking back into a time in my life when things had been simple, when the world had been one that I'd understood. I read through old posts for longer than I should have, wishing that—even though it was impossible—I could somehow go back to that time when I knew who I was and everything still made sense.

"Well?" Sophie asked me. It was hours later, and we were sitting on lounge chairs out by the pool, despite the fact that the day had turned cloudy and overcast. Sophie was wrapped in a throw she'd taken from the foot of her bed, and I was in the maroon sweatshirt that I'd now appropriated as my own.

She looked at me expectantly, and I knew she was waiting for details about my encounter with Teddy, but I shook my head and took a sip of my Diet Coke.

Sophie had returned to the Hamptons with two overstuffed bags of clothes, which according to her were desperately needed. When she'd come up here the first time, she hadn't packed very much or very carefully. And since Sophie was more fashionable than anyone else I knew, I understood full well how much happier she now was, freshly accessorized and dressed in clothes other than the repeating few I'd gotten used to since she'd been here. I was also happy that Sophie had brought her car, since now that Ford was here, access to Bruce's SUV might be limited. "Were your parents okay with you coming back?" I asked, trying to change the subject.

Sophie made a *so-so* motion with her hand, but her expression—even lit only by the pool lights—let me know she knew I was stalling and that I was going to have to answer her question eventually. "Kind of," she said. "They said I could, but I either had to get a job here or I had to go back to Putnam and work at their practice."

"Doing what?" I asked, since I had no idea what Sophie would do in a shrink's office. Her parents had pioneered a new version of couples' therapy this past year—it was called Couples Counseling Couples, and the couple met with both of Sophie's parents simultaneously—so maybe they were just really busy and needed Sophie to attend to people in the waiting room, or something.

"Who knows," she said. "I'd rather not find out. So I need to get a job."

"I could ask at the ice-cream parlor," I said, sitting up straighter, buoyed by this thought. Maybe if Sophie and I were working together, it wouldn't feel nearly as much like work.

Sophie made a face. "Not if Reid is working there," she said.

"Oh, right," I said, leaning back against my lounge chair again. "Did anything happen when he drove you home on the Fourth?"

"No," Sophie said. "But I could tell he kept trying to work up the nerve. It was *really* uncomfortable. And it's not that he's not cute, it's just . . ." She shook her head. "There's no *edge* there. I need someone with a little more angst. And you know I never go for the nice guys."

I nodded, thinking back over Sophie's last few relationships. This had certainly been true for the ones I'd known. The barista she'd had a fling with last month, I had never met, so I'd just have to take her word for it. "Well, I'm not saying that Reid's the one, but at some point you might want to rethink that policy."

"Maybe," Sophie said, giving me a smile. "But even if I'm not working there, you can still get me free ice cream, right?"

"Of course," I said, smiling back at her.

"Now what happened with Teddy?" she asked, and I knew she wasn't going to leave this alone any longer. I sighed and told her what had happened outside the Jitney stop.

"It was just clear that Hallie had talked to him," I said, feeling dispirited once again as I related the story. "I couldn't say anything to him that he was going to listen to."

Sophie shook her head, her long earrings jangling. "You know I was never Teddy's biggest fan, but it's also *not* okay the way she's using him like that."

"That's the weird thing," I said, swinging my legs off the seat and down to the ground. "I don't think she's only using him anymore. I think she actually likes him."

Sophie nodded, then folded her arms across her chest. "So you were doing all this just because you wanted to help Teddy," she said, and she didn't phrase it like a question. "Come on, Gem. Is this just because you want him back?"

"You want who back?" I whirled around to see Ford standing in the doorway of the pool house.

"Hey," I said, surprised to see him. I hadn't known he was in there—I'd just assumed he was still surfing—and I mentally rewound the conversation that Sophie and I had just had, trying to remember if I'd said anything super-embarrassing. "I didn't know you were home."

"I was working on the algorithm," he said as he pushed his glasses up and rubbed his eyes. "I needed a break." Then he set his glasses back down on his nose and raised an eyebrow at me. "Who do you want back?"

"Teddy," Sophie piped up from her lounge chair, causing Ford to turn and face me.

"You *do*?" Ford asked, looking surprised and—was I just imagining it?—a little disappointed.

"No," I said, glaring at Sophie. "I don't. I was just . . . um . . ."

"I'm not here," I heard a voice behind me whisper. I whirled around and blinked confusedly. There was a large camera in my face, totally blocking out whoever was behind it. "Seriously," the voice behind the camera said, louder this time. "Just go back to whatever you were talking about. Ignore me."

"Gwyn, give it a rest," Ford said as he walked over from the pool house.

The camera lowered, and on the other side of it was someone I recognized—Gwyneth Davidson, looking annoyed. "I was getting good stuff," she muttered. Then she turned to me with a smile. "Hey, Gemma! How's it going?"

I felt myself smile back. I hadn't seen Gwyneth for two years, but she looked pretty much the same. Unlike her brother, she was tiny, barely five foot. And whereas Ford had only turned into a hottie in the last few years, Gwyneth had always taken more after her mom, a former Miss Hawaii. She was petite but curvy, with long black hair and blunt bangs. Her heart-shaped face gave her an angelic look that I'd learned long ago was just a good facade. Maybe it was the influence of growing up among the Hollywood elite, but Gwyneth could be a master manipulator. "It's going okay," I said. "What's, um, with the camera?"

"Please don't ask," Ford said, shaking his head.

"Ignore him," Gwyneth said. "I'm filming a documentary this summer."

"Oh, right," I said, remembering Ford had told me that Gwyneth was at a workshop. "What's it about?"

"Hi," Sophie said, waving, and I realized a moment too late that although I'd been talking about Gwyneth for years, they'd never actually met. "I'm Sophie."

"Oh, Gemma's friend?" Gwyneth asked, smiling. "Awesome. Nice to meet you."

"Sophie's staying here for a bit," I said, and Gwyneth pulled out her phone.

"Good to know," she said, typing a note into it, her fingers flying across the screen. "Then I'll need a waiver from you too."

"A what?" Sophie asked.

"So what's this for?" I asked as I gestured to the camera. "What's the documentary about?"

"Well, after investigating multiple potential subjects . . . ," Gwyneth said as Ford snorted, then tried to turn it into a cough when his sister glared at him. "I've decided to take a boots-on-the-ground, fly-on-the-wall approach, and tell the story of what it takes to get a movie made in today's changing cinematic climate."

"Wow," I said, feeling my eyebrows rise. I hadn't understood most of what Gwyneth had just said, but it had sounded impressive.

"What does that mean, exactly?" Sophie asked, frowning.

"It means I'm making a documentary about Bruce," Gwyneth said. She was looking at Sophie, so I don't think she saw

Ford roll his eyes hugely behind her. "Really try to give people a look behind the curtain, so to speak."

"Uh-huh," Ford said, shaking his head. "Have you told Rosie about this?"

"I just got here," Gwyneth said, but I could hear she sounded nervous for the first time. Rosie did tend to have that effect on people. "I'll, um, talk to her soon. I might just talk to Bruce first, though."

"So what's this for?" Sophie asked as she leaned over to examine the camera. "Like, just for practice?"

"No," Gwyneth said, her expression growing more serious. "I'm trying to get this into a young filmmakers festival that screens at the end of the summer. It's really hard, supercompetitive. You really need to have a subject matter that grabs people, you know? It has to be *compelling*."

"I'm sure yours will be great," I said as encouragingly as I could. Personally, having been around Bruce and my dad for years as they tried to put their movies together, I was of the opinion that filmmaking was actually incredibly boring. But I thought it was probably wise to keep this to myself.

"Thanks," Gwyneth said, biting her bottom lip, "I appreciate it." Gwyneth usually never seemed to doubt herself about anything, and I had a feeling I was seeing a rare crack in her ultra-confident facade. It was also one of the reasons I wasn't as close to her as I was to her brother. Gwyneth was a little charmingly self-centered, and she had a tendency to just take whatever she wanted and think only about herself. When you pointed it out to her, she was always profusely apologetic, but I'd learned a long time ago that she always put herself first. She picked up her camera and turned to go inside, giving Ford a shove—it was their version of hugging—as she passed him.

"Back to it," Ford said, shooting me and Sophie a half-smile before adjusting his glasses and heading back into the pool house.

"Dinner?" Sophie asked as she pulled the throw more tightly around her shoulders.

"Sure," I said, casting a worried glance inside. I had a feeling we might not want to be there when Gwyneth told Rosie what her documentary would be about, especially since Rosie spent most of her time trying to keep Bruce *out* of the public eye. "But we probably want to go out."

"Lobster rolls?" Sophie asked hopefully as she stood up.

I shook my head immediately. Hallie had made sure that Josh and I had gotten spoiled ones on our first date, and the resulting fallout had been terrible enough that I wasn't sure when I would be able to have them again. "Anything else," I said, secretly hoping that Sophie wouldn't pick something like Indian, which she loved and I hated. "Your pick."

⚬⚬⚬⚬⚬⚬

"Is this Indian?" Ford called to me from inside the kitchen.

"Yeah," I said, as I untied my robe and tossed it on a nearby lounge chair. "Unfortunately." Sophie had taken me at my word that it could be her pick, and we'd gone to Mumbai the Sea, which she had loved, while I had eaten rice and plain naan.

"Help yourself," I said as I walked down the steps into the pool. I'd asked Sophie if she wanted to go night swimming too, but she'd claimed she was exhausted after going from the Hamptons to Connecticut and back again, and had gone to bed early. But I had seen the glint of the pool lights from my bedroom window, and I hadn't been able to resist.

"What were you doing at an Indian place?" Ford asked as he came out onto the pool deck holding one of the to-go containers and a fork. "You hate Indian."

"I know," I said as I started swimming, giving silent thanks to Bruce—or his pool guy—for getting the evening temperature so perfect. "But it was Sophie's pick, so . . ." I shrugged and ducked under the water, letting my hair flow out behind me, and then surfacing and smoothing it down.

"Well, it's pretty good, just so you know," he said as he sat down on one of the lounge chairs. I floated on my back and looked up at the sky, but it was still cloudy, and no stars were visible over the pool. "How did it go with Bruce's award?" Ford asked after a moment. "I assume fine, otherwise I probably would have been able to hear when his head exploded."

"It passed mustard," I said, swimming toward the side of the pool. "He couldn't tell anything had happened to it."

"I'm pretty sure," Ford said as he raised his eyebrows at me, "that the phrase is *passed muster.*"

I shook my head and rested my elbows on the edge of the pool. "What does that even mean?"

Ford set the takeout on the lounge chair and came to sit next to me, easing his legs into the water, a smile playing around the corners of his mouth. "I'm pretty sure—and by *pretty* I mean, like, ninety-nine percent—that it's a military expression. Civil War era, I think."

"No," I said, trying to hold on to the conviction I'd had only a minute beforehand. Somehow I felt that this would be easier if I were dry and on solid ground, though I couldn't have said why, exactly. "It's, like, when something is done, and it's easy—like passing someone the mustard. . . ." Even as I spoke, I was suddenly wondering if I'd been saying this wrong my whole life. Probably. Why had Ford been the first one to correct me? Had everyone else just secretly been making fun of me always getting my military expressions wrong? "Maybe you're right," I finally conceded, and Ford laughed.

He looked down at me and smiled, and I smiled back automatically. I thought about saying something—a joke, something to change the subject. I was suddenly aware that we were closer together than we normally were—and that I was wearing much less than I normally did around him. But somehow I didn't seem to want to do anything to change either of those things at the moment.

He leaned back on his hands and looked up, and for a moment I didn't feel the need to say anything, just stayed there in comfortable silence with him, the ocean crashing in the distance and the pool lights flickering and changing, impossible to pin down, as the water moved over them.

CHAPTER 8

"**O**kay," Reid said, looking around Sweet & Delicious and adjusting his baseball cap. "I guess maybe . . . that's it?"

I nodded and took a large much-needed sip of my iced latte. I had shown up an hour before the store's opening so Reid could show me the ropes. But considering he needed to consult the employee manual for almost everything, including how to use the employee manual, I wondered if Kendall had suggested Reid train me so that he also could get a refresher course. "I think I've got it," I said, hoping I sounded more confident than I actually felt as I looked around the empty shop, quiet except for the hum of the industrial freezer in the back. Most of my training—such as it had been—seemed to focus on it.

"Be careful in here," Reid had told me as we stood in the doorway of the freezer and looked around. It was actually pretty cool—a walk-in, with gallons of ice cream lining the shelves. There was a regular refrigerator in the back too, where the whipped cream and syrup and maraschino cherries were kept, despite the fact that they apparently were completely made of chemicals and could withstand anything (or at least this was what Teddy had told me the first time we'd gotten ice cream together and I'd ordered some). But the freezer was massive, seeming to stretch on forever—an illusion that was enhanced by the fact that it was pretty dark inside. There was a fluorescent light that flickered on and off, and maybe to combat this, a flashlight had been hung just inside the door. There was also a sweatshirt and a pair of fingerless gloves underneath the front counter for when you had to stay in the freezer for more than a few minutes—apparently, doing ice-cream inventory was a job everyone went out of their way to avoid.

"Careful?" I echoed as I looked around, exhaling to see my breath forming clouds. It was *cold* in there. We weren't even all the way inside, and I could feel goose bumps popping up on my arms.

"Yeah," Reid said. "Remember? The latch is faulty. The first time I got locked in here, I really didn't think I would make it out. The door is thick enough that nobody can hear you from the outside either. I was in here yelling for, like, ten minutes. Any longer and I might have lost a toe or something."

I shook my head. "I think frostbite takes longer than that." This was based on nothing except some movies I'd seen, but if people could survive overnight in the Arctic, it would seem that Reid could have managed half an hour in an ice-cream freezer. But even so, I had made a mental note to be extra careful when dealing with the latch.

And now my training was apparently done, and it was just Reid and myself, standing behind the counter, waiting for customers to arrive.

"Um," Reid said, glancing over at me and pointing at the neckline of my T-shirt. "Do you mind if I ask what that is? Is it like an iPod?"

I looked down at it and sighed. "No," I said. "I wish."

That morning, when I'd been trying to get some breakfast and not be late to my first day of work, I'd come down into the kitchen to find Bruce holding forth. He was lecturing the one person who had the misfortune to be in the kitchen then—Ford, who didn't quite look awake enough to understand what was happening—all about the diet his new nutritionist had put him on. It declared that the root of all nutritional evil was dairy, and so Bruce was putting a moratorium on it. He'd told us that he didn't want to see it in the house—no milk, no cheese, no pizza. When I pointed out to him that I was currently working in an ice-cream parlor, he'd just told me to be sure not to bring any of it home, much to Ford's dismay. Bruce had even set up the book his nutritionist had written, *Don't You Dairy!*, in the middle of the kitchen island as a reminder.

I'd poured out the coffee I'd just made, since there was no milk to put in it—I generally liked my coffee to taste as little like coffee as possible—and just planned on grabbing something before work. Bruce left to take a call, and I tried to follow, but before I could make it out, Sophie wandered in, yawning, and Gwyneth swept into the kitchen, exuding authority despite the fact that she was still in her pajamas.

"I'm so glad you're all here," she said as she dropped an overstuffed canvas bag onto the kitchen counter. "I'm already behind schedule, so the sooner we do this, the better."

"Do what?" I asked, wishing desperately for coffee as Gwyneth sat down next to Sophie at the counter and started rummaging in her bag. She came up with a mini iPad, unlocked the screen, scrolled through it, then handed it to me. "What is this?" I asked, as I squinted down at what looked like a contract. The language was dense and all of it seemed to be in legalese.

"Your release form," she said, back to rummaging through her bag again. "Everyone else already signed them."

"Is this for your documentary?" I asked, lowering her tablet, and Gwyneth nodded without looking up at me. "So why do you need me to sign one?"

"Oh, I thought I made it clear," Gwyneth asked, sitting up and brushing her bangs out of her eyes. "I want this to be a fly-on-the-wall documentary. Mostly, I'll be filming Bruce, of course, but you might be in it on the edges, and I want to make sure we're covered legally."

"I really don't think I'd sue you," I said as I squinted down at the form again.

"Even so," Gwyneth said, so I shrugged and signed with my finger next to the spot that was marked with a giant *X*.

"Make . . . Curt . . . Germ," Ford said, leaning over my shoulder as I signed *Gemma Rose Tucker*.

"Stop it," I said, glaring up at him while trying not to smile.

Ford was a genius at anagrams, and had told me years ago that, in his opinion, this was the best one for my name. Gwyneth took it from me and pushed it toward Sophie, who shrugged and signed.

"What does that mean?" Sophie asked Ford as she scrawled her looping signature, her eyebrows raised.

"Gemma's name," Ford said, an expression I knew all too well coming into his dark eyes. "What's your full name?"

"Sophie Jung Curtis," she said, looking from me to Ford. "Why?"

"Jung?" Gwyneth asked, still busy looking for something in her bag.

"Her parents are psychologists," I explained.

"Give me a second," Ford said. He crossed his arms and looked up—and it was like I could practically hear him thinking, his brain whirring faster than anyone else's.

"Or you could not," Gwyneth muttered. "I swear, this was old when we were kids."

"Heroic Pigs Unjust," Ford pronounced, looking triumphant. "You're welcome."

"That's what my name turns into?" Sophie asked, looking less than thrilled by this outcome.

"No," Ford said dismissively. "It's one of hundreds of options. But the best one, in my opinion."

"And you just did that in your head right now?" Sophie asked, sounding impressed. "What are some other ones?"

"Here!" Gwyneth said, reaching into the depths of her bag. She produced three white zippered pouches and handed them out to us. "If you could all wear these at all times, that would be *super* helpful."

I opened up the pouch and pulled out a small white object, perfectly square, like a postage stamp. It looked almost like a little iPod, particularly when I noticed it also had a clip on the back.

"What is this?" Sophie asked, beating me to the question.

"They're cameras," Gwyneth said with a smile. "Cool, huh? They're totally digital, wireless, the works."

"Just *how* much is Bruce sinking into this project of yours?" Ford asked, an eyebrow raised.

"Wait," I said, looking at Gwyneth. "You're going to be recording everything we do?"

"No," she said, shaking her head. "The camera faces out. So it's just recording from your point of view—your conversations and interactions. And of course, feel free to turn them off when you're doing . . . anything you wouldn't like me to see." She winked at me, then took the iPad back from Sophie and dropped it into her bag. "But if you could just keep them on the rest of the time, that would be awesome. And then every few days, give them back to me and I'll bank the footage and clear the device's memory."

"Are you going to be filming *any* of this yourself?" Ford asked, shaking his head.

"Of course I'll be filming," Gwyneth shot back. "But I can't be everywhere at once, can I?"

"But I still don't understand, if you're making a documentary about Bruce, why *we're* getting these," I said. Admittedly,

I knew almost nothing about documentary filmmaking, but this would seem to be generating a *lot* of footage for no reason that I could wrap my head around.

Gwyneth shrugged. "Bruce and Rosie and Gem's dad and everyone else already have them," she said. "I had extras. Plus, you never know what angles people are going to catch, or what things are going to be said that turn out to be, like, the whole crux of the movie. So this prevents that."

The three of us just stared at her, which Gwyneth seemed to take as a good sign, because she smiled wide, like we'd all just agreed with her. "Awesome," she said. "Thanks so much!" Then she grabbed her bag and headed back upstairs, already pulling out her cell phone and texting as she walked.

"Wow," Ford said, turning his camera over in his hands. "I can't believe my sister just outsourced the filming of her own documentary."

"I think it's kind of cool," Sophie said, clipping hers on the collar of her shirt, then moving her hair out of the way. "Kind of like a video diary, right?"

"A video diary someone else is going to read," I pointed out as I looked down at mine.

"I really wouldn't worry about that," Ford said. "She's going to delete anything that doesn't fit with her narrative." I considered this, then shrugged and put the camera on.

"Oh," I said now, looking at Reid, wishing I'd thought of something I could say. I wasn't sure if I should tell him that

I had a *camera* attached to my shirt. Reid was self-conscious enough even when his every move wasn't being recorded. "It's just, um, a device."

"Oh, right," Reid said, nodding a few too many times. I looked away and pretended to wipe some crumbs off the counter, just hoping he wouldn't ask any follow-ups. The camera blended in with my white shirt enough that you almost couldn't see it, and I just hoped that Reid's would be the only question about it.

My phone buzzed in my pocket, and as I pulled it out, I saw a text from Sophie.

> **Sophie Curtis**
> 9:15 AM
> Hey! How's work going?
> Can I borrow your pink bikini top?

I texted back immediately, not even trying to hide my phone, but setting it right out on the counter, since it wasn't like we had any customers. Which seemed fitting, considering it was nine A.M. Who wanted ice cream that early?

> **Me**
> 9:16 AM
> Of course!

I was about to put the phone back in my pocket again when I realized that Sophie hadn't been present for that morning's announcement about the house's new dietary restrictions. I had a feeling that the dairy ban wouldn't last long. Bruce was always fanatical about his diets in the beginning, but then he was cheating on them constantly and bribing you to bring him takeout. But since I was currently a guest in his house, and had brought my best friend (without his invitation) along with me, I thought it would be a good idea to go along with it, at least at first.

I texted her again.

Me
9:17 AM
Oh, and Bruce is on a
new diet—NO DAIRY!
We have to at least
pretend to follow it for a while.
So don't bring any
into the house, okay?

Sophie Curtis
9:18 AM
No problem! See you here later?

"Is that Sophie?"

I jumped and saw that Reid was looking over my shoulder.

"Sorry," he said, taking a step back. "I just . . . saw her name."

"Oh," I said, dropping my phone into my pocket. "Yeah. It was."

"Did she, uh . . ." Reid started, looking down at the

black-and-white floor. His face was slowly turning red and beginning to match his hat and hair. "Say anything about me?"

"Um," I said, looking longingly to the door for a second, thinking this would be the perfect time for someone to decide that they needed an ice-cream breakfast. I thought back to the conversation Sophie and I had had the night before, about how he wasn't edgy enough for her, and winced. "Not really." I didn't want to get any more involved in this than I had to be. Even though I knew how Sophie felt, I didn't want to have to be the one to tell Reid.

"Could you maybe talk to her about me?" Reid asked, and the expression on his face was so hopeful that I had to look away from it for a second. Was this how I had looked when I'd been holding on to the idea that Teddy and I could get back together? I suddenly felt retroactively embarrassed for two-months-ago Gemma.

"Well . . . ," I started, knowing it wasn't my place to tell him this, but also not having any idea how to get out of it. "Here's the thing. I—"

The bell over the door rang, and I had never been so happy to see someone entering an ice-cream parlor. It was a harried-looking father with three kids, all of whom had to sample at least four flavors before deciding.

After the kids had been served and they'd taken their cones to the wrought-iron tables outside, we had a steady stream of customers for the next two hours, which made the time fly by. I was also soon realizing that Reid's training left a lot to be desired, and I was pretty much learning on the job. And since we were scrambling to get the customers served, there really wasn't an opportunity for him to ask me more about Sophie's feelings for him, which I was very happy about. I knew I had to tell Sophie that Reid's crush on her had apparently not waned in the face of Sophie's lack of calling or texting him back. I figured she should know so that she could either bite the bullet and tell him she wasn't interested—or, failing that, be prepared for the eventual sight of Reid standing under her window, holding an iPod above his head.

When there was a momentary lull in customers, I ducked into the ice-cream freezer—ostensibly to get more cartons of vanilla and cake batter, but really to send Sophie a text. I knew I didn't have to worry about Reid finding me back here and questioning me more, since the employee manual had been pretty clear on the fact there was supposed to be an employee behind the counter at all times. I wasn't sure if Reid hadn't been aware of the policy the day before, or if it just explained why I'd been hired so quickly, but either way, the counter wasn't ever supposed to be empty, so I knew I could text in peace.

Keeping my foot wedged between the door and the wall, I texted Sophie that Reid obviously still liked her, and that she should either do something about it or be prepared for him to make a move. As I pressed Send and watched for a moment, already shivering, to see if she responded, I realized that my motives were partly selfish—I didn't want to keep getting put in the middle every time Reid and I worked together. But even so, it would probably be a good thing for Sophie to just make it clear to him how she felt. I waited for another moment, then decided that Sophie wasn't near her phone, because there was no response. Figuring that she was probably swimming or just napping in the sun, I dropped my phone back into my pocket just as I heard the bell over the door ring.

In case it was another large group, I grabbed the cartons of ice cream and hustled back to the front of the shop. "Reid," I said as I walked toward the counter, my arms already beginning to ache. "Are you okay, or—"

I stopped short when I saw who the customer was. It was Hallie. She was wearing shorts and a mint-colored sleeveless blouse, and her hair was up in a big, complicated bun. She had on perfectly applied red lipstick and looked like she'd just stepped out of a J.Crew catalog. She didn't seem happy to see me, but she also didn't look surprised.

"Look, Gemma, it's Hallie!" Reid said cheerfully. But then a second later his smile dropped, like he'd suddenly remembered things had changed. "I mean . . . um . . ."

"It's okay, Reid," Hallie said, giving him a quick smile. "Gemma and I are just going to have a little talk."

I looked between the two of them and realized that Reid knew. He was living with the Bridges, so it stood to reason it might have come up. Or maybe he'd found out when Hallie confronted him about the text I'd sent from his phone. Either way, it was clear he had been brought up to speed.

"Right," I finally said, mostly to put Reid—whose face was getting redder by the moment—at ease. "A talk."

"Okay, then," Reid said as he started to edge away from the counter, toward the door marked EMPLOYEES ONLY. There wasn't much behind it—it was basically just a hallway with cubbies and purse hooks, and a bathroom that we were not, under any circumstances, allowed to let customers use. "So I'll just—"

"No need to leave," Hallie said, her expression pleasant but her tone steely. "This won't take long." As I looked at her, impeccably dressed and put together, I couldn't help but wonder where the Hallie I'd known—the tomboy who lived in her flip-flops and frayed jean shorts—had gone, and when this version had taken over.

"I . . . actually needed to go to the bathroom, and . . ." Reid's voice grew fainter with every word until I couldn't actually make out anything he was saying. Then he turned redder than ever and started putting the ice cream I'd brought out into the front case.

"So I hear you talked to Teddy," Hallie said as she crossed the counter to stand in front of me by the register, where the serve-your-own chocolate and strawberry syrups were kept. "You were trying to tell him about how he shouldn't trust me."

"He *shouldn't* trust you," I said, crossing my arms over my white Sweet & Delicious T-shirt. "I wasn't telling him anything that wasn't true."

"And then, weirdest thing, I got a text from Reid here," she said, and as I turned to look back at him, Reid's face turned bright red, and he bent down over the ice cream—though I couldn't tell if he was organizing them or just trying to get his face to cool down. "But Reid said he never sent me a text. But that, lo and behold, you'd had his phone." Her voice was still pleasant, but I could sense the edge underneath it. I think Reid could too, because he started wiping down the counters and stress-whistling. "You shouldn't have interfered."

"Oh, I'm the one who's interfering?" I asked, feeling my anger starting to bubble to the surface once again. "Really? Why did you send a photographer to Bruce's house to take pictures of the award you had destroyed?"

Hallie shook her head. "What are you *talking* about?"

I had to give credit where it was due—Hallie was a much better actress than I was. For a second there I'd almost believed her.

Hallie took a step closer to me, and Reid's whistling got louder. "Listen, Gemma," she said, managing, as always, to make my name sound like an epithet. "I—" A pop song suddenly filled the ice-cream parlor. I recognized it, of course—it was a summer song by Call Me Kevin, the cheesy boy band that Sophie and I would sometimes sing along to at top volume when getting ready or driving around Putnam together. But I was shocked to hear it coming from Hallie's phone, since Hallie had only seemed to like hipper-than-hip bands with too many members who played obscure instruments.

She turned away from the counter and lowered her voice, answering in a murmur. I couldn't see Hallie's expression any longer, just her blue-and-white-striped cell phone case, with what looked like her initials monogrammed in the center of it. "Hi, Mom," she said, keeping her voice low. "Yeah, I'm babysitting tonight." Hallie glanced over her shoulder at me, then turned away again. "I'll be fine. Why do you need to know that?

Nothing's going to—" Hallie let out a breath and shook her head, and I could hear familiar mother-frustration in her tone. "*Fine*. It's thirty-two Mill Pond Lane," she said. "Okay. See you tomorrow. Me too." She hung up, dropped her phone in her bag, and turned back to me. "So like I was saying—"

"And like I was saying," I interrupted, "don't try and stop me from telling Teddy the truth."

Hallie just looked at me for a moment, then burst out laughing—a short hard laugh that didn't have any humor in it. "Oh, okay," she said. "We can play this game. Are you *threatening* me? You saw what I did to you this summer, right? You really want to do this?"

"I don't want to do anything," I said. I tried to keep my voice steady, but my heart was pounding hard, and Reid's increasingly loud whistling wasn't helping matters. "I just—"

"Why am I even bothering to talk to you about this?" Hallie asked. She looked at me scornfully. "I broke up you and your boyfriend of *two years*, and it wasn't even hard. I was lying to you all summer, and you had absolutely no idea. You thought we were becoming *friends*." She shook her head. "I mean, it was pathetic."

"Was it *pathetic* what I did to you five years ago?" The words were out before I could even think about what I was saying. "Because that wasn't particularly hard either." Hallie's eyes narrowed. "So if you're not going to get any ice cream you should just—"

What happened next was so fast that I almost couldn't process it at first—Hallie's hand reaching out toward the syrup, and then the red flying toward me. I looked down and saw what had happened—there was a streak of bright red strawberry syrup splashed across my white T-shirt.

Hallie looked down at the syrup bottle in her hand, then set it on the counter. Her face was flushed and she looked almost as shocked as I felt. Without saying anything else, she turned and walked out the front door, the bell ringing cheerfully as it swung behind her.

"Is she gone?" Reid asked, turning around. "Because—" He saw me and emitted a high-pitched shriek. "You're bleeding," he said, starting to turn pale. "Did she *stab* you? Oh my god. I'm not good with blood. I can't—"

"It's not blood," I said quickly, before Reid passed out on the black-and-white floor and I had to figure out how to revive him. "It's just syrup." I went to wipe it off, and proceeded in just smearing the already-hardening syrup into a handprint— a handprint that was directly on my chest. "Oh no."

"Oh," Reid said, blinking at the handprint on my shirt. "Yeah, that's not great."

"Um . . ." I looked around, like an easy fix for this would present itself. But even as I attempted to find a solution, I was still trying to get my head around what had just happened. Hallie had thrown *syrup* at me? Luckily, it hadn't hit the camera clipped to the neck of my T-shirt. I didn't even want to think about how expensive it would be to replace a mini-camera. Unluckily, it had hit directly across both of my boobs. "Maybe I could wash it off," I said, but a second later I remembered that my shirt was *white*. And probably the only thing worse that having a handprint on your shirt was having a handprint on your see-through shirt.

"You could wear this if you want," Reid said as he pulled out an apron from underneath the register, the kind I'd seen him wearing the first time I'd ducked into the store. The apron was pretty terrible—long and red and shiny-looking, like you could wipe it off. *Delicious,* it read in script that was the same font as the sign on the door. "There's a *Sweet,* too, if you want that instead."

I shook my head and motioned for Reid to give me the apron. "This will work." As long as it covered up the handprint, and I wouldn't be getting strange looks from customers all day long, I was fine with it. I put it on and tied the straps around my waist, grateful that the handprint was covered, and trying to ignore how the apron squeaked whenever I moved.

"Great," Reid said, starting to edge toward the bathroom again. "So I'm just going to—" As he was saying this, the door opened again, and a group of kids came streaming in, their parents in tow. "It's okay," Reid said, maybe seeing the look of panic on my face at the thought of having to handle all those customers myself. "I'll just take a break in a few minutes."

We were steadily busy for the next twenty minutes or so, a new wave of people coming in as soon as the previous customers were served. The muscles in my right arm—my scooping arm—were beginning to shake, and I'd started trying to sell people on the merits of soft-serve. At the very least, I reasoned as I rubbed my aching bicep while Reid rang up our latest customers, I might get toned arms out of this. Or at least toned arm.

I was actually glad that we were as busy as we were, because I found the routine motions were helpful when my thoughts were spinning faster and faster. If I'd been expected to carry on a conversation with Reid, I knew I wouldn't have been able to do it. I couldn't stop seeing Hallie's face, her scornful expression when she bragged about how easy it had been to break up me and Teddy. The pride she'd taken in lying to me all summer. Was I really going to just keep letting her get away with this stuff? And not only get away with it—let her keep gloating to my face about it?

"Okay," Reid said, looking hugely relieved as the bell jangled and the customers stepped out, maneuvering carefully with multistacked cones. "So if you can handle the front, I'll—"

"Actually," I said, feeling bad about interrupting him but knowing I needed to get out of there, if only for a moment. If I were still around Reid, my thoughts spinning like this, I knew that it wouldn't be long before I'd tell him everything I was thinking—which would then, of course, get directly back to Hallie. "I just need to step outside for a second. Okay?" I didn't wait for a reply, though it sounded like Reid whimpered softly as I ducked under the counter and walked outside, setting the bell above my head jangling. I didn't even bother taking my Delicious apron off. I just needed a moment to try and get my thoughts in order. I stepped outside into the bright sunlight and squinted against it as I paced in front of the building.

I couldn't quite believe what I was thinking, but the more the idea lingered in my head, the more it seemed like the only thing to do. I was thinking—maybe—about getting even. I hadn't thought this way since I was eleven, and it was startling to realize how quickly it was coming back. Was I really just going to let Hallie get away with everything she'd done—and was continuing to do? Was I just going to stand by and let it happen?

I realized I'd gotten almost to the coffee shop, and decided I should probably get back to my job. The pacing didn't seem to be helping either, just sending my thoughts around in circles. I had thought Bruce was on to something with his pacing around the pool, but clearly, it wasn't working for me. I turned back, and realized there was someone right in my path.

"Sorry—" I said as I tried to dodge around him, but he went the same direction as me. I was about to try to laugh, say something about how ridiculous this was when I realized I knew the person in front of me—it was Josh. "Oh," I said, scrambling to regain any sense of composure. Why hadn't I prepared for the fact that I might run into him? Why hadn't I bothered to put on even the smallest amount of makeup this morning? I tried to put my hands in my pockets, but then realized I was still wearing the ridiculous Delicious apron. I quickly untied the straps and pulled it off, holding it behind my back.

Josh glanced down at me, and his eyes widened slightly before he looked away. I looked down and realized the handprint across my boob had not magically disappeared. I opened my mouth to try to explain what it was doing there—I hadn't gotten as far as what that might be—when a gorgeous girl with long light brown hair materialized by Josh's side.

"There you are!" she said, smiling at him. She had two Quonset Coffee drinks in her hand—a blended drink and what looked like an iced tea. As I watched, my heart sinking, she handed Josh the iced tea and then let her hand linger on his. Josh didn't flinch or even look surprised, so it was clear this wasn't the first time this had happened. I suddenly realized that we were standing outside Quonset Coffee. And that Josh had been waiting for this girl when I'd gotten in his way.

"Thanks," he said, taking the iced tea from her with a smile—the first time in recent memory I'd seen him look anything but upset and hurt.

I bit my lip hard. So he was getting coffee with a beautiful girl. He'd moved on already. I should have known this was going to come at some point. I had just thought that maybe I'd have been able to explain myself better . . . or get him to understand where I was coming from. I hadn't realized my window would be slammed shut, and so quickly.

The girl didn't even look at me. She was focused on Josh, talking a mile a minute about the beach and plans to go paddleboarding. She was already starting to walk away, and Josh followed, but he shot me one last glance, his expression as blank as if he were looking at a stranger, as he slung an arm around the girl's shoulders. Then they turned and walked away together. I watched them go, feeling my eyes fill with hot tears as Josh got farther and farther from me, and then finally disappeared.

Four hours later I walked into the cool white expanse of Bruce's kitchen and collapsed onto one of the stools that ringed the granite kitchen island. My feet were killing me, my arms felt like jelly, and I had a feeling I smelled like the chocolate syrup I'd somehow managed to get into my hair. I had a new respect for anyone who worked behind an ice-cream counter, and had mentally pledged to start tipping much more—when I'd clocked out, I had left with a grand total of two dollars and a Canadian quarter to my name. I hadn't wanted to do the math of how many hours of ice-cream scooping it was going to take to pay my father back, because I had a feeling it would only depress me.

I hadn't been able to bring myself to ask Reid directly about the coffee girl—I had a feeling that it would make it back to Josh and/or Hallie immediately, and I'd already been embarrassed enough for one day. But when I'd tried to ask him veiled questions about people dating people, and people dating other people seriously, he hadn't understood me at *all*, and had just thought I was bringing up the Sophie question again. I'd tried my best to dodge it, but I think I'd left Reid more confused than when I'd started, and I still hadn't gotten any answers.

But even if I didn't have specifics, I had one answer—it was clear Josh wanted nothing to do with me. Knowing this did not make it any easier to accept, or stop my heart from hurting. If I hadn't been so exhausted, I would have been baking up a storm by now.

I rested my head on the cool granite, closing my eyes for a

second, wishing that I could just stay like that until the world started making sense again.

"Hey!" Sophie bounced into the kitchen, in my pink bikini top and cutoffs, looking thrilled to see me. "You're back! Finally. I have been so bored, I can't even tell you."

I turned to look at her without raising my head from the island. Bored sounded pretty good to me right now. I would have taken bored in a second over the complete exhaustion I was feeling now. "Where is everyone?"

"Gone," she sighed, and started listing people on her fingers. "Your dad went into the city to meet with that writer; Bruce and Rosie went to meet with someone about a permit or something; Gwyneth went with them for the documentary; and Ford—"

"Someone call me?" Ford ambled in, glasses on and hair rumpled—it looked like he'd been coding all afternoon. He went directly to the fridge and took out a bottle of water.

"Hey," I said, raising my head and sitting up.

"Whoa," Ford said, doing a double take at my shirt. "Gem . . . what's . . ." He gestured to my general T-shirt area, making me realize I probably should have changed immediately upon getting home. I'd had more than enough of people staring at—and being disconcerted by—my chest for one afternoon.

"Just don't ask," I said.

"I think I'm going to have to," Sophie said, staring at it as well. "Because, what?"

"I hope they at least caught the guy red-handed," Ford said, a smile playing around the corners of his mouth. Sophie burst out laughing, then looked at me and tried to flatten out her smile without much success.

"Sorry," she said, trying for serious, but not really pulling it off. "Um . . . are you okay?"

"It's a long story," I said as Ford gave us a one-handed wave as he continued on out to the pool house.

"Tell me," Sophie said hungrily, sitting on the stool closest to mine. "Seriously, I'm desperate for entertainment." As I looked at my best friend settling in, preparing to hear a story about a stain on my shirt—and looking thrilled about it—it hit me that usually back home, Sophie almost always had a boyfriend, sometimes two. It seemed like she was maybe having a little trouble filling the time.

"Are you still thinking about getting a job?" I asked, hoping the question didn't sound too insulting. But since it sounded like Sophie would only be allowed to stay in the Hamptons if she were employed, and I was in favor of keeping her here, I wanted to make sure that it was on her mind.

"Yes," Sophie said. "Anything, really. Well, anything where you don't need any experience." She leaned closer to me. "Is the ice-cream parlor still hiring? I could work with Reid. You know, probably."

"I can ask," I said, just hoping that if she did get hired, she and Reid would resolve things between them.

"So." Sophie pointed at the handprint. "Explain."

I looked down at it and shook my head. "It was Hallie."

Sophie's eyes widened. "Did she stab you?"

"No," I said, giving her a tiny smile. "It's just syrup."

Sophie shook her head. "That girl. She just doesn't stop, does she?"

"She doesn't," I said slowly. The thoughts that had been running through my mind all afternoon were starting to all point in one direction. I couldn't keep letting her do this to me. I couldn't let her get away with everything she'd done this summer. I had tried to make things up to her. I had tried to play nice. But where had that gotten me? Nowhere good. "Soph . . ." I started, a little hesitantly. "Remember when I said that I wasn't going to do anything to Hallie? That I was just going to let it all go?"

"I do," Sophie said, nodding. Her eyes were fixed on mine, and I was pretty sure she had an idea of where this was going.

"To hell with that," I said, feeling the anger starting to course through my veins, as potent as a drug (you know, so I'd heard). "I'm not just going to sit here and wait for her to do something else to me. I'm not going to let her get away with this. I'm done trying to make nice with her."

Sophie raised an eyebrow at me. "What are you saying?"

"I'm saying . . ." I started, then took a breath. "I'm going to get revenge on Hallie. I'm saying we take her down."

Sophie smiled at me. "Well, I'm in," she said. "But while we're getting revenge, can we also find me a job?"

"Of course," I said with a laugh. "We—" I stopped suddenly, an idea beginning to form.

"What?" she asked, raising her eyebrows. "What happened?"

"Come on," I said, sliding off the counter and picking up my bag. "I'm getting you a job." Sophie looked pointedly at my shirt, and I set my bag down again. "After I change."

CHAPTER 9

"**A**re you sure about this?" Sophie asked as we walked across the driveway of 32 Mill Pond Lane. "I mean, I have, like, no experience with kids."

"They're not that hard," I said, crossing my fingers as I said it, hoping that I wasn't getting Sophie into something she wouldn't be able to handle. "And I'll be around in case they get out of hand. Just a text away."

"I guess," Sophie said, and I could hear the doubt in her voice. "But maybe you could just ask if the ice-cream parlor needs anyone? And this could be, like, our backup?"

"Well, this might not work," I admitted as we climbed the four steps to the front door, painted a cool blue color. The house was a traditional-looking Hamptons beach house, gray clapboard shingles and white trim, bright red flowers in pots lining the steps. "So then we can always try Sweet & Delicious." Sophie nodded, biting her bottom lip, still looking unconvinced. I took a breath before I rang the doorbell, running through what I was going to say. I had a few different options, depending on who answered the door, but there was one scenario I preferred among all of them. I pressed the doorbell, which chimed softly, and a moment later I heard the unmistakable sound of small feet thundering toward the door and felt myself smile. It was the scenario that I'd been hoping for.

The door was flung open, and I looked down to see the identical faces of Isabella and Olivia, Hallie's babysitting charges, tiny agents of destruction, the girls who had purposely wrecked Bruce's house and broken his Spotlight award. "Hi there," I said, smiling down at both of them. "Remember me?"

Isabella's eyes widened—normally, I was hopeless at telling them apart, so it helped that she was wearing a monogrammed T-shirt—and she cast a worried look at her sister.

"Um," Olivia stalled, looking from me to Sophie. "I'm not supposed to talk to strangers?"

"Nice try," I said, bending down a little so I was at their level. "I just wanted to talk to your parents. Are they home? I thought they should know what happened that time I babysat for you. Before I charge them for all the damage you both did, that is."

"Gem," Sophie whispered under her breath. I glanced over and saw that she looked shocked by this, even though we'd gone through the plan on the drive over. But I suppose there's hearing about it, and then there's the reality of seeing someone blackmail a kindergartener. But Sophie didn't know just how horrible these girls could be. I knew it, and all too well. I shot her what I hoped was a reassuring smile, then turned back to

the girls, who had taken the pause to confer amongst themselves and were now presenting a tiny united front, arms crossed
and identical scowls on their faces.

"Prove it," Isabella said, her tone challenging.

"I'd be happy to," I said. "I just don't think you want to go
down that road. When your mom—"

"Dads," the twins interrupted, speaking in sync.

"Oh," I said, regrouping. "Okay. But when your dads hear
what I have to say, I don't think they're going to be too happy.
Or . . ." I let the word dangle like a promise.

"Or what?" Olivia asked, still trying for tough, but I could
hear the hope in her voice somewhere.

"Meet your new babysitter," I said, gesturing to Sophie, who
stayed where she was, raising her hand in a tiny unenthusiastic wave.

"Hey," she said. "Um. I'm Sophie."

"But Hallie's coming over tonight," Isabella said, frowning.

"She was," I said. "But you and your sister can just tell your
dads you don't want Hallie to sit for you anymore."

Both twins stared at me, then huddled together and had a
furious whispered conversation before turning back to us. "Who
even *are* you?" Olivia asked, eyeing Sophie skeptically. "Have
you been a babysitter before?"

"No," Sophie said. "Not exactly."

"Then why should we want you to babysit us?" Isabella
asked, folding her arms.

"I don't know," Sophie said, glancing at me, looking baffled.
"*I* don't even want to babysit you."

"Soph," I muttered, not wanting her to wreck this when it seemed close to working.

"Sorry," she said, glancing at me, then back at the girls. "I just thought you should know."

"So what were you planning on us doing tonight?" Olivia asked, and my heart sank. I could hear it in her voice—she and her sister were going to walk all over Sophie, just like they'd managed to do with me.

"I don't know," Sophie said with a shrug, apparently not picking up on this at all. "Watch TV? I brought my makeup bag."

The girls eyed Sophie's overstuffed purse, both looking genuinely interested for the first time. They exchanged a glance, then nodded. "Okay," Olivia said.

"Okay?" I echoed, looking between the two of them. "If we're agreed, then I won't say anything about what you did."

"Deal," Isabella said. "I'll go get my dads." Both she and Olivia turned and ran into the house, leaving the door half open.

"Can you handle it from here?" I asked Sophie, already starting to back away toward the car.

Sophie nodded, playing absentmindedly with the tiny camera attached to the strap of her tank top. "I'm a friend of Hallie's, and when she couldn't make it tonight, she sent me instead," she recited.

"And if you can," I reminded her as I took a step toward the SUV, "tell them that Hallie has been inviting her boyfriend over while she babysits." I was making this up, but I had gotten half my babysitting jobs back in Putnam from angry parents who'd found out their sitters were inviting boys over and then failing to look after their children while they made out on their couches. There seemed to be nothing that freaked out potential parents more.

"And if they ask why I'm an hour early, just pretend I got the time wrong."

"Right." I gave her an encouraging smile, then stopped when I saw that Sophie's expression was still doubtful. "What is it?"

"She deserves this, right?" Sophie asked, chewing on her bottom lip again. "Hallie, I mean?"

"Of course," I said automatically. I thought of Teddy breaking my heart in the aisle in Target, the raw expression of hurt on Josh's face, Bruce's shattered Spotlight award, the syrup flying toward me. "She does," I said firmly, and Sophie nodded.

"I'll call when I'm done," she said.

"Good luck," I said as I walked to the driver's door. "Text if there are any problems." Sophie nodded, and I saw the girls appearing in the doorframe again, with what looked like one of their fathers standing behind them. I got into the car and pulled out of the driveway, hoping they would just think I was Sophie's ride—which was not, technically, untrue. I drove for only a few seconds before pulling onto a side road and putting the car into park. I took out my phone and looked at it, waiting for a text from Sophie to arrive, for her to tell me we weren't getting away with this. But when one didn't come after a few minutes, I figured she was probably okay. I let out a shaky breath, then put the car in gear and drove back to Bruce's.

Hours later I was sitting on the sand, looking out at the waves in the moonlight. I'd had dinner with Ford and Gwyneth—our fathers and Rosie were still out, doing whatever they had been doing all day—but had been distracted, barely able to follow the conversation, despite the fact that it had been filled with insider gossip about movie stars. Instead I was looking at my phone every few seconds, waiting to see if there were any problems, and wondering if Hallie had actually shown up at the house, or if one of the twins' fathers had called her first. Either way, I wanted to be informed as soon as something happened, but my phone had remained quiet throughout the meal, leaving me to regret not getting some really premium gossip when it was on offer.

After dinner Gwyneth had gone to look at some of that day's footage, and Ford had headed into the pool house to code, but I'd been restless inside the house, not able to settle down enough to watch a movie or read a book. My thoughts were on what was happening with Sophie, and turning, more often than I would have liked, to Josh and the girl I'd seen him with that morning. Needing to try and escape all this, I'd headed out to my traditional thinking spot on the beach just outside of Bruce's, and had been there for the last hour or so. But now it was getting close to eleven, so I had a feeling that I'd hear from Sophie, needing a ride home, pretty soon.

"Hey." I turned to see Ford standing over me, wetsuit on, a longboard under one arm. "What are you doing out here?"

"Just thinking," I said. Even though it was dark—the only light coming from the moon and a little bit of spillover from the house—I was glad that Ford had his wetsuit zipped all the way up. It had been a few days of seeing him wearing his glasses and geeky T-shirts, and I'd almost totally forgotten about the ridges of his abs. Almost. "Are you going surfing?" The board and wetsuit would seem to be giant signs pointing to yes, but I'd never heard of anyone surfing at night before. Wasn't night when sharks ate people? "Now?"

"Night surfing is the best," Ford said as he laid his board on the sand and sat down next to me. "Back home I have a board that lights up. The LEDs go in before the glassing process."

I nodded, pretending I had understood the majority of the words he'd just said. "Isn't it kind of dangerous?"

"On these baby waves?" Ford scoffed. "Not exactly."

I looked out at the ocean, which suddenly seemed a lot more menacing than it had a few minutes ago. "But . . ."

"The problem, Gem," Ford said as he settled back on his hands, looking out at the dark water, "is that you've never been surfing. Despite all the offers you've had." He raised an eyebrow at me, and I knew he was talking about when we'd been in Malibu and I'd chickened out.

"I know," I said. "Maybe this summer?" I still wasn't sure about it, but surfing the waves of the Hamptons seemed a lot less intimidating than trying to surf Hawaii's or California's.

Ford just shook his head, smiling at me. "I've heard that one before." He sat up and leaned a little closer to me. "I just wish you'd have let me take you out there, even just once," he said. "Because there's no real way to describe it. You don't really even have time to think when you're out there; it's just pure instinct.

You're living in the moment entirely, and you learn to go with whatever comes. It's the most free I've ever felt."

I nodded without dropping my eyes from Ford's. I could have sworn it was suddenly warmer out on the beach, even though just a few minutes ago I'd been thinking how cold I was.

"And at night," Ford went on, looking away from me and toward the ocean in front of us, "it's all amplified. The crash and the roll of the waves, the sheer power of the ocean. And you're just going by feeling, letting your body guide you. It's . . ." He looked back to me, and I fought a sudden urge to look away from his eye contact. What was wrong with me? This was *Ford.* Why shouldn't I look at him?

Ford had trailed off and now he gave me a half-smile, and I tried to regroup and remember where I was. "Sorry," he said, shaking his head. "I tend to get a little carried away."

"No," I said, still trying to bring myself back to reality. "It's good. I mean, you made it sound really neat. Fun. You know." I was well aware that I sounded like an idiot, but multisyllabic words were not coming to me at the moment.

"Well, maybe one of these days you'll give it a shot," Ford said. "Despite the fact that it never really seemed like a possibility before."

"Maybe I will," I replied. I smiled at him, but then felt it fade as he kept looking right at me, his expression serious. All at once it felt like there was something crackling between us. Were we still talking about surfing?

Suddenly, unbidden, a memory flashed through my mind. My thirteenth birthday, Ford at fourteen, both of us on my dad's terrace as we looked up at the constellations. Ford had been telling me about light pollution, about all the stars you could see in Hawaii that were hidden in California. He was standing behind me, nearer than usual, pointing up at the sky. The lights of the Hollywood Hills were twinkling below us, and I was happy with everything—my birthday, the city lights, the way the air smelled like jasmine, and best of all, Ford, standing so close to me, telling me about the stars. He was showing me where Orion was, and I was looking up at it when he leaned down and kissed me.

We had never discussed it afterward, so I had no idea why he'd done it—a birthday present for an unkissed thirteen-year-old? Curiosity? Pity? At any rate, it had never happened again. I looked at Ford now, three years later, sitting next to me on the sand, in the dark, and was struck by this reality. We had *kissed*. At one point his lips had been on mine, his arms had been around me. And it had been a really good kiss, though I'd had nothing to compare it to at the time. I suddenly wondered if he ever thought about that moment.

I took a breath to say something—I hadn't gotten as far as figuring out what—when my phone beeped with a text.

Sophie Curtis
10:55 PM
All done here! Girls no problem. Pick me up?

"I have to go get Sophie," I said, turning back to Ford. Whatever had just been between us—*had* there even been something there? I wasn't entirely sure it hadn't just been a mix of my imagination and memory and moonlight—was gone now.

"And I should wire my spot before someone snags it," he said. He stood up, then extended a hand to me. I took it, and his fingers practically folded over mine. The Ford who had kissed me three years ago had been close to my height, and the fact that he was so much taller now was still sometimes hard to get used to. He pulled me to my feet like I weighed nothing, then dropped my hand. "See you tomorrow, Gem," he said, giving me another of his half-smiles. Then he grabbed his board and headed toward the water, running the last few feet and then diving in.

I watched the ocean for just a few moments after he dove under—I could see him only in glimpses, when the moon hit the shifting water just right. Even though I was trying really hard not to, I couldn't help but think about the opening to *Jaws*, which also took place in the water in the dark, with disastrous consequences. But, I reasoned, that was Martha's Vineyard, not the Hamptons, and Ford was not a naked blond girl, which always seemed to increase your chance of dying in any movie. Knowing that if I stayed, I would be imagining a shark had gotten him every time he disappeared, I turned and headed back into the house. I grabbed my keys off the kitchen counter and left out the front door, texting Sophie as I went that I was on my way. I was nearly across the driveway to the SUV when I stopped short.

"Dad?" My father was sitting in the front seat of the hybrid he had rented when he'd given up on trying to drive Bruce's sports car, finally admitting to himself that he wasn't going to be able to learn to drive stick *and* write a movie this summer. I squinted and took a step closer to the car. My father was sitting behind the wheel, the engine off, staring out into space. "Dad?" I asked again through the open window, louder this time.

"Oh!" My dad jumped and looked up at me. He blinked a few times, like he was struggling to remember who I was. "Gemma. Hello."

"Hi," I said, wondering why he was acting like this. "You okay?"

"Yes," he said. Then he shook his head, like he was trying to clear it, and got out of the car. "Sorry if I surprised you." He gave me a smile, but it didn't really reach his eyes, and I had the feeling he was miles away.

"How'd it go with the writer?" I asked, suddenly remembering that was where my dad had been all day—meeting with Brenda Kreigs about turning vampire erotica into something that could be shown in theaters with an R rating.

"Fine," he said, nodding a few too many times. "It was fine. I'm just . . . gathering my thoughts."

I looked at him, wondering if this was my opportunity. I had to tell my father what I had done five years ago. I needed to confess, especially since there was clearly going to be no happy reunion with Hallie to soften the news. And my dad and I were alone, I wasn't interrupting him in his work. . . . Was this the right moment? I tried to play out the conversation. My dad, yelling and disappointed. Me, trying to explain. Both of us upset.

And meanwhile, Sophie would still be waiting for me to get her. I'd tell him soon. Maybe tomorrow.

"Okay," I said, taking a step toward the car. "Well, I'm going to go get Sophie. I'll see you tomorrow?"

"Sure," my dad said easily, but I somehow had the impression he would have said this, with the exact same inflection, if I'd asked him for permission to get a couple of sweet tats. I tried to use this as proof that it hadn't been the right time, since my dad was clearly not up to paying careful attention. "Tomorrow."

I got into the car and started the engine, heading down Bruce's far-too-long driveway. But when I glanced back in the rearview mirror, I could see that my dad was still standing where I'd left him—keys in hand, standing in a shaft of moonlight, perfectly still, his expression faraway.

CHAPTER 10

"Okay . . . and can I also try the rocky road, the orange sherbet, and the peppermint stick?" I glared at the ten-year-olds across the counter from me. My second day on the job was not going a whole lot better than my first, but nobody had thrown syrup on me yet, so I was counting that in the plus column. I was exhausted again, and my arms, which were still sore from the day before, were positively screaming at me every time I had to scoop anything. I'd also learned quickly that lots of kids came in, tried every sample they could, and then left without buying anything. Apparently, there had been a motion to limit the number of samples to four, but people had complained enough that this had been lifted. Already, I could tell when someone was really trying to choose the right flavor or combination, and when someone was just scoring free ice cream. And when choices were this all over the flavor spectrum, it meant that there was no real decision-making going on—just freeloading.

"Do you need help, Gemma?" Darcy Santiago, my coworker for the morning, spoke up from where she was leaning on the back counter, utterly absorbed in her phone.

"No," I said as I reached for three small spoons, the kind we used for taste-testing. "I've got this."

"Cool," Darcy said, still not looking up from her phone. "Well, just let me know."

I scooped the three flavors out and handed them to the girl, who ate them in succession, pretended to consider, and then just told me, her friends behind her already starting to laugh, that she was so full from all the samples that she'd have to come back later. Then they ran out in a collective fit of giggles, and I closed the glass lid harder than I probably needed to.

Despite the fact that my job wasn't ideal, it seemed that Sophie's was, to my surprise, going really well. The twins had apparently loved her, and I realized why when Sophie told me they'd spent the evening watching premium cable and getting makeovers from Sophie's extensive makeup collection. And Sophie had been able to overhear a conversation between one of the twins' dads and Hallie, telling Hallie that her services would no longer be required. Sophie hadn't been able to hear everything clearly, but she definitely caught something about her bringing boys around as an explanation.

And since the twins were now without a regular babysitter, it seemed like this was now Sophie's job. When I'd driven her home, she'd told me about her hours and pay, and I tried not to wince at the fact that she was now making about three times what I was—she would have been able to pay my dad back for the bathing suit in no time.

I knew Hallie had most likely figured out it was me who'd sent Sophie to take her job—and if she didn't already know, she'd figure it out soon. But I had no regrets about it—it was the least Hallie deserved. And plus, this way I got to guarantee that Sophie could stay in the Hamptons. Win-win.

Sophie was sitting for them again today, and I'd spent most of our dairy-free breakfast trying to convince her that she needed to talk to Reid. Apparently, he'd texted a few times while she was babysitting, and Sophie hadn't responded. Reid wasn't working today, and I'd told Sophie that this would be perfect—she could talk to him, and he wouldn't be expected to go back to his job and continue to serve customers after she'd crushed his hopes. But she'd been vague about whether she was actually going to do this, and I'd eventually just let it go and headed into work. I knew she didn't want to talk to him about this, but the fact was she needed to tell him she wasn't interested, and I needed to not spend the summer dodging Reid's questions about my best friend's feelings.

"Does that happen a lot?" I asked as I absently wiped down the counters. Darcy nodded without looking up from her phone. She seemed nice enough, but I honestly wasn't entirely sure what she looked like, as she'd spent the entire morning looking down at her screen. She was actually pretty impressive—I'd watched her scoop ice cream, ring people up, and wish them a sweet and delicious day, all without looking up or pausing in her typing.

"Yep," she said. "They usually come in packs too. It's policy that we just give them the samples. I once had this one kid get, like, thirty."

"Seriously?" I asked.

"Yeah," she said with a shrug. "Nothing to be done about it." I nodded, and then there was near silence for a moment, just the whirr of the air conditioner and the sound of Darcy typing on her phone.

"Texting someone?" I asked after a few minutes of listening to her fingers tap her screen.

"Yeah," she said, actually looking up from her device and giving me a quick smile. She was pretty, with tan skin, hair in a braid crown, and dark brown eyes. "My boyfriend." She touched the screen, then turned the phone around to face me. "Isn't he hot?"

I looked at the image on the screen and felt my eyes widen. The picture was of a blond shirtless guy running with a football tucked underneath his arm, and it was in black-and-white. "So hot," I said, hoping that my voice didn't betray anything. Because I wasn't lying—he was incredibly hot. But it looked an awful lot like a picture from the last Hollister ad campaign. But maybe her boyfriend was *part* of the Hollister ad campaign, and this was how she was showing her support. "Is he . . . um . . . a model?"

"No!" Darcy said, but her smile had deepened, and I could see how pleased she was by this. "This is just him playing football with some friends by a lake. He sent it to me."

"Oh," I said. I nodded and paused before I asked, "So you didn't take it?"

"No," Darcy said with a sigh. "We haven't actually met in person yet. He lives in Philadelphia."

I nodded again and pretended to wipe down the counters. I wasn't sure how best to tell someone that they were probably being catfished, especially when you didn't know that person well at all. But I was prepared to bet all the money I had that the actual guy Darcy was texting looked nothing like the guy she'd just shown me.

"What about you?" Darcy asked. "Do you have a boyfriend?"

"No," I said, and I managed to say it without hesitating, like I had been doing earlier in the summer, when I was still having trouble accepting the fact that Teddy and I were done. "I did. But we . . . um . . . broke up right at the beginning of the summer."

"Oh, that's too bad," Darcy said, setting her phone all the way down. Apparently, relationship drama held her attention in the way that customers did not. "Were you guys together a long time?"

"Two years," I said, and Darcy's eyes widened. "I know," I said as I shook my head. For just a second I had a flash of a memory—the first time I'd seen Teddy, when I'd wandered into the Warblers meeting by accident. I had no idea then that saving the marsh warbler was one of Teddy's primary concerns, or that he would end up becoming the center of my world for two years. "But . . ." I said a little hesitantly, "it's not like it was perfect." I tried to think back to some of the clarity about Teddy I'd felt I was getting closer to earlier in the summer. It had not escaped my knowledge that it was a lot easier to have clarity about your ex when you were in the process of falling for some-one new. "I mean . . ." I stopped when I heard what I was pretty sure was a faint buzzing coming from the employee cubbies. I'd put my phone on vibrate, but I resolved to maybe switch it back to silent, since you could still hear it.

"That's you," Darcy said, picking up her own phone again.

I nodded and headed back, feeling like I should probably just keep my phone with me, since despite what all the signs in the tiny break room said, clearly there *were* cell phones behind the counter.

I reached into my bag for my phone, expecting to see maybe a missed call from Sophie, or one of her text monologues that always just seemed to descend into a series of emojis that didn't even make much sense. The last one I could remember had a picture of a cat, a slice of pizza, a dragon, and an airplane. But I felt my eyes widen when I saw that I had six missed calls. Four of them were from Rosie, one was from Ford, and one was from Gwyneth. Something was happening back at the house. The phone started to ring in my hand, and I saw it was Rosie. I an-swered immediately.

"Rosie?"

"Gemma." Rosie's voice was clipped. "I think you should get back here. Now."

CHAPTER 11

I screeched into the driveway, sending gravel flying in my wake, but not really caring. My call with Rosie hadn't lasted long—I'd started to panic that something was wrong with my dad, but she'd assured me he was fine. And then she said that I should get back to the house as soon as possible.

After I'd hung up, I'd had a quick negotiation with Darcy. I'd promised to work two shifts for her, her choice, and on less than twenty-four-hour's notice, in exchange for cutting out of my shift early and leaving her alone. She promised to clock me out so that management wouldn't know that we were breaking their "two employees present at all times" rule, and I thanked her profusely before grabbing my stuff and hurrying to my car. I'd tried my best to press Rosie for details, but there was a reason she was the long-time assistant of one of the most powerful people in Hollywood. She could be a stone wall when she wanted to, and apparently now was one of those times. I honestly had no idea what this could be about. Bruce wasn't married at the moment, so it wasn't like his soon-to-be ex-wife was torching his belongings on the lawn again.

I figured it was probably something to do with Ford or Gwyneth—and maybe Rosie wanted me there for support. I didn't think it had to do with me—I couldn't think of anything I'd done besides invite Sophie to stay without permission, and I couldn't imagine Bruce getting too upset about that. He'd nodded vaguely at Sophie in the kitchen that morning, which meant he was clearly getting used to her presence in the house, but hadn't yet wondered who she was, or why she was staying there.

I looked down at my phone and saw that while I'd been driving over, Rosie had texted me, just one word: kitchen.

I walked inside and headed directly for the kitchen, looking around the foyer as I went. The giant stuffed polar bear was still in the corner, but nothing else seemed amiss. "Rosie?" I called as I speed-walked toward the kitchen. "What's—"

I stopped short, feeling my jaw drop. There was cheese everywhere. *Everywhere.* There were platters on every surface of the kitchen, cheese baskets on the chairs, individually wrapped wheels of cheese stacked on the granite island. I literally couldn't see anything but cheese at first, which was why it took me a moment to notice that Rosie was also standing in the kitchen, and she looked furious. When she spoke, her voice was cold.

"Is this some kind of a joke, Gemma?"

"I . . . don't know," I stammered. Rosie was looking at me expectantly, like she was waiting for a response from me. "But I didn't have anything to do with it." I was still trying to process that Rosie was using this tone—the one she used to shoo away hangers-on and people posing as gardeners who tried to get scripts into Bruce's hands—with me. I also wasn't entirely sure why Rosie seemed so mad. I mean, it was just *cheese*. People sent huge quantities of strange stuff to the house all the time. The summer I was eleven, we'd all been up to our ears in apples, because for a moment Bruce had been attached to *Apple Man*, a superhero version of the Johnny Appleseed folk tale. It had, thankfully, fallen apart in development.

"Really," Rosie said, not phrasing it as a question. She pulled a card from one of the baskets and handed it to me.

To Bruce, it read in fancy curlicued handwriting, *with all best wishes for your new diet!—Gemma.*

I just stared down at the card, trying to get the words to arrange themselves into some kind of order that made sense. "But I didn't send this," I protested, looking up at Rosie. "I have no idea who . . ." But the rest of the sentence died on my lips. Of course I knew who it was. I should have known the second I walked in the door. This had Hallie written all over it.

"Bruce is not happy," Rosie said, crossing her arms over her chest. "You're a guest in his house, he asks you to respect his diet, and you throw it back in his face like this?"

"Rosie, it wasn't me!" I cried, walking around a huge wheel of Camembert to take a step closer to her. "I swear, I had nothing to do with it."

Rosie just looked at me for a long moment before her features softened a bit. "Really?" she asked, and I was relieved to hear that she phrased it like a question this time. "Because . . ."

"Don't mind me." I turned and saw Gwyneth edging into the kitchen, a camera up to her eye. "I'm not here. I'm just a fly on the wall." Rosie shook her head, and I moved away from Gwyneth, really not in the mood to be on camera at the moment. "Although," Gwyneth said as she panned from Rosie to me and back to Rosie again, "am I the only one who finds that phrase misleading? I *always* notice when there's a fly on the wall."

"Gwyneth," Rosie said, her tone resigned.

"Sorry," Gwyneth said from behind the camera, waving her arm at us. "Just ignore me. I'm not here."

"Rosie, I promise this wasn't me," I said, taking a step closer to her, trying to ignore both the wedge of Brie the size of my head and Gwyneth trailing behind me. "I'm pretty sure this is a practical joke. A . . . former friend of mine is mad at me. I'm positive this is her doing." I knew there was no other explanation for what this could be—this was retaliation for getting Hallie fired from her babysitting job.

Rosie nodded slowly, and I could see that she was starting to believe me. "You're going to have to explain it to Bruce," she finally said. "He was really disappointed in you, Gem."

I felt my heart sink. That was so much worse, really, than Bruce just being mad. "I'll tell him," I promised. "Where is he?"

"He left the house for a few hours," Rosie said as she gestured to the cheese. "He said he couldn't be around this much Gouda and be expected to stay dairy-free."

I nodded. "Understandable."

Gwyneth took a step closer to me, getting the camera

nearer to Rosie's face. "This is great stuff," she murmured. "Misunderstanding, anger, drama . . . and cheese. It's gold."

"Gwyn, give that a break." I looked up to see Ford coming in through the glass doors that led to the deck and snagging a piece of cheddar from a nearby platter. His T-shirt today read CAFÉ 3.14, above a drawing of a cup of coffee and a piece of pie. "We're all wearing these stupid cameras for you, so just let that be enough."

Gwyneth lowered her camera, looking like she was going to start arguing, but then just shrugged. "Fine," she said. "I have to go through some footage anyway. Mind if I take some with me?" she asked, gesturing to one of the cheese plates.

"I think we have enough," Rosie said dryly as she looked around. "And speaking of, Gem, could you do something with all this? I don't want it to still be here when Bruce gets back."

"Absolutely," I said, and Rosie nodded and turned to leave the kitchen. "And I'm really sorry," I called after her. She nodded and gave me a ghost of a smile before continuing out, which I supposed was the best I could have hoped for given the circumstances. I still couldn't believe that Hallie had done this—but I would have to get into that later. At the moment I had to figure out what to do with massive quantities of cheese, which was a problem I'd never been faced with before. I looked around, feeling overwhelmed by it all. It didn't seem right just to throw it away. But what was I supposed to do with it? Were there any cheese-focused charities that would be looking for a large donation? "Um . . ."

"Come on," Ford said, picking up a few of the larger wedges

and gesturing to me to grab one of the baskets and follow him. "I've got an idea."

✿✿✿✿✿✿

"**T**hank you," I said as Ford waved an arm out the window as we drove out of the parking lot of the Montauk Food Bank. "That was such a good idea."

Ford had told me he knew what we should do with the cheese, and after we'd loaded up the SUV (it took up most of the room in the backseats, storage area, and my lap), he'd driven us right here. The employees had seemed thrilled, and while I had a feeling getting gourmet cheese donations was probably not all that unusual in the Hamptons, the sheer volume of cheese we'd just donated probably set us apart.

"No problem," Ford said as he snapped off the air conditioner and rolled the windows down. It was one of the continuous arguments we had whenever we drove together. Ford only liked to drive with the windows down. His car in Hawaii didn't just not have windows, it also didn't have doors. He always said that air conditioning made him feel like he was in a bank. But he'd relaxed this policy when we'd driven over here, acknowledging that heat and sunshine was probably not the best thing for cheese.

"How did you even know about that place?" I asked as Ford turned onto the road that would take us home—and promptly slammed on the brakes. It was a two-lane highway that wound through the Hamptons and, as usual, there was bumper-to-bumper traffic.

"I volunteer there," he said, flipping down the sun visor and resting his elbow out the window.

I just looked at him for a moment. "You do?" This was brand-new information to me. Ford had never mentioned it before—which, I realized, I kind of liked. Teddy would have let you know—not in a braggy way, but let you know nonetheless—within an hour of meeting him if he'd been volunteering at a food bank.

"Sure," Ford said in an offhand manner. "It's not such a big deal."

"Well, it's really nice of you." I reached forward to turn up the volume on the radio, hoping this way we could at least listen to music and not one of Ford's weird tech podcasts. But I'd only scanned through a few stations before he reached over and turned it off.

"You want to tell me what's going on?" he asked. "Someone sent Bruce cheese, pretending to be you, as a joke?" He turned to look at me, which was pretty safe, since we weren't moving at all. "That's a *really* expensive joke."

"I know," I said. Truthfully, as far as revenge payback went, I wasn't really that impressed. Yes, Bruce was disappointed in me. But Rosie believed me, and I knew Bruce would come around. And she had left us with a bunch of snacks. If Hallie wanted to spend a fortune on cheese, I wasn't going to stop her. And this way, the less fortunate of Montauk were going to get some really good manchego.

"Some friend who you happened to tell about Bruce's diet," Ford went on, his voice heavy with disbelief.

"No," I said automatically. "I didn't—" I stopped short. How *had* Hallie found out that sending Bruce cheese was the one thing that would make him upset? I tried to force myself to remember if I'd mentioned something to Reid. I couldn't remember doing it, but I must have said something, even offhandedly. And then Reid must have said something about it to Hallie, not realizing that he was handing her a weapon. "It's kind of a long story," I finally said, when I realized Ford was still waiting for an answer.

"Well," he said, gesturing ahead of us, "it's not like we're going anywhere."

I looked over at him, sitting in a shaft of sunlight, half smiling at me. There was nothing but trust in his expression. I knew if I told him, it might change the way he looked at me—might forever alter what he thought about me. And I just wasn't sure I could risk it. "It's really complicated," I said, looking away from him and twisting my hands together.

"Sure," he said after a moment, and I could hear the hurt in his voice, the slight distance in his tone. "No worries."

We sat in silence, inching along for a few more minutes, until I couldn't take it anymore. "I do want to tell you," I blurted out. "Just not . . . now. Okay?"

"Of course," Ford said, glancing at me. "I'm here for you, Gem."

"Thanks," I said, reaching over and turning on the radio again, but then a moment later, snapping it off. "You know, I should probably call Sophie," I said, mentally picturing her forgetting about the no-dairy edict and walking into the house with a gallon of milk or something. This would *not* be the day for that to happen. "Just to make sure she remembers about the ban on all things dairy." I looked around for my phone, then remembered I'd left it back at the house.

"Go ahead," Ford said after the silence in which it became clear that I was not making a phone call. "I won't listen."

I felt myself smile at that, not sure exactly how he was going to pull it off. "I don't have my phone."

"Use mine." He gestured to the front cupholder, which was big enough to hold a 128-ounce soda. We'd measured once. "Code to unlock is 4362."

"You're telling me your code?" I asked, surprised, as I picked up his phone and unlocked it.

"I'll be changing it immediately, of course."

"Naturally," I agreed. I opened the keypad, then hesitated. I was pretty sure I knew Sophie's cell. Probably.

"What?" Ford asked, looking over at me still not making my phone call. "Out of juice?"

"I'll just call her when I get back," I said, setting his phone back down in the cupholder. "No big."

"Do you not know your friend's number?" Ford asked, sounding surprised but also a little gleeful. "Your *best* friend?"

"Not all of us have photographic memories," I pointed out. "Do you know my number?"

"Of course," he said, and when I raised my eyebrows, he rattled it off.

"Oh," I said, nonplussed. "Well, I would bet you anything

that *most* people don't know their friends' numbers. I basically only know my house line."

"You should do something about that," Ford said as he made the turnoff that would lead us down a side street and, hopefully, get us back to Bruce's before it got dark out. "Finally," he said with a sigh of relief as we actually started to move again.

"I bet you want to get back to the Galvanized . . . Metric . . . Algorithm . . ." I stopped, knowing I was probably getting most of them wrong.

"You mean the Galvanized Empathic Multipurpose Media Algorithm?" Ford asked, giving me a smile. "Yeah. Well, I need to try, at least. I've hit a bit of a wall."

"Let me know if I can help," I said, totally joking, since I knew absolutely nothing about coding or algorithms, except that I appreciated that they always seemed to know which city I should live in and which Skittles flavor I was.

"I might take you up on that," Ford said, and I noticed to my surprise that he was serious.

"Anytime," I said, and as I looked out the window, I saw that we were getting closer to Bruce's. "Thanks a lot for this," I said when Ford pulled down Bruce's ridiculously long driveway. "I really appreciate it."

"Anytime," Ford echoed as he put the car in park.

We headed inside, and Ford made a beeline for the pool house. I headed toward the kitchen, looking for some kind of nondairy snack, and saw the note that Rosie had shown me earlier. I was about to tear it up, but I stopped, folded it, and tucked it into the pocket of my jean shorts. I picked up my phone and was about to press the button to dial Sophie when I heard my dad's voice.

"Gemma!" I lowered my phone and frowned. It sounded like my dad was calling to me from his office, but I could hear him clearly in the kitchen, which was not a good sign. My dad wasn't a yeller. I could practically count on one hand the number of times I'd heard him really raise his voice. "Dad?" I called back.

A second later he appeared in the kitchen doorway, his cell phone in his hand and his face pale. For just a moment I worried something had happened to my mom—or, slightly less worrying, to Walter. I mean, they were in *Scotland*. Terrible things happened in Scotland. Men wore skirts to formal events, people painted their faces half blue and went around riding horses shirtless, they ate sheep intestines mixed with oatmeal, and occasionally people turned into bears. The last one seemed less probable, but still. "Is everything okay?"

"Did you . . . Did you . . ." My dad shook his head and closed his eyes for a long moment, pressing his fingertips to his eyes before exhaling and looking at me again. "Did you spend nine hundred and eighty-five dollars at a gourmet cheese shop?"

"No!" I said immediately. "Of course not. I—" A moment later I realized what was happening. Oh, *god*.

"Was it charged to your card?" I asked faintly, reaching out to hold on to the counter for support, even though I was afraid I knew the answer. Images flashed through my mind in a terrible montage—me, buying the replacement bathing suit with my dad's card in Sur la Plage, signing my name with a flourish. Realizing I'd forgotten the receipt in the bag. Getting it back when I was at Hallie's house—but now realizing that she'd had several days with my credit card receipt. Days in which she could have made a copy, taken down my numbers, practiced my signature. She hadn't spent her own money on cheese—she'd spent my dad's. And what she'd done was much, *much* worse than just making me look bad in front of Bruce. "The one that's linked to mine?"

"The one that's supposed to be for emergencies," my dad said, his face slowly starting to turn from white to red. "*Emergencies*, Gemma. Not bathing suits and cheese!"

"It wasn't me!" I protested. My father shook his head, and I rushed on. "I swear it wasn't. A . . . friend must have taken the information and done this. As kind of a—prank."

"I got an alert from the credit card company," he said. "And they said they checked with the cheese store. The person who ordered it over the phone had the number, your full name, knew your birthday and billing address. And you're telling me someone went to those lengths for a *joke*?"

"I'm so sorry," I whispered, my head still spinning, the number my dad had said—nine hundred and eighty-five dollars. Nine *hundred* and eighty-five dollars—whirling around and around in my thoughts and never getting any less terrible.

My dad just stared at me, and I could see in that moment that he didn't believe me. He thought I was lying. My father thought this was something I would do—order huge amounts of cheese on a whim and then lie about it. *Is it that different than spending three hundred dollars on a bathing suit?* a tiny voice in the back of my head whispered. *Really?*

"Dad, I *promise* I didn't do this." I heard my voice break on the last word, and my father's expression softened the tiniest bit.

"If you say you didn't, then I believe you," he said, albeit grudgingly. "But this is serious, Gemma."

"I know that," I said.

"You'll have to pay me back," he said, and I nodded, trying not to wince. I didn't even want to think about the math, how many shifts at the ice-cream parlor it would take me to pay my dad back for all the charges that had been made on his card this summer. "And I'm going to cancel this card. It really doesn't look like you're ready for this responsibility."

I nodded, even as I felt his words like a punch to my stomach. "I understand," I said.

My dad just looked at me for a moment longer, and I bit down on my bottom lip hard, trying with everything I had not to let myself start crying. "I really didn't expect this from you, Gemma," my dad said, shaking his head. I didn't need Rosie there to tell me this time—*disappointment* was written plainly across his face.

"I'm so, so sorry," I whispered, not trusting myself to speak any louder without my voice breaking again.

"Okay," my dad said, giving me a tiny nod. He turned and walked out of the kitchen, and I waited until he was gone before I felt my chin tremble and the first tear slide down my face. I pressed my hands into my eyes, making myself take deep breaths, trying to get control of myself. It was bad enough that Hallie had stolen my boyfriend and made me look like an idiot all summer. But to make my father stop trusting me—not to mention trying to make me look cruel to Bruce . . . It felt like a new low. Like she was taking this to a new, more terrible level than it had been at before.

I wiped the tears from under my eyes quickly, trying to gather myself. I could feel my sadness turning to anger. I had to make a plan—I had to do something. I couldn't just let this stand. But *what*? I wracked my brain for an idea—*anything* I could do so I could hit her back, and hit her hard—but absolutely nothing was coming to mind.

My phone started ringing—Sophie's ring tone—and I picked it up immediately, ready to tell her all about what had happened while she'd been babysitting all morning. "Hey," I said. "Guess what happened."

"Hi!" she said. "What?" Sophie must have been using a hands-free device—in the background, I could hear what sounded like the twins singing along with £ondon Moore's new song. It was the one that, on the radio, was nothing but a series of bleeps with the occasional word thrown in. Sophie wasn't listening to that version, and these six-year-olds were currently saying words that I had a strong suspicion their dads wouldn't be happy to have them know. I made a mental note to go through some babysitting basics with Sophie when she came home tonight.

"You're not going to believe it," I said. "Can you talk?"

"Maybe now's not the best time," she said. "I have the girls with me. Are you at work?"

"No," I said, suddenly remembering that, as far as Sophie was concerned, I was still supposed to be at the ice-cream parlor. "That's part of the whole thing. Have you texted Reid at all?"

"No," Sophie said with a sigh, and I could hear, in the background, the twins singing about "goin' to the pub, then goin' to the club." Maybe I could get Sophie to pretend that the song was about a country club. Or at least get her to start playing the bleeped version. "But I think you're right. I don't want to have to keep avoiding his calls, and it would probably be best to clear the air."

"Absolutely," I agreed, glad that Sophie had finally come around to this, and not only because it would make my work life more comfortable—but because the sooner Reid knew the truth, the sooner he could move on. "I think—" I was interrupted by a child's shriek that was so piercing, I held the phone away from my ear.

"Olivia, what is it?" Sophie asked above the wailing that had followed.

"Isabella bit me," Olivia cry-yelled.

"Well, bite her back," Sophie said as though this was the most obvious thing in the world. "Hang on a sec, will you, Gem?"

"Sure," I said, adding quickly, "but you might want to—" I was put on hold before I could tell Sophie that encouraging violence between siblings was maybe not the best way to go.

While I waited for her to come back, I could feel my Hallie rage bubbling up again as I went through how I would tell Sophie what had happened. Feeling the need to do something with my hands, I put my phone on speaker and started scroll-ing absently through my contacts. As I flipped through them, I decided that it was definitely Ford who was the outlier here. Because I really didn't know anyone's number—and I'd be will-ing to bet Sophie didn't either. I would be willing to bet that nobody else I knew—

I stopped short and drew in a breath. I realized there was a good chance that Hallie didn't know people's numbers either. And I could use that to my advantage.

"Back," Sophie said, sounding out of breath. "Man, those kids have sharp teeth. Aren't you supposed to be losing baby teeth by that age?"

"I don't know," I said quickly. "But listen, Soph. Um, what would you think about telling Reid today? As soon as you're done sitting?"

"Why today?"

"Here's the thing," I said, crossing my fingers that Sophie would be on board with this. She'd told me last night that she was with me, but that was before I was asking her to do any-thing. "Hallie did something really terrible to me this afternoon, and I think we might need Reid."

"What?" Sophie asked, sounding more baffled than suspi-cious.

"We might need him," I repeated, lowering my voice, despite the fact that there was nobody in the kitchen to hear me. I looked down and saw the camera clipped to my T-shirt's neck-line.

"Need him how?" Sophie asked. "Hold on." Her voice got

muffled, but I could hear her telling the twins to pipe down. "Back," she said. "What do you mean?"

"I mean," I said, "that we might need . . . to use him for something." I was trying not to think about this too hard, or I knew I wouldn't be able to go through with it. After all, Reid had done absolutely nothing wrong in this situation. But then, Josh hadn't either, and Hallie had certainly pulled him into her schemes. And he was her brother, who she presumably liked a whole lot more than I liked Reid.

"*Use* him?" Sophie asked, now sounding disapproving. "Gemma."

"Not in a bad way," I said quickly, though I really wasn't sure you could use someone and *not* have it be bad for them. "I just need you to tell him you have to talk to him at his house," I said. "I mean, the Bridges' house. Tell him you have to talk to him there, later this afternoon." Sophie didn't say anything, and it was like I could hear her hesitation seeping through the line. "I know," I said after a moment. "But I need you to get in there and get to Hallie's cell phone. And I obviously can't do it."

"What happened?" Sophie asked. "What did she do?"

"Something I need to get her back for," I said. "And quickly. Can you do this?" Even as I asked her, I remembered what Sophie had told me when she'd first arrived in the Hamptons and found out about the situation I was in—that she'd come here wanting a quiet, drama-free summer.

"If I do it," she said, "what am I even going to say to him?"

"I don't know," I said, realizing that there were lots of pieces to this that I hadn't thought through. "I'm sorry, Soph," I said after a pause in which neither one of us came up with anything. "Never mind. I'll figure something else out."

"No, it's okay," she said, surprising me. "I'll make it happen. I can do this."

I let out a long breath. I knew Sophie could—you can't date two people at the same school simultaneously unless you have a certain amount of moxie. "Thanks," I said. "Text me when you have the details?"

"I might have to call you," she said. "When I was texting this morning, the twins were yelling at me about some obscure driving law."

"It's a pretty big driving law," I said, scandalized. "And if there are kids in the car—"

"Call you later!" Sophie said as I heard the wailing start again, and then she hung up.

I set down my phone, then unclipped my camera and looked at it. I wasn't entirely sure this technology worked the way I was hoping it would, but there was only one way to find out. I clipped it back on and set out to find Gwyneth.

CHAPTER 12

"**A**re we set?" I asked as I paced nervously around the room. "Is everything okay?"

"You have to calm down," Gwyneth said from her seat in front of the monitors, shaking her head. "I mean, nothing's even happening yet."

"I know," I said as I forced myself to walk over and sit in the chair next to hers, trying to stop myself from fidgeting. I couldn't help but worry, if I was this nervous before anything was happening, how would I feel once there was actually something to be nervous about?

We were in what had been Bruce's third wife's closet—technically, a bedroom she'd converted to a closet. This explained why it was one of the bigger rooms in the house. Gwyneth had, I'd discovered when I'd gone looking for her, turned it into documentary central for the summer. There were three huge monitors on a desk, lots of complicated editing equipment that was intimidating even to look at, and cameras and microphones and assorted supplies stacked or scattered all over.

When I'd found Gwyneth, she'd been going through the footage on Ford's camera. "This is so boring," she'd groaned when I walked in, bearing a sugar-free Red Bull, her drink of choice. "Like, do you know how tedious it is to watch someone type numbers into a computer?" She pressed a button on her laptop. "Delete, delete, delete."

"I brought you a drink," I said, setting it on the table next to her, along with a glass filled with ice and a cookie.

"Aw, that's so nice," Gwyneth said with a smile. "What do you want?"

"Um, what?" I asked, a little taken aback, since her expression hadn't even changed as she asked this.

"You don't grow up surrounded by producers and not know when someone is trying to get something from you," she said, popping the top on the energy drink. "Not that I don't appreciate the gesture. But it's best just to come right out and ask."

"Okay," I said, blinking a little at the directness, but feeling that we might have just saved some crucial time. "I was wondering if it would be possible to see a live feed of one of the cameras—so that we could watch what someone was seeing."

"Of course," Gwyneth said. "But I'd never do that."

I felt my hopes—which had just been raised by finding out

that this technology could, in fact, do what I needed it to—deflate. "Um, why not?"

Gwyneth turned to look at me and brushed her bangs out of her eyes. "Because that contravenes the whole *point* of a documentary. The great thing about the cameras is that you forget they're there." I touched mine. It was true—I usually forgot it was even on until I got changed into my pajamas at night. "But if someone knows I'm watching what's happening as they're going about their day, it changes their behavior."

"But what if this doesn't have anything to do with Bruce or the movie?" I asked. "It would just be using the camera to help me, um . . ."

Gwyneth frowned and paused what seemed to be an endless stream of Ford typing so fast, his fingers were a blur. "Go on," she said.

I looked at Gwyneth for a moment, then took a breath. I needed her to help me with this. If she didn't, I had no other plans for how to get back at Hallie. And somehow, telling Gwyneth was a lot less scary than telling Ford. Maybe because we weren't as close, or maybe because, based on some things she'd mentioned, I had a feeling she'd once gotten back at an ex-boyfriend who'd wronged her. If not, she seemed to know a suspiciously large amount of facts about how long it took for shrimp to stink up a car.

I took a breath and explained, trying to go as quickly as possible while also not leaving anything out. Gwyneth listened, her eyes getting bigger as I got through what had happened the night of the Fourth, to today, with the cheese.

"Oh my god," she said breathlessly when I was finished. "I mean, you can't write that stuff! That's gripping! It's super-compelling. If it were a movie . . ."

"It's not," I said, glad that she didn't seem to be judging me, but also hoping that she'd still be on board with helping—otherwise, I'd just spilled my darkest secret for nothing. "So can you help?"

"I mean . . ." Gwyneth hesitated, then turned back to the monitor and twisted her hair up into a knot. Her hair was so long and thick that when she pulled the knot through, it just stayed there, like a crown on top of her head. "I'm not sure I want to be part of this. I mean, I know this girl did terrible things to you. But I have no issue with her."

I started to concede this point until I remembered it wasn't exactly true. "Well, she did steal your shoes," I said, crossing my fingers in my pocket, hoping that I wouldn't be taking the blame for this because I was the one who borrowed them in the first place.

Gwyneth whipped around to face me. "Which shoes?"

"The pink silk ones," I said, and I watched her expression slowly change, until it resembled Bruce's when he was about to fire someone.

"I'm in," she said, her voice steely as she turned back to the monitors. "Let's do this."

It had taken a number of phone calls to coordinate, but now we were there. Sophie had told Reid that she wanted to talk to him about something—she'd been vague about what—but that she couldn't talk while she was babysitting. It sounded like she'd steered the conversation so skillfully toward what she wanted that when Reid suggested they could just talk at the Bridges' house later on, it was clear he thought this was entirely his idea. She'd finished up with the twins and was now parked on the road outside the Bridges' house, testing her audio with us.

"Can you hear me?" Sophie asked. Her voice was a little muffled, but I could make out what she was saying.

"We can hear you," Gwyneth said, leaning down to talk into the phone she'd put on speaker on the desk. Sophie was wearing the earphones that went with her phone, but only had the one with the microphone attachment in one ear. She'd pulled her hair in front to camouflage the fact that she had one in, and then had run the cord down the back of her neck and into her collar. She was wearing a scarf looped around her neck, and we were just hoping people would think it was a fashion statement, to wear a scarf with jean shorts and flip flops in eighty-degree weather. The real reason was that the scarf would hide any traces of the wire, but we were hoping nobody would ever know that.

Gwyneth had spent about twenty minutes bemoaning the low-techness of this setup. Apparently, she had wireless earpieces that would have been undetectable—leading me to wonder, like Ford had, just exactly how much Bruce was sinking into his daughter's project. But since Sophie didn't have time to go back to Bruce's and get set up, we were trying our best to improvise.

"Okay, Sophie," Gwyneth said as she leaned forward to peer at her monitor. "I'm switching on your camera feed . . . now."

What had been just Gwyneth's screen saver—a picture of her favorite beach in Kauai—suddenly came to life. Everything went fuzzy, then the screen went black, and then we were both looking at Sophie's dashboard.

"Is it working?" Sophie asked. She waved her hand in front of the camera. "Did you see that?"

"We can see it," I said, leaning closer. "That's so cool."

"So, Sophie, keep in mind that the camera's at shoulder height," Gwyneth said. "If there's something we're going to need to see from your POV, you'll have to angle it up."

"Okay," Sophie said. The camera shook, and then we were looking at Sophie holding the camera out at arm's length to talk into it. "So you'll tell me what I'm supposed to be doing, right?" she asked. "You're not going to, like, abandon me when I'm in there?"

"Of course not," I said, but Sophie raised her eyebrows, and even though I knew she couldn't see anything except the camera, I was sure this was directed at me. Back when I was still trying to make amends with Hallie, Sophie had gone to get coffee with her, while pretending to be me (since I had been going under her name). She'd had an open call with me, her phone on speaker so that I'd be able to hear and text her if she ran into a problem. But I'd had to cut the call short when I ran into Reid, and it was clear Sophie hadn't forgotten about it. "I promise," I said, and Sophie nodded.

"Okay," she said, and then she disappeared from view on the monitors, and we were back to seeing from Sophie's point of view as the car started moving up the driveway.

"Wow," I said as I watched the footage move jerkily. It was the jolting camera motion of every found-footage horror movie, and it was starting to make me nauseous. "Is it always like this?"

"You should see Bruce's when he's been pacing around," Gwyneth said, shaking her head. "It's another reason why I don't ever watch live feeds. Too much of it that you can't fast-forward through, and pretty soon you're about to throw up."

"So it's not entirely about the integrity of the documentary?" I asked, raising my eyebrows at her.

"Not entirely," Gwyneth admitted. On Sophie's feed, the Bridges' house was coming into view, and Gwyneth let out a low whistle. "Nice place."

"So tell me what I'm looking for again," Sophie said as she pulled in front of the house. I noticed that Hallie's white Jeep was parked there, which most likely meant she was home—which, for our purposes, was perfect.

"It's a phone in a blue-and-white case," I said. "It has her initials on it." I'd been seeing her phone since the beginning of the summer, but I'd gotten my clearest view of the case when she had come to the ice-cream parlor and turned away from me to talk to Teddy.

"What if it has a security lock on it?" Sophie asked, and I saw her reach out and turn off the engine.

I was worried about that myself, but when Hallie and I had been hanging out—before I knew the truth—I hadn't remembered her ever needing to put in a code to unlock her phone. This might have changed, and I might be sending Sophie on a fool's errand, but I figured it was a risk I'd have to take. "I think we'll be okay," I said, and I heard Sophie take a deep breath and then let it out. "You'll be great," I added. "Just know we'll be here to help you if something happens."

"Okay," Sophie said, sliding out of the car. "Here I go."

I watched Sophie make her bumpy way to the front door, feeling myself start to get a little queasy—but I wasn't sure if this was from the motion of her minicam, or from stressing about what we were going to try to pull off. Sophie knocked on the door, and it swung open so quickly that I had a feeling Reid had been standing on the other side, not wanting to make her wait. I noticed with a pang that his hair looked freshly combed, and I suddenly wondered if we'd just accidentally raised his hopes by having Sophie come over. He looked happy and excited, and not like someone expecting to be told he was much better off in the friend zone.

Reid ushered Sophie in, and their exchange faded into background noise as I scanned every available surface I could see, looking for Hallie's cell phone. I recognized the house from the bonfire Hallie had thrown earlier in the summer, and I'd also been in it briefly at the Fourth of July party. It was where Josh and I had had our first—and, it now appeared, last—kiss.

"Do you see it anywhere?" Gwyneth asked, leaning forward to look at the monitor.

"No," I said. I was about to say something to Sophie about needing to move beyond the entrance hall, when Reid motioned her into the kitchen, and Sophie followed.

Reid was offering Sophie a huge list of beverages, and she started to slowly circle the large granite island in a way that I hoped looked even slightly natural. I was looking as hard as I could, but I saw only the normal kitchen-counter stuff—well, normal for places unlike Bruce's, since this one didn't have piles of scripts or propaganda about the evils of dairy, or someone filming a documentary in the background. There were stacks of newspapers, a bowl of fruit, and what looked like a mock-up of an invitation. I could only see part of it—it looked like Karen was throwing it, an event called Christmas in July—before Sophie took another step, and it passed out of view.

"I don't see anything in the kitchen," I murmured. I knew Reid wouldn't be able to hear me through her earphone, but I was still not talking at full volume, just in case.

"Maybe we should call it," Gwyneth said without looking at me, eyes glued to the monitor. "You have Hallie's number, right?"

"Yeah," I said, reaching for my cell phone and scrolling through my contacts. "Soph, we're going to call Hallie's cell to see if we can locate it, okay?"

Since I couldn't see if Sophie was okay with this—Reid was still listing all the beverages he could procure, including milk and tap water—I stopped on *Hallie Bridges*, and was about to press the button to send the call when Karen Bridges walked into the kitchen.

I felt myself pull in a breath involuntarily. I hadn't seen Karen in five years, and the last time I'd seen her, she'd been pale and miserable, heartbroken by what she believed my father had done to her. I leaned forward to try to get a closer glimpse through Sophie's camera. This Karen still had wavy blond hair, but whereas before it had been usually up in a bun with a pencil pushed through, it was now in a sleek bob. She was wearing the outfit I seemed to see on all Hamptons women my mother's age—a button-down shirt and khaki pants. She dropped an oversize designer tote on the island, and when she turned to say something to Reid, I could see that she had on a lot of delicate gold jewelry, and gold bracelets stacked on one wrist. She looked incredibly well put together, and even without knowing the brands, I could tell that most of what she was wearing was designer. But more than all that, Karen looked *happy*. It seemed to surround her like an aura, and you could see it in the way she threw her head back and laughed at something Reid said.

I felt a small lump rise in my throat as I watched her walk in and out of Sophie's camera range as she crisscrossed the kitchen, unloading a canvas bag with what looked like fresh fruit and ears of corn. Karen seemed like she was doing well. I still had no idea *what* she was doing, or how she had gone from Karen the struggling novelist to Karen with a beachfront mansion, but something had clearly gone her way in the last five years. And she looked happy. So maybe I hadn't totally ruined everything after all.

"Sorry," Reid was saying on Gwyneth's monitor and gesturing to Sophie. "This is Sophie. She's a friend of mine."

"Hi," Sophie said, but I could hear how high her voice was, and I knew she was getting a little freaked out.

"You're fine, Soph," I said quietly into the phone. "I'll talk you through this."

"So how do you know Reid?" Karen asked, smiling at Sophie as she pulled open the refrigerator.

"Um," Sophie said. I hesitated for a second before helping her to answer. Sophie couldn't exactly say she was friends with me—I had absolutely no idea what Hallie had told her mother about any of what had happened. I realized I was going under the assumption that she hadn't told her mother anything about five years ago or this summer, just like I'd kept my father totally in the dark. But Hallie had been close with her mother back then, so I had no idea what she'd shared with her.

"Say you met at the bonfire party Hallie threw," I said, hoping that this was just polite-mom small talk, and that soon she would leave and we could get back to the business of trying to find Hallie's cell phone.

"At Hallie's bonfire party," Sophie repeated. Her tone was upbeat, but I knew her well enough to tell that she was still nervous.

"Oh, wonderful," Karen said. "And what are you two up to now?"

"Say—" I started, just as there was a knock on the door. Gwyneth and I both turned away from the feed to see Bruce standing in the doorway, Bluetooth earpiece in one hand.

"Hi, ladies," he said. "How's it going?"

Gwyneth and I both looked at each other, and I was pretty sure we'd just had exactly the same reaction—that this was not the best moment for Bruce to drop in. We needed to be focused on what was happening on the monitor, and everything Sophie was dealing with at the Bridges' house—that we didn't really have time for this. "Hi, Daddy," Gwyneth said, turning to face him. "Gemma's just helping me with some documentary stuff."

"Ah," Bruce said. He stuck his hands in his pockets, looking uncharacteristically nervous. "Gemma? Could I speak to you a moment?"

I had a feeling this was about the cheese, and I suddenly felt nervous myself. I also knew that this was probably the worst time in the world to leave Sophie fending for herself—again—but after what Bruce thought I'd done to him, I didn't think I could tell him I'd just have to talk to him another time. "Of course," I said, pushing myself up from the table. "Um, just try to cover for me?" I whispered to Gwyneth, hopefully out of the range of Sophie's hearing. I figured I could make this really quick with Bruce, and then maybe even be back before Sophie realized I'd been gone.

Gwyneth nodded, but I could tell she looked a little freaked out. I hurried across the room and stepped into the hallway with Bruce, closing the door behind me.

"So," he said, clearing his throat. "About this afternoon—"

"Bruce, I'm so sorry," I said immediately. Not only because of the time crunch in the other room, but because I wanted him to know right away that I hadn't had anything to do with the cheese. "I swear it wasn't me who ordered all that cheese. It was a friend of mine. They were, um, playing a prank on me."

Bruce nodded. "Rosie said something about that."

"I'm really sorry," I said again. "I promise I wouldn't have done something like that."

"I know that," Bruce said, nodding. "And I apologize for thinking you would. You've always had such a good heart, Gem." I nodded, smiling without saying anything. If he knew what I'd been up to five years ago—or even what his daughter and I were up to right now—I wasn't sure he'd still think that. "Anyway," he said, putting his Bluetooth earpiece back into his ear, clearly having given as much time in his schedule as he could to this conversation. "I just wanted to make sure we were okay."

"Absolutely," I said, giving him a real smile and then starting to back toward the door.

"I still need to get your notes on my new project at some point," Bruce reminded me, and I nodded. It was what I'd had to trade him to get an invitation to his accountant's son's bar mitzvah, since the band playing at it was one of Hallie's favorites—back when I was still trying to get her to like me. Bruce was developing a project about a teenage girl, but apparently all the pitches he'd gotten in weren't working. "It's really not going well," he said, shaking his head. "We might need to go in a new direction entirely."

"Totally," I said, reaching behind me for the doorknob. "We can talk anytime."

"Thanks, Gemma," he said to me as he started down the

hallway, already touching his earpiece to answer a call. "Go for Bruce," he barked before he turned the corner.

I waited until Bruce was out of sight before I turned and dashed back into the room. "Are we okay?" I asked in a shout-whisper as I ran up to the monitors.

"Kind of," Gwyneth said in a cheerful voice that I didn't quite believe. "Sophie froze up a little when she realized you weren't there. The mom with the great hair went somewhere, and then Reid just started launching into it, telling her how he felt. Sophie cut him off before he could get that far, and she told him she just wanted to be friends."

"Wait, already?" I asked, leaning into the monitors. "Has she found Hallie's phone yet?"

"I understand," Reid said on the monitor. "I mean, if that's how you feel. I guess I was just hoping . . . when you said you wanted to come over here . . ."

"Poor guy." Gwyneth sighed, shaking her head. "He seems nice enough."

"Hey," a voice on the monitor said. A familiar voice. My heart started to beat a little harder, and I willed Sophie to turn in the direction of it. She did a second later, and there was Josh in a Clarence Hall T-shirt and running shorts. His hair was dark with sweat, and pushed away from his forehead. I hoped that maybe he'd just gotten sweaty from a long walk or something, since Josh had told me during the disastrous pool party that he'd torn his ACL and was on rest and relaxation for the summer—which meant that he should *not* have been running. I watched on the monitor as he crossed the kitchen, opening the silver fridge and grabbing a bottle of water from it.

"Wow," Gwyneth said breathlessly, suddenly sitting up a lot straighter. "Who is *that*?"

"Um," I said. I could feel myself getting defensive and territorial—until I remembered that Gwyneth didn't know about my history with Josh. "He's . . ." I thought about saying something. But really, what would I even say at this point? That he'd liked me once but now couldn't stand the sight of me? That she couldn't think he was cute, because he no longer had anything to say to me? "He's Hallie's brother, Josh," I said, then swallowed hard. I hated that this was the only way I could identify him now.

"He's *really* cute," Gwyneth said, eyes still fixed on the monitor, moving her head when Josh moved, as though that would somehow get Sophie to move as well.

"Where've you been?" Reid asked as Josh took a long drink of water while Gwyneth and I both watched, neither of us saying anything.

"Running," Josh said, wiping his hand across his face.

"But what about your ACL?" I practically yelled.

"But what about your ACL?" Sophie asked, and I clapped my hand over my mouth.

"Ruh-roh," Gwyneth said softly.

"Oh," Josh said, now looking right at the monitor—which meant he was looking at Sophie. "I didn't see you there. Sophie, right? The real one?" He asked this last question in the same bitter voice that I hated. And I also didn't feel prepared for how much I didn't like him calling Sophie by her name. I knew it was illogical—it was her name, after all—but he'd called *me* Sophie for a month, and even though it didn't make any sense, I didn't like it being used to address anyone else.

"Right," she said. "Sophie Curtis."

Josh shook his head. "I've heard that one before."

"How did you know about Josh's injury?" Reid asked, looking perplexed. Josh also turned to Sophie, eyebrows raised.

"Oh," Sophie said, and I scrambled to think of something, anything, Sophie could say that would be believable.

"Say you heard it from me," I said finally, realizing there was probably no other explanation.

"I think that . . . Gemma . . ." Sophie started, and as I watched Josh's face, it became closed off and angry.

"Enough said," he replied, his voice cold.

Gwyneth turned to look at me, eyebrows raised. "Did you two . . . ?" she asked. Before I could respond, Josh took a step closer to Sophie.

"So why are you here?" he asked, and it was like he'd suddenly remembered that Sophie was associated with me, someone to be suspicious about.

"I invited her over," Reid piped up, and I silently thanked him for it. "But I have a feeling Sophie probably wants to be going now."

"Yes," Sophie said.

"NO!" Gwyneth and I both yelled at the same time.

"I mean, no," Sophie amended quickly.

"No?" Reid asked, looking suddenly hopeful again.

"I mean . . . I just . . ." Sophie stammered.

"Bathroom," I said into the phone.

"Could I just use your restroom first?" Sophie asked.

"Sure," Reid said. "It's down the hall."

"Call it," Gwyneth whispered, snapping her fingers at me. "Call Hallie's cell. Now."

I started to press the button, then suddenly thought of something. I turned to Gwyneth, shaking my head. "I can't," I said, pulling my hand back. "Because she knows my number, and it'll come up on her caller ID."

"Use mine," Gwyneth said, thrusting her phone at me. With shaking hands, I typed Hallie's number into Gwyneth's phone as quickly as I could. We both leaned forward, listening, and the second we heard it ring, Gwyneth hung up. "It sounded like it was upstairs," she said.

"Great," I heard Sophie say to Reid. "I'll just be a second." She headed out into the hall and paused in front of the mirror in the foyer. "Guys?" she whispered into her camera, and it was a relief to get to see Sophie again, reflected back at us. Unfortunately, now I could see that she looked incredibly stressed. I think the last time I saw her look this on edge, she'd been dating two guys simultaneously while trying to study for finals.

"The phone's upstairs," I said. "It's okay. I know the layout of the house—I can talk you through it."

"But I'm supposed to just be going to the bathroom," Sophie said, looking increasingly freaked out. "They're going to know something's wrong!"

"No, it's okay," Gwyneth said, her voice soothing. I knew the tone well—it was the same one Bruce used when he was trying to talk actors into signing away their deal points, whatever those were. "You can do this. But you have to do it now. Gemma will help you."

"Of course," I said, jumping in, glad that Gwyneth was here, but wishing I were better at this. "So the staircase is just down the hall to your left."

Sophie nodded, then disappeared from the monitor as she started walking down the hall. She headed up the stairs, and I was incredibly grateful that I'd been upstairs in the Bridges' house before, because things were looking familiar—the curve of the steel staircase, the framed black-and-white family portraits that lined the walls. Sophie stopped on the landing. "Now what?" she whispered.

"Call it again," I said, gesturing to Gwyneth. She nodded, and a moment later I heard the faint ring of what I was pretty sure was a Lenin and McCarthy song. "Did you hear that?" I asked.

"I think so," Sophie said as she started down the hall.

"Hallie's room is at the end on the right," I said.

"Okay," Sophie said. She started moving down the hall, but then stopped when she was just outside Hallie's room. There was a wooden table in the middle of the hallway, a framed map of the Hamptons above it. And dropped on the table, a bit haphazardly, was a designer tote I recognized from Hallie carrying it earlier this summer—and next to it, her cell phone.

"Bingo," Gwyneth said.

"I see it," Sophie said. She reached down and turned over

the phone, and I could see the two missed calls from Gwyneth's number. Sophie slid her finger across the screen—only to be prompted for the lock code. *Damn it.* "What do I do?" she whispered, and I could hear the panic in her voice.

I leaned toward the phone to start to say something—that she should just leave, there was no point to this now—when Gwyneth waved me off.

"Which model is that?" Gwyneth asked. "Hold it up to the camera." Sophie did, and Gwyneth nodded. "Okay, Sophie, here's what I need you to do. Switch the phone to silent," she said, still using the same soothing tone, which was a miracle, considering how hard my heart was pounding, and how close I was feeling to panic myself. "And I'll call it again. When you answer, the phone will be unlocked. And as long as we keep the call open, you can do what you need to. Okay?"

"Okay," Sophie whispered, still sounding stressed, and I wondered if she'd realized what I had—that she'd now officially been gone a really long time for someone who was just going to the bathroom.

"I didn't know about that," I murmured as Gwyneth called Hallie again.

"Design flaw in that model," she said. "Ford told me they're fixing it with the next one." Sophie answered the phone immediately and then went right into the contacts.

"Change Teddy's first," I said, and Sophie pulled up his contact—I narrowed my eyes when I saw that his contact picture was a photo of him and Hallie, with more of her in the frame than him. Sophie deleted Teddy's phone number, replaced it with mine, then saved the contact.

"Sophie knows your number?" Gwyneth asked, sounding impressed. "That's a good friend." I was flattered by this myself, and silently promised that I'd memorize Sophie's so she'd never have to find out I didn't know hers.

"Are we set?" Sophie asked, her voice barely above a whisper.

"Wait," I said quickly. "Change my contact too. Otherwise, both might show up." Sophie scrolled through Hallie's contacts, found me, opened it up, and changed the last two numbers. "We're all set," I said. "Great job."

"Okay, hanging up," Sophie said. She went to put the phone down, then stopped, her hand hovering over the table. "Was it faceup or facedown?" she asked. Gwyneth and I just stared at each other. "Guys?"

"Faceup," I finally said, even though I had no clear recollection of this. "Just leave it faceup."

"Okay," Sophie said, leaning forward to put the phone down. As she did, I thought I saw something in Hallie's purse—a flash of green.

"Wait," I said, squinting at the screen. "Sophie—" But then Hallie's purse left the frame, and there was only the jerky movement of Sophie hurrying down the stairs.

"What?" Gwyneth asked me, eyebrows raised.

"Nothing," I said, trying to convince myself as I said it. For just a moment I had thought that Hallie might have my old Southampton Stationary notebook, the one I'd written all my eleven-year-old plans for her in. She'd made a mention of the notebook when we were on the beach on the Fourth, but I couldn't quite get myself to believe that she'd been carrying it around with her for the last five years. I'd seen something else, that was all.

"Sophie?" The voice—I was pretty sure it was Reid's—was coming from downstairs. Sophie started walking more quickly, the camera feed getting so blurry that I had to look away.

"Sorry," Sophie said as she reached the landing. Reid appeared mostly baffled, but I could see Josh leaning against the hallway wall, looking at Sophie with suspicion.

"I thought you went to the bathroom," Reid said, gesturing behind him. Sophie turned, and I saw that was where the bathroom was—it would have been *really* hard to get anyone to believe that she didn't see it and had gone wandering around upstairs looking for one there, instead.

"Right," Sophie said, stretching out the word, stalling while she waited for me and Gwyneth to come up with something. "Okay. You see . . ."

"Period!" Gwyneth yelled into the phone so loud, I was worried for a second that the boys would have heard it.

"So the thing is," Sophie said, and I could hear in her voice that she wasn't nervous any longer, now that she had a story to spin. "I needed some . . . personal things that weren't in the bathroom down here. So I looked for them upstairs. I hope that's okay?"

The boys nodded in sync, both of them starting to turn red.

"Right, sure, of course," Reid stammered. "Um, yeah, whatever you needed."

Gwyneth shook her head. *"Boys,"* she said, rolling her eyes. "Nothing else scares them so much. It was how I kept Ford out of my room for years. I just kept a box of Playtex by the doorway and it was like garlic to a vampire. He refused to even cross the threshold."

"So I should go," Sophie said as she slung her purse over her shoulder. "I'll see you, Reid."

"Yeah," Reid said. I'm sure he was trying to sound cool and collected, but I could tell—even with the somewhat scratchy sound quality—that he was crestfallen. "Sounds good."

"I'll walk you out," Josh said, and I wondered if this was him being funny, because the front door was about two steps away. If he'd said that to me, I would have been able to tell if this was one of the really dorky jokes he made sometimes, the ones that had been such wonderful, unexpected surprises. But if it was a joke, it didn't seem like Sophie got it, because she just followed Josh to the doorway. He held open the door for her, and she looked up at him. The moment stretched on and, staring at the screen, I willed her to just say good-bye and walk away. I wasn't loving the fact that they were still standing there together.

"I'm sorry about before," Josh said, leaning slightly against the doorframe. "I shouldn't have acted that way toward you. You had nothing to do with this."

"It's okay," Sophie said, and maybe she smiled, because Josh gave her a half-smile back, the kind that had once been directed at me.

"I'll see you around?" he asked. Even though it was almost exactly the same thing that Sophie had said to Reid, it seemed to me like there was an entirely different meaning behind it. Unless I was imagining things, which was a scenario I would have much preferred to believe at the moment.

"Sure," Sophie said, and I wished that Josh could have been wearing a camera, or that Karen could have chosen to have a mirrored door or something, because I couldn't tell from Sophie's tone what she thought about this, and what she meant by "sure." Was she being flirty? Polite? I had no idea, and the shaky cam view as Sophie started to walk across the driveway wasn't illuminating anything.

"You okay?" Gwyneth asked, taking a bite of the cookie as she nodded at my hands. I looked down and saw that I was gripping my phone so tightly, my knuckles were turning white.

"Yeah," I said, releasing my hands and shaking them out. I was fine. And I should be happy—we'd done what we needed to do and had pulled it off. I was going to get Hallie back for the cheese. This was good. It just didn't feel like it at this very moment, that was all.

"So *was* there something between you two?" Gwyneth asked.

I let out a breath before answering. "Not really," I finally said. "There was just . . . the possibility of something." That was the sad truth of the matter. I had liked Josh, and he had liked me, but we'd had only a few wonderful seconds after we'd kissed and before he'd found out the truth. There *might* have really been something there. But between the girl at the coffee shop and his possibly flirting with my best friend, it seemed like Josh was really no longer interested in there being anything between us. And while I could understand intellectually where he was coming from, it didn't stop it from hitting me like a punch in the gut.

"Okay," Sophie said, and suddenly she was there on the monitor, holding the camera out in front of her. "Are we good?"

"We're good," I said, smiling at her, even though I knew she couldn't see me. "Thank you so much."

"Meet you back at the house?" Sophie asked, and I could hear her car starting.

"Absolutely," I said, picking up my phone and selecting Hallie's contact. "We've got work to do."

CHAPTER 13

I looked at Sophie sitting across the lounge chair from me, and the phone that was between us. It was the day after Sophie had gone into the Bridges' house for me, and I'd promised to buy her iced lattes for the rest of July to thank her for it. She hadn't been happy that I'd abandoned her—again—when she was doing me a favor, but when I'd explained that Bruce had needed to talk to me, she'd understood. At least, she said she did. I could still hear a woundedness in her voice, and I just hoped it would blow over soon.

Gwyneth had promised to contribute ideas, but she'd been holed up all day working on her documentary. It seemed the deadline for submissions to this festival was looming, and Bruce was apparently not turning out to be as exciting a subject as she had hoped. I felt like I could have told her this from the beginning, but I had a feeling that would not be particularly helpful now. Ford was surfing, thankfully. He'd gone out early this morning, and even though it was getting close to four now, he still hadn't returned. Normally, I liked things better when he was around, but I wasn't sure how I would explain this without going into detail—why Sophie and I were texting someone, pretending to be that someone's boyfriend.

"So," Sophie said, looking down a little fearfully at my phone. "Should we just start? Or . . ." Her voice was hesitant, which was exactly the same way I was currently feeling. There was a piece of me that had started to worry we were crossing a line, but then I remembered Hallie had done the exact same thing to me with Sophie's phone. And she had made it seem like Sophie was in need of my help, which seemed equally bad, if not worse, than what we were about to do.

"Do you think she'll believe it?" I asked as I looked across at her. After all, if Josh happened to mention to his sister that Sophie had been upstairs—or if Hallie looked in her call log and saw she had a several-minutes' long conversation with a number from a Hawaii area code—she might be tipped off that something was wrong, or that she shouldn't trust her text messages.

We'd had fate on our side for yesterday and today, however, since I'd seen on Teddy's Friendverse that he'd gone to his cousin's lake house for the weekend. I knew from past experience that there was almost no cell reception there, and he couldn't send or receive texts, which gave us a window in which to do this.

"I think she won't have a reason not to," Sophie pointed out. "Not for a while, anyway. Teddy won't be able to text her. And you know Teddy well enough that you'll be able to imitate him pretty well."

I nodded, thinking. The plan had been to mess with Hallie. But I was beginning to wonder if we should do more. "Maybe we don't just mess with her," I said slowly. "It could be an opportunity to get some information."

"What do you mean?" Sophie asked.

"I mean, maybe try to get some answers, finally. Like about how they met in the first place. Like, *where*. Hallie somehow pulled this off, and we have no idea how." I could hear the frustration in my voice. It had been something that had been bothering me all along, but just in the background—how Hallie had known about Teddy to steal him from me in the first place.

Sophie nodded, looking impressed. "I don't know if we have anything to lose," she said. She looked pointedly down at the phone. "Ready?"

I took a deep breath and picked it up. "Ready."

⚒⚒⚒⚒⚒

Thirty minutes later I looked up from the glowing screen and blinked. It had gotten dark without me noticing, and my hands were cramping from the texting. Sophie had disappeared inside to grab a sweater once it got really cold. So I'd been on my own for the last few minutes, but the mission had pretty much been accomplished. At first, I'd been terrified Hallie would know I wasn't really Teddy—what if he'd told her about the cell reception issues? But it seemed like he hadn't because Hallie had responded immediately. Under the guise of reminiscing about how they'd first met, and by telling Hallie how beautiful she'd looked the first time he'd seen her (gag), I'd found out that Teddy and Hallie had met by chance (or so she wanted him to believe) at a park in Putnam. I didn't think I could get her to tell me which one without giving the game away. I'd also found out that their three-month anniversary was coming up, and I had used almost all my self-control not to fling my phone into the pool or smash it against the side of the house. Three months meant that Teddy had been cheating on me with Hallie for *weeks* before he got the nerve to break up with me in Target. I'd had to really work hard to make sure no anger or bitterness crept into my text replies, and I had been doing my best Teddy impression, careful not to let my turns of phrase creep in.

I had also found out, much to my dismay, that Hallie called Teddy "Bear" and apparently he called her "Panda," which was much, *much* more than I'd wanted to know. Teddy hadn't really called me anything except sometimes Gem—when we'd met, he had told me that diminutive nicknames were infantilizing and damaging to a relationship—or something. I had been so dazzled by him back then, I had mostly just nodded and agreed with him.

Hallie had to step away to go have dinner with her mother—apparently the "new project" was proving challenging. I had stared down at my blinking cursor after she'd written that, wondering if there was any way she would believe that Teddy didn't know what she was talking about. But Teddy had always been really on top of that stuff—asking about my mom's business, my dad's movies, Walter's fish. Even if he didn't remember, I knew Teddy would never admit to that fact and let himself look bad or uninformed. So I'd just texted an encouraging reply, and she'd promised to text back after dinner. It was after dinner, I'd decided, that I'd start taking things to the next level—after all, Hallie clearly believed I was Teddy.

I stretched, then stood up and headed toward the kitchen—my phone could use some charging, and it was starting to get cold out. I crossed the pool deck and slid open the glass doors that led to the kitchen, glancing at the pool house as I did. Ford hadn't come home yet, and I just hoped he'd be back soon, despite what he said about how surfing at night was perfectly safe. I just felt better when he was out of the water and accounted for.

I plugged in my phone, then looked down at Hallie's name, at the last exchange she and "Teddy" had had. Even though we'd stopped at a good point, it was like I could feel my fingers itching to do more. So what if Hallie had gone to dinner? Was there any reason her boyfriend couldn't keep texting her? They would be like little text presents for her the next time she looked at her phone. And Teddy had occasionally done this to me as well—I would sometimes check my phone and see I had about eight stream-of-consciousness texts from him, usually about the plight of the worker. So there was a precedent for this, after all. I picked up the phone and started to type.

> I'm hoping the next time we see each other,
> you'll tell me something really personal,

really

that you've never shared
with anyone. Will you join me on that journey?

I've always loved green. Why don't you wear it
more?
I think it would look gorgeous on you.

Do you like peaches? I can't think of
anything I like better. Except you, of course. ☺

Quick: favorite word? Mine's comestibles.

"I don't understand," Sophie said, looking up from the phone at me. I was still in the kitchen, rummaging around in the fridge to find something to eat for dinner and wishing that our pizza hadn't been thrown away in the cheese purge. "These are bad things?"

"They are to Teddy," I said with a smile as I gave up the pizza dream and brought a plate of leftover pad thai to the kitchen island where we'd gathered. I was betting on the fact that Hallie simply didn't know Teddy too well yet, and certainly nowhere near as well as I did. Which meant she had no idea the trap I was setting for her—no idea that Teddy was allergic to peaches, blue-green color-blind, and had a deep and abiding hatred of the word *comestibles* ever since it was the word that had gotten him kicked out of the national spelling bee when he was eleven.

"Oh, wait, she's writing back," Sophie said, suddenly sitting up straight.

"What did she say?" I asked, leaning over, my heart pounding. These last few texts did have me worried. If Teddy had told her any of these things about himself, it would be all the indication Hallie needed that she wasn't actually talking to her boyfriend.

Hallie Bridges

6:05 PM

I love that you're sharing with me like this, Bear.

Hallie Bridges

6:06 PM

I think it's proof we're getting closer.

Hallie Bridges

6:07 PM

My favorite color is brick red.

And my favorite word is ensorcelled.

(Which is how I feel about you. ☺)

"Oh, barf," Sophie said, looking disgusted as she pushed the phone away. "I so didn't need to see that."

"See what?" Gwyneth asked as she came into the kitchen, her camera under her arm. She headed right for the fridge, but then didn't open it, just rested her head against the silver door for a moment.

"Um, you okay?" I asked, getting more concerned the longer Gwyneth didn't move.

"Sure," she said in a manner that might have been more convincing if she hadn't been slumped against a fridge. "It's just this doc. I need something *compelling*. Something with *drama*. And all I have is Bruce yelling at people about getting him a permit for something, and trying to line up investors for his movie. It's making me fall asleep, which is a bad sign." She pushed herself up to standing and shook her head. "Very bad."

"I'm sorry," Sophie said, and I nodded. I wasn't sure what else to say, since none of my friends had ever had a boring-documentary problem before.

"Thanks," Gwyneth said, coming to sit with us at the island. She gave us a smile that seemed a little forced, but was there nonetheless. "What are you two up to?"

I pushed the phone across to her, and Gwyneth scrolled through the texts, her small smile growing as she read the exchanges. "Nice," she said. She set the phone down and looked at me for a moment, her head tilted to the side. "But do you really think you've gone far enough?"

"What do you mean?" Sophie asked, her brow furrowed.

"I mean . . . nine *hundred* dollars in cheese," Gwyneth said. "Charged to your dad. Not to mention my shoes. Not to mention your boyfriend."

"Ex," Sophie supplied.

"And whose fault is that?" Gwyneth asked. She picked up her camera and started fussing with the lens. "I'd push this as far as I could before she catches on."

I looked at Gwyneth, and I somehow felt that if she'd been here in the beginning of the summer, things might not have turned out the same way. She probably would have seen through Hallie in a heartbeat. "What are you thinking?" I asked slowly.

Gwyneth set down the camera, which was frankly a relief. She kept promising us that we'd get used to it—she insisted that everyone did, otherwise people on reality TV shows wouldn't behave nearly as badly as they did—but I still found it easier to speak to people when I could see their faces. "What does this girl look like?" she asked.

"Well, she's kind of tall," Sophie started. "With, you know, like, hair, and . . ."

"I've got a picture," I said, realizing that I could probably save us some time—and also, never to task Sophie with talking to a police sketch artist if we were ever witnesses to a crime. I opened up my pictures and scrolled through them. There were a number of me and Hallie from earlier this summer, and I stopped at one that we'd taken while attending (*crashing* might have been the more correct term) a bar mitzvah.

It was a selfie I'd taken of us while we were dancing up a storm to Lenin and McCarthy, Hallie's favorite band and the reason I'd gotten us in there in the first place. The lighting wasn't great, but you could see both of us clearly. Maybe it was because I was trying to steady my phone, or maybe it was because of something Hallie had said that I'd forgotten, but I was in the middle of cracking up, my eyes squeezed tightly shut and my head tipped forward in laughter. Hallie was half turned to me, smiling at me, looking like she was about four seconds from cracking up as well. We were leaning into each other, and Hallie's arm was slung around my neck. We looked happy. We looked like good friends.

"Here," I said, looking away from the picture and handing my phone to Gwyneth. If I kept looking at it, I'd start missing her—the Hallie who had never really existed. I forced myself to remember that even while we'd been laughing together, she'd been lying to my face and scheming behind my back. Technically, I'd also been lying to her, but at least my lying had been in an attempt to make something right.

Gwyneth looked at the picture, then up at me. There was something in her expression that told me she understood at least a little of what I was feeling, and I looked away, not wanting to have to see it. "So she's got good hair," Gwyneth said, looking at the picture critically, enlarging the image. "It's long?"

I nodded. "Very. And curly, though she straightens it sometimes."

Sophie shook her head. "That's *so* typical Teddy," she said dismissively.

"What is?" I asked.

"His *thing* with long hair," she said, rolling her eyes. "I couldn't even get Gemma to get a trim before they broke up. And can't we all agree that she looks much better now?"

"*Yes,*" Gwyneth said emphatically.

"Hey," I protested, feeling slightly insulted as I took another bite of my pad thai, wishing it were pizza. It also wasn't that Teddy had *prevented* me from getting a haircut, or anything. He'd just mentioned, on more than one occasion, how much he liked my long hair. That was all.

Gwyneth smiled. "Actually, that's perfect." She started typing on my phone, then pausing, then typing again. It wasn't until I heard the little beep of an incoming text that I realized she'd been texting Hallie.

"What are you doing?" I asked as I walked over to her. "What's perfect?"

"I'm just making a little style suggestion," Gwyneth said, still typing away. "It's not like she has to take it." I reached for my phone, but she turned away from me, still typing, fingers flying over the keyboard. For someone who was seven inches shorter than me, she was doing a very good job of keeping the phone out of my reach. She stopped typing, nodded, then handed the phone back to me. "See for yourself."

Teddy Callaway
6:15 PM
You know what I was just thinking about?

Hallie Bridges
6:16 PM
What's that, Bear?

Teddy Callaway
6:17 PM
The unrealistic beauty standards
society puts on women today.

Hallie Bridges
6:19 PM
I love how enlightened you are.

Teddy Callaway
6:19 PM

Somehow women are expected to conform
to a certain beauty standard.
But I've always found short hair
on girls to be the most attractive thing.

Hallie Bridges
6:21 PM
Oh. Really?

Teddy Callaway
6:21 PM
Absolutely. I was always
mentioning it to Gemma, but
she never changed anything.
Maybe she was too afraid to
be her own person.

Hallie Bridges
6:22 PM
Well, that's hardly surprising.

Teddy Callaway
6:23 PM
There would be nothing better to me
than a girl who has the courage
to challenge society's
preconceived notions of beauty.

I stared down at the text exchange, feeling my jaw drop.
After Teddy's last text, Gwyneth had attached pictures of girls
with pixie cuts—Emma Watson, Natalie Portman, and

Jennifer Lawrence. In other words, the only girls who had *ever* looked good with supershort hair. "Oh my god," I said, reading through the exchange again. I didn't like Hallie's jab at me, but at least Gwyneth (as Teddy) hadn't agreed with her. I could have used some fake-defending, but I didn't think that this was worth bringing up at the moment.

"What do you think?" Gwyneth asked, looking very pleased with herself as she picked up the camera once again and pointed it at me. "Think she'll do it?"

"Do what?" Sophie asked. I handed her my phone, and Sophie read through the texts. "Nicely done," she said to Gwyneth. "I think it's going to get into her head, at any rate."

"Hallie's not going to cut her hair," I said, but even as I spoke the words, I wasn't sure. I couldn't help but think, though, that if we did get her to cut her hair off—knowing full well Teddy hated short hair on girls—it would go a long way toward making up for the cheese.

"I wouldn't text anymore," Sophie said, sliding my phone away from me. "If you've just dropped something like that, I'd go silent. It'll make a bigger impact."

"Good call," Gwyneth agreed. I saw the logic in this, and pushed it farther away, out of reach, so I wouldn't be tempted to reply if Hallie wrote back. Sophie hopped off her stool, pulled open the fridge, and sighed. "Is there any dessert hiding in here? Or has everything been thrown away because it has dairy in it?"

"I've got some cookies in my room," Gwyneth said. "Chocolate chip with sea salt. Want one?"

"Do you really have to ask?" Sophie said with a grin as she closed the fridge.

"Gem?" Gwyneth asked me, eyebrows raised.

"I'm okay," I said, automatically reaching for my phone but then pulling my hand back. Sophie was right—I shouldn't keep this going. We'd left things in a good place.

"Suit yourself," Gwyneth said as she headed out. Sophie shot me a look as she went, one that clearly said, *What's wrong with you? Cookies!*

I gave her a smile, knowing that I'd probably find half a cookie on the desk in my room when I went up to bed. I reached for my phone again but didn't let myself go into the texts, just checked my e-mail and my Friendverse. Teddy was back from the lake, Reginald the Vegan still didn't understand why people ate bacon, and Abby West-Smith was linking to an online quiz where you could find out what flavor of ice cream you were. Abby had been updating her status pretty frequently, which I was happy to see, since she'd gone a bit radio silent in the beginning of the summer.

I found myself absently opening and closing different apps on my phone. I knew I should be feeling good about what we'd just pulled over on Hallie. But there was a piece of me that knew it would be so much more satisfying if Teddy had still been here. If he could be here in person when she started wearing green and talking about peaches. If, that is, she really had bought what we'd been telling her tonight.

I pulled up the page for the *Hampton News Daily* and waited for the very badly designed Web site to load. I was still checking it intermittently, just to see if the article with Bruce and his award would pop up. There hadn't been anything—which wasn't actually that surprising. Someone probably very smart at the paper had decided that a producer posing with an award he'd won several years before did not make for scintillating journalism. But in my perusing of the paper, I'd found myself getting weirdly invested in the local school board election, and so while I checked for anything about Bruce first, I always ended up staying on the site for longer than I'd care to admit.

I looked at the site, the text loading before the badly pixelated graphics, as usual. There didn't seem to be much that was new—more about the schism within the city council and the possible danger posed to a local bird habitat. But, unfortunately, no new reporting on the school board drama. I knew that if I ever ran into Andy Young again, I would tell him what I thought about his paper's shoddy coverage. I started to close out the window, when I saw that the picture on the bird habitat article had finally loaded.

I blinked, then leaned forward, not quite able to believe what I was seeing. I knew this bird. In fact, I knew more about this bird than I'd ever wanted to. It was as ugly as ever, but I had never been quite so happy to see the marsh warbler. I leaned closer to the screen, skimmed the article, then went back and read it over again.

This would do it. *This* would get Teddy back to the Hamptons. And then Hallie would look like a fool in front of him, which would cause a fight. I followed this thought to a logical conclusion, one that made me sit up straighter. What if I didn't just make her look ridiculous? What if . . .

What if I broke them up?

I felt my heart start to beat harder. If turnabout was fair play, surely she deserved that—after all, she had gotten Teddy to break up with me. My thoughts were spinning, and I wasn't sure I was up to figuring out an endgame at the moment. Right now I had to talk to Teddy. I started to call him, then hesitated. If he was screening my calls, he wasn't about to hear me out. I'd have to talk to him in person. I pocketed my phone and headed to the driveway, not wanting to tell Sophie where I was going, mostly because I didn't want her talking me out of it or asking me what my underlying motives were. I'd just text her once I was on the road so she wouldn't worry.

I stepped onto the gravel and saw the SUV parked in the driveway, two surfboards and a kayak strapped to the roof. Ford was standing on the running board, and he turned toward me when the front door slammed shut. "Hey, Gem," he said, undoing what looked like jumper cables around the boards. "Want to give me a hand?"

"Actually," I said, looking quickly into the garage and weighing my options. I didn't know how to drive Bruce's sports car, my dad's hybrid was gone—maybe he was working with the *Once Bitten* writer again?—and I couldn't borrow Sophie's car without having to tell her what I was up to. The SUV was the best answer, even though I had a feeling it would cost me a day's pay just to fill it up with the gas that would take me to Putnam and back again. "I need to use the car."

"Oh," Ford said as he lifted the surfboards off the SUV like they weighed nothing, and leaned them against the side of the house. "Right now?"

"Yeah," I said. Now that I had this information, I wanted to do something with it ASAP. I had to work tomorrow, and if I waited much longer tonight, by the time I got to Connecticut I'd be showing up at Teddy's door at midnight—which probably wouldn't help in the not-looking-crazy department. "I have to go to Putnam."

Ford's eyebrows flew up. "Tonight? Why?"

I hesitated, trying to force my brain to come up with some plausible excuse for why I needed to decamp to Connecticut immediately. But nothing came to mind, and the longer the silence between us stretched on—there was only the sound of the cicadas—I knew how much stranger I must have seemed.

"Does this have something to do with that thing you wouldn't tell me about?" Ford asked, tilting his head to the side. "That thing with the cheese?"

I nodded. "Yeah," I said. "So I really need to go. . . ."

Still frowning, Ford handed me the keys, which I immediately fumbled and dropped at my feet.

"Tell you what," Ford said, bending down and scooping them up. "I'll drive." He gave me a level look. "You talk."

CHAPTER 14

"Whoa." Ford just stared at me for a moment, then snapped the top onto his Slurpee cup.

"I know," I said. I started to reach for my own cup, now that Ford had put together his traditional Slurpee—Coke with a hint of cherry—but he waved me off and, as I watched, made me a perfect Gemma special—cherry with just a touch of blue raspberry.

I hadn't wanted to tell him the story, but it was becoming clear to me that I wasn't going to be able to keep it in, especially now that Gwyneth knew, and hundreds of dollars' worth of cheese were showing up at the house.

So as we pulled out onto the darkened highway, I'd told him the story. We weren't under a time crunch, so I'd been able to give him more detail than I'd given to Gwyneth. It had taken a while to tell—we were halfway to Putnam now, at a gas station we'd stopped at when both the gas and snack situation had started to get dire.

Ford hadn't said much as I'd talked, and I'd found it was actually easier than I'd thought it would be. It helped that we were in a dark car, driving down nighttime roads. I didn't have to look at him unless I wanted to, and he couldn't look at me for more than a second or two. But he hadn't denounced me or kicked me out of the car as I told him the truth about the worst of what I'd done, which seemed like a good sign, especially because I hadn't left anything out. I'd gone through the events of the past, then this summer, up to what had happened tonight, and my plans to get back at Hallie. The only thing I hadn't gone into detail about was the Josh stuff. I'd gotten right up to it, but then I'd suddenly felt strange talking to Ford about my crush and kissing Josh and how much it hurt me to see him with another girl. So I just said that I'd gotten closer to Hallie's brother as well, which, I rationalized, wasn't even technically a lie. It wasn't the whole story, that was all.

"Well, that was not what I was expecting," Ford said. He handed me my Slurpee cup, and I looked over at him, worried about what I would see in his expression. But, amazingly, there was no judgment. He just looked surprised and maybe even a tiny bit impressed. "I didn't know you had that in you, Gemma."

"It's not like I'm proud of it," I said, grabbing straws for both of us. "I thought I was going to make things better this summer, but—"

"You got outplayed," Ford said, nodding. "This Hallie girl was counting on the fact that you would believe what she told you."

"Yeah," I said slowly, still not quite able to grasp this had been Ford's whole reaction. I guess I'd expected him to be shocked or disappointed in me—not that he would just accept the situation and then move on to analyzing it.

"So you still want to be my friend?" I asked. I was trying for a joking tone, but even I could hear the worry and fear in my voice. "You don't hate me?"

"Gemma," Ford said, shaking his head as we reached the front counter and put our snacks—Doritos and frosted oatmeal cookies and peanut butter cups, in addition to the Slurpees—on the counter. "Of course I don't hate you. Don't be ridiculous."

I felt relief flood my body. It was like when you take a sip of hot chocolate and feel immediately warmer. "Really?"

"I just wish you would have told me," Ford said as he pulled out a ten and waved me away when I tried to put money down. "I could have helped."

I smiled at this as we walked back to the car, realizing how true it was. I probably should have gone to Ford the second I'd decided to get revenge on Hallie.

We got back into the car, and I put the drinks in the cupholders, and the snacks on the console between us. Ford and I both held the opinion that just because a drive is short does not mean it can't also be a road trip.

"So just to clarify," Ford said as he started the engine, "now we're going to your ex-boyfriend's house to tell him about a bird so that he'll come back to the Hamptons, because Gwyneth might have convinced Hallie to cut her hair."

"Well," I said, considering this. Then I nodded when I realized he'd basically summed it up. "Pretty much."

Ford laughed and pulled back out onto the highway. "I will say one thing about you, Gemma," he said, glancing over at me quickly. "You sure do keep life interesting."

I felt myself smile, even as I shook my head. "I'll be ready to go back to boring after this summer."

"Never boring," Ford protested, and when I stared at him skeptically, his face broke out into a smile, wider than his normal ones. "Maybe occasionally. But you didn't make a habit of it. Now where am I going?"

✺✺✺✺✺✺

"**O**n the left," I said, pointing to the driveway as Ford slowed the SUV. "Right there." I'd tried to tell myself as we got closer to Putnam that this would be fine. It was just me telling Teddy pertinent information that he would appreciate. It wasn't going to stir up any old feelings or anything. But as we drove up the driveway, and Teddy's house came into sight, it was like an onslaught of feelings started to cascade.

There was the tree we'd posed under for pictures before we went to the prom. There was the front step where Teddy and I had sat for hours, just talking, when we'd only been dating a few months and he'd accidentally forgotten his keys. It was just making me recall—more sharply than I'd anticipated—what it had been like to be with Teddy, not all that long ago.

"You okay?" Ford asked, shaking me out of this reverie as he parked in the turnaround.

"Fine," I said, a little surprised that he'd picked up on my mood. Ford just looked at me, and I remembered a beat too late that he had always been able to tell when I was lying. "A little nervous," I amended, "if you must know."

"You'll be fine," Ford said. "I'll be right here."

"Thanks," I said as I opened the door and slid out of the car, leaving my half-drunk Slurpee behind. I was beyond grateful as I walked up toward Teddy's front door that it was a Sunday. Both of his parents were bridge players, and they always played on Sunday nights. And I knew this well, because this was when Teddy and I would make out for hours at his house without having to worry about getting caught.

I made myself press the bell without hesitating. I knew that Ford could probably see me from the idling car and I didn't want to seem scared of talking to my ex-boyfriend.

"Coming," I heard Teddy call from inside, and then a moment later the door swung open. Teddy's expression fell a bit when he saw me, and it was clear I was not the person he expected—or wanted—to see. "Oh. Gemma," he said. "Um . . . hi. What's up?"

I could hear the wariness in his voice and knew that it seemed like I was fitting into every obsessive ex-girlfriend stereotype. I could practically hear what he'd say to his friend Reginald the Vegan over tempeh. *And then she just showed up at my house. Crazy, right?*

"Sorry to just drop by like this," I said, trying to keep my tone businesslike. The last thing I needed was Teddy telling people I was stalking him. With Hallie trying to get me back, she'd probably have him file a restraining order. "You just weren't answering my texts, so . . ."

Teddy let out a sigh. "Gemma. I thought we'd talked about this. You'll always be a cherished part of my life, but—"

"No, this isn't about us," I said. I tried to laugh, like the whole thought of that was just ridiculous, but I don't think I pulled it off. "I'm just surprised," I went on. I was trying my best to sound disappointed, but I was hampered slightly by the fact that I'd never even taken a single acting class. "I guess I just thought that you cared about the marsh warbler," I said, trying to sound both confused and hurt at the same time. "That's all." This acting thing was *really* hard. I would mention it to Bruce the next time he was grousing about meeting an actor's exorbitant quote.

Teddy's expression immediately became grave, the way I'd been hoping for, the way it always did when he was dealing with his favorite cause. "What do you mean?"

"I guess I thought you would have heard about it," I said as I pulled out my phone, which had the article loaded. "Look."

I watched Teddy's expression as he read it. I didn't need to read it over his shoulder—by this point, I practically had it memorized. The marsh warbler, which was native to Long Island, had a breeding ground that was being threatened by plans to expand a beachfront estate. (It went on to specify that while the plans *had* been approved by the local town council, vote-fixing and foul play was suspected. I'd learned, in my reading of the *Hampton News Daily*, that most of the articles were short on facts but long on drama.) The name of the estate's owner wasn't listed, just the architect and contractor. The article hypothesized that the expansion would decimate the marsh warbler population in Quonset, which in turn could damage the bird population as a whole. The article ended with a plea for the community to rally around the bird, and then got a little off topic with a digression about how we need to protect those who have been wronged through no fault of their own.

"I had no idea," Teddy said, looking stunned as he handed my phone back to me.

"That's why I was surprised you left the Hamptons," I said, crossing my fingers behind my back that this would work. "I just don't know if anyone is even doing something about this. All I could find was the one article, and it sounds like things are going ahead. I don't think anyone is going to put a stop to it. But of course," I said, after a small pause, "if you don't think it's that important . . ."

"It's not that," Teddy said, shaking his head. "You know how I feel about the warbler. But there are logistics to consider. When I was in the Hamptons, I had been staying with Hallie and her family, and I don't want to impose. . . ."

"I'm sure Hallie wouldn't mind," I said, all the while counting on the fact that she would mind, and very much. "Surely, she understands how important this is to you." Teddy nodded slowly. "I mean," I said, thinking of the Bridges' beachfront mansion, "I think they probably have enough rooms—" I stopped short, suddenly struck by a terrible thought. What if Teddy hadn't been in a guest room, like I'd just assumed? What if he'd been staying in Hallie's room? Did this mean that—were they . . .

All my focus on what I had to make happen in the next few minutes disappeared completely. Teddy and I had never slept together, which he thought was crazy, considering we'd been together for two years. But it had just never felt right to me for some reason. And Teddy had stopped bringing it up in the last few months we were together, which I thought was a good sign, like he was being respectful of my decision. But maybe it wasn't that at all—maybe it was just that he'd met Hallie, who wasn't always telling him about how Louis XVI and Marie Antoinette didn't sleep together for *seven* years, and how members of a particular New Guinea tribe didn't consummate their marriages until both people were thirty-five or there was a festival of the harvest moon, whichever came first. (Both these examples had come from a book my mom had given me when I started high school, *Wait, Wait, Don't Do It!*). Was this how Hallie had gotten Teddy to break up with me? I started to feel queasy.

"Gem?" I blinked up at Teddy. "Are you okay? You look a little pale."

"I'm fine," I said, trying to focus, but not without difficulty. "I was just . . . thinking about the poor warblers. . . ."

Teddy nodded, then ran his hands through his blond hair. "It's not that I don't care," he said, his voice rational, like the way he'd sounded in assemblies when he had to tell people that you had to buy tickets for the prom in order for there to be a prom. "But . . ."

"It just reminds me of that quote," I said, knowing that I was stabbing in the dark, but also knowing that I had to try something big, or I would have come all this way for nothing—just more embarrassment. "They were a wise person," I went on, since I had absolutely no idea who had said this. "So very . . . wise. Remember when you quoted them? Right before you chained yourself to the bulldozer?"

"'You must be the change you wish to see in the world,'" Teddy said slowly, recognition dawning. "Gandhi."

"Right, him," I said, nodding like I had remembered this all along. "You faced down a bulldozer to save the marsh warbler then." Teddy looked off into the distance. I wasn't sure, but I thought that this was getting through to him. I knew that I should just leave and hope for the best—like Bruce always said: *Get out while they're still listening to you.* "I know you'll do the right thing," I said, making my voice soft and hopeful, wishing once again I'd taken even a single acting class, or done anything on my dad's movie sets besides hang around craft services and try to get gossip from the hair and makeup crew. I gave him a smile, then started to go.

"Gemma," Teddy said, and I turned back. "I appreciate it." He leaned against the doorframe and smiled at me. "You always were so committed to the warblers. I'm just glad to see you haven't changed."

"Oh," I said, not exactly sure how to respond to this. What would Teddy say if he knew that I was currently pretending to be him and catfishing Hallie? If he knew what I was doing right now, that this conversation was part of a larger plan to make Hallie miserable? Also, aside from that, I wasn't sure if it was true. I was pretty sure I'd changed. Hadn't I? I looked away from him, confused. There was also the fact that Teddy was still looking at me, half a smile on his face, confusing me further. When he looked at me like that, I had trouble remembering we were broken up, that he'd cheated on me with Hallie. It was too familiar, too much like the way he'd looked at me when we were together. "I should get going," I said, feeling the need to get some distance from him, at least until I could try and sort out what I was feeling. I started to take a step toward the SUV, and Teddy squinted at it.

"Is your engine running?" he asked, sounding scandalized. "And is that a hybrid? Because otherwise . . ."

Ford chose that moment to lower his tinted window and shoot me an *everything okay here?* look. I nodded, then he gave Teddy a cross between a wave and a salute—maybe it was a surfer thing—before rolling the window back up.

"I, um," Teddy said, crossing and recrossing his arms, "didn't realize you were here with someone."

"Just Ford," I said. I'd talked about the Davidsons enough that Teddy knew exactly who Ford was—just not the parts about my crush or first kiss. I'd left those out. "I'm staying with his dad in the Hamptons, so . . ."

"So you two are staying together? In the same house?" Teddy asked, and for some reason, it looked like his cheeks were getting flushed, a dull red color.

"Yeah," I said slowly, wondering what was happening. "Along with my dad, his sister, his dad, his dad's assistant, Sophie . . ."

"Right," Teddy said, nodding a few too many times. "I just . . . He's the surfer, right?"

"Nationally ranked," I said, and I couldn't help a bit of pride from creeping into my voice.

"Cool. Cool," Teddy said again, his voice a little strangled.

"So, I'm going to go," I said, taking another step toward the car.

Teddy nodded and pulled out his phone. "I should probably text Hallie, tell her about this—"

"No!" I yelled this so loudly that I saw Ford's window roll down once again. Teddy was staring at me, perplexed, and I tried to regroup. I was thrilled Teddy hadn't gotten in touch once he'd gotten back into cell range, and I didn't want to do anything to wreck this now. "I mean . . . I wouldn't text her tonight. Maybe not tomorrow, either. You wouldn't want to get her hopes up until you've got your plans in place."

Teddy pocketed his phone. "You're probably right," he said with a nod. "Thanks."

I was on the verge of spilling it all right then—how Hallie had used him, that their whole relationship had started just to get back at me—but I bit my lip and stopped myself. "Hopefully I'll see you around the Hamptons," I said, taking another step toward the car.

"Maybe so," Teddy said, but I could hear the decisiveness in his voice, and I had to stop myself from grinning. I raised my hand in a wave, and he waved back, and then I hurried to the SUV and walked around to the passenger side.

"So that's the crusader?" Ford asked, putting the car in gear as I buckled myself in. "I have to admit, I thought he'd be taller."

I laughed at that as I picked up my Slurpee cup. "Oh, did you?"

"So how did it go?" he asked as he drove down Teddy's drive-way and signaled. "Victory?"

"I think so," I said, settling back into my seat and helping myself to some Doritos. "Time will tell." I looked across the car at Ford and felt myself smile. "Home?"

He nodded and headed back down the road that would take us to the highway. "Home."

CHAPTER 15

The next afternoon, I stared down at my phone, my hand shaking. I had a feeling I had just made a big, *big* mistake.

I'd gone right to bed after Ford and I had gotten home, and had kept my phone off all night, and then, feeling it might be an exercise in self-discipline, had kept it off this morning when I'd gone into work. There was also the added benefit of the possibility that if Hallie was texting Teddy, she was most likely getting frustrated with his lack of responsiveness. Which was *fine* with me.

Reid had been scooping at half speed, even as he told me repeatedly just how over Sophie he was, and how it really didn't bother him that she didn't like him that way. I'd tried to make it seem like I believed him, even though this couldn't have been further from the truth. It was during these soliloquies that I had to stop myself from reaching for my phone, just to have a distraction. But I knew if I had my phone on, I'd start texting

Hallie again, and I knew just what a delicate balance this had to be. One wrong text could upset everything.

Which was why I should have known better. I'd gotten back from work, and I had the whole rest of the afternoon ahead of me. I'd planned on seeing if I could pull Gwyneth away from the documentary long enough to ask if she wanted to go to the beach with me. But then I'd turned on my phone and seen these texts from Hallie:

> **Hallie Bridges**
> 11:05 AM
> Morning, Bear . . .
> **Hallie Bridges**
> 11:07 AM
> I'm just lying here missing you . . . wishing
> I was waking up next to you like before.
> Missing me?
> **Hallie Bridges**
> 11:07 AM
> xoxo

It was like someone had just punched me in the gut. It was exactly what I'd been afraid of—but here was proof. My hand tightened on my phone so hard that my knuckles started to turn white. I tried to talk myself out of it, tell myself that maybe they'd just slept *next* to each other, like Josh and I had done, but I couldn't quite make myself believe it. The proof was in Hallie's text, on my phone in undeniable type. I knew I shouldn't do anything, shouldn't react without thinking this through, but I was typing back and then sending a response before my rational side kicked in.

Teddy Callaway
2:15 PM
Actually, I'm not missing you. At all.
Teddy Callaway
2:15 PM
In fact, I think we should end it.
Teddy Callaway
2:16 PM
Bye.

It wasn't until the last text went through that I came back to my senses and clapped my hand over my mouth. I could see Hallie was writing back—and quite a bit, judging from how long her text bubble was showing she was typing. I turned the phone off before I could see what she wrote or would have to explain myself. Had I just wrecked this because I let my stupid jealousy get in the way?

"Are you okay?" I whirled around and saw Rosie striding into the kitchen, dressed nicer than usual. "You look . . . a little stressed," she said, and I glanced down and saw I was white-knuckling the phone again.

"Fine," I said, loosening my grip, trying not to play out the scenarios of what was happening on Hallie's end of the phone. "Just . . . thinking." I gestured to her outfit. "You look nice."

Rosie always looked pulled together, but she looked extra-professional at the moment.

"Thanks," she said, giving me a smile. "Bruce is having some investors over in half an hour or so. Snacks-by-the-pool kind of a thing. So you know what that means."

"I'll stay out of the way," I promised. Ford, Gwyneth, and I had been barred from being around business events ever since Ford and Gwyneth had started a food fight at one of Bruce's *very* important investor dinners, ruined two peoples' suits, and lost Bruce's financing on that movie. It had been a rule ever since, and one that I was happy to abide by.

"If this investor signs on, the movie can basically go tomorrow," she said, then shook her head. "Not that we're in any way prepared for that. But it would be a big deal."

"I will do nothing to wreck it," I promised. I lifted my hand. "Scout's honor."

Before Rosie could reply, Bruce stormed through the kitchen, cursing violently as he went. I watched him go, wondering if this was something work-related, or if he was just really craving dairy and taking it out on his nutritionist. Bruce stomped outside, then stopped, turned around, and stomped back in. "Rosie!" he yelled.

Rosie was already on her feet and hustling toward Bruce. The fact that she didn't know—and hadn't already taken care of—this crisis was troubling, to say the least.

"What is it?" she asked, and I headed toward them as well, hoping that whatever was going on would be so absorbing, they wouldn't notice me eavesdropping.

"I thought we got all the permits!" Bruce shouted. I noticed with a little concern that his face was getting steadily redder. "I thought everything was in place for the construction!"

"It is," Rosie said in a soothing voice—the same tone, I now realized, that Gwyneth had used on Sophie earlier. No wonder she'd been so good at it. "We're all set to start tomorrow."

"Then tell me why the contractor just called and said there was an intractable problem!" Apparently, the soothing voice would not be working on him today. Bruce started to storm out toward the beach, and Rosie followed. After a tiny pause I followed too, not wanting to miss out on whatever this was. I hustled to keep pace behind them as they walked around the side of the house and toward the beach on the edge of Bruce's property line.

"I had no knowledge of this. Nobody e-mailed me," Rosie said, speed-walking next to Bruce, already pulling out her phone. "We cleared it with the town council, so I don't know what could possibly—"

Bruce and Rosie stopped short, and a second later I did too. I felt my eyes widen. There, sitting on the sand, was a person surrounded by protest signs, as well as camping gear, who had chained himself to a backhoe. And that person was, without a doubt, Teddy Callaway.

"Hey, Gemma!" Teddy said, waving at me. "I took your advice. What are you doing here?"

Bruce and Rosie whipped around to face me, and I felt my stomach sink. "About that," I said. "Um. Ha. Funny story . . ."

CHAPTER 16

"Tell me again," Bruce said as he paced back and forth on the sand. We'd moved down the beach about fifteen feet from Teddy to discuss the situation and what to do about it. I didn't think that Bruce's face had gotten any less red—in fact, it had probably gotten even redder. And if his face color hadn't been enough to tell, from the tone in Bruce's voice, I knew he was really, *really* mad.

I knew this was probably the worst thing that could have possibly happened on the heels of the cheese debacle. But how was I supposed to know that *Bruce* was the estate owner threatening the habitat of the marsh warbler? His name had never been in the paper, because Rosie—and Bruce's lawyers—were very good at their jobs.

"That's my ex-boyfriend," I said, pointing at Teddy, who waved, clearly not reading the room—or beach—very well. "I talked to him yesterday about the marsh warbler. I just *encouraged* him to stick to his beliefs in trying to save it. I had no idea that it was your land, or that he was going to chain himself to any construction equipment. I swear."

Bruce let out a stream of curses again, and Rosie didn't even reprimand him, which let me know—in case I hadn't gotten it already—just how dire this situation was.

"I think what Bruce is saying . . ." Rosie started, maybe choosing to believe I'd never heard any of those words before. "Is that—"

"All I wanted was a helipad." Bruce sighed, shaking his head. "Is that so wrong?"

"Do you even own a helicopter?" I asked, a bit surprised I hadn't heard about this, since I was pretty sure that if Bruce did, Ford would have taken it out for a joyride already.

"Not yet," Bruce said, his voice rising again. "Not when I have nowhere to land it!"

"Okay, let's all calm down and think about solutions," Rosie said, using her soothing voice again. I was glad we all were wearing our cameras, because if Gwyneth thought that the documentary was lacking drama, this would certainly provide it.

"Well, we're going to call the police, right?" Bruce asked. "I have a vagrant on my lawn chaining himself to my construction equipment."

"He's not really a vagrant," Rosie pointed out, gesturing to Teddy, who waved again. "Gemma knows him. And your dad does too, right, Gem?" I nodded. "And I'm sure he'll leave when we ask him to."

"Um," I said, not wanting to draw any more attention to myself than I had to but also feeling pretty certain that that was not going to work. "I'm not so sure about that."

"He'd better," Bruce said. "This is private property, and—" He took a step toward Teddy and repeated this at full volume. *"Private property!"*

"Not to the marsh warbler, sir!" Teddy called back. Bruce took another step toward him, and Rosie grabbed his arm, pulling him back.

"Okay, let's just breathe," she said. "That means you, Bruce," she said in a tone that meant there wasn't going to be any arguing with her. "I think—"

"Hey." I turned around and saw my dad walking up the sand toward us. I would have expected him to look surprised or confused by the fact that Rosie was restraining an apoplectic Bruce, or even that we were all choosing to stand around on the beach while Bruce yelled. But my dad had the same vague dreamy expression that he'd had the night I'd talked to him in his car. I wondered if the script was just coming along *really* well. This happened sometimes when it was. Anything else could be going on—the house could be on fire—but when the writing was going well, he was in a totally different place, where everything was working out.

"What's going on?" He asked this in the *what's up?* sense, even though the actual question would seem to fit better here. Bruce pointed toward the campsite, muttering under his breath. "What's . . ." My dad took a step closer and squinted. "Is that *Teddy*?"

"There's a bit of a situation," I said, knowing this was an understatement but not sure how else to put it without using some of the kinds of words Bruce had earlier.

"Hi, Mr. Tucker," Teddy called across the beach. "Nice to see you again."

"Uh, hi," my dad said, waving to Teddy then turning back to me. His dreamy expression was gone, and now he just looked baffled. "Gemma, why is Teddy chained to a bulldozer?"

"Backhoe," I corrected, as though this would somehow make things better. "He's, um, protesting—"

"He's trespassing is what he's doing!" Bruce said, suddenly getting his momentum back again. "And when I call the police, they'll—"

"I'm not sure that's a good idea," Rosie interrupted him. She looked down at her phone. "We have the investors coming in twenty. Do you really want a police standoff going on in the backyard? In full view of the pool?"

Bruce just stared at her, and I watched him deflate slightly. "No," he muttered. "I don't."

"Exactly," Rosie said. "So we'll just handle this quietly. We'll move the meeting to a restaurant, the investors don't have to know anything is happening here, and we can keep the police out of it."

"But what if he's one of those ecoterrorists?" Bruce asked. "And he's here to destroy my house and shatter my peaceful summer, and—" He paused and turned to my dad, the anger suddenly gone from his voice, now all business. "There's an idea, Paul. What do you think? Kind of like a thriller?"

"Maybe," my dad said, still looking a little thrown by all this. "I can put together a treatment if you want."

Bruce nodded. "Get on that. We can call it *Blood on the Sand* or something."

"Or something," my dad echoed.

"We also have to think about the publicity," Rosie said, and I could see she was already scrolling through her phone. "The optics aren't in our favor."

"What about the polar bear movie?" Bruce asked, turning to my dad. "We'll throw an eco angle on that or something, right? Will that keep these people calm?"

"Bruce, you know we talked about that," my dad said, and I remembered the conversation when he'd told me he didn't want to write it. "I'm finished with those movies."

"We'll see," Bruce said, clearly not believing this. "Well—find something else we can do in the meantime so that we have some cover if this blows up at us."

"Already on it," Rosie said. She pointed at Bruce and my dad. "You two, go get ready. I'll handle this and make a reservation somewhere." Bruce just shook his head, glaring at Teddy, and Rosie said, "Now," in a voice that meant she wasn't expecting any arguments.

Bruce and my dad headed into the house, and I watched them go for a moment, hearing snatches of what I was pretty sure was Bruce talking about the plot of *Blood on the Sand*. I turned to Rosie, who had the phone up to her ear. She lowered it and pointed at Teddy. "I need you to try to get him to leave," she said. I took a breath to tell her I didn't think this was going to happen—when people chain themselves to things, it generally means they're planning on staying awhile—but she went on. "Or if that's not possible, find out what his endgame is. If there's any compromise or wiggle room. Let him know we're not going to call the police tonight, but we will tomorrow if he's still here."

I nodded. "Okay. And I'm really sorry about this."

Rosie just looked at me evenly for a moment. "I feel like you've been saying that a lot recently."

I felt my face get hot. "I know," I said. I tried to think of something I could say to make things better, but nothing was coming to mind. "But that's the last time you'll have to hear that from me this summer. I promise."

Rosie nodded. "Sounds good. Try to fix this, okay, Gem?"

"I'll try," I assured her as she started to walk back toward the house, already on the phone, no doubt with one of Bruce's publicists, trying to contain the damage before it started. I took a breath and walked over to Teddy.

He'd really done quite a good job setting up, I realized as I got closer. There was a folded tent, a sleeping bag, a lantern, and what looked like food and water rations. The food and water did make me a little nervous, though—exactly how long was he planning on living in the backyard?

"Hi," I said as I got closer to him. He looked up from the book he was reading and smiled at me.

"Hi, Gemma," he said. "Well, thanks to you, I'm here."

I swallowed hard. I wondered if there was any way to try to convince Teddy that I really didn't want any of the credit for this particular decision. "Is . . . Hallie excited about it?"

"Oh," Teddy said. He looked down and brushed sand off his sleeping bag. "You know, I haven't mentioned it yet. There's a lot to walk her through. I was waiting for the right moment."

"Totally," I said, my thoughts spinning. If Hallie didn't know he was here, that meant I (as Teddy) could be the one to tell her. Maybe my text hadn't ruined everything after all. First, though, I had to try to keep my promise to Rosie. "I was just wondering—is this the *only* place the marsh warblers are being threatened? Because it can't really just be this estate, right? Maybe some other ones need protecting . . . more." I looked out to the water, trying to come up with a more cogent argument, when I saw someone walking up the beach. As they got closer, I realized it was Ford, carrying his surfboard under his arm. He looked toward me, then changed direction and started walking toward us.

"Hey," Ford said as he got closer. His eyes widened when he took in the makeshift campsite. "Um, exactly how long was I in the water?"

"Ford, this is Teddy," I said, and Ford nodded.

"Nice to officially meet you," he said.

"Likewise," Teddy replied. He started to stand, only to be yanked back down by the chain attached to the backhoe. "I've heard a lot about you."

"Likewise," Ford echoed. He gestured to the setup in front

of him. "Is this to some end? Or are you just really against bull-dozers?"

"Actually," Teddy said, and I could hear in his voice that he was about to launch into one of his multiparagraph explanations. "I'm here as the lone voice who is standing up for the marsh warbler, a defenseless bird that has fallen victim to outsized greed and acquisitive desires. That—"

"Just to be clear," Ford said, turning to me. "It's my father whose greed is outsized here?"

"Oh," Teddy said, and there was a small pause. After a moment he said, "I swear this isn't personal. But if we keep putting our own desires above protecting those who need our protection, where will we be?"

"That's really wise," Ford said, nodding. "I'll think about that. But right now I—"

"Need to do that thing we were talking about," I jumped in, clearly to Ford's surprise. But I needed to act on this Hallie situation, and I didn't think I was skilled enough to text Hallie as Teddy, with the real Teddy right in front of me. "At the house? I'll be back," I said to Teddy. "I'll just . . . um . . ." I stopped talking when I ran out of words and nodded at him, then turned toward the house, Ford following behind me.

He'd only gotten a few steps before he turned back to Teddy. "I've got to get out of my surf gear, but I'm sure we'll catch up later, man—especially since you're, you know, camping out at my house."

"I'd like that," Teddy said, nodding again. Sarcasm had

never been something Teddy had really gotten, and it was clear now that he thought Ford was being totally sincere.

Ford nodded and took a few steps away, only to pivot and face Teddy once again. "You know, you'd be welcome to use my shower and bathroom," he said. "I'm just in the pool house, so it's not like you'd be going inside the house or anything. And I promise I wouldn't tell Bruce—it's not like this is some ploy to get you to leave."

"That's really nice of you," Teddy said. "Thanks. I appreciate it."

"Well, I guess your pep talk worked," Ford said when we were out of earshot. "I bet Bruce isn't happy about this."

"You bet right," I said, turning on my phone again. "Rosie told me to get him out of there, but I'm not sure that's going to be possible."

"I would say not," Ford said, deadpan. "What with the chains and all."

My phone had come to life, and immediately it started beeping nonstop—I had five text messages, all from Hallie.

Hallie Bridges
2:30 PM
WHAT?!?
Hallie Bridges
2:31 PM
Teddy, what do you mean?
What are you talking about?

Hallie Bridges

2:32 PM

Is this about Gemma?

You know you hadn't been happy

with her for ages. Remember?

Hallie Bridges

2:33 PM

Did Gemma talk to you? Is this her doing?

Hallie Bridges

2:34 PM

I think we should talk. Are you in Putnam?

"You're blowing up," Ford said, nodding down at my phone. He gave me an even look. "What's happening?"

"Curiosity question," I said as I started to text back. "If Hallie knew Teddy was here, how long do you think it would take her to get here?"

"Ten minutes," Ford said immediately.

I smiled at that. "You don't even know where she lives."

"I don't have to," he said. "Based on whatever you told me, this girl's coming here by helicopter if necessary."

"Too bad we don't have a place to land it," I said, and Ford smiled.

"If she's coming, I'm making myself scarce," he said as he walked toward the pool house. "Call if it looks like fisticuffs are about to break out. I'll back you up."

"Fisticuffs?" I called after him, and heard Ford laugh as

he walked into the pool house. I looked down at the text I was writing, then finished the exchange.

Teddy Callaway
2:36 PM
Not in Putnam.

Hallie Bridges
2:36 PM
Where are you then?!

Teddy Callaway
2:37 PM
Here.

I took a breath, dropped the pin, and looked down at the time, wondering if Ford and I should have put some money on this. The clock started now.

CHAPTER 17

Eight minutes later a white Jeep careened into Bruce's driveway in a spray of gravel.

I was glad that Rosie had hustled Bruce and my dad off to the investor meeting, because if Hallie was as upset as I had a feeling she was, I didn't want to give her an opportunity to start talking about all kinds of things I'd rather she didn't—like the fact that I'd spent all of June pretending to be someone else.

I didn't even wait for her to ring the bell but pulled open the door and then promptly bit my bottom lip, hard, to stifle my reaction. Hallie was standing on the front step. She was wearing a Kelly green dress and matching flats. Her makeup was perfectly done, but I didn't notice any of that at first. The only thing I could see for a minute was her hair—or complete lack thereof. The long curls that had flowed over her shoulders and back were gone. Her hair was now cut in a pixie, with a tiny fringe in front. I couldn't quite believe it for a second, even though the proof was right in front of me. But Hallie had chopped off her hair. It was *gone*. She didn't look bad, I realized, after I began to get accustomed to it. She just looked really, *really* different. As I stared at her, at the huge amount of hair she'd cut off because of a lie I'd told her, I started to wonder if we'd gone too far.

"Gemma," Hallie said, and I could hear the strangled anger in her voice, the fury she was trying to contain, probably because she knew she had to go through me to get to Teddy—which she was probably also very unhappy about having to do.

"Hallie," I said. "I've been expecting you."

"Is Teddy here?" she asked, adjusting the bag on her shoulder and crossing her arms over her chest.

"He is," I said, nodding. "Did you want to say hi or something?"

Hallie stared daggers at me, and it was like I could see the effort it was taking her not to start screaming. "Why is he here?" she asked, practically biting off the words. "I thought he went back to Connecticut. Is he staying here?"

"I think that's his plan," I said. "But I promise, it's not like I invited him or anything."

Hallie let out a short laugh, the kind designed to show someone that you *didn't* find something funny. "Right," she said. "I'm so sure, Gemma." She shook her head. "I suppose you've told him everything," she said, and though I could tell she was trying to just toss this off, I could hear it in her voice—the fear that this was true. "You've told him all about me."

"You mean, did I tell him that you started dating him to get revenge on me?" I asked. "No, as a matter of fact, I didn't. I thought you should be the one to tell him he's just been a pawn."

"Well, I don't think that's going to happen," Hallie said. "Teddy doesn't need to know about that. We have a real connection now, and that's all that matters. Who cares why we initially got together?"

"I think Teddy might," I pointed out.

"I know you were behind this," she said, glaring at me. "I'm sure you had this plan all worked out. But I can tell you right now, it's not going to work. Teddy is *done* with you. It was beyond easy to break you two up. I actually thought it was going to be a challenge."

I swallowed hard. I didn't want her words to have any effect on me—because who knew if she was even telling the truth? But it felt like someone had just poured salt on a still-healing wound. "I don't believe you," I said. I tried not to let it show, but even I could hear the hurt in my voice.

"Believe what you want," Hallie said. "But you can't break up a couple who's totally happy. Not unless someone is already bored and looking to get out." I blinked hard, trying to hold back the hot tears that were forming behind my eyes. I had started to feel bad about what we'd done to Hallie—the haircut, the texting—but not anymore. Now I was beginning to regret we hadn't tried to convince her to get a tattoo. "So," she said, lowering her sunglasses—oversize designer frames—over her eyes. "Will you please get Teddy for me?"

"I think you might have to go to him," I said. "You'll find he's a little tied up right now."

Hallie pushed her glasses up and stared at me. "What's that supposed to mean?"

"Oh, nothing," I said. "Want to come on back?"

I could see Hallie hesitate a moment. She probably figured she was safe out in the open, but didn't want to come into a house I could have booby-trapped. "Fine," she finally said as she stepped over the threshold. "Where is he?"

"In the back," I said as I closed the door behind her. I led her across the foyer, and I saw her look at the giant polar bear—it was pretty impossible not to—but she didn't comment on it or ask any questions, just folded her arms more tightly as she walked with me into the kitchen. "Hungry?" I asked, stopping by the kitchen island. "Maybe for some cheese?"

The sides of Hallie's mouth twitched, and then she regained her composure—but not before I saw a glint of triumph in her eyes. "Maybe another time," she said. "Teddy is . . . ?"

"Follow me," I said as I led the way through the kitchen and past the pool. Ford was standing in the doorway of the pool house, toweling off his hair, and I saw him do a double take when Hallie walked by.

Hallie? he mouthed silently to me. I don't think Hallie saw, because she was looking fixedly ahead, like she was trying to pretend I wasn't actually standing next to her, like maybe I didn't actually exist. It was the same way Bruce acted when his unpaid interns were around.

Yes, I mouthed back to Ford, raising my eyebrows at him for good measure.

Haircut! he mouthed to me, and I smiled at him before we passed out of view and crossed onto the beach.

"By the way," I said as we walked along the side of the house, "I meant to tell you. I *love* your haircut."

"Thanks," Hallie snapped. "Where's—" At that moment, though, she must have spotted Teddy and the backhoe, because she stopped abruptly. "Tell me this isn't about that stupid bird," she said, disbelief in her voice.

"I would," I said. "But I don't want to *lie* to you." Hallie rolled her eyes hugely then started walking across the sand. "Say hi to Teddy," I called after her. I watched her get closer to the campsite. Teddy jumped to his feet when he saw her, only to be yanked back down again by his chain. Even from this distance, I could tell that he was nervous. I took a few steps closer, but I knew I wouldn't be able to get close enough to hear what was happening without them seeing me—and, most likely, telling me to go away. But I *really* wanted to hear how this was going to go down.

"Hey." I whirled around and saw Ford was standing right behind me.

"I didn't even hear you coming," I said, and Ford smiled.

"They used to call me the ninja when I was a kid," he said. I just looked at him skeptically, since I was pretty sure I would have remembered that. But before I could reply, he nodded toward Hallie and Teddy. "Want to hear what's happening over there?"

"Yes," I said, "but I'm not going to be able to get close enough. Not without them seeing me."

"Did you know Dakota wanted to be a beekeeper?" Ford asked, raising an eyebrow at me.

"Um. No," I said, thinking that this was a very strange time for a round of stepmother trivia. "Neat."

Ford shook his head. "Follow me," he said. "And *try* to be quiet."

Before I could respond to this, Ford was already doubling back toward the house. I wanted to point out that he was heading the wrong way, but I didn't want to draw attention to myself. I followed behind him as he hugged the side of the house, and then took a little path that I wouldn't have noticed if he hadn't started down it. It led to two wooden structures with slats. They were right next to each other, about the height of phone booths, maybe a little wider. I noticed they were about fifteen feet from the spot of Bruce's proposed helipad, but I'd never noticed them before, as they were masked by the trees right in front of them, and blended in with the landscaping.

Ford put a finger to his lips and pulled open the doors of one of the wooden structures. I hesitated before stepping inside. "Are there actual bees in there?" I asked. I wanted to eavesdrop, but not *this* badly.

Ford shook his head and said in a low voice, "There never were, don't worry. Dakota had these built but then divorced Bruce before she actually got any bees. Thank *god*. Apparently, it was the trendy thing to do that summer and, knowing her, she would have gotten them and then lost all interest." He nodded toward the inside of the building, and I stepped in.

It was cool and dark in there, lines of sunlight filtering in through the slats. It still had the smell of new construction—of sawdust and wood. Ford let the door swing shut, and then it was *really* dark in there. He tapped my shoulder and then pointed over to the side of the bee hut (or whatever its proper name was), where I could see there was the largest opening in the slats. When I took a step closer, I found that it looked right out onto Teddy's makeshift campsite. I glanced over at Ford, who was standing a little behind me—it was small enough in there that we really couldn't even stand comfortably side by side. I'd been expecting him to leave once he'd showed me the place—he had algorithms to write, after all—but he stayed where he was, close enough to me that I could hear him breathing. Trying not to let this distract me, I leaned forward toward the opening.

Teddy had moved to lean against the backhoe, maybe so he wouldn't be that much shorter than Hallie, who was standing in front of him and who didn't look happy.

"I just don't want to break up," Hallie was saying, her voice trembling. "Whatever you're thinking, we can sort it out, right?"

"What are you talking about?" Teddy asked, sounding genuinely baffled.

"I . . . Do you want to end this?" Hallie asked, her voice cracking.

There was a tiny pause, then Teddy said, "I . . . No. I don't. Do you?"

"No," Hallie cried. "But I guess . . . I mean . . ." She let out a breath that I could hear from where Ford and I were standing.

"Oh, thank god. I was so worried. . . ." She turned away from him for a moment, and it was like I could see her actively pulling herself together. "I don't know why you didn't just tell me you were going to be here," Hallie said in a voice that sounded like she was trying hard to stay calm. I leaned farther forward, listening as hard as I could.

"I should have . . ." Teddy started, and for just a second I was thankful for all the assemblies he had led and the meetings he had chaired over the years. It had gotten to the point where Teddy waved off the microphones that were offered to him. His projecting had always been good, and I'd never been so happy about it.

"Is there something going on?" Hallie blurted out, and I could hear it again, the struggle to keep herself composed. "With Gemma?"

"Of course nothing's going on with Gemma," Teddy said after just the tiniest of pauses. "She came to see me last night, and she was telling me all about the warbler, and—"

"She was at your *house*?" Hallie's voice rose at least an octave, and I backed away slightly from the door. "I guess I just don't understand," Hallie said, her words coming faster and faster, "why you have to be *here*. Where Gemma's only a few feet away."

"I can't help where the marsh warbler needs to be protected," Teddy said. "I have to go where I'm needed."

"It just . . . seems very convenient," Hallie said. "And I'm sure it was *Gemma's* idea, wasn't it?"

"All Gemma encouraged me to do was to remain true to my

ideals," Teddy said, speaking slowly, and I knew him well enough to know that he was getting frustrated. "Do you want me to turn my back on the cause?"

Hallie looked away, and even from this distance, I could see her taking deep breaths, like she was still trying to compose herself. When she looked at Teddy and spoke again, her voice had lost its edge. "Of course not, Bear," she said. "You know I love your commitment to your beliefs. I just wish you had told me, that's all."

"I understand and I apologize," Teddy said, and I could hear the relief in his voice. "Can we start over?"

"Absolutely," Hallie said, her tone happy again, and I felt my stomach sink.

Was that *it*? All that work, and they had a tiny fight that resolved itself that quickly? I turned to look at Ford, who was right there behind my shoulder. *Really?* I mouthed to him, and one side of his mouth kicked up in a smile.

Wait, he mouthed back to me.

I returned to the scene on the beach. Hallie was now sitting next to Teddy, on the sand, spreading her dress around her like she was going to a picnic in the '50s. She smiled at him, and Teddy smiled back, and the beat went on just a bit too long. Finally Hallie said, "Do you like my dress?"

"Yes," Teddy said quickly. "It's really nice. Really . . . pretty. You look great, as always."

"It's *green*," Hallie said, a little bit of tension in her voice. "I just bought it. And I wore it for you."

"Ah, yes," Teddy said quickly. "Green. And it looks great on you. But then, everything does." Even though nobody could see me doing it, I was not quite able to stop myself from rolling my eyes at that.

"You're sweet," she said, reaching up to touch his face. "Are you doing okay out here? I feel like I should bring you provisions or something."

"I'm fine," Teddy said, and as I watched, my eyes narrowing, he slung an arm around Hallie's shoulders. "I've got some supplies."

"Well, I'll have to bring you some real food," Hallie said. "Or should I say, some *comestibles*?" She smiled up at him, and Teddy just gave her a tight smile in return. Hallie paused, clearly confused by his lack of reaction, then added, "Maybe even a peach pie?"

"Oh," Teddy said, sounding distinctly unenthusiastic. "Uh, it might be best if you don't. Thanks, though."

"Sure," Hallie said, but I could hear the frustration in her voice, and I felt myself start to smile just a little bit. "So, what are you thinking—how long will this last? Are you going to still be here next week? Are you going to be able to come to the benefit?"

"That's out of my control," Teddy said.

"So you might still be here in a *week*?" Hallie asked, her voice rising. "We've been planning this benefit all summer. Are you still going to be out here on my birthday?"

"I don't know," Teddy said, shaking his head, "but I would think that you would recognize the importance of—"

"This benefit is very important to my mother," Hallie said. "And—"

"Then why isn't she using the money for a more worthy cause?" Teddy shot back.

"What, like the marsh warbler?" Hallie asked scornfully, and I felt myself smile for real.

"Yes," Teddy said quietly, with wounded dignity. "Something like that."

"I think maybe I should go," Hallie said in a way that made it clear she was expecting Teddy to protest this and demand she stay.

"That might be best," Teddy said, and even from fifteen feet away, I could see the shock and hurt pass over Hallie's face.

"Fine," Hallie snapped as she got to her feet. She picked up her bag and started to walk away. She'd only gone a few steps before she stopped and turned back to Teddy. "I guess I just thought you'd at least *mention* my hair," she said. Her tone was full of bravado, but even I could hear the vulnerability underneath it.

"It's nice," Teddy said, after a pause. "It's . . . a real change."

"That's it?" Hallie asked, and I could hear the quaver in her voice.

"You know that I'd never try to dictate your appearance or infringe on your personhood," Teddy said, and even without turning my head, I could practically *feel* Ford rolling his eyes behind me. "But . . . I've never liked short hair on girls. I guess it's just a vestige of patriarchal thinking, but—"

"Wait," Hallie interrupted, taking a step closer. "What did you just say?"

"I was talking about the patriarchy," Teddy said, and I could tell that he was just warming to his theme. "About how vestigial notions of beauty are—"

"No, before that," Hallie said. "You said you didn't like short hair on girls?"

"Much as it pains me to admit to," Teddy said. "I don't. But you . . . you look very . . . um . . ."

"Oh my god," Hallie said slowly, and it was like I could practically hear her thoughts whirring as she began to put things together. "Do you even like peaches?"

"I'm allergic," Teddy said apologetically. "So while it's a sweet offer, I just—"

"*Oh* my god," Hallie said, her voice rising. She turned away from Teddy—which meant she was now looking directly at the bee huts.

Ford and I stepped to the side at exactly the same moment, trying to get out of sight. We were pressed up against the back wall of the hut, and Ford's arm was above me, resting on the wall. We stayed just like that for a moment, perfectly still. I couldn't help but think about how this was the closest I'd been to Ford in a long time—probably since the night he kissed me, three years ago. And then, we certainly hadn't lingered this long.

It was like I could feel his heart beating against my back, and he smelled like the ocean and dryer sheets and cinnamon rolls—a smell that was familiar to me, though I didn't know from where. One of the slats of light was crossing his face, just over his eyes, and I looked up at him—when had Ford gotten so tall?—at the light passing over the planes of his face, his tan skin, his freckles, his black hair sticking up in imperfect spikes. And though I knew there were other things I should be focusing on right then, for a moment I just wanted to stay right there, in the bee hut with the dust motes floating in the shafts of sunlight. I wanted to stay there, with Ford pressed so close to me, his arm above me, almost around my shoulders if it was just a few inches lower, our breath rising and falling in sync. I would have liked to have just stayed in that moment, but then I heard Hallie say my name, and the spell was broken.

"What about Gemma?" Teddy asked. Teddy could roll with— or at least pretend to be interested in—most conversations, so the fact that he sounded this baffled showed how many unexpected turns this conversation had taken. It occurred to me then that you probably would really regret chaining yourself up to construction equipment when having arguments with your girlfriend—because even if you wanted to walk away, you couldn't.

"She . . . she . . ." I watched as Hallie let out a long shuddering breath, like it was taking all her effort not to curse me out. "Nothing," she finally said. "Just . . . tell me your number again, Bear? I'm afraid I might have deleted it."

I looked over at Ford, who nodded, then pushed open the door to the bee house inch by inch, until it was all the way open. He held it for me, and I ducked under his arm. We both crept quietly around the side of the house again, until we'd reached the pool deck and I felt like I could start breathing normally.

"So she put it together," Ford said. "Impressive."

"Inevitable," I said. "I knew it wouldn't last for long." I looked up at him as we walked. Now that we were out in the afternoon's bright sunlight, it was like that moment of us standing so close in the darkness was fading away, until I wasn't even sure if I'd imagined it or not.

"Well," Ford said, and smiled down at me. "I should get back to it. This algorithm isn't going to write itself."

"Right," I said. "The Graduated Elemental . . . Mechanized . . ." I trailed off, waiting for Ford to jump in and finish it, but he was just looking at me, waiting.

"Go on," he said, and I could tell he was enjoying this. "Then what?"

"I think you should simplify the name anyway," I said, choosing not to continue floundering for the name I couldn't seem to keep straight. "Make it an acronym or something."

"There's an idea," Ford said, again smiling at me for some reason, probably still laughing at my attempts to name the algorithm. He turned back to the pool house, calling over his shoulder as he went, "And what you were looking for was the Galvanized Empathic Multipurpose Media Algorithm."

I was glad I'd stopped when I had—I would never have gotten that. I was starting to head back inside when I heard my name called.

"Gemma." It wasn't shouted, just stated, but with enough authority to get my attention. I turned and saw Hallie crossing the pool deck toward me and looking surprisingly composed, and totally calm—but as she got closer, I saw that her hands were clenched into fists.

"Leaving so soon?" I asked. "Now that's a shame."

Hallie walked up to me but stopped when she was about a foot away. She just looked at me for a moment, then shook her head. "I think I underestimated you," she finally said, a note of surprise in her voice. She shouldered her bag and gave me an even look. "I won't do it again."

I felt a chill, suddenly wishing she would have hurled insults or threats at me instead—both would have somehow been less disturbing than whatever was happening now.

"I'll show myself out," she said, crossing to the glass doors that led to the kitchen. She slid one open, then stopped and turned back to me. "And Gemma?" she said. Her tone was pleasant, but I could hear the threat underneath it. "Watch your back."

CHAPTER 18

"So *then* Chaz was going to come and spend the weekend here, and just when he was about to get on the train, guess what happened."

I looked up at Darcy from where I had been scraping some excess ice off the sides of the freezer case. I was doing this by choice, since Darcy had been talking about her "boyfriend" for the last hour, and doing menial labor was all that I could do to stop myself from yelling out something along the lines of *He's not real! You're being catfished!* every time Darcy asked my opinion.

It was a very slow Thursday night, which meant that the store probably didn't need to be employing three of us to work when there were very few customers coming in. It probably didn't help that there had been an unseasonable cold snap, which was keeping people away from the ice-cream parlor.

It had been two days of Teddy living on the beach, still chained to the backhoe. But he was using Ford's shower on the sly, so it wasn't like he was impossible to be around. I'd mostly been avoiding him, since my feelings were not exactly clear at the moment. Gwyneth, however, was paying him lots of attention, interviewing him for the documentary. She claimed that since she was making a documentary about Bruce's work, and Teddy was currently getting in the way of it, he was a relevant subject. Rosie had backed down on her threat to call the police, and Bruce's strategy at this point seemed to be to wait Teddy out, ignore him, and not give him the attention that calling the police to forcibly remove him would.

I hadn't heard anything from Hallie since she'd been at the house, and though I'd spent the first day bracing myself for another cheese onslaught, nothing had happened, which had been enough to let me relax. Maybe, despite her threat, she was giving up.

And even though she had told me to watch my back, I was feeling distinctly like we were ahead. Sophie and Gwyneth certainly seemed to think so, if their reaction when I told them about the haircut was any indication.

"I don't know," I finally said to Darcy when I realized her question about the lack of Chaz wasn't rhetorical, and that she was actually waiting for an answer.

"I'll guess," Reid piped up, sticking his head out of the walk-in freezer. Reid was so scarred by his near-death experience (at least, according to him) that he was doing inventory with the door propped open (which I'm sure was not good for the ice cream) and would yell out to us every few minutes to make sure we were still there in case he *did* somehow get locked in again. "It's just good sense to have a freezer buddy," he'd explained when I'd asked him about this, despite the fact that I was pretty sure this was just a term he'd made up and not an actual thing. "Wait," Reid said, frowning as he looked from me to Darcy. "What was the question again?"

"I was just telling Gemma that my boyfriend was going to come to visit for the weekend, but at the last minute he had to cancel. I was seeing if she could guess why."

"Let's see," Reid said, screwing up his face in concentration. "He . . . got mugged and lost all his money. And his memory. And so he forgot where he was even going in the first place, and why."

"Close." Darcy sighed. "Just as he was running for the train, he tripped and broke his femur. So now he's in a cast and not able to get anywhere for at least two weeks."

"Oh, that's too bad," I said, mostly to the containers of ice cream. I'd given up on asking Darcy why they didn't just Skype or video-chat, since she always seemed to have a new, not particularly plausible reason. And if she believed it, I wasn't sure it was my place to burst her bubble. I personally thought that her first clue should have been that this guy was claiming his name was *Chaz*.

"I know." Darcy sighed, pushing herself up to sit on the counter and examining her nails. "It's really going to put a crimp in those football games he plays with his friends. You know, the one I showed you a picture of? I guess I'm just sad because I really thought this was going to be the weekend it all finally worked out, you know? And—"

I heard an incoming e-mail beep, and I reached in my

pocket for my phone just as Darcy pulled hers out. "Mine," Reid called from the closet. When neither of us responded, he added, sounding concerned, "Freezer buddies?"

"We're here," I called back. "Don't worry."

"So anyway," Darcy said, and I could tell that I was about to be hit by another Chaz anecdote. I briefly considered seeing if I could switch jobs with Reid, but Darcy was already launching into it. "We were talking the other day—and by talking, I mean e-mailing—and Chaz . . ."

The bell over the door jangled, and I had never been so happy to have a customer. "Hi," I said brightly, standing up and dropping the ice scraper. "Welcome to—" I stopped when I saw that it was just my dad, embarrassingly taking pictures of me with his phone. "Stop it," I muttered, and even though I couldn't see it, I had a feeling my cheeks were turning the same color red as my Delicious apron.

"Hi, I'm Gemma's dad," my father said much too cheerfully to Darcy. "What's good here?"

"Hey," Darcy said, waving. "Nice to meet you." Her phone beeped, and she looked down at it. "You mind if I go on break?" she asked. "I want to send Chaz an e-mail."

"Sure," I said. Across the counter from me, my dad smiled. "You can handle this place all by yourself, huh?"

I shook my head. "It's not like we're in the middle of a huge rush, Dad."

"But even so," he said, taking another picture and causing me to hold up my hand in front of my face. "Your first job! I'm proud of you, hon."

"Thanks," I said, feeling my cheeks heat up just a bit more. "Can I get you something?"

"Mint chocolate chip, if you'd be so kind," my dad said, and I reached for one of the sugar cones automatically—my dad had, on more than one occasion, voiced his displeasure with the very concept of cups. In his opinion, you had to also be able to eat the vehicle that ice cream came in.

"Hey, Gemma—" Reid stuck his head out of the freezer and then smiled when he saw my dad. "Oh, hi," he said cheerfully, like he recognized him. "Nice to—" A second later, though, his smile faded and his expression just became confused. "Um," he said, "I mean . . ."

I looked to my dad, trying to figure out what was happening, but my dad was now looking down, apparently very interested in counting out his change.

"What's going on?" I asked Reid, only to see his head disappear back into the walk-in.

"I can't hear you," Reid called to me. "I'm in the freezer."

I shook my head at this, deciding to attribute it to Reid's general weirdness. "Here," I said, handing my dad the mint chocolate chip cone and shaking on some chocolate sprinkles for good measure. "On the house."

"Well, in that case," my dad said, dropping a ten into the tip jar. He took a bite and nodded. "Wonderful," he pronounced. "And *very* well scooped."

"Glad that I could help you," I said. "We try our best here at Sweet & Delicious."

My dad nodded, took another bite, then said, "Gem . . . if you're not too busy, could I talk to you about something?"

"Sure," I said. I gestured around to the empty store. "We're *really* not busy, as you can see." I looked at my dad closely and realized that he seemed nervous. And that the words *talk to you about something* had never been followed by anything good. Was I in trouble? I could feel myself start to sweat. Had my dad found out about the Hallie stuff? I hadn't shown her out myself—who knows what she might have gotten up to as she walked from the kitchen to the front door? Was he blaming me for the fact that Teddy was still camping out on the beach and antagonizing Bruce? "Um, what's up?"

"I was just wondering," my dad said, after clearing his throat a few times, "how you might feel about me . . . starting to date someone."

"Oh," I said. The first emotion I felt was pure relief that I wasn't in trouble. I wasn't sure my relationship with my dad could handle something else, particularly on the heels of the nine hundred dollars in cheese. But then I started to process what he'd just told me. I'd tried to broach this subject myself at the beginning of the summer, and my dad had basically shut me down, acting like it wasn't even a real possibility. But maybe my words had had an impact after all. "I think . . ." I started, a little haltingly. My dad and I were *not* good at talking about stuff like this, and it felt like I was finding my way as I went. "That it would be great if you found someone who makes you happy."

My dad smiled at me, surprise and relief on his face. "Thanks, hon," he said. "I appreciate it."

I suddenly wondered why this was coming up now—and if this was a rhetorical question, or if there was a specific someone he was thinking about dating. "Um," I started. "Are you . . . I mean, is there someone that you—"

"Help!" Reid called from the direction of the freezer. "Gemma? Darcy? Freezer buddies? I think I'm locked in!"

"It sounds like duty calls," my dad said, and I nodded.

"I should probably go help him." My dad took a few napkins from the dispenser and started to head toward the door. "Dad, we can talk more about this later, if you want," I said. I wasn't sure that it would be the most comfortable conversation for either of us, but I wanted him to know that I wasn't going to use this interruption as an excuse to never talk about it again.

"Sounds like a plan," he said.

"And," I said, before I could lose my nerve, "there's something I need to talk to you about. When we have a moment?" There was a piece of me that just wanted to confess everything here, and hope that in the presence of my coworkers, he wouldn't yell at me too much. But I also knew that I'd been holding on to this secret for five years—I owed it to both of us to find the right time to tell him.

"Sure," my dad said with a nod. "You know I'm always here to talk, Gem." He gave me a smile and headed out the door, and I went back to the freezer to rescue Reid.

I pulled the door open and found Reid hopping from foot to foot in the middle of the freezer. "What are you doing?"

"Trying to keep warm," he said as he walked past me and into the shop, blowing on his hands. "That's *so* much better."

"I thought you had the door propped open," I said as I followed him out. "What happened?"

"I think it was when I came out and saw your dad," Reid said, flexing his fingers like he was trying to find out if they still had feeling in them. "I must have kicked aside the doorstop."

I was about to reply to this, then something occurred to me. Had I told Reid he was my dad? But a second later I let it go. He'd probably overheard it when my dad introduced himself to Darcy. "Well, I can finish the inventory if you want," I said, since Reid was still shivering theatrically.

"That would be great," he said just as Darcy came out from the break room, pocketing her cell phone.

"Back," she said cheerfully. "Chaz says hi."

"That's, um, nice of him," I said, restraining myself from saying anything else as I headed back toward the freezer. Before I'd gotten too far, though, I felt my phone buzz with a text. I looked down at it and felt my breath catch in my throat as another text message sound—I couldn't tell if it was Reid's phone or Darcy's—chimed.

Hallie Bridges
Look what I've found!

She'd attached a picture of the green Southampton Stationary notebook. It was bent and the cover had faded, but I recognized it. There was my eleven-year-old handwriting across the front. This was the notebook that had my plans in it. So she'd kept it after all—it was here, with her in the Hamptons.

Hallie Bridges

I really think your dad might like
to take a look, don't you?

Hallie Bridges

I bet it would be a real page-turner.

I could feel that I was starting to break out in a cold sweat. Hallie sending this notebook to my dad before I could tell him myself was the worst scenario I could imagine. So I needed to tell him, and tonight. Maybe—

"Hey, Gemma, are you working tomorrow?" Reid asked, interrupting my train of thought.

"No," I said, still staring down at the picture on my phone. "Why?"

"Because I was supposed to work a job for the catering company, but I forgot I was scheduled here," he said. Reid was avoiding my eyes, and his voice sounded nervous—maybe because he was asking me for a favor. "I didn't, um, know if you would want to work it for me?"

"Oh, I'm working that," Darcy said, brightening. "Some kind of benefit or something? Usually means good food."

"Wait," Reid said, his face falling, like he'd suddenly

remembered the situation. "You might not want to do it, though. It's at, um, the Bridges' house."

"Why, what's wrong with the house?" Darcy asked, suddenly looking worried. "Is it haunted or something?"

I looked up at him, feeling hope flare in my chest. If I was on the Bridges' property . . . if I was there catering this event . . . I might be able to get the notebook back. And then when I was sure that no horrible relic from the past was going to pop up, I could tell my dad when I felt ready to. "You know, I think I'll be okay," I said to Reid, trying to sound like I didn't desperately need to do this. "Hallie and I are . . . fine." I looked at Darcy and saw she still looked alarmed. "It's not haunted," I reassured her.

"And you and Josh?" Reid asked tentatively.

I swallowed hard. I was torn between really wanting to see Josh again and not wanting to face the reality of the fact that when I did see him, he might be with another girl. Just when I would think I was over him, or he would fade from my mind, suddenly I'd get a flash of memory to the time we'd spent earlier this summer, and I'd be back to missing him, feeling the hollow ache in my chest, and knowing that I had probably wrecked my chance with him. "It'll be okay," I finally said, trying to make myself smile, but giving up when this proved too challenging.

"Great," Darcy said, smiling at me. "We'll have so much fun! Wear a black shirt and black pants. And I'll text you the information on how to get there. And then we can work out our serving plan!"

I didn't want to tell Darcy I could get there myself, that I knew the layout of the house pretty well. I figured it would probably be better not to reveal that right now.

"Great," I said as I headed back into the walk-in, making sure to prop open the door, my mind already racing with possibilities, and putting together plans, none of which focused on ice cream. "I'll be ready."

CHAPTER 19

"**S**o usually, nobody wants ice-cream sandwiches until they've eaten the passed appetizers and dinner," Darcy was telling me as we stood behind the ice-cream sandwich station. "But then again, sometimes people do," she added. "So we have to be set up and ready the whole time. Which is kind of annoying. But you can get some good people-watching in."

I nodded like this was riveting information, but my eyes were scanning the crowd, looking for my opportunity. Darcy may have thought I was there to serve ice-cream sandwiches with her, but I really only had one goal—find the notebook and take it.

"People-watching," I repeated. "Got it."

We were set up just outside the huge white tent that had been erected on the lawn behind Hallie's house. Why we were the ones *outside* the tent, when we had frozen things we needed to keep cool, was a mystery that had not been explained to me. I also hadn't wanted to ask, since the woman running the catering company, The South Fork—its name was plastered on every available surface, just in case you might have forgotten it—was really tall, with hair in a terrifyingly neat bun, who was walking around the edges of the event clutching her iPad and barking into a headpiece. I really didn't want to even be on her radar if I could avoid it.

The party—at least from what I could see from the outskirts—looked pretty great. There were beautifully dressed people milling about, cater waiters in black silently holding out trays of appetizers, and gorgeous white flower centerpieces on every table. The only thing that was a tiny bit off was the printed banner that was stretched over one side of the tent. *A Benefit for the Hamptons Historical Society!* was printed in beautiful cursive. *And the Marsh Warbler!* read the clearly handwritten message squeezed on next to it.

When I'd left that afternoon, I was leaving a deserted house—except for Teddy, who was still living on the beach and doing his part for an endangered bird. As a result, I had a feeling he wouldn't be making an appearance here today. Sophie was babysitting, my dad was in the city working with the *Once Bitten* author, and Bruce and Rosie were apparently investigating their options—quietly—in terms of what they could do to get rid of Teddy without generating negative publicity, or giving even more attention to his cause. Gwyneth was going with Bruce to film this, and Ford had been gone since early that morning, heading out before dawn to the Montauk surf break.

I'd seen Karen already—but it didn't seem like she'd seen me. At any rate, she hadn't said anything if she recognized me.

She seemed to be spending most of the party in motion, moving from group to group, keeping the event going. She looked lovely, wearing a gold dress that shimmered in the late-afternoon light. I'd also seen Hallie, in a flowing pink maxi dress with gold necklaces layered on top, and matching gold flats. Her hair, I had to admit, looked really chic, and seemed to bring out her features more, making her eyes look huge. If she was upset about the fact that she'd basically been conned into the haircut, it was not apparent to the outside observer.

While we'd been getting our station organized, Darcy had explained the setup to me, about the freshly baked cookies that guests could choose to make up their ice-cream sandwich, while I only half listened, my mind trying to figure out the best way to get into the house. The fact that I was this close and not yet inside was making me as jumpy as if I'd just gotten a quad latte instead of my single shot. I needed to get up to the house, get the notebook, and get out of here, hopefully without attracting any attention, and before Hallie realized that I was working there.

"So that's about it," Darcy was saying, and I snapped back to attention, crossing my fingers I hadn't missed anything too important. "Do you have any questions?"

"I think I've got it," I said, nodding, hoping she thought I'd been paying attention this entire time. "It seems really—" I looked up and lost track of whatever I'd been starting to say. Josh was walking past the ice-cream station. His eyes were fixed straight ahead, like he was deliberately not looking in my direction. He had always looked incredibly cute when he was dressed up, and this was no exception. He was wearing a crisp white shirt and khaki pants. Maybe it was because of the contrast of his shirt, but he seemed even more tan than when I'd last seen him. And maybe because I was so distracted by how good he looked, it took a moment for me to notice that there was a girl next to him. It wasn't the girl with the long brown hair I'd seen him with outside Quonset Coffee. This was a different girl, which was somehow worse. She had strawberry-blond hair up in a knot on top of her head, and seemed to be touching his arm way more than necessary as they walked by.

Josh's eyes flicked over to me just as they passed, and I started to give him a hopeful smile, but it died when I saw the coldness of the stare he gave me. He looked away from me a moment later, but it was enough to leave me shaken. It almost would have been better if he'd continued to ignore me—then I could have at least pretended he didn't hate me as much as he very clearly did.

"You okay?" Darcy asked, and I looked over at her, trying to focus.

"Yes!" I said quickly. "Sure. Fine."

"Excuse me?"

Darcy and I both looked to the front of the stand, where a very small—and familiar—person was standing, looking impatient. "Can I have an ice-cream sandwich?"

It was Olivia—or Isabella. I'd never been able to tell them apart, and when I'd asked Sophie how she was managing, she'd looked perplexed by this. "But they're so different," she'd told me. "When you get to know them, it becomes obvious." I was willing to take Sophie's word for it, since the only other time I'd attempted to get to know the twins, they'd willfully destroyed Bruce's house.

"Sure," Darcy said with a big smile. She clearly didn't know who she was dealing with, and had just assumed there was a sweet kid in front of her. She gestured to the cookies. "Just pick which ones you want, sweetie."

The twin chose her cookies, then gave me a nod. "Gemma," she said, her tone cool.

"Hi," I said back without much enthusiasm. The appearance of these girls had never meant anything good. I looked over her shoulder—it was rare to see one without the other—but didn't see another twin. "Where's your sister?"

The twin hooked a thumb over her shoulder, gesturing vaguely behind her as she considered her ice-cream options. I followed her gesture and saw the other twin, pulling on the hand of the person standing next to her. My eyes traveled up and I realized, with a shock, that I recognized her—it was Sophie. I just looked at her for a moment, trying to make the pieces fit. Sophie had told me she was babysitting, but not that she was attending this benefit. I would have thought she might have mentioned it, considering it was a benefit at Hallie's house. But she hadn't said anything, just left the house this afternoon with a cheerful wave, asking if I maybe wanted to get pizza for dinner. I watched her clearly not going wherever this other twin wanted to drag her. She was having an animated conversation with someone—I couldn't see who, as they were blocked by a cater waiter holding out a tray of appetizers. I tried to tell myself it wasn't a big deal. That Sophie probably didn't know who was throwing the benefit, or she surely would have mentioned it. It probably just—

The cater waiter moved, and I could suddenly see who Sophie had been talking to. It was Hallie.

I reached down to steady myself on the table, feeling like the world had just started spinning. This didn't mean anything. It didn't. It couldn't.

But without wanting to, I suddenly remembered Sophie asking me if Hallie really deserved this. The fact that Hallie had Sophie's cell phone the morning after the Bridges' Fourth of July party. And the fact that Hallie had been able to find out a *lot* of things, many of which still hadn't been explained—like how she somehow knew that Bruce wasn't eating cheese. I didn't even want to think it, but the pieces were stacking up faster and faster. Had Sophie somehow been in league with Hallie this whole time?

"You okay?" I looked down to see the twin, now holding an overstuffed cookie-and-ice-cream sandwich, looking up at me and frowning.

"Yeah," Darcy said. "You're looking a little pale, Gem."

"I just . . . Maybe it's the heat," I mumbled, knowing that this was not a convincing reply, but not feeling able to come up with anything else at the moment. The twin in front of us shrugged, clearly having exhausted her interest in this conversation, turned, and ran back toward Sophie. She was still in conversation with Hallie and as I watched, horrified, Sophie threw her head back and laughed at something Hallie said.

"Maybe you should get out of the sun for a moment," Darcy said, still looking at me, concerned. "I'm worried you'll overheat like Reid did last week when we were working at a barbecue." It seemed that between the sunstroke and the freezer burn, Reid was really not having a great summer in terms of extreme temperatures.

"Maybe," I said, trying to figure out how I could use this, since one of the rules we'd heard the most about from Scary Headset Lady was that we were never—under any circumstances—to go inside the house.

Darcy slid over the lid on the giant cooler that contained our ice cream and looked down at it. "Why don't you get some more ice?" she asked. "Catering is set up in the kitchen," she went on. "We're allowed to go inside if the quality of the event would be compromised otherwise. And I think melty ice cream definitely counts. You could just hang out in the AC for a bit before anyone notices. Just so you don't overheat." She gave me a smile, and I was suddenly so grateful for Darcy. It occurred to me that she deserved a real boyfriend, and not whoever it was she thought she was dating.

"That's a great idea," I said, trying not to sound too excited about this and remembering that I was supposed to be suffering from heatstroke. "I'll go right now."

"Just don't go beyond the kitchen," Darcy said, suddenly looking worried. "Like, you could get in real trouble for that." She took a step closer to me and lowered her voice. "Apparently, there was this string of thefts last year, and it turned out it was the employee at a catering company. Not this one," she added quickly, like she was worried I would think we were working for a shady operation. "But still. They got *super*strict after that."

"Right," I said. "Got it." The notebook had once been my property, so I certainly didn't think it would technically be stealing. But even if it was, I no longer cared. I had to get it, and quickly. Out of habit, I reached for the purse I'd stashed under the table.

"You can leave that here," Darcy said. "I'll keep an eye on it."

"Right," I said, rolling my eyes at myself. "Sorry. Thanks." I took my phone from it, tucked it into my back pocket, and then nodded at Darcy, trying to look like I was currently suffering from heat exhaustion. I started walking up toward the house. I wanted to run but didn't let myself, since I had a feeling that might attract attention I didn't need.

The late-afternoon sun was hanging low in the sky, and the glare was making it hard to see. I squinted as I tried to weave among the partygoers, wishing that sunglasses had been part of our approved catering uniform. I thought I was doing okay—stepping around clusters of beautifully dressed people, all of whom seemed to have very full glasses in their hands—when there was suddenly somebody crossing in front of me, right in my path.

We crashed into each other before I could stop, or pivot in the other direction, and I was thrown off-balance, windmilling my arms to try and stay upright, but not succeeding. I wobbled over and hit the ground hard in a totally undignified move. It was like I could feel the eyes of everyone at the party on me, and my face was suddenly really hot—which might actually be helpful, if I needed to try and sell the "overheating" story.

"I'm so sorry, love," a British voice from above me said. A hand was extended in my direction—from the guy I'd crashed into—and I grasped it and was pulled to my feet. I was about to apologize when I realized, with a start, that I recognized him.

"Hey," I said, blinking at him. It was Andy Young, the *Hampton News Daily*'s photographer, the one who'd come to the house to take pictures of Bruce. But he certainly hadn't been British when I'd met him before.

"Oh," he said, sounding surprised. His accent was still in place, and I realized he had just recognized me too. "Hi," he said, now sounding like he had before—that is, totally American.

"Andy, right?" I asked. I looked to see if he was wearing his press pass or carrying his camera, but he was dressed like all the other guests.

"Right," he said, flashing me a quick smile before starting to walk away. "Nice to see you again. . . ."

"So that article never ran," I said, hurrying a few steps to catch up with him. He blinked at me, and I added, "The one about Bruce Davidson's award?"

Andy Young gave me a smile that didn't quite reach his eyes. "Well, you know journalism," he said. "Who can predict these things?"

"Come on," I said, folding my arms over my chest and looking him in the eye. "You can just admit you never intended to run a story at all, and that Hallie sent you to take that picture."

Andy blinked at me. "Who?" he asked, sounding legitimately baffled. Maybe I'd underestimated how good an actor he was, because I almost believed him.

"Hallie Bridges?" I prompted. When he still looked blank, I gestured around me. "This is her mother's house."

"Oh, right," he said, nodding. "Right." I noticed his accent was back to being shaky again, moving back and forth across the Atlantic. I narrowed my eyes. Something about this—about him—just wasn't adding up. "Well, must be going," he said, giving me a nod and then practically speed-walking away from me.

I watched him go, frowning. I knew I didn't have time to deal with it right then, but I'd have to try and figure it out later. Right now I had to do everything I could to get the notebook back.

I walked toward the house, trying to project authority I didn't quite feel like I was on some catering emergency, nodding at some of the other black-clad people I passed. It must have been convincing enough, because some of them even nodded back at me as they hurried to the party, bearing trays of appetizers.

I stepped inside the house and looked around. Hallie probably had the notebook in her room, which meant I needed to get upstairs. But now that I knew this was forbidden, I'd have to be especially quick—and stealthy—about it.

"Right behind you," someone snapped at me, and I jumped out of the way. A stressed-looking cater waiter carrying a tray piled high with sliders was heading through the kitchen and outside. He turned back and looked at me, frowning, and I knew that despite my all-black ensemble, at some point soon I'd be recognized as the ice-cream sandwich girl—which meant that there was no reason for me to be hanging out in the kitchen.

I started to move toward the staircase, keeping an eye on the kitchen and the two people who were currently standing over the prep area, assembling veggie towers and chicken on skewers lightning-fast. When I was sure that they weren't looking my way, I speed-walked toward the stairs. I knew that the clock was ticking on this. If anyone saw me right now, I was done for. And if the Scary Headset Lady saw that there was only one person manning the ice-cream sandwich station for too long, she might start asking questions. Also, I didn't want to raise Darcy's suspicions at all. She'd already proven herself to be remarkably easy to fool, but I knew at some point if a cooldown and ice run took me half an hour, even she would start to wonder what was going on.

I walked up the stairs as fast as I could while still being quiet, walking down the white-painted hallway hung with the Bridges' family pictures. I stayed close to the edge of the wall, since Ford had once told me—I hadn't wanted to ask why he knew this—that this was the way to walk if you didn't want to be detected. Apparently, the floor never squeaked against the wall. I knew exactly where Hallie's room was—at the end of the hall. I was almost there when I heard laughter coming from one of the rooms, the door cracked open just an inch.

I froze, my heart pounding hard. I was still in the middle of the hallway. If someone came out now, I was totally exposed, a sitting duck. I was too far away from any of the rooms to run into them, and too far away from the stairs to make it back down again and pretend I was on some approved catering-related errand.

The laughter sounded again from the room, and in the crack that the door was open, I saw Karen pass by. She was talking to someone I couldn't see, but I could hear it in her voice—how happy she was. It was like when I'd seen her on Sophie's feed. She looked radiant. And even though I knew I should get out of there, continue on down the hall to Hallie's room before I was caught, I found I couldn't quite move. One of my biggest worries had always been that I'd wrecked Karen's life beyond repair. And to see her now, in her mansion, looking gorgeous and happy, was putting to rest a lingering fear of mine. I still had no idea how it had come to be. But the fact that she was here—however she had managed it—was lifting a weight from my shoulders, one that had been there for a long, long time.

"Of course you would say that," she said, laughing. "Oh, my darling. What am I going to do with you?" She passed the crack in the door then, and I heard the distinct sound of kissing. That was enough to get me moving down the hall again. While I was happy that Karen had found someone, it didn't necessarily mean that I needed to see old people making out.

I hurried down the hall to Hallie's room. The door was ajar, and I checked over my shoulder before easing it open. I held my breath as I glanced around, but the room was empty. I didn't turn the light on, but I could see that it looked the same as the last time I'd seen it—the night Hallie had invited me over to her bonfire, and she'd still been pretending she didn't know who I really was and that we were actually friends.

Even though I knew I didn't have time for it, and even though I didn't want to, my eyes slid over to her dresser. Of course the picture of us that had been there before—the one we'd taken together at the bar mitzvah—was gone. I didn't know why I was even surprised, really.

I focused on the task at hand. I had to grab the notebook and get back down to the ice-cream sandwich station—with ice—before anyone got suspicious. I looked around, trying to think where Hallie would have put it, when I saw Hallie's purse on the armchair in the corner, the same designer tote where I had first thought I'd seen it. Could it really be that easy?

I crossed quickly over to the chair and looked inside the bag. There it was, lying faceup, next to a lip gloss and a handful of change. I pulled it out, feeling my heart start to pound with anticipation. But a moment later I realized it wasn't mine. It was the same color, but it was a newer version, and my handwriting wasn't scrawled across the front. What was this? I let out a breath and started to flip through it.

The first pages were blank, and I flipped faster and faster until I came upon a page with writing on it.

HI, GEMMA was written across two pages in huge block

print. I was just staring at this, confused, when the lights snapped on.

I looked up and saw the Scary Headset Lady standing on the threshold of the room. And behind her, leaning against the doorframe and smiling at me, was Hallie.

CHAPTER 20

"Look," I said, in my best I-swear-I'm-not-a-criminal voice, "I think this is all a misunderstanding."

"A *misunderstanding*?" Scary Headset Lady—whose name, I had learned in the last few minutes, was Blair—glared at me. We were still in Hallie's room, though I had left the notebook behind and stepped away from the purse. "You were found inside the house of our client, where you were explicitly told not to go. Not to mention that you were inside one of the closed bedrooms going through the contents of a purse!"

When she put it that way, I could see how this really, really didn't look good for me. "The thing is," I said, "I just . . ." I glanced over at Hallie, who raised an eyebrow at me. She looked incredibly pleased with herself, and I could just *tell* how much she was enjoying this. She had baited me into this. She had probably found out from Reid I was working. . . . My stomach suddenly clenched.

Unless she'd set that up too. She'd gotten him to get me

here so I would be in the exact spot I was now . . . in *really* big trouble. She'd set a trap, and I'd walked right into it.

"The last thing I want to hear," Blair said, shaking her head, "is that one of my workers is making our clients feel in any way unsafe." She turned to Hallie, whose expression immediately changed. She now looked concerned and a little shaken, and it was good enough that I had no doubt Blair was buying it. "Miss Bridges, I'm so sorry about this. And I'm sure my employee . . ." She looked at me.

"Gemma," I supplied, hating that I had to do this, but not seeing any alternative.

"Gemma," Blair continued, frowning at me, "is very sorry as well. She will be disciplined for this. You don't have to worry about that."

"Oh, good," Hallie said faintly, like she had been rattled by this whole experience. "Thank you. You think you can trust people. . . ." She let the sentence trail off, but not before she looked at me significantly.

"Please turn out your pockets," Blair said to me, and the heat rushed to my face once again. It didn't matter that I knew I hadn't stolen anything—this was *really* embarrassing.

"I don't think that's necessary . . ." I started, but Blair gave me a look that made it clear this wasn't a discussion. I turned out the lining of both my pants pockets, which—of course—were empty, except for my cell phone.

"All right," Blair said, apparently satisfied that I hadn't, contrary to all appearances, stolen anything. "Please take your things and leave. You will *not* be compensated for today."

I nodded, glad that this whole thing seemed to be ending. I really didn't like getting in trouble—even though Blair had no real authority, I still didn't like that I'd gotten on her bad side. "Okay," I said as I started to leave. "I'll just—"

"So is she fired?" Hallie asked from the doorway, eyebrows raised, looking disappointed. Blair turned to look at her, and Hallie's expression immediately became more contrite. "I mean . . . I was just wondering what the consequences would be."

Blair pursed her lips. "Well," she finally said. I wondered if I should speed things up by saying that I had no desire to work for the catering company again, so it really wasn't a big deal for me. "I know she strayed out of bounds, but nothing was taken. So I think maybe just a sincere apology and leaving early without pay should suffice."

I took a deep breath, wondering if I offered to quit, I could be spared the "sincere apology" part. I wasn't sure I was going to be able to get through one of those to Hallie and make it sound at all believable. But before I could speak, Hallie interrupted.

"I mean, I certainly don't want to tell you how to do your job," she said. "But . . ." She bit her lip, like she was incredibly conflicted about this. "I would really feel more comfortable if you would search her bag before she left. After all"—here Hallie lowered her voice to a whisper, but one designed to carry, since I could still catch every word—"this may not have been the only time she did this today. It might just have been the only time she got caught."

I rolled my eyes at that. "Fine," I said. "Check all you want. There's nothing there."

"We'll see," Blair said, pursing her lips at me again. They made me lead the way downstairs, I guess so that they could make sure I wasn't grabbing stuff once their backs were turned. I could feel my face flame as we walked through the kitchen and down to the tent.

It wasn't like I was handcuffed or anything, but it must have still somehow been very clear that I was in trouble and going somewhere against my will—people kept turning and looking at me, and even though I hadn't done anything wrong (well, not *really*), I was starting to feel like I had by the time I made it back to the ice-cream sandwich station.

"Hi!" Darcy said cheerfully. A second later her smile faded as she looked behind me. "Um, what's going on?" She looked at me again, her brow furrowed. "Wait, where's the ice?"

"It's kind of a long story," I muttered, looking down at the perfectly manicured grass.

"Your bag?" Blair asked, and I looked over at Hallie, who shot me a smile as I reached under the table and pulled it out. I couldn't say why, but I didn't like that she was smiling at me, not one bit. I handed it over to Blair, just as my phone buzzed in my back pocket. I took it out and saw I had two texts from Sophie.

Sophie Curtis

5:55 PM

Hi! Did I hear you were at that benefit thing too?
Crazy!

Sorry I missed you! I had to take the girls home
for dinner, but are we still on for pizza later?

Sophie Curtis

5:56 PM

Also, I dropped my gift bag off in your
purse—it was pretty heavy.

Would you bring it back home for me?

As I read the last text, I felt my stomach plunge. I had a
feeling I now understood Hallie's satisfied smile—and that I
was still in the trap she'd set, and everything had been planned
for this moment. I realized I'd just been set up. "Wait—" I started,
as Blair pulled out a canvas bag I'd never seen before out of my
purse. "That's not mine," I said immediately.

Hallie smiled at me sadly. "Isn't that what they all say,
though?"

Darcy was watching all this, her expression confused, and I
was glad for the small favor that nobody seemed to want an ice-
cream sandwich at that particular moment. "What's going on?"
she asked slowly, looking at me like she'd never seen me before.

"Is this yours?" Blair asked Hallie, holding the canvas bag
up. *Thank You!* was printed on the side in stylized cursive.

"It's the gift bag for the event," Hallie said, back to using
her shaken voice. "I guess maybe she found one? It's not a big
deal. She can just have it if she wants it that badly. . . ."

"You took a *gift bag*?" Blair asked me, sounding horrified.
She looked more upset by this than anything else that had
happened in the last few minutes.

"No!" I said, feeling the need to defend myself, even though all the evidence was being manufactured and stacked against me. I turned to Darcy. "Darcy, did you see a girl with brown hair—my friend Sophie—drop this bag off in my purse?"

"Well . . . no," Darcy said, looking disconcerted. "I mean, I saw your friend. She asked if you were working here. But then I had to make, like, five sandwiches in a row, so I didn't see . . ." Her voice trailed off, and she looked between all of us, clearly not sure what was going on or what she should be saying. "I mean . . ."

"Look, my friend just dropped that off," I said, glaring at Hallie. "There's no need . . ."

But even as I said this, Blair was shaking out the contents of the gift bag onto our table. It looked like the typical gift bag stuff I'd seen Bruce bring home—gift certificates and makeup samples and a T-shirt. But then a small cloth bag, the kind you keep expensive jewelry in, rolled out, and Hallie gasped. "That's mine," she said faintly. "That's . . . not part of the gift bag."

"I didn't—" I started, but Blair held up her hand, clearly not interested in hearing it.

"What's going on?" I looked over and saw that Josh was walking up to the table—as if this wasn't quite embarrassing enough already. The only small favor seemed to be that Josh was alone—the girl with the topknot was nowhere to be seen.

"Nothing," Hallie said quickly, no longer looking quite as comfortable. "Can you make sure Mom has everything she needs? Because—"

"No need to worry," Blair assured Josh. "This will be taken

care of. There will be no theft from my employees that goes unpunished."

"Theft?" Josh asked, sounding flabbergasted. He looked at me in shock. "You stole something?"

"No," I said. I looked right at him. "I didn't." He looked back at me for a moment, and I could see confusion in his eyes. But it also seemed like he—maybe—believed me.

Josh turned to Hallie, his arms folded. "What is this?"

"It's nothing," Hallie said, starting to look really discomfited. "You really don't need to be here. I can handle this."

"Don't you want to open this?" Blair asked, holding up the cloth bag. "We'll need to know the contents if you want to press charges."

It was like the world went fuzzy around the edges for a moment, and I grabbed on to the edge of the table for support. Press *charges*? Was Hallie—had she just framed me for an actual crime? Was I about to be *arrested*? I tried to remind myself to breathe, and then tried to remind myself just how to do that.

"It's okay," Hallie muttered as she picked up the bag and dropped it into her dress pocket. "I don't want the party to be ruined."

"Totally understandable," Blair murmured, looking relieved.

"But I want her gone," Hallie said, pointing at me. "And I want her fired."

I saw Josh look at Hallie sharply, but she was looking right at me, her expression cold. "No need," I said, picking up my purse, leaving the discarded contents of the gift bag spread out on the table. "I quit." Next to me, Darcy looked more confused than ever, like she was waiting for someone to step in and tell her what was going on. "Sorry, Darcy," I muttered. I knew I was leaving her short-handed, but I knew I wouldn't be able to stay there for one minute longer without starting to cry or screaming at Hallie.

"It's okay," Darcy murmured, still looking caught off guard by the events that had just occurred. She was probably missing working with Reid, when all she had to deal with was sunstroke.

I shouldered my bag and looked at Hallie, who stared back at me. I could feel my anger bubbling inside me again, threatening to spill over. This felt like she'd taken things to a new level. This was beyond humiliation and haircuts. This was something else. "Happy?" I asked her, my voice dripping with sarcasm. I didn't wait for a reply, just shook my head and started to leave. Before I turned away, though, I saw Josh looking at me, his brow furrowed, like he was trying to figure out what had just happened.

Join the club, I thought as I walked away as fast as I could. And I made it almost to my car, parked on the side of the street, before I let myself burst into tears.

CHAPTER 21

I hadn't gone back to Bruce's. I'd felt too wound up, and I worried that if I went home, I would find myself yelling at the wrong person or accidentally breaking something. Instead, to try and calm down, I'd gotten an iced latte from Quonset Coffee and taken it to the beach, but picked a spot away from Bruce's house. I wanted to be far from anyone I might recognize. I knew I was getting funny looks from people—the girl dressed all in black at the beach, like Ford in his Goth phase—but at the moment, I didn't care.

I took a long drink of my latte and dug my bare toes into the sand. In front of me were two girls who looked around ten. I watched as they passed a magazine back and forth on the towel they were sharing, both of them laughing. I wanted to tell them to enjoy it while it lasted. Before long they'd be turning on each other and tricking each other into questionable haircuts, and one would be trying to get the other arrested.

Every time I thought about the events of the afternoon, it

was like I could feel my blood pressure—and my temper—rising. So Hallie had meant what she'd said when she'd warned me to watch my back. I just hadn't realized she'd go this far. And then to be humiliated like that, in front of everyone at that party, in front of Darcy, and Josh . . .

I could feel the adrenaline start to course through my body, like I was preparing for a fight. I looked out to the water, trying to take deep breaths, and found myself wishing that I had taken up running, that I'd actually done it any of those times that Bruce and I had said we were going to but instead just went for bagels. In movies, at least, people were always running to burn off their excess anger and frustration, and then returning calmer and more clearheaded. I realized suddenly why Josh had gone for a run that day I'd seen him in the kitchen through Sophie's camera feed. I got now why he might even risk damaging his ACL again.

As soon as I'd thought this, I realized there might be a way for me to sort out what had happened today. I set my iced latte cup down and pulled out my phone, pressing the button for the contact even as I got to my feet and was walking back toward the parking lot.

"Gwyneth?" I asked when she picked up. "Are you around? I have a favor to ask you. . . ."

⚬⚬⚬⚬⚬

Gwyneth turned in her chair to face me, and raised an eyebrow. "Just so you know, this is *far* outside the scope of the documentary," she said.

When I'd first asked her, I'd expected her to argue with me again, like she had when we were trying to get to Hallie's phone. I'd actually expected *more* of a fight, since this would be watching someone's feed without their knowledge. But Gwyneth had agreed almost right away, to my surprise—but I was not, apparently, going to get by without a lecture about her ethics. "I know," I said, looking down at my hands.

"I just want to put it out there," she said as she turned back to the monitors again. "This has nothing to do with Bruce or the movie. It sounds like you just want to spy on the girl who's supposed to be your best friend."

I sat back, stung by that—maybe because there was some truth in it. I knew I could have asked Sophie what had happened, but I was feeling truly confused, and like I had no idea who I could trust—even the people I'd thought would never ever betray me. "I don't want to spy on her," I said after a moment. "But I almost got arrested today, Gwyn."

Gwyneth waved this away. "They never would have gotten the charges to stick," she said with confidence. "The evidence was entirely circumstantial. And—"

"That's not the point," I said, shaking my head. "I just have to know how it happened. Because either Sophie's in on this . . ." I said, struggling to get the words out. I hated to even be thinking them. "Or somehow Hallie pulled her into this without her realizing it," I said, feeling my anger start to bubble again as I said it. "And I just need to know."

Gwyneth looked at me for a moment then nodded. "Okay," she said. Her expression changed into a grin. "The *drama*," she enthused as she turned back toward her computer. "I mean, you can't write this. It's *way* more interesting than watching Bruce moan about the fact he can't have a helipad." She typed rapid-fire on her computer for a few minutes, and then I realized I was looking at a frozen image of Sophie staring at herself in the mirror, with bedhead, looking tired.

"So this is from when she turned on the camera this morning," Gwyneth said as she started to scroll through the feed. I watched as the images flew by, my best friend going about her day at incredibly fast speeds. Gwyneth slowed it down a little when I appeared, but still not enough to make out what was being said—but there we were, talking in the kitchen this morning, probably making plans to get pizza later, then Sophie waving at me as she headed out the door. Gwyneth sped up the feed again as she drove over to the twins' house, then babysat for a while—for Sophie, this seemed to consist entirely of watching soap operas along with the girls, all three of them seeming equally engrossed. I was beginning to understand why they liked her babysitting style so much.

Gwyneth slowed down the feed to normal speed as Sophie and the twins arrived at the Bridges' house. The twins ran off to two people who I assumed were their dads, and then it seemed like Sophie wandered around for a bit, sticking to the edges of the party. I could practically feel her unsureness creeping through the footage. Sophie really wasn't great at being alone, which was one of the reasons that she always had a boyfriend. Her current state of singledom was a very rare occurrence. And then, with horrible timing, like my train of thought now had predictive powers, Josh showed up in frame, smiling down at Sophie.

"Can you . . ." I asked, then cleared my throat, as my first attempt at speaking had come out scratchy. "Can you turn up the volume on this?"

"I can do my best," Gwyneth said as she hit keys on her keyboard. "The audio on these things isn't the best. When I'm just filming Bruce, I usually have a boom mic. . . ." But she must have been able to figure something out, because a moment later I could hear much better—scattered party sounds and people laughing and talking, but I could also hear Josh and Sophie.

". . . surprised to see you here," Josh was saying. I couldn't help but notice that he looked happy to see her. Every time since I'd seen him at the Fourth, he'd been unhappy and angry when he saw me, and I'd almost forgotten what happy Josh looked like.

"Yeah," Sophie said, and I wished once again that I could have seen her expression. I couldn't tell through the mic on her camera what she was feeling about this. "I'm babysitting, so . . ."

"Oh," Josh said, nodding. "Got it. I was wondering. I thought maybe you were here with . . . Gemma." He pronounced my name like he was still getting used to it, and still didn't like the sound of it.

"No," Sophie said, and I could hear her surprise. "I don't think she's here."

Josh pointed, and then Sophie turned, and I saw myself, across the tent, in the sunshine, saying something to Darcy as we organized the cookies. Sophie turned back to look at Josh, but his head was still turned in my direction.

"He's *really* cute, isn't he?" Gwyneth asked as she leaned back in her chair. "Is he dating anyone?" I started to tell her about the two girls I'd seen him with that summer, when Sophie's feed got shaky as she started to walk again, and I totally lost whatever audio we had as she passed an incredibly loud group of people, all of whom seemed to be talking at once.

When the feed settled again, I saw that Sophie and Josh were now in a far corner of the tent, where it was less crowded, and I wondered whose idea it had been to walk there. I realized I didn't like either possibility.

"So," Josh was saying, and he was suddenly much more in the frame. I realized, with my heart sinking, that this meant he was now standing closer to Sophie. "I don't know if you're busy . . . but would you ever want to get coffee or dinner sometime?"

The words hit me like a punch to the gut. Josh was asking Sophie out. Josh, who had for a brief shining moment been *my* Josh, was asking out my best friend. I leaned forward so far that I was practically touching the screen, just as it went dark. There was still some movement, and then a muffled sound, but I couldn't hear anything. "What happened?" I asked, staring at the screen like this would get it to suddenly show me something. "Gwyn? What's going on?"

"I have no idea," Gwyneth said, hitting various keys, and turning the volume—which was now just muffled static—up as far as it would go. "I think she accidentally put her bag over the camera," Gwyneth said. "The feed is still going, so it's not like it cut out. I just think she's accidentally blocking it."

I nodded, feeling my heart pound. *Was* it accidental? Or did Sophie not want anyone to see or hear the rest of the conversation? I hated that I was thinking this way—that Hallie had gotten me to this point of distrusting the person I'd once trusted the most.

Gwyneth scrolled through the footage—all blackness— until Sophie must have adjusted her bag again. I could see the party, and then the twins, as Sophie was bending down to talk to them. One of them pointed in the direction of the ice-cream sandwiches, and Sophie must have agreed, because the twin ran out of frame. "I don't want ice cream," the twin that had remained behind was whining. "I want a cupcake!"

"Okay," Sophie said, not sounding particularly invested in this problem. "So do you see any cupcakes? Because—"

"Did you want a cupcake?"

Sophie must have turned toward the person who was speaking, because suddenly they filled the frame, and I instinctively recoiled—it was Hallie. She was smiling at Sophie like she'd just seen an old friend.

"Oh," Sophie said, and for once I didn't need a mirror to tell how she was feeling—totally thrown, not to mention nervous. "Um, hi there. I . . . uh . . ."

"Hallie!" the twin shrieked, hugging Hallie's legs tightly. "I missed you! Do you have any cupcakes?"

Hallie laughed at that, and so did Sophie—and I realized that must have been what I saw when I saw them laughing together. "Sure," Hallie said easily. "I think there are some going around on the catering trays. I'll keep an eye out for you."

"I'm really sorry," Sophie said haltingly. "I didn't know this benefit was at your house—I wouldn't have said I could babysit if . . ."

Hallie shook her head. "Sophie, it's okay," she said, her voice kind. The Hallie I thought I'd been friends with earlier in the summer was back, and it was painful to see. "I know you didn't have anything to do with this whole . . . situation. You've just been dragged into it against your will. And I'm sorry."

I felt myself bristle at that characterization, and Gwyneth looked over at me, eyebrows raised. "Damn," she said, shaking her head. "This girl is *good*."

"Well . . . thank you," Sophie said, and I could hear that it sounded like this was starting to sink in. "I appreciate that."

"Of course," Hallie said, her voice sweet and friendly. I could feel myself start to sweat, just looking at her guileless expression. Sophie was walking into a trap, and she had no idea. "And . . . I mean, despite everything else, I'd actually really like it if we could be friends. I understand if you don't think that can happen, but . . ." She let her voice trail off, and then bit her lip. I silently urged the Sophie on-screen—which was ridiculous for several reasons, including that this had already happened—to just agree with her and walk away.

"No, I'd like that too," Sophie said.

Hallie smiled like she was relieved. She glanced over toward the ice-cream sandwich station for a moment, and I wondered what she was seeing—was this the moment I'd headed up to the house? I willed Sophie to turn in that direction, but a moment later Hallie was back to facing her again. "Um, I brought you a gift bag," she said, holding it out a little shyly. "You might not want it. It's stupid. I just thought—"

"No, that's really nice of you," Sophie said, sounding pleased as she reached out for it. "Thank you."

"Well . . . thanks for giving me a shot," Hallie said, sounding grateful. "I appreciate it."

"This is really heavy," Sophie said as the feed shook slightly, and she must have hoisted it onto her shoulder. "Always a good sign, right?"

"Totally," Hallie said with a laugh. "Do you have a bag or something you could put it in? Or somewhere you could leave it? I know it's going to be a pain to carry while running around after the girls."

"Back!" The other twin had returned, carrying a dripping ice-cream sandwich with both hands. Hallie said good-bye and headed out of frame, and I watched Sophie turn toward the ice-cream sandwich station, where I no longer was—and it was like I could practically hear her thought process, thinking the idea that Hallie had planted in her head was her own.

She started across toward the station where Darcy was now trying to deal with a growing line, and I sat back in my chair. "It's okay," I said, and Gwyneth paused the footage, shooting me a sympathetic look. "That was all I needed to see."

I thanked Gwyneth and headed downstairs, my head spinning. So at least Sophie hadn't been conspiring against me with Hallie—unless they were the greatest actors in the world, in which case, I was giving up and going home. But she'd still just allowed herself to be played like a fiddle. She'd let herself be used by Hallie, and I'd almost gotten arrested as a result.

I tried to go to my room, but after pacing the perimeter a few times, I was feeling claustrophobic. I headed down to the pool, where I'd seen Bruce pacing on more than one occasion, finally feeling like I understood him a little more.

"Hey!" I turned and saw Sophie heading toward me, a smile on her face. I realized she had no idea anything out of the ordinary had happened once she left. "You never texted me back! Are we getting pizza? I've been thinking about it all afternoon."

I just looked at her and tried to make myself take deep breaths. But even so, I was getting mad. And though I knew it was Hallie I was really mad at, not Sophie, I couldn't stop some of my frustration from spilling over onto her. "I haven't had time to think about pizza," I said, hearing the angry, condescending tone in my voice, but not able to stop myself, even as it was happening. "Thanks to you and your gift bag."

Sophie's eyes widened, and she took a step back. In all our years of friendship, we'd never really fought—we'd had little arguments, over movie theater snacks and which boy band member was the cutest and how you pronounce the word *caramel*—but nothing major. "What are you talking about?" she asked, sounding confused and defensive. "Did you bring it for me? I assumed it would be okay. . . ."

"Well, you assumed wrong," I said, and filled her in on what had happened. Sophie's eyes went wide as she listened, her jaw dropping when I got to the part about pressing charges.

"Jeez," she said, "I had no idea. I mean . . . how was I supposed to know? Hallie just offered me this gift bag, so I took it to be polite. And I didn't think—"

"No, you didn't." The words were out of my mouth before I could stop them, and even as I spoke, I knew I should stop myself. "You were telling Hallie how you wanted to be *friends*. And—"

"Wait. What?" Sophie asked, her eyebrows flying up. "How did you know that?"

"Because I just watched your camera footage!" I practically yelled this last part. I hadn't realized how loud I had gotten until the pool house door opened and Ford stuck his head outside.

"Um . . . is everything okay?" he asked, looking from me to Sophie, his expression concerned.

"Fine," Sophie said. She gave me a *what the hell?* look as she walked past the pool and headed toward the beach. I followed, and when we were out of earshot of the pool house and the rest of the house, she turned to me. "What are you talking about?" she asked, her volume going right back to what mine had been. "What do you mean, you watched my footage?"

"Good evening, ladies." We both turned and saw Teddy waving at us from his campsite. I had pretty much forgotten Teddy was there—and so had Sophie, judging by the look on her face. Apparently, we weren't out of earshot of protesters claiming squatter's rights.

"Hi, Teddy," Sophie said, unenthusiastically. I waved, and Sophie and I walked farther down the beach, away from him. "What do you mean?" she asked me a little more quietly.

"I mean," I said, knowing that there was no way to get out of this, since I'd just admitted it to her, "I had Gwyneth show me your footage."

Sophie's face turned red—though with anger or embarrassment, I couldn't tell. "You were spying on me?"

"How is this any different than what Gwyneth is doing?" I asked. But even as I said it, I knew the answer.

"Because she's going through it and deleting whatever doesn't fit with her documentary," Sophie said, her voice rising again. "She's not going through it looking for . . ." She paused, her eyes narrowed. "Why did you even look at it in the first place?"

"Because," I said, "I saw you talking to Hallie, all buddy-buddy at the event, and then the gift bag that you put there shows up in my bag. . . . I thought that maybe you and Hallie—"

"Oh my god," Sophie said slowly, shaking her head. She was looking at me like she wasn't quite sure who I was. "Are you freaking kidding me? I really can't believe this," she said hollowly. "Are you honestly telling me you don't trust me?"

"I do," I said. "I just—"

"If you needed to spy on me, that means you don't trust me," Sophie said. She let out a long breath. "I swear, this *thing* between you and Hallie has gotten so far out of hand, I don't even know what to say anymore."

"I know," I said quickly, "but—"

"*Do* you know?" Sophie asked, looking directly at me, fixing me with her gaze. "Because the Gemma I used to be friends with would never have mistrusted me. She wouldn't have been spending all her time planning on how to hurt someone. She spent too much time with her stupid do-gooder boy-friend—"

"Hey—" I started, but Sophie kept going.

"But she never would have behaved like this!" Sophie stopped and shook her head. I took a deep breath, trying not to let myself start crying. Sophie's words had hit me hard—mostly because I knew they were the truth. "You know, we've barely done anything fun this summer?" she went on after a moment, her voice quieter. "We could have been enjoying spending our time together, instead of—"

"What did you want me to do?" I asked more quietly now, but not rhetorically. I actually wanted to know. "Was I sup-posed to just walk away from what she did?"

"Yes," Sophie said as though it should have been obvious. "Exactly."

I shook my head. Even though I knew that a lot of what So-phie was saying was right, there was a part of this I knew she didn't—couldn't—understand. "I think that's easier for you to say," I said, "because you've never . . . I mean, in your relation-ships, you're not . . ."

"What are you saying?" Sophie asked, her voice quiet. "That I don't understand because I wasn't in a relationship with a selfish *jerk* for two years?"

"No," I said, deciding to just ignore the dig at Teddy, "but you've never been in a long-term committed relationship. You don't know what it's like to be in love, Soph. And so maybe you don't get why I had to do what I did."

"Look, I have been in relationships," Sophie said, her voice breaking, "so don't tell me that I don't understand."

"Then why were you flirting with Josh this afternoon?" I blurted it out, not knowing I was going to, and I heard my own voice shake when I said his name. "I saw you guys. And he . . . he asked you out, and—"

"Yeah, he did," Sophie said. She shook her head and crossed her arms. "But I told him no. Because I wouldn't do that to you, and I thought you'd have known that. Give me a little credit at least." She turned to walk inside.

"Soph—" I started. I could feel that I was on the verge of tears and like everything was spinning out of my control, moving too fast for me to get ahold of it.

"Just . . ." Sophie turned back to me, shaking her head. "Just leave me alone for a while, okay, Gemma?"

I watched Sophie walk inside, away from me, not once looking back, and I brushed a hot tear off my face. My first instinct was to blame this on Hallie, and while she had been a part of it, the truly honest part of me knew this was my fault.

"Gem?" I heard Teddy calling to me in the darkness. Not wanting to have to keep shouting, probably in the hearing range of all the people just trying to enjoy the Quonset beach sunset, I walked a few steps toward him.

He was sitting next to the backhoe again, in front of his lantern, which was turned on low—there was still some light from the sun, which hadn't totally set yet. He gave me a sympathetic smile as I got closer to him. "It looked like you guys were arguing," he said. He patted the ground next to him in a circular motion. "Want to talk about it?"

The thought of talking about it with someone really was appealing. Sophie was normally the person I talked about things with, and I didn't have that option in this case. But I realized a second later that I didn't think I wanted to talk about it with *Teddy*. He'd never been a huge fan of Sophie, and I didn't want to hear him say anything bad about her. Also, in order to truly explain what we'd been fighting about, I'd have to go into a lot more than I wanted to at the moment.

"No," I finally said. I could see in the lamplight this had surprised him, as well. "I think . . . maybe I'm just going to go inside." I gave him a nod and started to walk away. Even though it was still early, and I hadn't had dinner yet, suddenly the thought of just getting into bed, pulling the covers over my head, and waking up when things made sense again, was very appealing.

"Gemma." I'd only gone a few feet when I heard Teddy's voice, and I turned to him. "You know I'm always here, right?"

I nodded. I could have pointed out that he'd basically guaranteed this when he'd chained himself to construction equipment, but I knew that wasn't what he meant.

"Yeah," I said, giving him my best attempt at a smile. "Thanks."

I started to walk to the house again, but before sliding the door open and heading inside, I turned back. You couldn't see him from the house, but I was pretty sure I could see the light thrown off by his lantern. I'd expected to feel comforted by this, but somehow it was just irritating me, and I didn't know why. I looked at it for a moment longer before stepping inside and slamming the door.

CHAPTER 22

I barely slept that night.

Whenever I did close my eyes, all I could see was Sophie looking at me like I was a stranger, telling me truths I didn't want to hear but nonetheless couldn't ignore. And when I did manage to drift off, I had strange dreams about running from people I couldn't see, not even sure why I was running, just feeling somehow that I needed to—but always turning up in dead ends.

When I woke up, though, I knew what I needed to do. It was clear to me now. I'd hoped that I'd be able to go back to sleep, but at six A.M., after an hour of staring at the time on my bedside clock, I gave up, and headed downstairs. I was about to make some breakfast, when I found myself looking outside—at the beach and Teddy's tent. And before I even knew I was going to do it, I was walking outside toward him.

I'd expected the tent to still be zipped shut, and Teddy to be sleeping, but he was up, sitting cross-legged in front of the opening, looking out at the water.

"Hey," I said as I approached him. It felt like I'd just had a huge pot of coffee—I was amped up and jittery. I hadn't even asked myself if this was a good idea, and I realized I didn't care if it wasn't.

"Gemma," Teddy said, looking surprised but not unhappy to see me, his voice still a little crackly from sleep. "Good morning. What's—"

"You *cheated* on me." I blurted it out, and I saw Teddy draw back slightly, looking confused. Clearly, having an argument with his ex-girlfriend at the crack of dawn while chained to construction equipment had not been in his plans this morning. "You lied to me. For months. And then when you did break up with me, you didn't even have the courage to tell me the real reason." It felt so good to finally say this to him, and I realized as I did that while I was angry, it wasn't raw and painful anymore. It felt like I was getting over him. Not fake getting over him, because I was crushing on Josh, but actual getting over him.

"I'm sorry," Teddy said immediately. "I . . . wish I had done some things differently. But—"

"And then you show up here," I interrupted, not wanting to lose my nerve, "and never once even ask me if I'm okay with it. Or Hallie," I acknowledged, realizing for the first time that this had been really unfair to both of us.

"The marsh warbler—" Teddy started, looking increasingly discomfited.

"I don't need to hear about the marsh warbler," I said,

realizing as I did that I should have said it two years ago. "Here's something you might want to know—I actually don't care about the marsh warbler." Teddy's eyes widened in shock, and I felt myself smile.

"You're not yourself," Teddy said, frowning as he looked up at me. I just shook my head, not knowing how to tell him that this *was* me—and that the version he was used to seeing was the fake. "Is this about Ford?"

"Ford?" I echoed, surprised. "Why would you—"

"I'm not blind, Gemma," Teddy said, shaking his head. "I can see what's going on."

I took a breath to tell him there was nothing happening with me and Ford, but then I just let it go. I didn't owe Teddy anything, least of all answers about my love life (or lack thereof). "See you around," I said as I turned to walk back to the house. Even though Teddy wasn't saying anything, I could practically feel his surprise radiating toward me in waves. I felt myself smile as I passed the pool. That had been scary—and the kind of thing I normally would have never said to Teddy—but it had felt good. It had felt like I was being really honest with him, maybe for the first time in two years.

I slid open the door to the kitchen. The house was still quiet, and I fully expected to be the only one awake—which was why I jumped when I saw Ford sitting at the kitchen island with a bowl of cereal.

"Morning," he said, raising his spoon to me in greeting. He was wearing shorts and a T-shirt, and was reading a book, his glasses slightly askew on his face. "What are you doing up?"

"I could ask you the same question," I said, not wanting to get into the discussion I'd just had with my ex—or how Ford's name had come up. I turned away from him, took a bottle of orange juice out of the fridge, and poured a glass.

"I'm going back over to the Montauk break," he said. "It was, like, *killer* there yesterday." He dropped into his surfer cadence, which made me smile—the very act of which felt unfamiliar on my face, like I hadn't done it in a while.

I took a sip of my juice and placed it on the counter, then I shivered and rubbed my hands up and down my arms.

"Cold?" Ford asked. "I'd lend you my favorite sweatshirt, but it seems to have gone missing. . . ."

"I'll keep an eye out," I said around a giant yawn.

"Gwyneth told me about yesterday," Ford said, and I was glad for once that his sister was such a gossip—it saved me from having to go through the whole recap again. "And then I couldn't help but hear you and Sophie by the pool."

I nodded. I knew I should probably be embarrassed that we'd been fighting loudly enough for Ford to overhear, but I somehow couldn't find the energy to care. There were too many other things going on at the moment. "Yeah," I said, rolling my juice glass between my palms. "Not my favorite day of the summer."

"So what are you going to do?" Ford asked. "What's the plan?"

I couldn't help but smile again at that as I dropped two slices of bread into the toaster. It really had been a comfort to have someone who was always looking ahead and focusing on the next step, rather than judging me for my actions or telling me what I should have done differently. I took a breath and told him what I'd been thinking about ever since I'd gone to bed the night before. "I think I'm done," I said, liking the way that it felt to be saying it. "I'm walking away. I've had enough."

"Wow," Ford said, leaning back slightly, like he was trying to get a better view of me. "That's big."

I nodded. It was the only thing, the only course of action that had felt right, as I'd had another long sleepless night—it was starting to feel like a summer full of them. But unlike in the beginning of the summer, it didn't feel like Hallie would be winning, or that I would be meekly walking away. Now it felt like the strong thing to do, somehow, to leave before I wrecked everything I still cared about. "I know."

"I will say," Ford said as he picked up his spoon again, "that at least from movie-related evidence, revenge never ends well for anyone."

"Not ever?" I asked, surprised, trying to think about all the revenge movies I'd seen, all the ones that Ford had made me watch, most of which seemed to be subtitled and incredibly violent. But surely, there had to be *one* in which someone got revenge and was happy about it, and felt good about their choices by the end of the movie. Right?

"Not that I can think of," Ford said. "It just always seems to lead to bigger problems."

I let that sink in for a moment, then I shook my head. "You might have mentioned that."

He gave me one of his half-smiles. "I figured it was something you'd have to find out for yourself. So you're done, huh?"

I nodded. "I am. And I'm going to finally tell my dad what happened that summer when I was eleven. It's time he knew the truth. And he should hear it from me."

"Wow," Ford said again as he put the spoon back in the bowl and pushed it away from him slightly. "It's like revelation day around here." He raised an eyebrow at me. "But not in the end-of-the-world biblical sense. Hopefully."

I smiled at that. "Maybe while I'm at it, I should also tell Bruce that I was the one who broke his most expensive bottle of wine when I was eight. What about you?" I asked, peering into the toaster to check on the toast's progress. "Is there anything you want to confess?" I expected Ford to smile at that, or make a joke.

Instead he just looked at me for a moment and then adjusted his glasses and cleared his throat. "Actually," he said, sounding uncharacteristically nervous. "The thing is, Gem—"

Ding! My toast popped up. I looked over at it instinctually, but then I looked back to Ford. "What were you . . ." I started, but Ford was already in motion, getting up and crossing to put his bowl in the dishwasher.

"Nothing," he said easily. "Another time."

I nodded and opened the fridge, wishing that some sort of nondairy butter had been invented, before giving up this dream and taking out some jam. "So what are you reading?" I asked as I crossed over to where Ford had been sitting, and pulled out a stool for myself. "Something good?" Ford's book choices were usually either biographies of inventors or mathematicians who

I'd never heard of, or technical manuals for various computer systems that really did not appear to be written in English. But even so, I leaned closer to the book, which was open, faceup on the counter.

"No," Ford said, and he started hurrying to me. "That's not—"

I turned the book over and felt my eyebrows fly up. "Not you too," I said as I looked at the cover for the paperback edition of *Once Bitten*. "Seriously?"

"What?" Ford said, but I could tell he was blushing. "The paper's not here yet. And I wanted something to read while I ate breakfast."

I looked down at the cover and shook my head. "I can't believe my dad's adapting this," I said, trying to avoid making a face but not succeeding. "Ugh."

"What's she like?" Ford asked. "The author?"

"Brenda Kreigs?" I asked, reading the name off the cover. I shrugged. "He hasn't really said. So I guess, fine."

"Well," Ford said, raising an eyebrow at me, "I can leave that with you if you want."

"Please, don't," I said with a laugh as I pushed the book away from me. "I don't want to lose my appetite."

"So now what's the course of action?" Ford asked even as he started back toward the pool house door. "Are you going to tell Hallie you're done? Or just fade out?"

"I think I'll just go radio silent," I said, and Ford nodded. "Honestly, I would be happy to not have to deal with any of the Bridges ever again." Even as I said it, I knew it wasn't totally true—at least not where Josh was concerned—but saying it felt like a step in the right direction. And if Josh was asking out my best friend, it was clear that he no longer had any feelings for me—even friendly ones. I should just accept that and let it go.

"I'll see you later," Ford said as he slid open the glass door and started to walk to the pool house.

"Hope the waves are good," I called back to him. I concentrated on evenly spreading the jam on my toast and *not* reading the book that was in front of me. Because if I did, I would be forced to admit that my dad had read it too, and I wasn't sure I wanted to go there. I was considering going back upstairs for my phone, just to have something to do while I ate, when Ford burst back into the kitchen.

"Hallie's last name," he said, talking fast, sounding out of breath. "It's Bridges?"

"Yeah," I said slowly, wondering what was going on. "Are you okay?"

"What's her mom's name?"

"Karen," I said, still not understanding any of this. "Why?"

Ford flipped the copy of *Once Bitten* around so that it was facing him, and grabbed a paper napkin and a pen from the counter and wrote something out, then looked at it for a moment and shook his head. "Wow," he said, sounding shocked. "I'm actually disappointed in myself. It's an *anagram*. And it's been in front of me this whole time."

"What are you talking about?" I asked. Ford pushed the napkin over to me, and as I read it, I felt my breath catch in my throat.

BRENDA KREIGS
KAREN BRIDGES

'd told Hallie that I was going to her house. I didn't want to give her time to set up something against me, so I waited until I was just a few minutes away before sending my text.

Me
6:02 AM
Hey. Need to talk.
On your beach in five minutes.

The whole drive over, my thoughts were spinning. Karen was the *Once Bitten* author. My dad had been working *very* long hours with the *Once Bitten* author, which meant . . .

Were my dad and Karen back together? Was *Karen* who he had been talking about when he'd asked me if I was okay with him dating someone? I couldn't believe that my dad would have started dating Karen again and not have told me. But how else to explain the dreamy happiness that had settled over him as soon as he'd started to work on this script? I thought about how we hadn't been communicating all summer, about how many secrets I'd been keeping from him. I supposed I shouldn't have been this surprised that he was doing the same thing to me.

I parked right in Hallie's driveway this time, trying to focus on what I had to do.

She was already on the beach when I got there, wearing

Teddy's yellow OCCUPY PUTNAM shirt and leggings. Not even that long ago, the sight of her wearing it probably would have bothered me. But this morning it was just something I noticed, not something I really cared about.

"What?" she asked as I got closer to her, her hands on her hips. "You know it's early, right? I don't really appreciate being summoned like this."

And I didn't appreciate being framed for larceny, but I decided not to say it. Being done with this meant being done with those kinds of remarks. I waited until I was standing in front of her, and then I said, "Brenda Kreigs."

Hallie's face went pale for a moment, but then she regrouped, and unless you'd been watching for it, you might have missed it entirely. "Who?" she asked, almost convincing enough to believe.

"Your mom's pen name," I said, and when Hallie took a breath, her expression incredulous, I continued. "Just don't waste your time denying it. I know, okay?"

Hallie folded her arms across her chest. "So what are you going to do with that information?" she asked, and I could hear—maybe for the first time since this had all started—the real fear in her voice.

"Nothing," I said, and Hallie let out a short laugh.

"Sure," she said, shaking her head. "Like I'm going to believe that. You already ruined her career once, and now—"

"Which is exactly why I'm not going to do anything," I said. "The last thing I want to do is to hurt her again."

Hallie just looked at me, head tilted to the side, like she was trying to figure this out. "Then why tell me this?"

"I guess . . ." I started, then took a breath and went on. "I just wanted you to know there's a line I'm not going to cross." Hallie rolled her eyes. "Look," I said, "We both have something that can hurt our parents. You have my notebook. I know about your mom's name. Maybe we both decide to walk away."

"Mutually assured destruction?" Hallie asked, raising an eyebrow. "It's very cold war of you."

"You can do whatever you want," I said with a shrug. "Go ahead and show my dad the notebook." I hesitated here. Would this actually be easy for her? Did Hallie know about our parents? Were she and my dad already hanging out? "But just know that I'm not going to do anything."

Hallie looked utterly thrown by what had just happened, but like she was trying very hard *not* to look that way. I gave her a half-smile and turned, heading up the beach and back to my car. I'd only gotten a few feet before I turned back. "And you should tell Teddy the truth yourself," I said. "I promise I won't. But you should do it. He deserves that."

I walked to my car, but before I got in, I turned back to look at Hallie. She was still looking into the distance, but it seemed like—maybe—she was considering what I'd said.

⁂

"**A**re you sure you're supposed to be here?" Darcy asked, chewing her bottom lip.

I looked at her as I unfolded my Delicious apron. "Why not?" I asked. It was midafternoon, and I was coming to relieve her from the morning shift; I'd be working with Reid, who hadn't shown up yet. After I'd seen Hallie on the beach, I'd gone back home and taken a long nap. When I'd woken up to get ready for work, Sophie was already babysitting. There was a piece of me that was glad she hadn't been in the house. Being in a fight with Sophie was so unfamiliar to me that I really didn't know how to navigate it. But there was another piece of me that hated myself for even thinking this way, aware of her comings and goings and hoping that we wouldn't overlap.

My dad had been locked in his study, working, which I was also relieved about. It bought me just a little more time before I had to confess. But I had decided—I was going to do it after work.

I was also trying to sort out the fact that he was most likely dating Karen. Was I supposed to bring it up? I knew it wasn't like he *had* to have told me, but the fact that he hadn't was bothering me.

So I'd been glad for the excuse to leave the house and take my shift at the ice-cream parlor, even if it would mean working with Reid. Ever since the catering job, I really wasn't sure how much I could trust him.

"Well," Darcy said, and I could see that she was starting to blush. "I mean . . . because of what happened yesterday. I mean, weren't you fired?"

"I quit," I clarified. "And that was just the catering thing. It has nothing to do with the ice-cream parlor."

"Oh," Darcy said. "Okay. I guess I didn't understand."

"How are we looking?" I asked, mostly just to change the subject to *anything* else, including how well stocked we were on ice-cream flavors. I really didn't want to have to relive the events of the day before. I'd be thrilled if everyone could just collectively forget them, though I had a feeling this wasn't that likely.

"A little low on the blueberry cheesecake," Darcy said, peering down into the case. "And we could probably use another rocky road, just to be on the safe side."

"Got it," I said. Darcy started to head toward the freezer, but I shook my head. "I'll go get them," I said. I gestured to the empty store. "It's dead here anyway."

"Thanks, Gemma," Darcy said. Her phone beeped, and she pulled it out of her pocket. "That's Chaz," she said, frowning down at it. "We've been having *such* a hard time getting in touch with each other. I'm just going to text him back. . . ."

"Take off early," I said as I headed toward the walk-in. "Reid will be here any second. And I'll be able to hear the bell if anyone's coming in."

"Really?" Darcy asked, looking disproportionately grateful. "That would be amazing. Because we haven't talked—I mean, texted—in such a long time, and it would be nice to really catch up, you know?"

"Totally," I said, restraining myself, as ever, from enlightening her to the reality of her situation. "Tell, um, Chaz I say hi."

"I will," Darcy said, already ducking into the break room and grabbing her bag. "Thanks, Gemma! I owe you one."

"See you later," I called as I grabbed the sweatshirt from under the counter and headed into the walk-in. I very carefully propped the door open with the stepladder. I was pretty sure I wouldn't need it to get either the blueberry cheesecake or the rocky road. But I'd rather have to strain to reach something a little bit than accidentally get trapped in here.

I found the rocky road easily enough—it was one of our most popular flavors, and on the lowest shelf for easy access. The blueberry cheesecake, however, was proving elusive. It was a seasonal promotion, which meant I had no idea where it was kept. I was kneeling down to look at the bottom shelf, wishing that someone had instituted an alphabetizing system, already feeling goose bumps start to pop up on my arms, when I thought I heard the bell above the door jangle. "Hello?" I called, straightening up a little. I didn't want to go all the way out there if it was only Reid. It was always that much harder to head back into the freezer once you'd gotten warm again.

When I didn't hear anyone respond, I pushed myself to my feet. The last thing I needed was a customer feeling ignored—or, more worryingly, someone deciding to rob the place. "Hello?" I called again toward the crack in the door.

"Hi," a voice called back. It was familiar. I couldn't be certain, but I was pretty sure it sounded like Josh.

I started to cross toward the door as it swung open, and there he was—Josh, standing in the doorway of the freezer. It was unexpected enough to see him there that it took a moment for me to wrap my head around it. "Hey," I said, and I noticed that as I did, I could start to see my breath. "Uh, Reid's not here yet."

"No," Josh said. He looked at me, then took a breath. "I actually wanted to talk to you." He took a step forward, and as he did the door swung shut behind him, knocking aside the ladder.

"*No!*" I yelled, darting toward the swinging door as fast as I could. But even as I reached for it, I knew I was too late.

I was locked in the freezer. With Josh.

CHAPTER 23

"**A**nd you're sure nobody can hear us?" Josh asked from the opposite side of the freezer.

I shook my head. Despite my already telling him this, Josh had spent the last ten minutes yelling at the door. I was just trying not to panic. I kept telling myself that Reid would be here any moment and he'd let us out. Josh had sent him multiple texts telling him that when he got to work, he needed to go straight to the freezer immediately. I was just hoping nobody would knock over the shop in the absence of any workers behind the counter. And also that Reid had been wrong about how long it takes for hypothermia to set in.

"But Reid will be here soon," I said, noting with some distress that my teeth had started to chatter on the last word. I'd put on the sweatshirt—Josh had insisted I take it—but it really wasn't doing all that much to keep me warm. The fact that I was in jean cutoffs and flip-flops probably wasn't helping either.

Josh looked across the freezer at me, and I rubbed my hands up and down my arms. It wasn't that I was mad at Josh—it was an innocent mistake. Most freezers weren't potential death-traps—but I still wasn't sure why he'd come to talk to me in the first place, since all we'd done so far was discuss freezer logistics. After a moment of silence, I looked back at him. This was pretty much the opposite of an ideal situation, but I couldn't help thinking that it was the first time in a while that he wasn't trying to get away from me, shutting me out, or glaring at me. I would never have wished for this situation, but it made for a nice change.

"I'm sorry," he finally said, and I noticed that his teeth were starting to chatter a little too. "I should have been more careful when I opened the door."

"You didn't know," I said with a shrug. I tried not to notice that my muscles were already starting to feel stiff. I immediately regretted doubting Reid about his quick-onset frostbite theory. It was *cold* in here.

"I just . . ." Josh said. It looked like he was having difficulty speaking, but I honestly wasn't sure if the reason was the subject matter or the fact that I could see his breath every time he exhaled. "I guess I just wanted to talk to you about yesterday."

"Ah," I said. I flexed my fingers a few times and hopped from foot to foot. I knew it wasn't the most attractive of moves—it probably just looked like I had to go to the bathroom—but I was starting to go numb if I stayed in one spot too long. I shook my head. "I didn't steal anything."

"I believe you," Josh said. "I guess I'm just trying to understand what happened. That's all."

I looked at him. It wasn't like I hadn't seen him since the night of the Fourth. But each of the times I'd seen him had been fraught and stressful. Even though this was the opposite of a peaceful environment, it was like I could actually see him, the Josh I remembered, for the first time in what felt like a while. "I think you should talk to Hallie," I finally said. I knew that I could tell him right then and there what she'd been up to all summer, how she'd hurt me, what she'd pulled him into, how she used him. But only a few hours ago I had decided I was done with all that, and I certainly didn't think being done with it included selling her out to her brother, however tempting that might be.

Josh nodded, then rubbed his own hands together and blew into them. "It would *really* not be a great day for Reid to be late," he said.

"Or call in sick," I added. "He hasn't responded to your texts?"

Josh shook his head. "How are your telepathy skills?" he asked, deadpan, and I felt myself smile.

"Rusty," I said, and Josh smiled back. It only lasted for a second, though, before he looked down at the floor again. I bounced up and down on my toes, trying to think warm thoughts. Sandy beaches, hot asphalt, boiling water. It didn't seem to be working, though. I was starting to shiver, and I'd lost feeling in one of my toes. It was my pinkie toe, so it's not like it was really important or anything, but still. I would have preferred to have feeling in it all the same.

"How . . . how are you doing?" Josh asked, and it looked to me like he was starting to shiver as well.

"Okay," I managed. "You know. F-fine." My teeth had started chattering too much to really speak, and I pressed my lips together, trying to stop them from moving.

"Did you . . . ever take any first aid courses?" Josh asked, and I just shook my head. I didn't understand where the question was coming from, but maybe this was his version of small talk. Maybe he was trying to keep things between us as boring and platonic as possible. In which case . . . mission accomplished. "I did," he said, and I could have sworn that he started blushing. I wanted to encourage him to keep doing it—it was probably helping to keep him warm. "Um, I was a . . . Boy Scout."

I couldn't stop myself from smiling at the image of that. Josh must have seen, because his blush got more pronounced. "Shut up. Anyway. Um . . . from what I can remember about preventing frostbite and hypothermia . . ."

"Yes?" I asked, suddenly beyond grateful that Josh possessed this kind of knowledge. I'd taken a babysitting training course when I was thirteen, but all that had covered was how to call the poison control hot line, and also how to prevent children from consuming things that were poisonous.

"Um . . . the best thing to do in situations like this is to utilize body heat."

"Great," I chattered, waiting for him to tell me how to do that. Josh just looked down at the ground, and I suddenly understood what he meant—and also why he was blushing. He meant our *combined* body heat. "Oh," I said, nodding a few too many times. "Okay. Um."

"So is it . . ." Josh started as he gestured across the freezer to me. "Can I . . . ?" I nodded, and he crossed the freezer to me, standing closer than he had since the night of the Fourth, the night that he'd given me the best kiss of my life. He cleared his throat. "Okay," he said again, and now that we were close together, I could see the flush in his cheeks, even under his golden tan. "The parts of the body that possess the most heat are the neck and the, um, stomach."

I blinked, and nodded a few times, trying to get my head around the idea. I had seen Josh's stomach when we'd been swimming together, and his abs were almost as impressive as Ford's—but it would have been superweird to suddenly start touching his stomach in an ice-cream freezer. I looked up at him, and I had a feeling we were both thinking the same thing. "Neck?" I asked just as Josh said, almost at exactly the same time, "Neck."

"Okay," he said, rubbing his hands together again. "Go ahead. Whenever you're ready."

"Oh," I said. I hadn't realized I would be going first. But then I suddenly remembered Josh opening up car doors for me and pulling out chairs. He had always been a gentleman, and apparently, the fact that we were both slowly becoming human Popsicles wasn't going to change that. "All right." I rubbed my hands together, trying to get some heat back in them. "So do I just . . . ?" I asked, moving them toward his neck.

"Like this," Josh said, taking my hands and putting them on either side of his neck. He winced when my hands touched his skin, but I had a feeling it was because they were cold, not because he couldn't stand to have me touching him. At least, I hoped.

His Boy Scout training must have been good, because his neck, while not hot, was warm, certainly warmer than my hands, and it was like I could feel them start to defrost a little. I could feel his pulse beating just underneath my palms, and I looked over his shoulder at the containers of coffee and vanilla bean, trying not to think about how strange this was. If I'd looked up at him, we would have been close enough to kiss. "Okay," I said after a few moments, taking my hands back. "Your turn."

"It's really okay," Josh said, even as I noticed with some alarm that his lips were starting to turn blue.

"Don't be silly," I said, and I reached for both of his hands. They were like blocks of ice, and that was all I was thinking about as I placed them on either side of my neck. I tried not to flinch as they hit my skin, but I now felt I understood Josh's reaction—they were so cold, it was painful.

"Are you okay?" Josh asked, and I looked up at him.

"Fine," I said, trying to smile, instinctively putting my hands on the outside of his to try to keep them there, to get them warm. But a moment later it hit me what an intimate position this was. I didn't want to think about it, but I was suddenly having flashbacks to the last time we'd been this close—when we'd been kissing each other for all we were worth.

"Your turn," Josh said after a moment, lifting my hands up and placing them on his neck again—but a little higher this time, almost underneath his jawline.

Maybe it was just my body reacting on instinct, sensing his body heat, but I was moving closer to him before I even realized I was doing it, so I was almost pressed up against him. I didn't try to move away after I'd realized what I'd done. It was like I was too cold to be embarrassed.

I knew this was pretty much the opposite of an ideal moment. And maybe the cold was going to my brain, because without really thinking about it, I said, "Josh? I'm really, really sorry. I hope you know that. I never meant to hurt you."

Josh looked down at me, right into my eyes. And it seemed—though this might have just been wishful thinking—that the anger I was used to seeing in his expression was beginning to dissipate. He nodded but didn't take his eyes from mine. "Gemma Tucker," he said slowly, like he was trying out my name.

I nodded, feeling his pulse underneath my fingers. We were so close, just a breath away. "You've got it," I said.

He looked at me for a moment longer, then gave me a smile. "It's nice to meet you," he finally said.

I looked into his eyes, and for a minute it was like I forgot all about being cold. I searched his expression, trying to figure out what was happening here. Was anything happening here? The silence went on, suddenly becoming charged. Josh tilted his head just slightly to the side, and I felt my pulse start to race. I stretched up toward him as he tilted his head down to me. I closed my eyes—

"Hello?"

My eyes flew open, and I saw the door swing out. Reid was standing in the doorway with Kendall behind him, both looking very confused.

I dropped my hands from Josh's neck and took a step back, still trying to understand what was happening—and what had just almost happened. In other circumstances I probably would have jumped away, but I didn't currently feel capable of moving that quickly. I suddenly realized what this probably looked like—the two of us pressed together in the freezer.

"Hey," Reid said, looking baffled by the whole situation. We left the freezer and walked in a group back out into the ice-cream parlor, and it was like I could practically feel the heat flooding through me, despite the fact I'd never really thought of Sweet & Delicious as being all that warm.

Josh left pretty quickly after that, Kendall telling him to run his hands under tepid water as soon as he got home and to avoid being chilled for the next several days. She sent Reid down the street to Quonset Coffee to get some hot tea. And then she turned to me, her expression concerned. "Are you feeling okay?" she asked.

I nodded. What I was really feeling was incredibly confused as to what had just gone on in there with Josh. But I had a feeling Kendall might not appreciate that much information. And now that I was no longer trapped in the freezer, I was feeling much better. "I am," I said, wondering if maybe she'd give me the day off to recover.

"Oh, good," she said with a relieved smile. A moment later, though, her smile disappeared. "You're fired."

CHAPTER 24

walked my bike along the side of the road, my thoughts spinning. I had just been fired. And if I hadn't quit the catering
job, I would have been fired twice in the past twenty-four hours.
It was really not a great track record.

It seemed that Kendall had been intending to have a "serious conversation" with me about my behavior at the benefit.
That morning Blair had given her the rundown on her poten-
tially felonious employee. But when she'd arrived to find the
store deserted, and me in a compromising position in the freezer
with a non-employee, apparently her decision was made. She
didn't want to hear that I'd just been getting ice cream when
the door closed, and wouldn't even listen to Reid as he tried to
explain why he'd been late (he'd accidentally set his phone to
military time again, and hadn't realized he was late until he'd
happened to see a clock). She told me how much trouble the
store could have gotten into if Josh had gotten seriously hurt in
the freezer (she didn't seem to care that much about me), then

went into all the things that could have happened with the store just sitting empty. Then she told me that my employee T-shirts would be coming out of my paycheck, and not to return for my shift the following day. I was just glad that nobody else had been around to see it. Especially Darcy—if she'd seen me get fired and almost-fired two days in a row, I wasn't sure her opinion of me would ever recover.

I slowed my (literal) roll as I started to think about the consequences. Now that the reality of the situation was sinking in, I was going to have to deal with the fallout. It wasn't like I was going to miss working at the ice-cream parlor all that much, but it was still embarrassing to be *fired*. Mostly, I was dreading having to tell my dad. He'd been so proud that I'd gotten this job. And I hadn't even lasted long enough to collect a paycheck. Also . . . I slowed even more as something else occurred to me. How was I supposed to pay him back for the cheese—and the bathing suit—if I didn't have a job? After disappointing my dad in various ways all summer, I really didn't think I needed to add to it.

Also—what had just been about to happen with Josh? My thoughts were flying in every direction, and I kept having to steer my bike back toward the sidewalk. For a second I let myself replay the moment, Josh's head tilting down to mine . . . Out of nowhere, though, I found myself thinking of Ford. Which was crazy, but even so, I couldn't seem to stop him from surfacing.

Needing to stop this train of thought, I tried to make

myself concentrate on what I was going to do about the job—or lack thereof. By the time I was just a few minutes away from Bruce's house, I had come up with a plan. I wouldn't tell my dad just yet that I'd been fired. I'd find another job first so then I could just tell him I'd become much more interested in something else, and maybe I wouldn't even have to go into the circumstances of leaving my last job. This plan buoyed my mood, and when I felt my phone buzz with a call in my back pocket, and I saw it was Ford, I answered with a cheerful, "Aloha there!"

"Gemma." Ford's voice was more serious—and angrier—than I'd ever heard it. "What did you *do*?"

I stopped dead in my tracks. "What?" I asked, suddenly wondering if news of my firing had somehow gotten to Ford. Had Kendall put it on the Internet or something? Wasn't that private information? "What, um, are you talking about?"

"Where are you?" Ford asked, which was not at all an answer to what I'd asked him, which was starting to make me even more nervous.

"Um, I'm almost to Bruce's," I said, picking up my pace. "Down the road. What's going on?"

"I'm coming to you," Ford said, but then hung up before I could ask him any more questions. I got on the bike and started riding, holding my phone in one hand, just so I could see if Ford called or texted again. I had no idea what this was about, but I was getting the feeling it was about more than my being fired from the ice-cream parlor. But *what*? I hadn't even done anything wrong recently. Unless Karen had told my dad about how I'd gotten Hallie to cut her hair. I figured this was most likely it, but a moment later doubt crept in. Why would Ford be calling me about that?

Before I could come up with an answer, Ford was flying down the road toward me on his skateboard. And even though I knew there was a lot more going on at the moment, I couldn't help but notice how cool he looked, bending backward on the board as he took the curves of the road. I got off my bike and stood next to it, and when he got close to me, he jumped off and somehow kicked the board so that it popped up and he caught it. "Hey," I said, trying not to let him see how impressed I'd just been with his board-kicking move. "What's happening?"

Ford took his aviators off and looked right at me, his dark eyes searching my face. "You didn't have anything to do with this?" he asked. "Because I wouldn't have told you if I'd thought you were going to turn around and do this."

"Told me what?" I asked, and I could hear my voice rising. Someone really needed to start using some nouns or adjectives around here, and the sooner the better. "I have no idea what you're talking about."

Ford looked at me for a moment longer, then nodded and tucked his aviators over the collar of his T-shirt. He pulled out his phone and handed it to me. It looked like the home page of an Internet gossip site I would sometimes visit if there was nothing happening on Friendverse. I squinted against the glare to read it, and as I did, I felt my jaw drop.

***Once Bitten* Shocker!**

The author of everyone's favorite sexy vampire series has been revealed! "Brenda Kreigs," as it turns out, is just a pseudonym for Karen Bridges. Bridges published a single book half a decade ago that was pulled largely because of widespread rumors she had plagiarized it. And far from living a quiet life on a remote island, as her publicity department would have you believe, Karen Bridges is living the high life on her royalties, with a townhouse in Manhattan and an estate in the Hamptons. The news has not been confirmed with her publisher, but it was obtained by someone who would know the truth—a daughter of one of the main players, currently living in the house where production on the movie adaptation is being set up, was our source.

I looked up at Ford, struggling to breathe normally. "It's not true," I said, shaking my head as I read it over again. There it was, as clear as anything—the direct accusation that I had been behind this. "I promise, Ford, I would never have done this."

Ford nodded. "I didn't think you would," he said. He let out a long breath. "But this is really, really bad, Gem."

I closed my eyes for a moment, wishing I could just go back to a time when things made sense. I opened them again when I realized I no longer knew when that was. Before Teddy had dumped me, probably. When my life had gone along in a much less dramatic fashion.

"It was Hallie," I said, realizing I shouldn't even have wondered who was behind this. I made myself try to keep breathing. So much for mutually assured destruction. Why hadn't I foreseen this—that Hallie would preemptively drop *my* bomb to make me look bad?

Ford let out a low whistle. "She'd really do this to her own mom?"

"It seems like it." I should have seen it coming. She'd been willing to hurt Josh—apparently, she was willing to hurt her mother too. "I . . . went to see her this morning after you left. I told her that I knew, but that I wasn't going to do anything about it." Ford started to shake his head, and I added quickly, "I meant it like a peace offering! I wanted to show her I was done."

"And she turned around and used it against you," he said. He let out a long breath. "You might want to reconsider that whole 'walking away' thing."

"Weren't you the one who just told me that revenge never leads to anything good?"

"Well, that was before she might have derailed Bruce's movie." My head snapped up, and I stared at him. "Apparently, one of the conditions of her giving him the rights was that her identity be totally protected. You should see how many lawyers are already at the house. If she wants to pull out of this, and keep her option money, it looks like she can."

"But . . ." I started, trying to understand what was happening. "But it wasn't me!"

"Everyone thinks it is, though," Ford said, shaking his head. "And the perception might be enough."

We just looked at each other for a moment, and I could feel myself on the verge of tears. Ford started to walk toward the house, carrying his skateboard, and I followed, walking my bike. I still quite couldn't believe this was happening. It was one thing for Hallie to mess with me. It was another to mess with Bruce, and my dad, and even her own mother. I wanted nothing more than to talk to Sophie about it—except for the fact that I was currently fighting with my best friend, and she clearly didn't want to talk to me.

"How bad is this?" I asked, my voice small.

"Bad," Ford said, shaking his head. "I wanted to get you before you walked into the house. I think it might be best if you avoid Bruce and Rosie for the time being."

"Shouldn't I explain that it wasn't me?" I asked as we reached the driveway and started walking up it. "I mean, won't they believe me?"

Ford winced, and I realized that Hallie had been playing a long game much better than I had. Bruce and Rosie might have believed that the cheese wasn't from me—but if I tried the same line again, they probably wouldn't. She'd turned me into the Girl Who Cried Innocence, and I hadn't even realized I'd walked into her trap until it was too late. "I'd maybe just go talk to your dad," Ford said, and as we approached the house, I realized he was leading me around to the side entrance, the one where all Bruce's deliveries and bribes were sent.

"I can't even go through the front door?" I asked, feeling my stomach sink as I followed behind Ford.

Ford just shook his head. "*I don't even want to go through* the front door," he said. "Have you ever encountered a pack of lawyers who've been pulled away from their golf courses and spinning classes?" He gave me a half-smile. "None of them want to be here, and most of them are in shorts. It's *really* not pretty." I tried to smile back at that, but I gave up when it turned wobbly halfway through. Ford held open the door for me, and I stepped inside. I was still trying to understand how Bruce's—which had felt like my home only a few hours ago— now felt like a minefield, a place I had to carefully tiptoe through. I didn't like it, not at all.

I realized that Ford had picked the perfect door to get me back in—my dad's office was just down the hall. "Thanks," I said as I walked up to the door. I tried to think about how I would tell him I appreciated it—not only the heads up, but for being on my side throughout the whole Hallie thing and never once judging me.

"You'll be fine," he said, and then after a moment added, "eventually. I'm sure. You'll pass mustard." I felt myself smile at that for real. "I'll see how far I can get with Bruce and Rosie," he said. "Let me know how it goes with your dad." I nodded, and Ford gave me a quick hug before heading down the hallway that would take him to the main part of the house.

I took a deep breath, then knocked on my dad's door. "Yeah?" I heard from inside. I didn't want to give him the opportunity to tell me not to come in if I announced myself, so I just pushed the door open.

My dad was sitting on the couch in his office, reading something. He looked up when I came in, and his expression was not one of pleasure at seeing his only child. He did not look happy to see me, in the least. In fact, it looked like his expression as I walked in was one filled with dread. "Dad," I said immediately, figuring that I needed to get in front of this as soon as possible, explain my side in things. "Ford told me what's going on. But I swear, I never told that Web site about Karen. I promise. I would never have done that to her. I wouldn't have hurt her that way."

My dad just looked at me for a long moment, then nodded. "I see," he said. He lifted up what he'd been reading, and I saw now that it wasn't a book. It was a very familiar green notebook, one I'd last seen when I was eleven. "Then do you mind explaining this?"

CHAPTER 25

I just stared at it and realized that I'd been outplayed yet again.

I should have known that if Hallie was going to throw my bomb, she was of course going to throw hers too. She was hitting me with everything she had, and I had nothing left to fight back with.

"Where?" I asked, when I trusted myself to speak again. "I mean, how . . ."

"It came by messenger twenty minutes ago," my dad said, setting the notebook in front of him on the table. "Made for some interesting reading." He turned to look at me, and I could see his eyes were red. I also heard a tone in my dad's voice I hadn't heard in years—he was mad at me. He was *furious*.

"I . . ." I started. I was not prepared to talk to my dad about this right now. Yes, I'd planned on telling him today. But I'd planned on bringing back ice cream for both of us to soften him up, and then introducing the subject in the right way. Not like this. Not being ambushed by it. Not with him learning this from someone else. "So the thing is . . ."

"Is it true?" my dad asked, standing up and turning to face me.

There was nothing else to say. It was the secret I'd been keeping from him for five years, and I hadn't even been the one to tell him. "Yes," I said, looking at my hands so I wouldn't have to see his reaction to this, the disappointment that I could practically feel coming off him in waves. I took a big shaky breath, feeling the need to at least try to explain myself, though I wasn't sure if that would do any good at this point. "I was afraid you and Mom were going to split up for good," I said. My voice was wobbling, and I just hoped I'd be able to make it through this without starting to cry. "So I did . . . those things. But I've always regretted it. And actually this whole summer, I've been trying to—"

"So it was you," my dad said, and I felt tears spring to my eyes when I heard his voice—full of heartbreak and disbelief. "You were the one who started that rumor about Karen. Gem . . . that was you?" His voice broke on the last word, and I looked at my dad; then a second later, I wished I hadn't. This was miles beyond all the other times he'd been disappointed in me. This was something I wasn't sure we would be able to come back from.

"I'm sorry," I said, and I was crying now—I couldn't help it. The way he was looking at me, like he didn't know who I was, was breaking my heart. "I'm so sorry. I never imagined it would go that far. . . . I just wanted—"

"I can't believe you did this," my dad said, his voice rising. "And that you would keep it a secret from me—"

"What about the secrets you've kept from me?" I was blurting out these words before I'd even thought about what I was going to say. "Like the fact that you were dating Karen five years ago. Like . . ." I hesitated, then figured I had nothing to lose, and went ahead and said it. "Like the fact you're dating her now."

My dad just blinked at me for a moment, like he was as surprised as I was that we were having this conversation—that we were having *any* kind of a real conversation. "I . . ." he started, then adjusted his glasses. "I'm not talking to you about this."

"I know," I said, and my voice broke, even as I made myself say the words. "Of course you're not. We *never* talk. It's like you just want to be in my life when it's fun and easy." My father and I just stared at each other, and I wondered if he was feeling what I was—that we were in completely uncharted territory at the moment.

"Well, it's certainly neither of those things right now," my dad said, his voice tired and broken. "I need some time alone, Gemma. I'm still trying to get my head around what you've done."

Just like that—hearing how disappointed in me my dad sounded—it was like my anger deflated, leaving only the terrible sadness from before. I swallowed hard and wiped at my cheeks. When I managed to speak, my voice was cracking. "I just . . . I only . . ."

"Please." My dad shook his head. "Please leave my office. I can't even look at you right now."

I bit my lip hard, and nodded. "Okay," I whispered. I started to walk toward the door, hoping with every step that my dad would call me back, say it was okay, show me that he'd be able to forgive me, tell me that we could actually talk about things. I had my hand on the doorknob, trying to think if there was anything at all I could say that might help me explain why I'd done it. But in a moment of terrible clarity, the kind that never seems to come until it's too late, I realized that there was no explanation. I'd done cruel things that had directly impacted my dad's happiness, and then kept them a secret for five years. He didn't have to find out like this—because I'd had five years of opportunities to tell him the truth. I'd just been too much of a coward. And because I'd wanted to avoid a scene just like the one I was currently in.

"Gemma?" My dad's voice was cold now, all the emotion leached from it, which was somehow the worst thing of all. "Close the door behind you."

My last shred of hope gone, I forced myself out the door and shut it behind me. I leaned back against it for a moment, trying to get myself to think. Bruce and Rosie thought I'd betrayed them, and were furious with me. My dad couldn't stand to even be in my presence. I'd been fired twice in two days. I was fighting with my best friend for the first time ever, with no resolution in sight. Hallie had managed to wreck or damage all the relationships I cared about the most. She had won.

She'd told me she had, on the beach the night of the Fourth, and I realized now that I should have believed her. I shouldn't have even been trying to get revenge. I should have just accepted it then and there. She'd told me to go on home to Connecticut, and I should have just listened and saved everyone a lot of heartache.

A thought occurred to me suddenly, and it was like a single ray of sun piercing a pitch-black sky. I didn't have to be here, in this house, where nobody wanted me. I could just remove myself from the equation.

I pushed myself off my dad's door and hurried down the hallway, just wanting to make it to my room, throw my stuff in a bag, and get out. I wasn't going to stay here a minute longer, the place where I hurt people over and over, and made things worse when I was trying to fix them. I was out of there.

I was going home.

CHAPTER 26

I hit the lights, tossed my quilted duffel on my bed, and looked around the room.

I'd only been gone a month and a half. But somehow it seemed like I hadn't been there in a very long time. Before pretending to be Sophie. Before meeting Hallie again. Before Josh. And because so much had happened, the room felt like it belonged to someone younger and more naive. The piles of discarded clothes on my chair were from someone who'd packed hoping for the best, planning on a quiet summer at the beach, thinking she was just going to have a nice time in the Hamptons with her dad.

I'd called a cab from Bruce's, then gone directly to the train station. I hadn't even looked at the schedule, just waited with my duffel on the platform until one showed up. I'd called another cab when I got back to Putnam, and as I opened the front door, I was beyond grateful that I knew our alarm code—3474—also known as *F-I-S-H*. I'd written Ford and Gwyneth an e-mail from the station, and texted my dad on the train, saying that I was going to stay with friends for a few days, and that I was sorry. I saw that he'd read the message but hadn't responded, which had left me with a horrible churning in my stomach, one that I wasn't sure was ever going to go away.

I kicked off my flip-flops and crossed to my bed. It seemed like being upright was getting harder with every step I took. I shoved the clothes that hadn't made the packing cut onto the floor, then pulled back the covers and crawled into bed, not bothering to get undressed. I hadn't realized how exhausted I was until I let my eyes close.

≈≈≈≈≈

It's a rainy day. Hallie and I are sitting on the floor of her beach house, listening to the rain hit the roof, and the occasional ping! as drops fall through the hole in the roof and into our sand castle bucket that we've repurposed for the moment. Our parents are doing research at the library, which sounds so boring, neither of us asks for any information, and it wouldn't have crossed my mind to, not then. I'm still in the happy haze, not realizing there's a ticking clock on all this—but especially on Hallie, sitting next to her as a friend, without ulterior motives.

We've played Monopoly, Go Fish, War, Sorry!, and Battleship. We're down to the last two games in the house's collection—chess and dominoes. Hallie is trying to teach me chess while I set up the dominoes in long curving rows.

"You have to think at least two moves ahead," she's saying as she frowns at the board, pushing her hair behind her ear.

"Preferably three. You have to anticipate your opponent's move, plan for it, and act accordingly. If you're reacting to the present circumstance, you've already lost." She shrugged and scratched a mosquito bite on her shoulder. "At least that's what my dad said. He taught me to play. Got it?"

I hadn't really been paying attention, but I nodded like I had been. "Sure," I said as I worked at balancing the dominoes on the house's uneven wooden floorboards. "Anticipate. Opponent. Got it."

"And do you understand about lateral moves?" Hallie asked. She usually had a lot of patience, but I had the distinct sense I was testing hers today.

"Totally," I said, nodding. "I guess I'm just confused about the point of it all."

Hallie laid the queen down on her side. "Checkmate," she said.

I nodded and then felt myself smile. I flicked the lead domino and watched as they crashed into each other, one tapping the next, until they'd all fallen down. "So it's pretty much the same thing?"

Hallie shook her head, but I could see that she was smiling. "No," she said, a laugh hiding somewhere in the back of her throat. "Mine requires skill."

I gestured to the fallen dominoes all around us. "But mine was way more entertaining to watch." I grinned at her. "Right?"

opened my eyes and looked around, immediately squinting them into slits—not only was bright sun streaming in through my windows, but it appeared I'd gone to sleep with the lights on. And all my clothes on, which explained why the waistband of my jean shorts was currently digging into my hip.

I sat up in bed and, once my eyes had adjusted, peered at the numbers on my bedside clock—it was ten A.M., the following morning. I'd slept for over twelve hours, which might explain why I was currently so hungry. I decided to go downstairs— maybe Ford had picked up food, or maybe he'd managed to sneak in some dairy. . . . I started to roll out of bed and then realized, all in a rush, where I was. I wasn't in the Hamptons. I was at home in Putnam, because I had managed to mess up everything in my life, possibly irreparably. I closed my eyes for a moment, but knew, somewhere deep down, that nothing would be solved by going back to sleep. I sighed, then forced myself to get up.

Twenty minutes later I'd taken a long shower and gotten dressed in clothes I hadn't brought with me to Bruce's—I'd been wearing the same suitcase's worth of outfits for so long now that this was disproportionately exciting. I'd combed out my wet hair but hadn't dried it yet as I wandered around my room. It felt a little bit like I was an anthropologist, examining a past civilization with an objective eye. How had I never noticed before just how many pictures there were of me and Teddy? Pictures of him, and him and me, covered almost every available surface. There were a few of me and Sophie, and one of me and my parents, but that was it. Who was the girl in all the pictures, the one who looked like me, who was just smiling at him adoringly? I really didn't like to see it. I was pulling down all the pictures I'd pinned up or stuck into the corners of my mirror when I heard the doorbell ring.

I froze, thinking fast. I hadn't figured out much of a plan beyond "go back to Putnam and figure out a plan later." I wasn't sure how long I was going to be able to stay there while keeping both of my parents in the dark. If the circumstances were different, I probably would have been able to tell them both that I was staying with the other parent, and bet on the fact that they wouldn't check with each other. But since my mom was in *Scotland*, I wasn't sure my dad was going to just believe I had joined her there—not without at least a phone call to discuss logistics. I didn't want to answer the door and expose myself as being home, in case it was a friend of my mom's or something—but wouldn't all her friends know she was away for the summer?

The bell rang again, and I decided to answer it—after all, if someone had seen my light on all night, the jig might already be up. I took the stairs two at a time and headed directly for the front door. "Coming!" I called as I pulled it open.

Sophie was standing on the other side, carrying a tray with two iced lattes and a white pastry bag. "Hi," she said, giving me a slightly nervous smile.

"Hi," I said, smiling automatically in return. I stepped back and opened the door wider for her to come in. I was surprised that she was there, but I wasn't sure I'd ever been happier to see my best friend.

"Sorry for just showing up like this," she said as she led the way to the kitchen—Sophie knew my house as well as her own. "I just . . ." She set the coffees down on the kitchen counter and turned to me, twisting her hands together. "I'm really sorry," she blurted, and I shook my head.

"No, *I'm* sorry," I said immediately. "I'm the one who needs to apologize. I should never have distrusted you. Or spied on you. You've done so much to help me this summer, and I'm not sure I ever even thanked you."

Sophie gave me a trembly smile. "Are we okay?"

I nodded. "Yes," I said, and it felt like someone had just lifted a giant weight off my back. No matter what else was happening, Sophie and I were okay. I had my best friend back. We hugged, and then Sophie pulled a plastic cup out of her carrying tray.

"For you," she said, and I noticed that it was my iced latte summer usual—soy with vanilla—and that *GEMMA* was written in giant letters along the side. "I had them put your name on it this time," she said, and I felt myself smile. "Just in case."

"Thank you," I said, taking a long drink. Sophie pulled bagels and cream cheese out of the white paper bag, and I felt my stomach rumble just looking at them. "This is great," I said, as I pulled down plates for us, and Sophie pried the lid off the cream cheese. "Dairy," I said as I picked it up, marveling at the sight. Then I set it down, suddenly remembering something. "But . . . um, aren't you supposed to be working?"

"I called in sick," Sophie said with a shrug. "It felt weird to be in the Hamptons when you weren't there."

"So you know what happened, then?" I asked, knowing the answer even as I said it. I had a feeling it would have been hard to miss the phalanx of lawyers that had stormed the place. Sophie nodded, and I bit my lip. "Was everyone still really mad at me?"

"More confused than anything else," she said, taking a bite of her bagel. "Ford told me what really happened," she said. "Not that he would have needed to," she added quickly. "I knew you wouldn't have done that to your dad or Bruce."

"I wish they knew that," I said quietly. We ate in silence for a moment, and then I said, straining to be upbeat, "Well, we'll just have to make the rest of the summer here really great."

"Absolutely," Sophie said, her voice matching mine in the same faux-cheerful cadence.

"We can totally have fun here," I said with confidence I really didn't feel. "Who needs the Hamptons?"

"Exactly," Sophie said, nodding, her tone not getting any more convincing. "I mean, who wants to stay in a stupid mansion on the beach? Ugh."

"Right," I said. We looked at each other and then both started laughing.

"Well," Sophie said, shooting me a smile, "I'm sure people here will be glad to know we're back. You'll have to text Abby West-Smith."

I frowned at Sophie and then said around a mouthful of my bagel, "Why would I text her? I've never even met her. She's your friend."

Sophie's eyes widened. "I've never met her. I always thought she was *your* friend."

We stared at each other in horror for a moment, and then I

realized what it had to mean. Sophie must have too, because we both said in unison, "Hallie."

⸳⸳⸳⸳⸳⸳

"**W**ow," Ford said half an hour later. We were video-chatting, Sophie and I on my laptop, Ford on his iPad. When we'd realized what was going on, I'd suggested we turn to the closest thing we had to an IT expert. "I have to say, I underestimated her. This is beyond what I thought she was capable of." We'd told him the situation, and Ford had looked up the Friendverse profile of Abby West-Smith. It hadn't taken him long to find out that it was a fake account—her friend numbers were padded out with automated and corporate accounts, her biographical data didn't check out, and she had really only interacted on the site with me and Sophie—and, more recently, Teddy.

"But we've been friends—" I started.

"*Friends,*" Sophie amended, putting air quotes around the word.

"For, like, four years," I finished. "Hallie was . . . She was doing this four years ago?" She'd been spying on me this whole time? The thought, frankly, was making me nauseous.

On-screen, Ford nodded and adjusted his glasses. "She's been playing a long game," he said grimly. "I guess we can assume that this is how she found out about Teddy in the first place."

I nodded. My head was spinning, but it was at least nice to get an answer to my question—just *how* Hallie had known so much about my life. It turned out that the whole time I'd been feeling sorry for poor catfished Darcy, Hallie had been doing the exact same thing to me.

"And that's probably how she found out about the cheese," Sophie said, shaking her head.

"Right," Ford said, leaning closer to the monitor. "So I think what you're going to want to do is defriend her immediately, and—"

"But I never put anything on Friendverse about the cheese," I said slowly. I really hadn't been on it much at all this summer. "Why would I have done that?" I tried to think back on it. "I called you, didn't I?"

Sophie shook her head. "I just think you texted me." She pulled out her phone and started scrolling through it. "Yeah, you texted me not to bring any cheese into the house because of Bruce's diet."

"But it's not like Hallie would have seen your text," I said, now more confused than ever. "She had your phone way before that."

"Wait," Ford said on-screen, leaning forward. "Hallie had your phone?"

"Yeah," Sophie said. "After the party on the Fourth. She gave it back to Gemma, though."

Ford shook his head. "I wish you would have told me this before. Okay, Sophie, we're going to do a diagnostic to see what's going on."

I took a step back so Sophie would have a clear view of the monitor while I half listened, my thoughts spinning. Ford talked Sophie through the steps, and they discovered that while Hallie had Sophie's phone, she'd installed software on it that took screenshots of her texts and then had them forwarded to a blocked account—presumably Hallie's.

I listened to Sophie freaking out about this and Ford trying to talk her down, and wondered when this would ever end. When I'd stop being surprised that Hallie was doing something terrible to me. When she'd stop getting my friends involved.

"So what was she *doing* with my texts?" I heard Sophie ask, sounding increasingly freaked out. "Some of them were, um, private."

"Barista?" Ford asked knowingly, and I wondered if there was anyone Sophie hadn't spilled her romantic saga to. Probably even Teddy knew, being as he was the definition of a captive audience.

I closed my eyes for a moment. I thought about my decision to walk away and end this thing. I thought about how I hadn't known how entrenched in my life Hallie had become, that she'd been doing this for four years now. And who was to say, even if I walked away, that it would stop? And then I thought about checkmate, and dominoes. And I wondered if there was a way I could end this—if I didn't just topple one piece, but everything at once. If I set everything up and then knocked it down so Hallie wouldn't be able to do this ever again. It was an extreme option, but I thought it might be the only way to stop this once and for all.

I focused back on Ford and Sophie. Ford was explaining how Sophie would be able to reboot her phone and eliminate the spyware, when I stepped forward, into the frame. "Actually," I said, looking at Ford, and then at Sophie. "I think we should leave all this stuff. Leave the spyware on your texts, keep being friends with Abby West-Smith."

"What?" Sophie asked, sounding shocked.

"Why?" Ford asked, leaning forward, his eyebrow raised. "What are you thinking?"

I took a breath, then let it out before I spoke. "I think I might have an idea."

CHAPTER 27

Two days later I stood on the front step of Bruce's, about to ring the bell—I'd left my keys behind on the hall table when I'd fled back to Connecticut. Sophie had returned to the Hamptons immediately, so as not to raise any red flags for Hallie. But I'd waited, wandered around my empty house, and tried to offset my growing boredom by putting plans into place.

I wasn't sure if it would work. But I knew I had to try and do one last thing. And after that, if Hallie wanted to keep messing with me and my friends in perpetuity, then I would give up—or possibly look into getting a restraining order. But I would have known I'd given it my best shot.

Ford had called and given me the go-ahead that morning, and I'd boarded the train to the Hamptons trying to be as incognito as possible, a baseball cap pulled low over my face, and sunglasses on during the whole ride. He'd told me it would be okay to head back—Bruce and Rosie had left to meet with a foreign investor who'd apparently gotten nervous about all the negative publicity the *Once Bitten* movie was attracting. Ford thought they'd be gone the better part of a week, which meant the coast was clear for me to return. And I'd gotten a very stiff e-mail from my dad, telling me that he was going to California for the next week to clear his head and get some work done on the script. I could tell from the tone of the e-mail that he really wasn't anywhere even close to forgiving, or forgetting, what I had done, and that our fight was still clearly on his mind.

And Gwyneth had been sending happy chatty e-mails—despite all the chaos at home, things apparently were going great with her documentary. Maybe the drama that wasn't good for Bruce was great for Gwyneth. She'd also mentioned, as an aside, that my dad had signed on to write the polar bear movie.

When she'd sent me the e-mail, I'd read it over and over, trying to square this with how against it my dad had been all summer. It wasn't just that he didn't want to write *In the Nick of Time*—it was that he didn't want to write any of those movies anymore. It wasn't until I'd read it a third time that the penny dropped. This was what he was doing to get back in the studio's good graces after his daughter had almost derailed its movie. It was my fault he was doing it, and this, on top of everything else, was making it hard to sleep at night.

I hadn't heard anything from Josh, though I'd been checking my phone more than I probably should have been. It wasn't like I'd really *expected* to hear from him, or anything . . . but there had been a moment between us in the freezer, hadn't there? It had at least seemed like the possibility of a new beginning, that we might be able to start fresh, with no secrets or mistaken identities between us. But the more time that passed without hearing from him, the more I'd resigned myself to the fact that I probably wouldn't. It seemed, at the very least, that he didn't hate me quite as much as he had before. And maybe I'd have to take that and be satisfied with it.

I reached out and pressed the doorbell just as I heard someone coming around the side of the house. I turned around and saw Teddy, looking more tan than ever, carrying his rolled-up tent and biodegradable backpack.

"Gemma," he said with a smile. "Hi. It's been a while."

"Right," I said after a moment, realizing that Teddy, in his warbler protection mode, must not have realized I'd left, gone back to Connecticut, and then returned again. "Well, I was just in a place where that would have been hard. I mean, I couldn't really . . ."

"I understand," he said, holding up his hand in a we-don't-have-to-talk-about-it gesture. He gave me a serious, understanding look. "I know I hurt you, Gemma. And I get that it might have been too painful to have to see me on the regular."

I started to answer this, but then just nodded, figuring it was probably just easiest to agree with this. Teddy *had* hurt me. He *had* broken my heart. But I had been a different person then—I'd been the girl in the pictures, the one I didn't even recognize now. "So the protest is over?" I asked, realizing this was the first time I'd seen Teddy standing upright and not chained to construction equipment in quite a while.

"Yes," Teddy said, giving me a wide smile. "That all got sorted."

"Great," I said, nodding. I waited for him to tell me why—how, exactly, this had been resolved. "What happened?" I asked after a moment when nothing was forthcoming.

"Bruce and I had a talk one night," Teddy said, his voice earnest. "And it turned out we were actually on the same page about a lot of things. And he ended up optioning my life rights. Isn't that cool? Apparently, he was working on a script about a teen girl, but it wasn't coming together, so he moved on. Now, he's developing a movie about a teen activist. I'm going to consult."

"But . . ." I said as I stared at him. "What about the marsh warbler?" I asked just as a Hamptons taxi pulled into the driveway in a spray of gravel. The driver, who looked around our age, honked the horn, put the car in park, and then immediately started texting.

"Gotta go," Teddy said, sliding on his fair-trade sunglasses. "I guess you're leaving too?" he asked, looking down at my duffel bag, eyebrows raised.

I opened my mouth to set him straight, but then thought fast. Presumably—and only because I hadn't heard anything different—Hallie and Teddy were still together. Which meant they would still be in communication. And it was crucial, at least for a while, that Hallie believe that I'd gone back to Putnam and stayed there. "Right," I said, nodding and taking a step away from the door. "Gotta go."

The front door was flung open, and Sophie was standing behind it. "Hi," she said, smiling wide when she saw me. "You're—"

"Just leaving," I said, waving at her. "So, um, thanks for everything. But back to Putnam I go."

Sophie frowned. "Wait," she said, and I didn't blame her for being incredibly confused. "What? You just—"

"Bye now," I said, cutting her off as I reached out and pulled the door shut.

Teddy shook his head. "Sophie always was a little clingy, wasn't she?"

I nodded, even as I had to bite my lip hard not to argue with him. "Yeah," I said. "Totally."

"Well, I'm sure I'll see you around," Teddy said, shouldering his bag. "Or probably at Hallie's birthday party next week, right?"

I felt my eyes widen. Teddy had just given me a gift, and it didn't even seem like he'd realized it. "Right, absolutely," I said, remembering that as far as Teddy was concerned, Hallie and I were just old friends. "The party on . . . um . . ."

"Saturday," Teddy filled in for me as the driver honked the horn again without looking up from his phone.

"Right, of course," I said, nodding. "I wouldn't miss it."

"Great," Teddy said. "See you then, Gem." And before I could prepare myself for it—or even react—he leaned toward me. I think he was aiming for my cheek—but maybe it was habit, or the fact that we'd kissed thousands of times—but Teddy turned his head and kissed me, his lips brushing mine. I started to kiss him back automatically—but a second later I realized what I was doing and broke away from him.

Teddy was looking down at me, his expression puzzled but

not unhappy. "Gem—" he started just as the driver leaned on the horn again.

"Bye," I said quickly, taking another step away from him. Teddy looked at me for a moment longer, then nodded and turned to walk down the driveway. I watched as he got into the car, and it sped out of the driveway as fast as it had sped in.

I turned and pulled open the door to find Sophie still standing on the threshold, her eyes wide. "What the heck was that?" she asked.

"I didn't want Teddy to know I wasn't heading home," I said, stepping inside and hauling my bag with me. "In case he told Hallie."

"Not that," Sophie said, waving this away. "I mean, when he kissed you."

"Nothing," I said, realizing that, of course, Sophie had been watching through the window. I dropped my bag by the foot of the stairs. I wasn't sure why Teddy had done it—but it hadn't felt like all the other times we'd kissed, which I hadn't been expecting. Maybe because it had come out of the blue, but I'd felt . . . nothing. "I don't know why he did that," I said, trying to keep my voice from betraying any of the confusion I was currently feeling. "But he's leaving for good?"

Sophie nodded. "It's about time. So I guess he saved that swamp pigeon?"

"Marsh warbler," I corrected automatically, then hesitated. I was not sure at all that Teddy had actually done this, which was bothering me more than I'd realized it would. "Is Ford around?" I asked.

"He was surfing earlier, but I think he's back now," she said. She pulled out her phone, and her face turned pale. "Crap. I was supposed to be babysitting, like, forty-five minutes ago. I'll see you tonight?"

I nodded, and Sophie grabbed her purse off the hall table and headed for the door.

"Tell the twins hi for me," I called after her, mostly because I had a feeling that it would annoy them. Sophie nodded and waved at me over her shoulder as she went out toward her car. I headed to the kitchen, since that was usually where most people in this house could be found. Sure enough, the fridge door was open, and I had a feeling I knew who was behind it. I gave it a push and heard a familiar "*Ow!* Dude, what?"

The door swung closed, and there was Ford, his hair sticking up in his post-surf-shower spikes. His expression changed when he saw it was me, his annoyed look disappearing. "Hey," he said, smiling at me. "You're back."

"Just now," I said. "Didn't mean to scare you."

"I figured it was Gwyn, home early," he said, shaking his head. "She's been beyond out of it for the last few days—I think it's documentary fog; she's trying to meet her deadline. So I figured she'd just walked into the door or something."

"How has it all been going here?" I asked. We'd discussed the plan two days ago, and Ford had said he'd look into some of the possibilities, but we hadn't talked much about it since.

"Good," he said, nodding. "I think it's going to work. Want to reconvene tonight when we're all here?"

"Sure," I said, then looked around, even though it was clear we were the only ones in the kitchen. "Is Gwyneth around?"

Ford shook his head as he started to head for the door that led to the pool house. "She's out," he said. "No idea where. But she told me she'd be back tonight." I nodded. That wasn't so unusual in this house—it wasn't like we all kept track of one another's comings and goings—but I was still curious. "So let's meet up tonight in the war room, okay?"

For just a second I hesitated. I had a feeling he meant his pool house. But this was a house of Bruce's, so you could never be sure just what kind of ridiculous rooms they contained. His last place in L.A. had a meditation garden, for reasons that never even seemed to be clear to Bruce. "The war room," I repeated slowly.

Ford nodded. "The pool house," he clarified. "We'll order pizza or something. I'm pretty sure that's the traditional food when plotting someone's demise." He raised an eyebrow at me, and I felt myself laugh. He slid open the glass door but then turned around and gave me one of his half-smiles. "I'm glad you're back, Gem." Then he headed over to the pool house, and I took a breath before walking back into the foyer, grabbing my suitcase, and heading upstairs. I had some planning—as well as some unpacking—to do.

᠅᠅᠅᠅

"Okay," I said later that night after the four of us—Sophie, Gwyneth, Ford, and myself—had worked our way through two pizzas and an order of garlic knots.

"So thanks to Teddy, we know that Hallie is having her

birthday party on Saturday. I'm thinking that's where it might make the most sense to do this." I looked over at Ford. "Is there any way to find out more details?"

Ford adjusted his glasses and raised an eyebrow at me. "I can hack," he acknowledged. "But I can't exactly just Google 'Hallie's birthday party where is it.' I'm going to need a little more than that."

Sophie sat up a little straighter. "I can find out," she said. She didn't look thrilled about the prospect, which meant I was pretty sure I knew what her strategy was here.

"Reid?" I asked. Sophie nodded, and Gwyneth's jaw dropped.

"Wow," she said, shaking her head. "That's taking one for the team."

"I'm not going to *date* him or anything," Sophie said as she reached for the last slice of extra-cheese. "I'm just maybe going to let him think I might."

"And there's really no chance you could actually like him?" Gwyneth asked, leaning closer. Ford cleared his throat, opened his laptop, and started typing busily. I had a feeling we'd just reached his girl-talk threshold.

"No," Sophie said, taking a huge bite of pizza. I tried not to make a face. I hated cold pizza, but Sophie loved it. We'd had multiple arguments about it over the years. "He's just so nice, you know? I need someone with darkness and secrets and mystery. Reid's just . . . Reid."

"Poor guy," Ford said, shaking his head.

"I promise I won't lead him on too long," Sophie said. "Just enough to get the details on the party."

"While you're doing that," Gwyneth said, "I'll start doing the Hallie edit of the footage. I'm sure there's going to be enough."

"Sorry to interrupt your documentary for this," I said, biting my lip. It was one of the things I'd been most worried about when I'd first proposed this plan—that it would be pulling everyone away from stuff. Sophie told me repeatedly that she wouldn't mind having to miss babysitting the twins for a few days, but Ford had work to do on his algorithm, and the last time I'd talked to Gwyneth, she'd claimed to be at a "critical juncture" with her documentary. "And the algorithm," I added quickly to Ford.

Gwyneth waved this off. "Bruce is gone," she said. "And plus, it hasn't exactly been shaping up the way I'd hoped. It turns out my dad's work actually is pretty boring. My mom had been saying that for years, but I thought she was just bitter because she didn't get the beach house."

"And," Ford added, "I think this is actually going to be a great test of the Galvanized Empathic Multi—"

"Stop," Gwyneth groaned, as she tossed a crust in his direction. "I really cannot stand to hear you say those words any longer. Please change the name to something better, or get an acronym or something. I'm begging you."

"Anyway," Ford said, after catching the crust and chucking it back to his sister, "it's going to be the first time I'll actually be able to try it out. Hallie just became our first beta tester."

"And, um," Sophie said, frowning, "what exactly does that mean?"

"Well," Ford said in a tone I already recognized as one that meant he was going to get really technical and jargon-heavy very soon. "The algorithm will mine her metadata, and—"

"Please," Gwyneth said. "In English."

Ford thought for a second, then said, "The algorithm is going to go through Hallie's online digital footprint. Everything public—I'm not going to dig unless we have to. But when you have a large amount of data like that, patterns emerge. Stuff people thought they were cleverly hiding suddenly becomes totally obvious. It's really beautiful, actually. We're defined totally by our choices, even ones we don't realize the significance of at the time."

"And, Gem?" Gwyneth asked, turning to me. "You're going to be keeping up the misdirection?"

I nodded. It was part of the strategy I'd discussed with Ford and Sophie when I'd proposed we not let Hallie know we were onto her. I'd suddenly become a lot more active on Friendverse, updating my status a couple of times a day, always about how bored I was in Putnam. And Ford had showed me how to change the location feature so that it would seem like my status updates were coming from Connecticut, not the Hamptons. Sophie and I had also been texting a lot, about how we missed each other, and how I was giving up entirely, because Hallie had so decisively won. It meant that we were actually talking on the phone a lot more now, since texting anything real was now impossible. "Still at it," I said. I picked up my phone and saw that I'd gotten a handful of likes on a selfie I'd posted earlier that night. One thing I'd done to pass the time when I was back in Connecticut was to take pictures around Putnam, in different outfits, so that it would look like I was actually there when I wasn't.

"Great," Sophie said, looking around, starting to smile. "I guess we have a plan. Saturday."

"Well, it's not ideal in terms of timing," Ford said. "But it's not undoable. And speaking of, I should get back to it. You're all welcome to stay, except Gwyneth."

"Thanks," Gwyneth said, standing up and stepping hard on his foot as she crossed to the door. "But I should actually go too. I have, um, some calls to make. You know." She gave us all a wave, then hurried out of the pool house and back to the mansion, already pulling out her phone as she walked.

Sophie and I told Ford good-bye—though I had no idea if he even heard us, as his eyes had glazed over and he'd gone into what I recognized as his coding trance—and headed out together. I stepped into the warm humid night, the lights from the house reflecting on the pool, the sound of the waves crashing just a few feet away, and was more grateful than ever to be back there.

"What's going on with Gwyn?" Sophie asked as we walked up to the house, neither one of us hurrying.

"I don't know," I said, glad that she was wondering about this too—proving that we were both just a little too interested in other people's business. I know Ford thought it was her documentary, but I knew what deadline stress looked like, and this wasn't it. "Gotta be a guy, don't you think?"

"Totally," Sophie replied without missing a beat. When we got to the house, I glanced back into the pool house for just a second. I could see Ford in silhouette, hunched over his laptop, fingers flying over his keyboard. "What's going on there?" she asked, nudging me with her hip.

"Nothing," I said immediately, turning away from Ford and sliding the door closed.

"But something could," Sophie said, her voice full of confidence I wished I could feel. "If you wanted it to."

"I don't know," I said, glancing involuntarily back toward the pool house before making myself turn away and cross the kitchen with Sophie, through the foyer where the ridiculous polar bear was still standing like a very large furry butler. We started up the stairs together, and by the time we'd reached the first landing, I'd gathered my thoughts a little more. "I just wouldn't want to say anything without knowing for sure how he felt."

"I could talk to him," Sophie said, brightening at the prospect. "Oh, please, let me? I've been watching my parents do it forever. They can get information out of people without them even realizing it."

"Maybe just save that for Reid," I said with a laugh as I made a mental note never to see either of Sophie's parents in case I ever needed a therapist in the future, which I really might after this summer. Sophie just raised her eyebrows at me, her look clearly saying *Really?* I nodded. "It's like Gwyneth talks about," I said. "About how the act of observing something changes it. I don't want Ford to have to start thinking about how he might or might not feel, because someone put the idea in his head." Sophie nodded, and it looked like I was maybe getting through to her. We stopped at the top of the stairs, but Sophie was not peeling off for her own bedroom yet, clearly knowing that I had more to say.

"I guess . . . if I had some sign of how he felt, something that was independent of anyone pressuring him for an answer . . . that would be a different situation. But until I have that, I don't want to mess something up that's really good."

Sophie nodded, and I knew she wasn't going to push the issue any further tonight. She headed down the hall to her bedroom, but before going inside, she said to me, "But just because you have something good now doesn't mean something else couldn't be even better." She smiled at me, gave me a *think about it* look, then went into her room.

I turned and walked down the hallway, Sophie's words echoing in my head. I had a feeling that she was right. But I also had a feeling that maybe now was not the best timing. Of course I was thinking about Ford—but also about Josh and Teddy. My thoughts kept returning to the pictures of Teddy all over my room, and the way Josh had sounded when he'd said my real name in full for the first time. It all seemed to add up to the fact that I needed to figure myself out before I could figure out how I felt about a guy. With this resolution firmly in mind, I brushed my teeth, updated my status once more about how bored I was in Connecticut, and got into bed.

But as I closed my eyes and tried to go to sleep, I found that I kept thinking about a pair of kind dark eyes and a three-year-old kiss.

CHAPTER 28

"Okay," I said into my phone as I walked down Quonset's main street, glancing into Sweet & Delicious long enough to see that Darcy was working—her version of it: checking her phone while Reid cleaned the inside of the ice-cream case. "Cinderella is in the castle."

There was a pause on the other end, then Sophie said, "Wait, remind me what that one means again?"

We'd started using spy lingo for our various tasks, despite the fact that Ford had told us repeatedly that it actually drew *more* attention to what we were saying, since normal people never talked about the weather in Malaysia, or which directions the fountains faced in Rome, in addition to not being efficient at all, since everything had to be repeated and clarified. But while all that was true, the lingo was also fun to say.

"Darcy's inside," I said as I stepped out of the stream of foot traffic and a little closer to the nearest storefront window, pretending like I was interested in the truly hideous flowered sundresses on display.

"Great," Sophie said. "Okay, I'll go wave the cape." I thought hard. I knew what that one meant, I was pretty sure. It just wasn't coming to me at the moment. "I'll get Reid out of there," she clarified after a few seconds of silence on my end. "But five minutes is all I can guarantee. More than that and he might just hang up on me and give me a horrible excuse later. You know how crazy he is about that job."

"I know," I said. In addition to firsthand experience, Sophie had told me from her recent info gathering on Reid that he'd become even more worried about getting fired after I'd been shown the door. Apparently, after being fired from his internship at the start of the summer, he'd developed a huge fear about it happening again. "Okay. I'll let you work your magic."

"Talk soon," Sophie said, then hung up.

It had been a busy few days. Sophie had gotten back in contact with Reid, and it had been incredibly easy for her to get intel on Hallie's party. We now knew that it was taking place on Saturday on a rented boat, and that The South Fork was going to be catering it again—which was why I was here, about to drop in on Darcy and just hoping what I was about to do wouldn't be too obvious. I checked my watch. Reid was still cleaning the ice-cream case, which meant Sophie hadn't called yet. I took the window of time I had to send her a text.

Me
2:19 PM

Hey, Soph. Any chance you're coming
back home soon? It's so boring here in Putnam!
What's going on there? Anything interesting?
Text when you can! Xoxo

When I looked back into the ice-cream parlor again, Reid
was looking down at his phone and saying something to Darcy,
who only glanced up at him. I felt my heart twist as I watched
Reid hurry out toward the break room. His face was flushed
and happy, and it was like I could see it plainly written in his
expression—just how much he liked Sophie. I waited until he
was gone, then stepped through the door of the ice-cream
parlor.

"Hello there and welcome to Sweet & Delicious," Darcy said,
still to her phone. "What can I—?" She looked up at me, and her
eyes widened. "Gemma," she said, giving me a nervous smile,
like she wasn't sure if she was allowed to be happy to see me.

"Hi, Darcy," I said cheerfully, and hopefully like I had nary
an ulterior motive in mind.

"It's so good to see you. I thought you'd gone back home."
She leaned over the counter and lowered her voice. "I was so
sorry to hear what happened," she said. "I mean, I totally didn't
think it was right. Just because you were making out with
someone in the freezer. I mean, that's no reason to fire someone."

"I wasn't making out . . ." I started, then realized I probably
didn't have time to set her straight. "Right," I said, nodding.
"So unfair, right?"

"Totally," Darcy said, still keeping her voice low. "It hasn't been the same here without you."

"So listen," I said, leaning a little closer. I had a feeling that more small talk was probably a good idea, so she wouldn't get suspicious, but I wasn't sure I would have enough time for that. Apparently, when Sophie had called Reid at work the day before, he'd only talked to her for forty-five seconds before he'd yelled "Look, a bear!" in what Sophie described as possibly the most unconvincing voice ever, then hung up. "I was just wondering if you were going to be working for the catering company this Saturday. The party on the boat?"

Darcy nodded. "Yeah," she said. "Some kind of birthday? They want ice-cream sandwiches, that's all I really know. And I wasn't working, so I figured it would be a good way to get some extra money." She smiled at me, her cheeks turning pink. "Did I tell you that Chaz is coming? And I wanted to take him to that really *nice* mini-golf place. You know the one I mean? With the windmill?"

"Right, that one's awesome," I said, knowing full well that if there wasn't time for small talk, there certainly wasn't time for a Chaz-disillusionment lecture. "I was just wondering . . ." I leaned a little closer still, and Darcy leaned in to meet me. "Would I be able to work that in your place?"

Darcy paled and drew back. "Um, I don't know, Gemma," she said. "I mean, it didn't go so well last time, remember? And I really don't want to get in trouble."

"I promise you won't," I said quickly. "If anyone is going to get in trouble, it'll be me—I'll take all the blame."

"But . . ." Darcy said, her brow furrowed. She was looking toward the door, and I had a feeling she was desperately wishing for a giant group of kids to come in, all now demanding multiple samples, just so she could get out of this conversation with me.

"I guess it's just been hard," I said, my voice soft, "ever since I got fired. You know, with no job or, um, sense of purpose. And remember when I covered for you so you could text Chaz? And you said you owed me? And it was actually because you weren't here that . . . well . . ." My voice trailed off as I shrugged, letting my words hang between us. I tried to tell myself that this wasn't quite blackmail. Darcy *had* said she owed me one. And who knows, I might not have gotten fired after all if she'd been there to let me and Josh out of the freezer. If anything, it was more like *guilt*mail.

"Oh," Darcy said, nodding, her eyes wide. "Right. I guess I forgot about that. Um . . ." She looked around, like she was worried the ice-cream parlor was bugged, and when she spoke again, her voice was low. "So how would that work, exactly?"

"I'd just say I was you when I showed up," I said, incredibly relieved that she was getting on board with this. "They didn't check IDs or anything last time, remember? Just crossed our names off the list. You won't get in trouble, I promise."

Darcy nodded, then smiled at me. "Okay," she said. "You can take my shift. It'll actually give me more time to spend with Chaz!"

I looked at her smiling hopeful face and realized that the

moment was probably here. "Darcy," I said gently. "There's been something I've been meaning to tell you about Chaz. The thing is—" The bell over the door rang violently, and a huge family—it looked like there were four kids and two nannies—piled into the shop. "Another time," I said, taking a step back toward the door.

"I'll text you the info," Darcy said, already looking overwhelmed. "Reid!" she called toward the break room. Since the last thing I wanted to do was to have Reid report back to Hallie that he had seen me, which would mean that I was not, in fact, biding my time in Connecticut, I ducked out of the store, giving Darcy a quick wave that I don't think she saw.

I let the door close behind me, and I slipped on my sunglasses. That had gone pretty well. I just hoped everyone else's plans were working out just as smoothly, since Saturday was rapidly approaching. I started to head back to my car—normally, I would have stopped for an iced latte, but I was trying to keep as low a profile as possible—when I almost crashed into someone heading the opposite direction.

"Oh, I'm so sorry," the person I'd almost run into said.

"It's okay," I said automatically. I could see now that it was a guy—a really cute one. And he looked familiar, somehow. I pushed up my sunglasses and felt my eyes widen. The guy in front of me was tall and tan, with blond hair and chiseled features, his left leg in a walking cast. I had seen a picture of him once, in black-and-white, playing football. "Chaz?" I asked, not quite able to believe it.

"Oh," he said, looking surprised but not displeased. "Um, yes, that's me. I guess you know Darcy? I was just coming to surprise her?" I suddenly noticed that he was carrying a bouquet of flowers, and he looked nervous.

"Yeah," I said after a slightly-longer-than-normal pause, still trying to get my head around this—Darcy hadn't been getting catfished, and I had. Darcy's relationship was actually everything she'd told me it was. "Um, we used to work together. She's inside."

"Great," he said, giving me a smile that truly belonged in an ad for teeth-whitening strips. "Nice to meet you."

"You too," I called after him a moment too late as I watched him square his shoulders, take a breath, and head into the ice-cream parlor. I turned and walked back to my car, wanting to give Darcy and Chaz their privacy—well, as much privacy as they could get in front of a passel of kids, their nannies, and Reid. But I found that I kept smiling as I unlocked the car and got in. It seemed that sometimes things were what they appeared to be after all. And after a summer of subterfuge, this was more welcome than I'd realized it would be.

⸙

Four days later—or "T-minus one," as Ford was insisting on calling it—I sat out by the pool, my feet in the water of the deep end. It was late; I knew that I should be in bed, preparing for everything that was going to happen tomorrow night. But every time I closed my eyes, all I'd see were the lists of things that still needed to be accomplished, and things I hadn't done yet. So I'd decided that if I was going to be kept awake, I might as well be outside.

I didn't want to jinx it, but it seemed like everything was on track. And we were getting even more access than we'd planned—the day before, Reid had asked Sophie to the party as his date. She had accepted immediately, and it made things easier for us. I would be there in Darcy's place, but this would mean that Sophie would be there too, keeping an eye on things and reporting back. Gwyneth was going to give me her final edit on a flash drive in the morning—she'd wanted to tweak some last things. I'd seen some early cuts of the footage she was assembling, and it seemed like it was going to be enough—especially since the algorithm hadn't performed the way Ford had imagined. He'd emerged that morning from the pool house, where he'd pretty much spent the last few days, even forgoing his morning surf sessions to monitor the algorithm's progress. He had sat next to me at the kitchen counter, where I'd been devouring a maple-bacon donut (we were all taking advantage of Bruce's absence by eating whatever we wanted).

"Sorry," he'd said, and behind his glasses, I'd been able to see how tired he'd looked. "I thought that the algorithm was going to come through for us with something."

"Nothing?" I'd asked, trying not to sound too disappointed, even though my heart had been sinking.

Ford had shaken his head. "I think she was just more careful than I was planning on," he'd said. "Maybe if I had more time . . ." He'd let the sentence trail off, then broken off a piece of my donut and popped it into his mouth. He'd looked disappointed enough in himself that I hadn't even protested this. "But I'm really sorry, Gem. I thought I was going to be able to get you something."

"It's okay," I'd said reassuringly, even as I'd moved the rest of my donut out of his reach. "Gwyneth's stuff is plenty damaging. We'll be fine."

Ford had nodded, but then he'd pushed himself away from the table and started back toward the pool house. "I'm going to keep working," he'd called.

"Ford, get some sleep," I'd called after him. But he had just gone back inside and shut the door, his usual signal that he was working and not to be disturbed. But since it was now the night before, it would seem that he hadn't found anything.

Even without anything from the algorithm, I was feeling confident about things. It looked like we were in good shape. And I'd gotten an e-mail that evening from my dad, telling me that he was having productive meetings with his team (his managers and agents, not the Dodgers) and was planning on being in L.A. another week. He still didn't sound happy with me, not by any stretch, but the e-mail also wasn't quite as frosty as his first few had been. But it was clear that the fight we'd had in his office—and the issues we hadn't resolved—were still hanging unspoken between us.

I moved my feet in small circles under the water, flexing and then pointing my toes. I knew I should probably go in and get some rest, but I just wanted to savor the moment—the calm before the storm that would be coming tomorrow.

"Gem!" I turned to see Ford standing in the doorway of the pool house, holding his laptop, looking stunned but happy. "I . . ." He looked down at the screen, then back at me. "I think I might have something."

I started to get up, but Ford was already crossing over to me, sitting next to me by the pool but not putting his feet in the water, maybe so he could be sure to keep his laptop out of splashing range. "I thought you said there wasn't anything," I said.

"There wasn't," he said, the sides of his mouth turning up in a smile. "On the surface, at least. I started digging deeper. When did she say her anniversary with Teddy was?"

I reached for my phone and scrolled back through the fake correspondence with Hallie, back when she believed I was Teddy. "May eleventh," I said, not quite able to stop myself from rolling my eyes, since their anniversary was the day they met, despite the fact that Teddy had very much still been my boyfriend then.

Ford smiled wide, the kind I wasn't used to seeing from him. I had a feeling that his lack of big smiles related to all the years he'd been in heavy-duty orthodontia. But whatever the reason, I liked it that they weren't so frequent. It made the times he did smile big seem to mean more. "Exactly," he said. "Do you know what you were doing on May eleventh?"

I shook my head. "No idea."

"Your status update on Friendverse was, and I quote, '*Ugh, so don't want to do this today. SUCH a drag.*'" I just stared at

Ford, trying to put this together with whatever he was trying to tell me. "It's the day you took the SATs," he said, and I nodded, then shuddered.

"Okay," I said, still trying to understand the relevance of this. "And?"

"And you'd been updating about that quite a bit leading up to them," he said. He looked at me over his glasses, his expression apologetic. "I had to look at your metadata too," he said. "Sorry, Gem."

"It's fine," I said easily, partly because I was still not exactly sure what metadata actually was.

"Anyway, you and Teddy had an exchange on Friendverse about how you weren't going to see each other that afternoon."

"Ah," I said, feeling my cheeks get hot. It had seemed normal at the time, but with a little bit of distance, this level of codependence was really starting to bother me. "And?"

"And that's the afternoon they met 'by chance' at Putnam Park, where Teddy had told you he would be."

I nodded, waiting for the smoking gun to show up. So Hallie had stalked my Friendverse feed to find out when Teddy and I—who had spent almost all our time together—would be apart. It was creepy, but not exactly surprising at this point. "And?" I finally asked, after failing to see what Ford had been so excited about.

"And," Ford went on, "that was the same day New York schools had an SAT test as well."

"Okay. So Hallie didn't take that one. She'll just take it in the fall." I was planning on taking it in the fall again as well, as

I had admittedly slacked off on the vocabulary-memorization part of the verbal.

"But that's just the thing," Ford said, and I could tell from his tone that he was now getting to the good stuff. "She did take it. Her school published a list of their top SAT scorers in some alumni fund-raising thing. And Hallie's on there."

I just stared at Ford as this all started to come together. "So she . . . hired someone to take the test for her?"

Ford shrugged. "At this point I don't know what she did. But Hallie wasn't taking that test on the eleventh. Someone was, but not Hallie. She couldn't have been, because Hallie was in Putnam, pretending that her meeting with Teddy was accidental."

"Oh my god," I said breathlessly. I just looked at Ford, and I could tell we were both thinking the same thing—this was *really* big.

"I know," he agreed. "The algorithm came through after all."

I tried to smile at that, but my thoughts were racing. This was beyond what Hallie and I had thrown at each other all summer. This wasn't just haircutting, or even trying to derail Bruce's movie. This was college-rejection, expulsion-level, ruined-future stuff. "I . . ." I started, then pulled my feet out of the water and hugged my knees. "I'm not sure I want to do anything with this." I registered the shock on Ford's face, and went on. "I . . . just think I maybe need to sit with it for a few days. I don't want to use the nuclear option unless we have to."

Ford nodded. "Fair enough," he said, and though I couldn't be sure, I thought I detected a look of relief on his face. "Okay, we'll hold it until we need it."

"But thank you," I said quickly. "I mean . . . it's amazing that you were able to catch it."

"Well, technically it was the algorithm."

"But you wrote the algorithm," I pointed out.

Ford smiled at that. "Fair point." He looked over at me. "You ready for tomorrow?"

I took a deep breath and then let it out. I knew the answer to that immediately. I was. It was what I'd been moving toward since the moment I saw Hallie on the train platform, even though I hadn't known it then. "Yes," I said. Whatever happened tomorrow, I was ready for it. "We should get some sleep," I said, and Ford nodded.

"Good idea," he said. "Big day tomorrow."

But neither one of us made any move to leave, we just sat there in comfortable silence. I looked at the stars above me and tried to memorize it all—the sound of the cicadas, the waves crashing, the knowledge that Ford was right there next to me and that neither one of us felt like we had to speak right then. I just took it all in, enjoying the peace while I still could.

CHAPTER 29

"Darcy Santiago," I said to the flustered-looking woman with the clipboard, making sure to sound bored and, hopefully, not at all suspicious. "Ice-cream station?"

She scanned the list of names, and I crossed my fingers and held my breath. Most of the other caterers had arrived a few hours before to prep, but since there wasn't much to do on the ice-cream station, Darcy had the latest arrival time. I'd walked across the ramp to the boat along with some guests, all of whom were beautifully dressed and bearing gifts. Everyone's eyes had slid right over me, since I was very clearly not an invited guest. I was wearing all black and carrying an overstuffed backpack, and I hadn't brought Hallie a present—at least, not the kind she'd be expecting.

I'd followed the instructions Darcy had given me, and made my way belowdeck, where the catering staff was getting everything ready. It didn't look like Blair was working today, which was a huge break for me. Even if none of the rest of the catering staff had remembered me, I knew I would be spotted by her right away. Everyone's stress level seemed a little bit high, and I had a feeling that it had something to do with the fact that people were basically having to run up one of two very narrow staircases, trays in hand, trying not to jostle the food too much or spill anything. But everyone running around and being stressed meant that nobody was really paying attention to me. I'd found a closet that seemed to contain mostly a huge amount of white life preservers, neatly stacked, and had dropped my backpack in the far corner. I was going to check in, just so no red flags would be raised that Darcy wasn't there. But I had no intention of actually serving any ice-cream sandwiches today. Hallie and her friends would just have to get over it.

It seemed like everything was a go. Gwyneth had given me the flash drive that morning. I had hoped she'd be watching the live feed of my or Sophie's camera, but she'd told me she would be busy during the party—but that she'd leave the feed running on the monitors, and Ford had promised to check in occasionally in case we needed help. I wasn't sure what he was going to be able to do from land, across town, but it was at least nice to know there was going to be someone minding the store.

I had made sure to be hidden from view when Reid came to pick Sophie up. Though if Sophie was actually trying not to lead him on, it would seem to me that she would have worn pretty much any other dress than the one she'd chosen. She looked beautiful, but it was not the dress you wore when attending a party with someone you only wanted to be friends with.

I looked back at the woman, who was still scanning her list and felt my pulse start to race. Was this about to end before it even started?

"There you are," the woman said with a relieved sigh as she put a check mark next to Darcy's name. "Wonderful. You know where to get set up?"

"Absolutely," I said, my voice full of confidence. I gave her a nod, then turned around and headed directly for the closet where I'd stashed my bag. Just as I reached it, I felt the ship jerk beneath me, followed by a loud clanging metal sound. I heard the faint clapping of people above deck, and realized that the ship was pulling out of the harbor. Come what may, I was now stuck on this boat with Hallie and the rest of her guests for the next four hours.

I pushed open the door and ducked inside, hitting the lights and locking the door behind me. I went right to my bag and pulled out what Gwyneth and Sophie had decided I needed to wear tonight—a long beaded dress that had once belonged to Bruce's last wife. It was gorgeous, and much more formal than anything I'd ever worn before. I pulled my hair down from my ponytail, and was just glad that nobody had wondered why the girl in charge of the ice-cream sandwich station had been wearing quite so much eye makeup. I changed quickly out of my black uniform and into the dress, then stepped into the heels I was already regretting as the ship rolled underneath me.

I stuffed my uniform into my backpack and pulled a tiny clutch out of it, then hid the bag behind the life jackets once again. Then I took a deep breath and let it out. It was go time.

I eased open the door, looking through the crack until I could see I had a window. I darted out, shut the door behind me, and looked around.

My heart was pounding as I pressed my back against the corridor. On the boat above me, I could hear music and laughter and conversation, the sounds of a successful party. It seemed like everyone was having fun—for the moment, at least.

I checked that the coast was clear, then continued down the hallway to the staircase that would lead me above deck, trying to look like I'd been here all along, a guest who'd just lost her way. I had been expecting to need to psych myself up for this, talk myself into it, but now that the moment was here, I found it wasn't necessary. I knew I would get in a lot of trouble for this. I knew I was about to burn all my bridges. But I was ready. It would be worth it.

I headed toward the stairs and walked up them carefully, holding my long beaded dress out to the side so that I wouldn't trip over it—that was not the kind of entrance I was hoping to make.

I stepped onto the deck of the boat and felt my jaw drop. I hadn't been able to see much of the party when we were unloading in the kitchens downstairs, but it was absolutely stunning. The tables were all done in white and blue, with white peony centerpieces and tiny blue twinkle lights all around the deck of the boat. The entire deck was filled with people, everyone dressed in their best beachy formal-wear. I saw a group of older people—probably Karen's friends—but mostly it was people my age, everyone laughing and talking in clusters. The music was just loud enough to keep everyone's energy up, but not loud enough to get in the way of conversation. There were cater waiters in black pants and jackets—the same outfit I'd ditched in a closet downstairs—carrying around trays of miniature burgers, tiny individual pizzas, and meticulously decorated cupcakes. *Happy Birthday, Hallie* read the hand-lettered sign hung just above the blue-and-white cake.

As I took it all in, I had to admit that it was the perfect party.

I just hoped everyone was enjoying it while it lasted.

I pulled my shoulders back and made myself walk through the party like I'd been invited. One of the cater waiters shot me a sharp look as I passed, and I had a feeling I'd just been recognized, but I kept my eyes straight ahead as I walked. I passed a picture strung along the boat's rails. *Hallie's 17th!* it read. In the picture, she and Teddy cuddled on the beach while the sun set behind them, Teddy beaming down at Hallie while she smiled at the camera serenely.

I ripped it down, dropped it to the floor, and stepped across Hallie's face as I made my way to the back of the boat.

There weren't many guests here, and I could see why. It was where the electronics station was set up—the DJ's laptop, the sound board, and a mess of wires and cords underfoot. As promised, it was currently deserted.

I looked across the boat and saw her. Hallie was standing in a group of people, her head thrown back in laughter. It radiated off of her—just how pleased she was with herself.

I reached into the clutch and pulled out the only other thing in there—a small silver flash drive.

I looked across at the guests, and when I was sure that nobody was paying any attention to me, I slipped the flash drive into the USB port of the DJ's laptop, then pretended I'd seen someone I knew on the side of the boat, and walked purposely over there.

Once we'd found out from Sophie the relevant information about the party (like where it was taking place), it hadn't been hard for Ford to find out who had been hired to DJ and run the media for the party. Gwyneth had gotten in touch with him, and found him nicely uncommitted to his job. In exchange for a few hours' free use of the professional-grade sound-mixing equipment Bruce had provided her with, the DJ had agreed to take a break at a very crucial moment, and then "accidentally" use the media on the wrong flash drive. I leaned over the railing of the ship, looking at the lights back on shore starting to glow in the twilight. All I really had to do now was wait and stay out of Hallie's sight until the big moment. I'd set up all my dominoes, and now I would get to watch them all come crashing down.

In my peripheral vision, I saw a waiter circling with a tray of sparkling waters, and when he passed me, I reached out and grabbed one, making sure to avert my gaze. But he just let me take one and then he moved on, and I let out a relieved breath as I took a big gulp. I slowly turned around to face the rest of the party, and then moved myself casually off into a darker corner. The last thing I wanted was to be spotted early. I didn't need Hallie thinking something might be about to happen, and then double-checking things. I caught a glimpse of Sophie and Reid through the shifting crowd. Sophie was laughing at something Reid was saying, leaning into him as she did. Reid looked beyond pleased about this, his smile shy but proud, his expression thrilled.

I wasn't sure Sophie needed to sell it that much—after all, she was already on the boat. But as I watched them for a moment, I wondered if there was maybe a piece of her that was having a good time. I hoped so, not only for Reid's sake, but for hers—it was high time Sophie fell for someone nice.

I was scanning the crowd, looking for Hallie, when I saw Josh across the boat, leaning on the railing as well, his expression serious. He was in a dark suit and a tie, and I felt my breath catch as I looked at him. I was suddenly remembering my hands on either side of his neck, the way we'd stood so close in the freezer. I knew I couldn't go and say anything to him—I'd blow my cover for sure—but I just watched him for a moment, standing alone, wondering if he was thinking about me at all, maybe even wishing I was there with him.

But not even a second later a girl approached him, her back to me, and she put her hand on his shoulder. I felt my hopes wilt a little, and I knew I shouldn't even really be surprised. I'd seen him with two girls already this summer, after all. I didn't think this one looked familiar, though. She was on the shorter side, with black hair up in a messy knot. Josh smiled at the girl, and as he leaned down to kiss her, I saw her face. My heart felt like it stopped for a second, and I grabbed on to the railing to steady myself.

It was Gwyneth.

I just looked at them for a second longer, then had to turn away. I couldn't even get my head around what was happening. Gwyneth and *Josh*? How had they even met? How long had this been going on? And I realized, the pieces coming together like the answer to a terrible puzzle, that this was why Gwyneth had been so dreamy and unfocused lately. Josh was the boy Sophie and I were sure she'd been talking to. And the fact that she was here as his date was the reason she had told me she would be busy tonight.

I couldn't help but feel a stab of betrayal. After all, Gwyneth had known I'd had a history with Josh, didn't she? I tried to force myself to sort through the thoughts whirling around in my head. I realized, my stomach sinking, that I hadn't told her. She had asked me once, I was pretty sure, but I had avoided the question and hadn't gone into any details. And I remembered Gwyn commenting, every time she saw Josh on a video feed, just how cute he was. It was too much to take in, and even though they were all the way across the boat from me, I felt like I needed to not be in the same space as them at the moment. The deck of the boat was big, and open to the elements, but it was still starting to feel a little too claustrophobic, like the walls were pressing in on me.

Even though I knew I would be risking blowing my cover by bumping into someone who could recognize me, I walked across the deck, keeping my head low. I ducked into the interior of the boat, noticing just how much nicer these hallways were than the ones belowdeck. There were helpful signs pointing in the direction of the ladies' room, and I followed them, just feeling like I needed a place to be alone and gather my thoughts. If I hadn't been worried about getting recognized, I might have gone back down to my life jacket closet. Unless there was a serious maritime disaster—in which case I'd have much bigger things to worry about—I had a feeling nobody would bother me down there. But since I knew that wasn't a great option, I pushed open the door to the ladies' room.

Thankfully, it was empty. The last thing I needed was to bump into Hallie. I walked quickly to one of the two stalls, locked the door, and leaned my back against it, trying to find my composure again.

Why was this bothering me so much? I'd seen Josh with two other girls this summer, not to mention I'd seen him hitting on my best friend. Why was Gwyneth different? I knew the answer to the question as soon as I'd asked it of myself. It was in the way Josh had smiled down at her before he kissed her. At one point he'd smiled at me that way. This wasn't dating someone because he was mad about what I'd done to him, or because he was trying to make me jealous. This had absolutely nothing to do with me. He had moved on.

I let out a breath, then checked the time on my phone. I couldn't spend all night in the bathroom, upset over guys who no longer liked me. There were bigger things going on here, and I had to keep my eye on the prize. I adjusted the straps on my gown and made myself stand up straighter, then pushed the door open and stepped back out into the bathroom.

There was a woman standing in front of the mirror, pulling something out of her clutch. I stepped forward toward the mirror just as she lifted her head. Our eyes met in the reflection, and I drew in a sharp breath.

Karen Bridges was standing next to me.

CHAPTER 30

I felt my pulse start to race. I didn't think I could turn and run from the bathroom, not without really attracting attention to myself. I quickly looked away from the reflection, pretending to search through my bag, wondering if there was a way to get out of this. After all, Karen hadn't seen me since I was eleven. Who was to say she would even recognize me?

"Gemma?" Her voice was hesitant, like she was expecting to be told otherwise. But there was really no getting out of this now. Feeling as close to facing a firing squad as I ever had in my life, I turned around to look at Karen.

It was the first time I'd really seen her up close—and in person—in five years. But all the other glimpses I'd gotten of her this summer hadn't misled me. Karen looked great—older than when I'd known her before, of course, but still wonderful. But more than her hair or makeup, she just seemed—as she had when I'd seen her before—*happy*. But I had a feeling that running into me was about to diminish that glow, and fast.

"Hi," I finally said, my voice coming out shaky. "It's . . . um . . . nice to see you."

"I didn't know you were coming," Karen said. It was with some relief that I noticed her tone didn't sound accusatory or confused—it was pleased, if anything.

"Yeah," I said, my eyes searching her face, trying to figure out what she knew. This whole time, I'd never been able to pinpoint just how much Hallie had told her mother. I wasn't sure what she knew—everything? Nothing? Somewhere in between?

"Well, I'm so glad to see you," Karen said, smiling at me. "Hallie mentioned that she'd started spending time with you this summer."

I nodded, even though my mind was racing. It didn't seem like Karen knew much. Maybe Hallie was keeping her in the dark, like I had tried to keep my dad in the dark. "Yes," I finally said, trying to stay on the vague side of things. "We've been hanging out a little."

"I'm so glad," Karen said. Her smile seemed genuine, like there was nothing behind it but happiness that two childhood friends were reconnecting. She dropped a lipstick back into her bag, which was made by a designer whose name I'd seen in magazines, but never in real life. Then I realized that I no longer had to wonder about how she was affording things like the dress, or the diamonds in her ears and on her finger, or the designer purse in front of me—because I knew she was actually Brenda Kreigs.

Oh my god. I realized with a sickening twist in my stomach that there was one thing I was sure Karen did know—she thought it was me who leaked her name and got the movie derailed. "Um . . ." I started, feeling my palms begin to sweat. I knew I had to do this, but that didn't make it any easier. "Karen. I . . ." It was starting to feel physically difficult to form words, like my throat was strangling them before I could get them out.

"Yes, Gemma?" She turned to me, her expression slowly growing concerned. One look in the mirror at my own reflection was enough to tell me why—it looked like I was on the edge of throwing up.

"I . . . I just wanted to tell you. About that thing—they said I was the one who told people that you were really . . . I mean—" I took a breath to try to speak more coherently, but Karen just held up her hand.

"You don't have to say anything," she said as she shook her head. "It's all fine. I promise."

I just stared at her. It didn't seem like she was saying this passive-aggressively, or like she didn't mean it. She seemed to be totally genuine—which was, at the moment, baffling.

"No," I said slowly, wondering if she hadn't understood me. "I . . . I need to apologize." As I said it, I realized how true it was. I hadn't done what she thought I had—but I'd done much worse things to her years earlier. It was an apology that was going to come five years too late, but I was finally going to try to do it. "I hurt you . . ." I started, and as I opened and closed my clutch's clasp, I could see my hands were shaking. "I never should have done it. And it's not just that. Five years ago, I—"

"Gemma." Karen's voice was still kind, but it was firm. "I really don't need to hear it." I opened my mouth to tell her what I was trying to say—maybe using more actual words this time—but Karen continued on before I had the chance. "Honestly. You just have to forgive people, in the end."

This was so not what I had expected to hear that I blinked at her. "You do?"

She nodded. "I went through a time when I was . . . holding on to a lot of anger. And it didn't do any good. It was toxic and eating me alive. And so I let it go."

She said this with a note of finality, and a smile, like that was all there was to it. "That's it?" I asked after a moment of waiting to make sure nothing else was coming.

"That's it," she said. "You just have to forgive and walk away." She looked at me for a moment longer, then crossed behind me to the door, touching me briefly on the shoulder, the diamond on her finger catching the light and reflecting it back. She turned to me and gave me a smile. "Take care, Gemma." Then she stepped out the door, leaving me alone in the bathroom with my thoughts, which were more confused than ever.

I stared at my own reflection—the smoky eyes, the borrowed dress, the party hair that had survived its time in a ponytail. But then I looked closer. I saw the dark shadows under my eyes, and how nervous and stressed I looked. Karen's words were reverberating in my head, and for the first time I let myself wonder what would happen if I just called this off.

I knew all the rational reasons why we should stick to the

plan—like the fact that everyone had put so much time and effort into helping me with this. But . . .

The thought of just calling this off, deciding not to do it, letting Hallie have a great birthday celebration, and spending the evening dancing with Sophie (and Reid)? It sounded so much better. As soon as I pictured the alternate way the evening could go, I realized how much I didn't want to go through with this. I wanted whatever kind of happy peace Karen had been able to achieve. I didn't want to keep carrying this anger toward Hallie with me forever.

And it wasn't that I was giving up, or that she was winning, or any of the distinctions I'd felt the need to put on this earlier. It was just me deciding to let it go. Deciding not to deliberately hurt someone any longer. And as soon as I made the decision, I immediately felt better.

I pushed myself out of the bathroom door, keeping my head up, realizing now that we weren't going to do this, I didn't have to worry about being spotted by Hallie. Well, I supposed I still did in case she tried to have me kicked off the boat or thrown in the brig or whatever it was they did to party-crashing guests when the party wasn't on dry land. But that all still sounded preferable to going through with what we'd been planning. I felt more sure of the decision with every step I took, and it was like a weight was slowly being lifted off my shoulders. After all, I'd already ruined Hallie's twelfth-birthday party. I didn't need to wreck her seventeenth.

As soon as I was back on the deck of the boat, I pulled out

my phone. This was all scheduled to start in ten minutes, so I really didn't have much time. I saw that Gwyneth was now standing by herself against the railing on the other side of the boat. And even though I didn't have to worry as much about being recognized, I didn't want to have to waste time trying to explain what I was doing there in case I was spotted. I ducked back into my darkened corner and called Gwyneth.

I saw her pull out her phone, smile, and then answer. "Hi, Gemma," she said, her voice happy. "What's up?"

"Hi, Gwyn," I said. "I'm across the boat from you."

"Oh," she said, and she turned around and gave me a small wave, then turned back to face the water again. "I should have told you I was coming! But Josh kind of asked me at the last minute, and it was a little bit of a whirlwind, so . . ."

I knew there were other things going on right now that I really had to deal with, but I couldn't stop myself from asking, "So how did that happen? You and Josh?" I tried to make it sound like his name was just one of many I said, and one that didn't hurt me to say it in the context of him and someone else.

"Well," Gwyneth said, and I could hear through the phone how pleased she was to get to tell the story—their story. "I think it was the day you went back to Connecticut. He came to the house looking for you."

I felt my heart leap at that, even though I knew rationally that it probably wouldn't make any difference. "He did?"

"Yeah," she said. "But I told him you'd gone home to Connecticut for the rest of the summer—because that's what you'd said in your text," she said, sounding maybe a little defensive.

"Anyway . . . we just got to talking. And we hit it off. He's a really great guy."

"I know," I said quietly. I tried not to let myself wonder why Josh had come to see me—or what he'd come to say. Quite possibly it was to yell at me for almost giving him frostbite. But I had a feeling that wasn't it. It didn't seem, however, like I was going to get to find out. "So," I said, trying to focus on the actual things that were happening now—not theoretical conversations that hadn't ended up happening. "I think we need to call this off."

"What?" Gwyneth's voice was suddenly sharp again, the Josh dreaminess gone from it. "What are you talking about?"

"I mean, I've changed my mind," I said as I started to sidle over to the DJ station, which was still empty. "I'm just going to get the flash drive back, and—"

"I'll do it," Gwyneth said, cutting me off. "The DJ knows me, so he'll know I mean it if I tell him to change the plan. But he might just think that you're a party guest who found out. It's better if I talk to him."

"All right," I said, then pulled my phone away from my ear to check the time. "But we have to hurry, okay?"

"Don't worry," Gwyneth said, and I could see she was already heading toward the DJ station. "I'm handling this."

"I'm just sorry I made you put in all that work," I said, realizing that Sophie was probably going to kill me when I told her she also probably didn't need to be on a date with Reid at this very moment. Hopefully, she'd let me buy her frozen yogurt for the rest of the summer to make up for it.

"No worries," Gwyneth said, and I saw she was almost to the

DJ station by now. But it looked like there was someone approaching at the same time—someone who I assumed was the DJ, since nobody else at this party was walking around with a huge pair of headphones around his neck. I squinted for a moment, trying to see if the headphones were even connected to anything, then gave up. "After all," Gwyneth said, "it gave Ford a chance to test out his Global . . . Earthly . . . uh . . ."

"Galvanized Empathic Multipurpose Media Algorithm," I recited, and then was immediately stunned that I'd gotten it right. Maybe I'd been hearing it long enough and had just absorbed it by osmosis or something.

"I told Ford," Gwyneth said as I watched her make it to the DJ station. "He needs an acronym. I have to handle this. I'll talk to you later."

She hung up, and I started to put my phone away. And then I froze. I selected the notes feature, then typed out the words, then deleted all but the first letters. It was an acronym. I put the letters together and suddenly realized what it was, what it had been, this whole time. Galvanized Empathic Multipurpose Media Algorithm. G-E-M-M-A. *GEMMA.*

I could feel my cheeks get warm as my thoughts flew in all different directions, like a firework exploding. Could this just be a coincidence? A second later I dismissed this. Ford was one of the most methodical people I knew. He wouldn't call his algorithm that unless . . . which meant . . .

I felt like my head was spinning, and I wished I could somehow stop everything else that was happening and just sort out what I was feeling. But I'd told Sophie that what I'd really wanted was a sign—something without prompting or interference. Some way to know how Ford felt about me. And there it was—he'd named his algorithm after me.

I glanced over at the DJ station again and saw Gwyneth walking away. I caught her eye, and she gave me a discreet thumbs-up. I let out a long breath. I'd stopped it, and now I could just enjoy the party while, hopefully, not making it too obvious that I was here. Things would be okay. I was going to let this—the whole thing with Hallie—go. And it actually felt pretty good. I unlocked my phone, about to call Sophie and see what she thought this Ford revelation meant, when I realized there was someone headed right toward my corner of the ship.

It was Teddy. And a second after I realized this, he was right in front of me, standing close. "Teddy," I said, taking a step back. "Um. Hey there." I wasn't sure, at this point, what Hallie had told him—maybe everything. I wondered if Hallie had sent him—and if I was about to be kicked off this boat. At the very least, I might be asked to go back downstairs with the rest of the catering staff. Which would be fine—my heels were killing me anyway. I braced myself for him to ask me what I thought I was doing there, but Teddy just took a step closer.

"Gem," he said, his voice soft. "I thought you'd gone back home for the rest of the summer."

"Well," I said as I realized there was nowhere else to go—I was backed into a corner, literally. "Um, not exactly."

"I'm glad you're here," Teddy said, talking over me, and I realized he hadn't even been listening to my response. "I wanted to talk to you."

"Oh," I said. I looked over his shoulder, eyes scanning the room for Hallie. I had a feeling that it would *not* be a good thing if she realized I was here when she spotted me in a dark corner with Teddy. "Okay."

"Do you . . ." Teddy started, then hesitated. This was enough to snap my focus back to him. Teddy *never* hesitated. Teddy spoke in paragraphs, not sentences, and always eloquently, if occasionally long-windedly. I suddenly worried that this wasn't about Hallie—maybe it was about the kiss.

"What?" I asked. I couldn't help but noticing, over Teddy's shoulder, that the large cake, with blue-and-white icing, was being carefully carried forward on a table to the center of the room. I knew it was getting close to the moment that "Happy Birthday" would be sung—when our plan had still been on, we'd timed it that way. But I had a strong feeling that Hallie would probably want her boyfriend by her side, and not huddled in the corner with his ex, when that was happening.

"Do you think we made a mistake?" Teddy blurted all at once, no longer sounding like his confident self. "Do you think that maybe we should have stayed together?"

I just stared at him. These were the words I would have given almost everything to have heard at the beginning of the summer. But now they were just complicating an already complicated night. "Where is this coming from?" I asked.

"I don't know," Teddy said, looking right at me with those eyes that used to make me melt. "You were so great about the marsh warbler protest. And now, without you . . . I'm worried I'm losing myself. You've always been my true north, Gemma, always keeping me aware of my principles. I guess I've just started thinking. I know I've accomplished a lot in the last two years . . . but maybe that was because you were by my side."

"Teddy," I said, shaking my head. "I just . . ." I suddenly realized that I'd been lying to Teddy. Not just this summer, although that was certainly true. But for a lot of our relationship—pretending I liked the marsh warbler, pretending I was interested in his causes, never really demanding he see me for who I was. And Josh had walked away from me the second he'd learned the truth about who I was.

I realized with a sudden understanding, like the final piece of a puzzle was fitting into place, that the only person who hadn't judged me through any of this, who'd accepted what I was doing and who had helped me out—was Ford. And suddenly I wanted nothing more than to tell him that.

"I have to go," I said, pushing past Teddy, who seemed very surprised by this.

"Go?" he echoed, sounding stunned. "But . . ."

I didn't wait to hear what he had to say, I just walked quickly across the deck. I needed to find a quiet place where I could talk to Ford. I'd go back to my life jacket closet if necessary. I pulled out my phone and selected his contact, looking for just a moment at his picture, Ford making a face at me in a maroon hoodie—

I stopped walking, and I enlarged his contact photo. He was wearing the sweatshirt I'd taken as mine, because for some reason, I'd loved the smell it carried. And it had made me feel safe in a way that had nothing to do with the sweatshirt itself.

It was because it had been Ford's. Which was one more reason I needed to talk to him as soon as possible.

I was almost to the other side of the deck when the music stopped playing and the lights went down. I looked around for Gwyneth and saw her standing by herself at the side railing. Josh, Hallie, and Karen were now gathering around the enormous cake, and people dressed in catering uniforms were starting to put unlit candles on it. A video screen was starting to descend automatically, and people were already turning toward it.

"All right," the DJ said, his lack of excitement palpable in his voice. "Let's take a look back at tonight's birthday girl, Hallie Bridges!"

The guests burst into applause just as I reached Gwyneth's side. I turned to face the water so that my back would be to Hallie—I was almost directly across from her, and that seemed like a dangerous place to be.

"Are we good?" I asked Gwyneth quietly, still looking out at the water. When she didn't respond right away, I looked over at her. "Gwyn?"

"Sorry," Gwyneth said, but she didn't really sound sorry, and I noticed that she was pulling out her phone and switching it to video—like something was about to happen that was going to be worth filming. "But this was just crucial to the narrative."

"What narrative?" I asked, starting to feel panic building up in my chest. "Gwyneth, what are you talking about?"

"Well, the stuff about Bruce was *really* boring," she said with a grimace. "But the whole thing with you and Hallie made for great drama. I realized it a while ago. That's why I had to leak Karen's real identity. I knew you and Hallie needed that extra push to see things through."

I just blinked at her for a moment, trying to make this fit. "It was *you*? I thought it was Hallie. . . ."

"I know," Gwyneth said with a smile. "It's great stuff. Wait till you see it. Between that and what's coming, there's no chance I'm not getting into this festival now. Isn't that great?"

"But . . ." I felt my panic grow as I realized what everyone was about to see. "You have to stop this," I said, as I turned around to see the footage starting to play.

Hallie looked at the screen, and even with the lights dimmed, I could see she was smiling. Teddy had at some point made his way back over to her. I wanted nothing more than to not be here for this, about to witness it, but I knew if I tried to go belowdeck now, I would just draw more attention to myself. And we were on a *boat*—where was I supposed to go?

Hallie's face filled the screen, a frozen close-up, and the guests all clapped. Then she became unfrozen, and her face changed as she scowled. Then the video cut to Hallie in the ice-cream parlor, glaring at me, telling me that I'd regret staying, then throwing strawberry syrup toward the camera. Gwyneth had slowed that part down, and I flinched as it filled the screen.

By now I could see some of the guests whispering to each other, trying to figure out what was going on. Hallie was looking around, like she was trying to stop it, and her eyes landed on me. I took a step back and realized I was now up against the railing.

"*I suppose you've told him everything,*" the Hallie on-screen was saying, and Hallie looked away from me and back to the screen. "*Teddy doesn't need to know why we initially got together,*" she was saying, and I watched the Teddy on the boat lean down and whisper something to her. He looked furious. "*It was beyond easy to break you two up. I actually thought it was going to be a challenge.*" I could hear the low murmur spreading through the crowd, and Hallie was still staring up at the screen, her hand over her mouth. I wanted to look away, but I found I couldn't. It was like watching a car crash in slow motion. "*Watch your back,*" video-Hallie was saying to me from the screen. Hallie was rolling her eyes and calling the marsh warbler a stupid bird, and then she was smiling wide as I got in trouble, making sure I would be fired. This was where the cut I'd seen with Gwyneth ended, and I braced myself for the lights to come up, and for the fallout.

But the footage kept going, shots I'd never seen before. Teddy was sitting on the beach at night, smiling at the camera—which meant he was smiling at me, reaching over to brush a lock of hair from my face. This cut quickly with shots of Teddy telling me how much I understood him and his causes, how he didn't think Hallie did in the same way. And then Teddy outside of Bruce's driveway, leaning over to kiss me. The video ended on a close-up of Hallie's face in an ugly scowl. In beautiful cursive *Happy Birthday, Hallie!* scrolled across the image *Xoxo, Gemma.*

The lights came on, to utter silence. Nobody seemed to know where to look, and the caterers were standing awkwardly by the cake, clearly not sure what to do with the fact that the vibe had just changed so completely.

"*You.*" Hallie, her face tear-stained, was stalking toward me. "This was you. Are you happy?"

"No," I said, very aware that an entire boatful of people was now looking at me, and some were raising their phones and starting to take pictures. "I didn't—"

But before I could get very far with this, Hallie reached over and pushed me, hard. I was surprised enough by this that it took me a moment to react. I dodged out of the way, thinking that maybe my life jacket room would be a good possibility after all, when Hallie grabbed my arm.

"Stop it," I said, pulling my arm back. "Don't—"

"Oh, I'm *sorry*, Gemma," Hallie said, and the composure she'd kept such a tight lid on all summer was off now—this Hallie looked furious, her rage unleashed, and on the verge of tears again. "Did that hurt you?"

"Really," I said, trying to disengage myself from her. I'd never been in a fight in my life, and I didn't want to have my first one be in formal-wear and heels, in front of a group of on-lookers. "Just—" I was planning on saying something calming and rational, but that's when Hallie grabbed my hair and yanked it. "*Ow!*" I pushed her away, and she stumbled back a few steps, then came running toward me again.

I put up my hands to block her, but she crashed into me with enough force that I lost my balance on my heels and felt myself wobbling backward. I shoved myself forward, toward her, just as Hallie came at me again. I was losing my balance—but in the split second I had to think about it, I grabbed her arm and pulled. If I was falling over, I was taking her with me. It was only as gravity started to take over that I realized we were both headed for the cake.

We hit the table, and I felt frosting cover my whole right side. It was in my hair, it was all over my dress—and now it was in my face, because Hallie had grabbed a handful and was smearing it across my cheek. "Stop it!" I yelled, trying to get up, but my hand slid in the frosting on the ground, and I fell back again. Hallie laughed, and without thinking, I picked up a handful of the cake and flung it at her, hitting her right across the face.

She lunged forward for me just as I grabbed what little of her hair I could. *"Ow!"* I heard her yell just as I yelled, "Stop!"

"Girls!"

I froze and looked up. My dad and Karen were standing over us, both looking horrified. I was suddenly snapped back to reality, and all too aware of the situation I was in.

I was covered in cake and frosting, in a formal dress, fighting on the ground. And my father—along with lots of people I didn't know and several I did—had all seen it.

"What are you doing?" Karen asked, and I could see she looked angrier than I had ever seen her. "Answer me, Hallie."

"Gemma," my dad said, his voice equally confused and furious. "What's going on here?"

"Um," I said as I tried to wipe some of the frosting off my face. I carefully pushed myself up to standing, since I'd lost one of my heels in the fight. "I—"

"What is he doing here?" Hallie asked, looking at my dad, her eyes wide.

"Yeah," I said, suddenly realizing that for once Hallie and I were on the same page about something. "What happened to California?"

"Well," my dad said. He turned to Karen, and I saw the two of them exchange a loaded look. Hallie glanced over at me, and despite the fact that half her face was covered in frosting, I could tell she was as thrown by this as I was.

Karen took a step closer to my dad, and I noticed the diamond on her hand again, the one I'd seen in the bathroom. Except this time, I paid attention to what finger it was on.

"Dad?" I asked hesitantly. This really wasn't happening. This *couldn't* be happening. If this was happening, my life as I knew it was essentially over.

I watched as my dad slid his arm around Karen's shoulders and took a breath. "We actually have something to tell you. . . ."

I looked at Hallie in horror, and I saw the same expression reflected back at me.

This was happening.

ACKNOWLEDGMENTS

First and foremost, thank you to Anna Roberto. The amount of thanks you properly deserve would go on for pages, and this book is long enough already. So I will just say that I am so grateful for your endless patience, support, and wonderful notes. I'm so lucky to work with you.

Thank you to my wonderful agent, Emily Van Beek, who is beyond amazing and lovely.

Thank you to Jean Feiwel and all the wonderful people at Macmillan: Lauren Burniac, Kathryn Little, Ashley Halsey, Caitlin Sweeny, Ksenia Winnicki, Mary Van Aiken, Nicole Banholzer, and Molly Brouillette.

Thank you to Rich Deas for another gorgeous cover!

Thank you to Rosa Lin for all things *hermano*.

Thank you to Rachel Cohn, Leslie Margolis, and Jordan Roter, the best writing pals a girl could ask for.

Thank you to Robin Benway, for all the work days and the Diet Cokes.

And finally, thanks to Mom, Jason, Amanda, Katie, and Murphy.